Praise for Fiona Lowe

"The first in the Wedding Fever series is a fun, romantic romp in a quirky small town. Anni and Finn are well matched in both wits and stubbornness. Their journey from enemies to friends to lovers is one that will keep readers turning pages."
—*RT Book Reviews*, 4 stars, on *Saved by the Bride*

"With the perfect mixture of romance, sadness and Australian/American wise-cracking, *Boomerang Bride* is one of the best romance novels this reviewer has read in a long time."
—*RT Book Reviews*, 4.5 stars

"I love wedding stories, and after reading Lowe's debut Carina Press novel last year, I knew I was in for a special treat with the new Wedding Fever series... I'm really excited to read the upcoming books."
—*The Book Pushers* on *Saved by the Bride*

"I'd recommend *Saved by the Bride* to anyone who wants a good romance with a fun story."
—*Harlequin Junkie*

"*Saved by the Bride* is a well-written romance. I loved reading about Finn's parents' story. And the amazing love story interwoven in the main story of Finn's sister was an added bonus. RITA and R*BY award winning author Fiona Lowe yet again brings this brilliant romance to her readers and other lovers of romance!"
—*Romance Book Paradise*, 5 stars

"*Saved by the Bride* has such a wonderful humour and sense of fun about it. Fiona Lowe, you have created a couple, and a town, that you just can't help but cheer for."
—*My Written Romance*

Saved BY THE Bride

FIONA LOWE

CARINA
PRESS™

Recycling programs for this product may not exist in your area.

ISBN-13: 978-0-373-00224-5

SAVED BY THE BRIDE

Copyright © 2013 by Fiona Lowe

Edited by Charlotte Herscher

www.CarinaPress.com

Printed in U.S.A.

Dear Reader,

I'm so excited to bring to you the first book in my Wedding Fever trilogy. Many small towns are struggling, jobs are disappearing, young people are moving away and places that existed as agricultural centers are looking at new ways to reinvent themselves. When I was writing *Boomerang Bride*, Matilda sold her wedding dress and she and Peggy Hendrix started a small wedding business. This got me thinking about creating an entire small town that was ALL about weddings.

Welcome to Whitetail! It's a small town languishing on the edge of a pristine north-woods lake and home to an electric group of people who love nothing more than throwing a great wedding for their own. Of course, Whitetail is in Wisconsin because I used to live there and I know it well. The north woods are a very pretty part of the state dotted with lakes and fishing cabins. It's beautiful but it's isolated and a sensational place to spend a summer. Annika and Finn's story kicks off the trilogy but the townsfolk are all introduced and across the series many of them get their own love story in *Picture Perfect Wedding* (ebook August 2013) and *Runaway Groom* (ebook January 2014). I hope you enjoy getting to know the supporting cast of the romantic leads: Nicole, the hairstylist from Affairs With Hair; Melissa, who runs the Northern Lights Boutique; John Ackerman, the owner of Whitetail Market and Video; and Mrs. Norell, the vibrant senior with pink hair who has an opinion on everything. I hope you fall in love with Whitetail as much as I did and revisit it often!

For photos, the book trailer and more information about the Wedding Fever trilogy please visit my website at www.fionalowe.com. I love hearing from my readers and you can contact me at fiona@fionalowe.com or hang out with me on Facebook (fionaloweromanceauthor) and @fionalowe on Twitter.

Happy Reading!

Love,

Fiona x

Dedication

To my family who support and believe in me
even when the "Crows of Doubt" are pecking wildly.

To Joan, Nicola and Rachael who are always
on the end of an email and happy to listen
and to brainstorm with me.

Many thanks to Rechelle for her passionate,
patient and detailed descriptions of thermography,
and for an insight into the intricacies of
wedding invitations. Any errors in the story are mine.

To Serena for the cheerleading
and grammar assistance.

Mega thanks to Charlotte whose perspective
smooths out the kinks in the manuscript
and helps my characters shine.

ONE

WHO KNEW THAT being a klutz and combining it with a distrust of wedding bouquets could lead to a black eye?

Annika Jacobson automatically touched the four-day-old berry-colored bruise with its spectacular vivid yellow edges with the tips of her fingers as if that would will it away.

"Stop it." Nicole Lindquist from Whitetail's Affairs with Hair leaned forward and captured her hand. "I've concealed it with makeup but if you keep tapping it with your fingers, you'll ruin all my hard work."

"Sorry." For the thousandth time in ninety-six hours, Annika asked herself why she hadn't just caught the damn flowers. Everyone outside the old Whitetail church knew that Jennifer would throw her bouquet to her best friend and they'd all discreetly taken a step back so it could happen. She'd known it too and had thought she was up for the task but at the last minute she'd panicked and moved sideways, thinking it would leave Melissa wide open for the catch. In her own inimitable, uncoordinated style, she'd misjudged it completely and the only thing she'd caught was a wad of firmly packed tulip stems to the cheek. Stems which packed a hell of a punch. All in all it had capped off a day she'd been dreading for months.

Not that she didn't think Jennifer's marriage was a good idea, it totally was. Jennifer, unlike herself, had been born to be married and Carl was a great guy, but their wonderful wedding, where the town had made them celebrities for the day, had been their last day in White-tail. They too had joined the parade that led out of town toward jobs in Madison, Milwaukee, the Twin Cities and beyond. Their departure made the economic situation very real and meant that after a decade, she was the only member of her graduating class still living in Whitetail. Financially, she was barely holding on herself because personalized calligraphy was a luxury few in town could now afford and her almost nonexistent bank account had her seriously worried. Reggies, the biggest employer in the town, had been shedding jobs for a year and had now pulled out completely. The business park lay idle and her beloved town was shriveling before her eyes—slowly languishing on the curve of a pristine northwoods lake.

Sadly, beauty and fresh air didn't pay the bills and the town desperately needed a new industry to survive. She thought of her two overdue rent notices and knew deep in her heart she needed a regular job to survive. A job so she could stay in Whitetail where she belonged.

"I'm just nervous, is all." She glanced around at the other four expectant faces, the core group of the White-tail Chamber of Commerce who'd joined her in the lim-ousine for moral support. At least they thought it was moral support. Annika felt it was more along the lines of making sure she didn't back out of "the plan." Just the thought of "the plan" made her sick to her stomach so she tried to joke. "At least this party's full of out-of-staters and no one will have read about my epic failure in *The Bugle*."

Melissa Bergeron, the owner of the Northern Lights Boutique and the woman who'd lent Annika the evening dress she was now wearing, made a funny face as if she was trying not to laugh.

"What?"

"They might have seen it in the online edition."

Annika's stomach rolled on acid and not much else. "Since when does *The Bugle* have an online edition? I thought Eric was still learning how to use the Guttenberg press?"

"His grandson, Joshua, is home for the summer and as part of his IT project to get the seniors online, he's taken the paper to the web, complete with a subscription deal," said John Ackerman, the proprietor of Whitetail Market and Video. "This week's the inaugural edition and Jennifer's wedding video is the first click-through feature."

"Joshua's wonderful and he made everyone at the center have a practice," said Ella Norell, a vibrant senior with a passion for gardening and cake decorating. "Anni, you looked quite pretty before you sprawled on the grass."

Annika almost dropped her head into her hands before realizing she wasn't allowed to do that because it would ruin her hair and makeup. Life was so much easier wearing her ink-stained jeans and pulling her hair back in a ponytail. So she gave a shuddering sigh instead as that was the only option open to her. After twenty-nine years she knew she couldn't hide how uncoordinated she was from her small hometown, but the world didn't need to know.

The internet knows. "Oh, God, why did it go live this week? The video's probably been uploaded everywhere and someone at the party will have seen it."

Nicole nodded in sympathy. "Don't worry. Just think of it as more of your exemplary community service."

When Annika was twelve and on a 4-H hike, she'd

organized a group of girls to carry out an injured Sally Tomie on a stretcher made of sweaters. On their arrival back in Whitetail, both the town and her often-distracted parents had gushed with pride. Annika had been "helping out" ever since.

"Me being suckered by treacherous tulips wasn't part of any plan to get Whitetail on the map."

Neither was the town's current plan of having her gate-crash an engagement party hosted by the head of AKP Industries from Chicago, which was being held at his vacation house on Lake Whitetail. Sean Callahan's company had bought the business park from Reggies and as the mayor's volunteer assistant, she'd made numerous telephone calls, sent emails and even snail-mail letters requesting an appointment to discuss the future plans for the park. Without a business plan the town would die and she was determined not to let that happen. She'd put in hours of work but all she'd got back was silence. Utter, devastating silence.

At an emergency town meeting held two days ago when then-mayor, Donna Wakeen, had unexpectedly blown off the town by running away to Chicago to a job that paid, Annika had suddenly found herself appointed acting mayor despite a thousand reservations of her own including the accusatory internal voice that said, *You need to focus on your career.*

She'd silenced the voice, accepted the temporary position and while looking for a way to move forward, she'd posed the general question, "What is Whitetail good at?"

The town, on a post-wedding high, had replied exactly that. Weddings.

Nicole had told everyone how Hobin, Wisconsin, had been successful with weddings and they only had a red barn for receptions. Annika had pointed out that surely

Wisconsin only needed *one* small town for weddings. Nicole had enthusiastically argued that as Whitetail was close to the Minnesota border, they were in the perfect position to attract couples from Minneapolis/Saint Paul and they had a lot more to offer than a barn. Then she'd waved a glossy magazine article about Bridget Callahan's engagement.

Despite John Ackerman's opinion of the family—"worst vacationers ever. They never spend a cent in the town"—suddenly everyone was pushing Annika to use Donna's invitation to attend the engagement party and go convince the bride-to-be to have her wedding in Whitetail.

"It will put us on the map just like Chelsea Clinton did for Rhinebeck," Mrs. Norell had claimed, and the town had enthusiastically agreed.

Annika thought the plan to be utterly insane. The daughter of a billionaire who'd never supported Whitetail wouldn't even consider getting married in a tiny northwoods town. No, she'd be having a glitz-and-glamour wedding at a venue like Chicago's Museum of Contemporary Art.

Just like yours was going to be.

She banished the thought so fast she almost gave herself whiplash. The town's outrageous wedding plan wasn't hers. Whitetail needed real jobs with a long-term future but as Sean Callahan hadn't accepted any of her offers to take a meeting, she had no choice but to resort to gate-crashing his daughter's party. When she finally did meet him, she wouldn't be talking about weddings—she'd be talking about the business park and the future of Whitetail.

Al, the owner-driver of Whitetail's Feel Like a Star car and carriage service, brought the limousine to a halt near a clearing in the dense pine trees. He turned to them and said, "The gates of the Callahan property are just up ahead. The four of you need to get out and I'll collect you all after I've delivered Anni to the front door."

Annika's heart kicked up. This crazy plan was actually happening. *Breathe in, breathe out, breathe in, breath out.*

Nicole, her eyes shining and with a smile that broke through the strain of grief which had circled her since the start of the year, tucked a stray strand of Annika's hair into place and gave her face a final dust of powder. "Don't be nervous. We've made you look so amazing we hardly recognize you. You're going to fit right in with those Chicago socialites."

Mrs. Norell added, "Anni, just remember Tess in the movie *Working Girl*. She gate-crashed a wedding and talked business. Oh, Harrison Ford was gorgeous back then."

Annika was too stressed to point out *that* was the movies and the eighties, where as this was real life. Her real life.

John gave her a supporting smile tinged with hubris. "You might mention that my fruit and vegetables are equal to what their cook brings in from Chicago."

"John, she's going to be talking about weddings," said Melissa as she adjusted the strapless dress. "Tell Miss Callahan I can order in any number of wedding dresses."

"Out," Al said firmly. "Leave the poor girl alone."

They scrambled across the seats and out into the sweet evening air and a minute later Al drove the vehicle through the open and imposing gates with their monogrammed *K* in the center, up the long drive and came to a stop halfway around the circle. As he opened the door for her, he said in his best chauffeur's voice, "This is the Callahan's cabin on the lake."

She gave him a tight smile. "Thanks, Al."

The property was closer to the town by boat than by car and she'd never been here before. She moistened her lips and stepped out, and as she was smoothing down her dress it hit her that not only was she a walking example of the Whitetail Chamber of Commerce, she carried the expectations of the entire town on her now bare and nervous shoulders. Her stomach spun like the spin cycle of the washing machine she couldn't afford. Why had she let the town talk her into this?

Jobs and the future. Your future.

As she watched the limo pull away and disappear down the wide sweep of driveway, she took in a deep breath and turned to face the Callahans' lakeside cabin. She instantly wondered if the rich took pleasure in irony. She supposed a small and simple fishing cabin might have existed once, but not anymore. The setting sun cast a golden glow on an imposing classic American house with a silvery-gray cedar-shake exterior, white windows and a shingled roof, and it reminded her of an era long passed. Four enormous stone chimneys rose majestically but only those with an eye for detail and some knowledge of architecture could tell they also marked the spot where the original house ended and the huge modern extension started.

The house—Kylemore, according to its copper nameplate—loomed above her, its steeply pitched roof dwarfing her and her bravado.

She smoothed down her dress and squared her shoulders. She could do this.

Then she laid eyes on the headset-adorned security guard. Her stomach lurched so hard it almost tugged her sideways. *Crap. Security.* It hadn't occurred to her to factor that into her plans.

A tremble started in her toes but then, out of nowhere, part of the 4-H pledge rolled through her brain, stalling the wobble at her knees. *I pledge my heart to clearer thinking.* She took in a calming breath, letting the sight of the sparkling water on the lake soothe her. As steadily as one can in three-inch heels, she walked purposefully to the front door with her head held high and a smile pasted on her face. "Good eve—"

"Name."

The security guard barked out the word so loudly, so unexpectedly and so very un-Wisconsin-like, that she wavered precariously on her heels as her composure fled. "Ann...Donna Wakeen."

Damn, damn, damn. She stifled a groan. She'd practiced over and over what she needed to say and now the first time she'd opened her mouth she'd gone and fluffed it.

Distract with chitchat. She smiled again and this time her cheeks ached as she tried to keep the edge of anxiety out of her voice. "You must be from Chicago."

A grunt was all she got as he studied his clipboard and followed with, "You're not on the list."

I'm not on the list!

Don't panic yet. She opened the ridiculously small but exquisitely beaded evening purse and pulled out a folded piece of thick, embossed paper. Paper she knew cost a fortune because a calligraphy client had once asked her to price it. "Here's my invitation."

The stone-faced man stared at it impassively. "You're not on the list which means I can't let you in."

Her heart pounded against the figure-hugging bodice of the dress. It had never occurred to her that holding the invitation wouldn't be enough to gain entry. Frantically trying to think, she crossed her fingers in the folds of her dress. *Forgive this bending of the truth. It's for a good cause.* She tried to peer at his list. "Oh, dear, aren't I? My P.A. assured me she'd telephoned and given the RSVP. Clearly there's been a miscommunication."

His dark eyes showed no emotion and he turned away, speaking into the mouthpiece of his headset. Annika strained to decipher the words but his voice was a low and unintelligible rumble and all she caught was "Donna." He turned back. "You got your cell on you?"

She smiled brightly. "Yes."

He nodded and then said "yes" into his mouthpiece before looking directly at her. "Neiquest or Callahan?"

"Pardon?" She had no clue what he was talking about.

He spoke slowly, his expression shrewd. "Are you friends of the Neiquests or the Callahans?"

Understanding dawned. "Oh, right, um, the bride's father." *Well, that's kind of close to the truth seeing the impossible-to-contact Sean Callahan is the reason I'm here.*

He tapped his clipboard. "Your phone's not ringing."

"Ah, no. Should it be?"

"If you were Donna Wakeen then, yeah, it would be."

He flicked some gum with his tongue, the action of a man in total control and holding all the keys to the kingdom. "The dispatcher just rang the number and got her voice mail. I don't know who you are, lady, but no one gate-crashes a Callahan party on my shift." His stance widened to block the doorway and his hands moved to his hips. "I'll be asking you to leave now."

She could hear the animated sounds of the party and she was so very close to her goal and yet so very far away. Desperation flooded her. "This invitation was for the mayor and she couldn't come and—"

"Do you need me to escort you off the property?" His expression was granite.

Her cheeks burned with mortification. "No. Thank you, I can find my own way."

"Good." He continued to stare at her as if she was a June bug he could squish whenever he chose.

With her confidence in tatters, she somehow managed to muster up her dignity, turn very slowly on her heels and stalk down the blacktop into the fast-fading light. As the pine trees enveloped her and the noise of the party became a low buzz, a smolder of fury burned inside her, slowly gaining heat. What did manners cost? If that was the caliber of the staff Callahan hired then she wondered at the type of person this billionaire was. Easy—undeniably rude!

The balls of her feet burned and with a rough tug she pulled off her sandals and sank down into soft pine needles. Okay, so she'd tried to use another person's invitation to gain entry but only because Callahan hadn't responded to any of her communications. Why had she even thought he might? According to older residents, the Callahans had been coming to Whitetail for years but unlike most other vacationers, they'd kept themselves aloof from the town. Each summer they buzzed the lake with their powerboats and Jet Skis, and every Thanksgiving they cut down a Christmas tree and, without a backward glance, headed back to Chicago.

Always taking, never giving.

The smolder ignited into a hot flame that quickly took hold until a fire raged. Damn it all, good people were hurting and this family *owed* her a meeting. Owed Whitetail a meeting. She'd always been good, always done the right thing, and her dealings with AKP Industries were no different. She'd gone through all the correct channels and what had it got her? Squat. Now the town had gone to enormous lengths to get her ready for this party so she could meet Sean Callahan, and she didn't need to imagine their reaction if she returned without meeting him—she could taste their disappointment in her already. She hated letting people down.

She heard a band start up followed by cheering. Given the volume of noise and combining it with the fact it was a warm and balmy summer night, she knew everyone was dancing outside. She should be there. Not dancing but mingling outside in the crowd and finding the man she needed to meet.

Outside. The thought rocked her. Most people would be in the garden, leaving the house fairly empty. With a determined pull, she strapped her dainty shoes back on her feet. There was more than one way to skin a cat so there was more than one way to get into that party.

She just had to find it.

FINN CALLAHAN DOWNED his third Leinenkugel, and wondered how much longer he had to stay at his sister's engagement party. After months of living and working in Mexico and becoming used to a more casual dress code, he found that his tuxedo clung to him as tight and constricting as a straitjacket. The starched collar of his shirt scratched and itched, and with an abrupt pull, he undid the offending bow tie and shoved it into his pocket.

Why on earth had Bridey wanted a formal engagement party? The question immediately begged a bigger one—why did she even want to get married? It wasn't like either of them had been raised to actually witness any benefits from the institution. He took another slug of his beer, wondering what was going on in his sister's pretty head that made her insist the party be up at the lake. This meant his long-since-divorced-but-still-acrimonious parents had to spend an evening together in a house they'd once shared and his second stepmother now considered to be very much her own. Happy families didn't come close.

After the stiff smiles and overly bright attempts at conversation by the current and ex-wives of Sean Callahan had worn him down, he'd retreated to the library because it was the only room in the house he liked. It was the one place Sean had left untouched during the massive renovation. Quiet and tucked away in the back corner, it meant he was unlikely to be disturbed, but it also gave him a partial view of proceedings. From here he'd know when to reappear so as not to miss the toasts.

He gazed out one of the many windows, past the live band in full swing out on the terrace, past people dancing on the floating dance floor under the stars and toward the lone twinkling light in the middle of the lake. He smiled at the faint yellow glow, loving what it represented—*his* island and *his* cabin. A real cabin, unlike this monolith that his father had built to impress and in the process lost the soul of Grandpa's place.

He checked his work email on his phone—nothing from Henrico so thankfully no disasters at the new plant. Still he wouldn't mind one if it got him out of Kylemore. He ate a club sandwich from the platter that Esther—the indomitable housekeeper—had brought in for him and then he looked for something to read. A vast array of women's magazines were scattered across the low table along with an angling magazine and a bunch of plastic toy building bricks. When he'd been a kid, his father had never allowed him in here to read, let alone play. He turned away from the toy bricks and crossed the room to the wall of bookshelves. With a practiced eye, he quickly found *Adventures of Huckleberry Finn*.

He settled into the wingback chair in the far corner of the large room and the book fell open to his favorite scene, read to him so many times by his grandfather. As he reread the well-known words he could hear Grandpa's booming voice telling the story and the noise of the party fell away.

A soft thud made him look up. A beaded purse lay on the rug. He immediately heard a louder thump followed by a heartfelt, "Ohh, shit! Ouch."

He was instantly on his feet and just in time to see a long, creamy leg pointing ceiling-ward into the room with the back of the knee pressed against the window-sill. Five brightly painted red toes peeked out of a ridiculously high-heeled shoe and a pair of manicured hands gripped the sill as the leg tried to bend to find purchase. A grunt of effort reverberated as loudly as a bass drum and he glimpsed a head, saw the second leg appear and then the head vanished.

Someone was doing an exceptionally clumsy job of trying to climb through the window. He should've been outraged but then again most thieves didn't raid homes dressed in evening wear. The absurdity of it added an extra something to what so far had been a very long evening. Someone had obviously drunk far too much champagne so instead of calling security, he decided to check it out himself.

He raised the window higher and leaned out into the shadows. He couldn't make out much more than the outline of what he assumed was a woman's body lying upside down against the side of the house. He couldn't see anyone else. "Most people use the door."

A gasp shot through the air followed by a beat of silence. "I'm not most people." The Midwest accent combined resignation with attitude—an intriguing combination.

"Exactly what are you doing?"

"Do you think we could leave the explanations until after you've helped me up? My head's about to explode from too much blood."

"I guess that's an option." His gaze slid along the curve of one fully exposed leg and then snagged on the clear view of white, cotton panties. He took a second look to make sure he'd seen right. He couldn't even remember the last time he'd seen plain, classic briefs, and combined with evening wear, well, it was just wrong. The luxurious material of the dress demanded French lace or a skimpy thong, not utilitarian cotton. Even so, he suddenly felt hot, which was ridiculous, and he quickly pulled the dress over both legs to cover her up. Standing to one side, he gripped her wrists and pulled. Her legs moved sideways, knocking into his head.

"Whoa, what are you doing? I'm slipping. Just pull me straight up!"

The bossy tone, not unlike the one Bridey had used when she'd demanded he attend her party, irritated him and he started to regret his offer of help. He much preferred women who didn't say very much. "Listen, Legs, I was trying to spare you an element of indignity."

A strangled sound that was half groan and half laugh floated up to him. "I left dignity behind at the last mile post. Do whatever. Just get me up."

He knew exactly what he had to do but he wasn't certain she was going to like it. "Hold the windowsill with your left hand." Keeping a firm grip on her right wrist and losing the battle not to take a second peek at the utilitarian underwear, he managed to maneuver himself so he stood between her legs. "Wrap your legs around my waist."

"Excuse me?" Her voice rose an octave.

He grinned at the fact he'd made her take-charge tone waver, but she had absolutely nothing to worry about. Not only did he prefer women who didn't readily offer up opinions, he was also very fond of breasts. Legs had never really done it for him. "Relax, it's pure physics. We're using my weight to counterbalance yours."

"Oh, God, I did say do whatever, didn't I?" She suddenly let out a shriek. "Quick, the sprinklers just came on!"

Her smooth, warm legs came in hard and fast against his body before she crossed her ankles behind him. His blood pounded south. *Just physics, right?*

He tugged firmly on her forearms, as much to bring her straight up as to banish his body's response to her. It had been weeks since he'd reacted like this to any woman and they'd been women he'd been able to see. Why the hell was this happening with one he couldn't see?

A moment later, with her legs gripping him even harder, a flash of wet, emerald-green bodice appeared, followed by even more creamy skin. Then, framed by sodden mousy-colored hair filled with pine needles and twigs, vivid blue eyes stared straight at him. Eyes that reminded him of cornflowers and kaleidoscopes. Eyes that seemed to be having a great deal of trouble focusing. She swayed backward.

"Don't faint on me. Take a deep breath." Instinctively he put his arm around her waist to steady her and the action brought her hard up against his chest. She smelled like fresh pine, summer flowers and simpler times. He leaned back, suddenly needing to keep some distance.

She gulped in air, her chest heaving, and suddenly her eyes cleared, filling with relief. "The room's stopped spinning."

"That's a good start." Her legs continued to grip him like a vise, draining his blood from his brain. Somehow, he managed to choke out, "You can probably put your feet on the ground now."

Thick, chestnut lashes blinked and droplets of water splashed against her pale cheek. He watched, fascinated, as a flush crawled up her neck, staining her skin pink.

With lightning speed, she dropped her legs, slid off the windowsill and stood tall and dripping on the rug. Despite being soaking wet and bedraggled, "Legs" held herself with an air of composure that matched the vestiges of style and coiffure which were sharply at odds with the fact she'd entered the house in a questionable way. He couldn't detect a single strand of guilt.

She tugged at her dress, straightening it as if she scrambled through windows every day, and then she hit him with a clear and direct gaze. "Thank you very much, Mr., er…"

No apology. Interesting. He decided to wait and see how she played it. "Finn."

"Thank you, Finn."

She spoke clearly and with no sign of a slur, which immediately ruled out drunkenness as the reason she'd attempted to climb through the window in such an inept way.

Her gaze darted around the room as if she was trying to get her bearings. "This is a lovely room."

"I like it." He closed the window, his blood now fully back where it belonged—oxygenating his brain. "By the way, most people come through a window head first, legs last."

She nibbled her bottom lip. "Yeah, my game plan was a bit off and gymnastics was never my strong suit."

Again, it wasn't an answer he'd expected and her apparent honesty disarmed him. He took a closer look at her face, seeking any expression that told the real story. She wasn't pretty in the conventional way although under the mess of makeup, she had good bone structure. He noticed a dark smudge near her eye. "Have you hurt your cheek?"

"Oh, God, can you see that?" She touched the top of her right cheekbone and let out a low wail. "Sadly, it's not mascara but an almost-healed black eye from when I missed a catch."

He couldn't help himself and laughter won out. "So gymnastics *and* ball games aren't your thing?"

Her mouth tilted up into a self-effacing smile, joining him in the joke. "To be honest, it's all sports including crossing the road."

He couldn't help grinning at her. "And yet knowing that, you tried to climb through a window in an evening dress?"

"It's always important to give it your best shot." Her hands came up to grip her arms and she took a shivery step toward the throw rug on the couch. "Do you mind?"

Her question momentarily jolted him out of his intrigue and activated his manners. "Sure, go right ahead." He'd get her warm and *then* drill her. He poured a shot of Scotch from the crystal decanter and handed it to her.

She stared at it for a moment before accepting the glass and downing it in one gulp. Her pupils instantly dilated to wide, jet discs, almost obliterating the piercing blue. Coughing, she sank onto the leather couch and gasped out, "Water?"

He squirted some soda into another glass and she swallowed it all. "Better?"

"It burns all the way down."

"That's the general idea." He sat down next to her. "Who are you?"

She hesitated for a moment as if battling with herself. "Donna."

"Donna, who?"

The blue eyes suddenly flashed with silver. "Finn, who?"

He could have told her he was Finn Callahan, third generation of the Chicago Callahans, previously of County Clare, Ireland, and currently heading up the Mexico division of AKP Industries, but the fact she didn't seem to know him was oddly liberating. "Just Finn."

She nodded slowly, as if acknowledging the surname-less pact. "So, Finn, why are you hiding out in the library in the middle of a party?"

The perceptive question hit hard. Over the years he'd honed a variety of tactics when faced with family occasions and the fact she'd worked out so fast that he was hiding, rankled. This woman with her round, bright eyes should be apologetic and grateful instead of questioning him. "Given your unorthodox entrance, *I'm* the one that should be asking the questions."

She shrugged and a knowing smile creased into round cheeks. "It's well known that guilt makes us grumpy."

"In that case you should be as grumpy as hell."

She tilted her head in consideration of the accusation. "Maybe, but mostly not."

"And how do you figure that?"

"Sometimes breaking a few rules is what has to happen so fairness can prevail."

"That's an interesting philosophy." One she shared with his father and some of his business associates, but not him. A stickler for the rules, he always argued the point of what constituted fair and to whom.

He passed her the platter of sandwiches with the intention of relaxing her so she'd say something to give him a clue as to why she was here.

She picked up two sandwiches and unlike most women he knew, bit deeply into one as if she hadn't eaten in days.

"Tell me how this philosophy is working out for you."

"It's a recently adopted attitude and I'm still ironing out the kinks. Basically, I'm feeling my way." She smiled, but her eyes twinkled with purpose. "So why you are here?"

The answer was as complicated as it was easy. "Business." *Family and commercial.* Sadly, the two couldn't be separated and he knew which one he preferred. "And you?"

"Same."

He tried not to frown, wanting to keep his disbelief hidden. Bridey had insisted that the party not be filled with AKP contacts unless they were her friends or long-time personal friends of the family. Granted, he'd been in Mexico a lot lately but if Donna was a friend of his sister's, surely she would have mentioned Bridey's name by now. "What sort of business?"

"Um, warehouses."

She bit her lip again and his gaze zeroed in on a bead of moisture while his brain kicked him hard. *Focus.* "You don't sound very certain."

"It's complicated is all." She pushed some escaped strands of hair behind her ears, the action quick and decisive. "So if you're here for business, you'd know Sean Callahan?"

And we're getting warmer. The mention of his father's name sent a thousand warning flags up in his head. "Sure."

She picked at the second sandwich. "He's a hard man to get hold of."

And he was, but why would she know? *How* did she know? Everyone at AKP had been sworn to secrecy about company matters especially with the Mexico expansion. Was she a spy from Paper Again, a rival company who'd been trying to get information on the new plant? *Nah.* He immediately ditched the idea because as a spy she was incredibly inexpert.

A rogue thought pinged into his mind and took hold. Unless of course this whole "damsel in distress" thing was an act to sucker him in. After all, he'd been rescuing birds, animals and women since he was a kid so deliberately setting him up for help would be the perfect way to get to his father. Hell, it had already worked up to this point. He'd pulled her into the house, into his arms, warmed her up and fed her!

He cursed the unauthorized internet news article about him published a few months back that had basically said, "the soft side of Finn Callahan." God he hated the press.

Press! The thought exploded in his head with the clarity of a brilliant cut diamond. This was just the sort of thing a tabloid reporter would do to get an exclusive. The last thing he needed right now was the press sniffing out dirt on him or finding out that Sean had been missing some important AKP meetings. He still didn't understand what was going on in his tycoon father's head but if the shareholders got wind of it in this financial climate, it would send jitters through the stock prices. He sure as hell didn't need an article about how it took one generation to create a company, the second generation to increase it and the third to lose it.

His gut seethed but he didn't have enough evidence on "Legs" just yet so he had to play it cool and detached. Pretty much how he played all things family with his father. He gave her an encouraging smile. "I guess you just have to know how to contact him."

"And you do?" She'd leaned forward slightly, her face alive with interest.

Bingo! Ms. Donna had just made a fatal mistake in her almost perfect modus operandi—an enthusiasm for her target. All that was left to do was expose her by reeling her in, hook, line and sinker. "I've got his private number."

Excitement zipped and fizzed in Annika, following fast behind the effects of the Scotch, which was warming her up in the most delicious way, but in the process making it really hard to concentrate. Finn was making it really hard to concentrate.

From the moment she'd slammed into his broad chest and looked into those questioning coal-black eyes, she'd been out of her depth. At five foot eleven inches, she was used to being taller than some men but Finn had the height of a basketball player, and the solid bulk of a toned athlete. She felt tiny in comparison, which was unusually disconcerting. That and the fact she'd wrapped herself around him like a pole dancer. Just thinking about it made her hot and bothered, which was silly because she knew from the tips of her bruised toes and to the apex of her dented heart that tall, handsome men, dark or blond, spelled disaster for her. All men really.

Thank you, Ryan. When she'd returned to Whitetail

after that heart-hammering debacle she'd decided that the more handsome the man, the easier he was for her to resist. Granted, Whitetail hadn't thrown up any opportunities for her to test her theory in two years, but Finn in his tailored tuxedo slotted perfectly into the top category of "beyond gorgeous" so he was a perfect test case.

Attraction aside, her biggest problem was that she'd been out of her depth before she'd met Finn. The fact she'd even considered that she could pull off a stealth entry to the house was a testimony to her desperation. When she'd ruined the perfect look that the town had gone to so much trouble to organize for her so she could blend into the party, she'd immediately wanted to flee. But perhaps the Gods of Fairness really did exist and had finally deigned to intervene. She wanted to pinch herself because given everything that had happened up to this point, she couldn't believe she was actually sitting next to a man who not only knew Sean Callahan but knew how to contact him.

Yes! She gave a silent squeal. He'd been remarkable in his lack of concern over her illicit entry, avoided the obvious question of, "What the hell are you doing?" and had been generous with food and drink. She wasn't going to second-guess why he hadn't handed her over to security—she'd just accept it as a gift. She was absolutely certain he'd help her meet Sean Callahan, CEO of AKP Industries.

Working hard to keep her mind on the game and not on the sharp, clean scent of his cologne as it mixed in with something essentially masculine, she did everything she could to sound casual. "His private number? Wow, you must be really close to him."

"Not really." The words sounded unexpectedly curt

but then he shrugged, softening the tone. "Business is business."

She didn't really understand what that meant because in Whitetail all business involved a community connection but she brushed it aside as being irrelevant to her needs. "So you can get a message to him?"

He raised his brows and gave her a cat-who-ate-the-cream smile. "I can."

She tried to rein in the quivering anticipation that leaped in her belly. It was all to do with being close to getting Sean Callahan's private number and nothing to do with the way the peak of Finn's top lip said, "Kiss me."

Nail the deal. "I've been trying to meet with him for weeks."

"To discuss," he raised his fingers, wiggling them like quotation marks, "warehouses?"

It seemed an odd gesture but she nodded enthusiastically. "Do you think you could arrange a meeting with him for me?"

He rubbed his chin thoughtfully, the soft sound of the rasp of stubble the only noise in the room. "I suppose I *could* set that up."

Please, please, please. "But will you?"

He stretched his arm along the length of the couch and all the hair on her body rose in a delicious tingle. She held her breath as she scanned his face, everything hanging on his reply.

"Yes."

Relief poured through her, setting up a euphoric swirl, and this time she couldn't stop the squeal of delight from erupting from her lips. "Thank you. You have *no* idea how much I appreciate this."

"Oh, I think I do." His palm curved around the back

of her neck, his fingers winding their way into the fallen tendrils of hair.

She stilled as the warmth of his hand built on the heat from the Scotch, and then like a fireball it exploded into jubilation. Her head spun even faster than when he'd pulled her into the room, and she pressed her hand to his chest to stop herself from falling forward. "You're right. You've made me incredibly happy. Thank you."

His eyes, like unfathomable pools of ink, stared down at her, hypnotically, as if pulling her toward him. She automatically leaned in, kissing him gratefully and briefly on the cheek.

Like a slow-motion sequence, his head dropped forward, his hair tickling her forehead and then his lips touched hers, their pressure firm and coaxing.

Shocked surprise hurtled through her and the tiniest part of her said "Stop now" but it was silenced by the alcohol in her veins and the sheer joy that she'd secured the interview. *It's just a kiss.* What did it matter if it was with a virtual stranger—it made a crazy sort of sense given everything that had preceded it this evening.

And it had been such a long time since she'd been kissed.

She opened her mouth under his and sighed. He tasted of malt, of hot, starry summer nights and a tantalizing sense of long-lost joy. With her hand still pressed against his chest, she curled her fingers under the gaps between the studs of his formal shirt, and the tips met hot skin and taut muscle. Her breath hitched and her palm itched to feel more.

His hands slipped down her neck, caressing her bare shoulders and journeying along her arms—the touch leaving a trail of intoxicating bubbles that joined together into an effervescence of unadulterated need. She ached in a way she'd forgotten she could, and all the while his tongue continued its invasion of her mouth in the most delicious raid that had her reconsidering the antisocial behavior of pirates.

One of his hands rested on the top of the zipper at the back of her dress while the other cupped the weight of her breast through the beaded material. Her nipple immediately rose, pushing against the constraints of the bodice, and tingles dived deep. *More*.

She leaned in closer but he suddenly whipped his hand away from her breast, and was gripping the tops of her arms. Her breast sobbed, her mind snagged and suddenly she was being hauled upward. Her feet hit the floor hard. The next moment, Finn broke all contact, spinning away from her and striding straight toward the decanter.

As her breathing slowed and her vision started to clear, it took her wet and throbbing body a few seconds to catch up with her brain. When it did, it was met with a comprehensive list detailing *all* the reasons why Finn stopping the kiss was a seriously good idea. Not kissing strangers was a basic safety rule up there with looking both ways before crossing the street. Plus she was here on a mission for the town and she couldn't let herself get sidetracked by sex. The tiny rebellion of reawakened womanhood was duly reprimanded and squashed.

He silently handed her a drink which she accepted with an unsteady hand and with no intention of drinking it. If one Scotch had her considering getting naked with a complete stranger then she didn't need a second one. Finn downed his fast, his face a complicated crush of expressions, none of them easily readable. He placed the low-ball glass on the credenza and shot her a tight smile. A very different smile from the one he'd worn when he'd laughed with her over her lack of athleticism. That one had lit up those inky eyes like moonlight breaking through cloud, before carving into high and handsome cheeks, and weaving its way through sexy stubble.

This is officially awkward. Her mouth dried as she tried to think of something casually clever to break the stained silence, but she came up empty.

"Donna, how far are you prepared to go to meet with Sean?"

Okay, this was good; aberration over and now it was back to business. She could do that. She'd hoped to speak with Sean Callahan in Whitetail but if the only appointment she could get was in Chicago, then she'd go there. "Just tell me and I'll do it."

Black brows drew in so fast she almost heard them snap as they dug a deep V into the bridge of his long, straight nose. Every ounce of graciousness vanished. "And then I suppose you'll write about it."

Write about it? His change in demeanor had her second-guessing herself but using the logic that they were talking about a meeting, she realized that a detailed report for *The Bugle* was probably a good idea. "I'll give an interview first."

"I bet you will." Disgust slashed his face and he pressed a button near the fireplace before sweeping up her purse. With deft fingers he undid the clasp and upended it.

"Hey, what are you doing?" Lipstick and her phone tumbled onto the floor and she scrambled for them, her heart racing in shocked surprise. She had no idea what had just happened but every part of her told her it wasn't good.

Finn reached her phone first and held it high. "You're

not getting an interview, and you're sure as hell not getting any photos of me in compromising positions."

Photos? She stared at him wondering if he had some sort of mental problem. "What are you talking about?"

A steely expression stole all the humanness from his face and he stared at her like a thunderous, black angel with evil intent. "You can drop the innocent act because with a mouth like that, you're not innocent at all, are you? What was the plan? Sex on the couch or the credenza with a photographer secreted at the window?" His lips thinned and barely seemed to move. "I don't know who you're working for but you better hope they've got bail money."

Her heart hammered in her chest as she tried to make sense of his words and his complete character change but it was like she'd tumbled into a parallel universe. Everything looked the same but it was all oh so very different. "I have no clue what's going on inside your head but you're barking mad." She lunged for her phone.

He caught her shoulders and held her firmly at arm's length, as if she was a child. The slight creak of a door opening jerked his gaze up and beyond her.

She turned her head as far as she could, given his viselike grip on her, and saw a tall, silver-haired man striding into the room.

Sean Callahan. Annika instantly recognized him from the magazine picture Nicole had shown her. This was who she'd risked a concussion for. This was the man she had to speak to and she had to get to him before Finn said anything. She had to get free. Thinking fast she weighed her options—she could knee her captor in the groin but instead she chose the next one. Lifting a foot, she aimed a sharp kick squarely to his shin.

"Shit." His hands fell away from her shoulders.

Ignoring the pain that ricocheted along her own leg, she bunched up her long skirt and ran toward the man who held the future of Whitetail in his hands. "Mr. Callahan, I'm so sorry to do this to you on your daughter's engagement but I need to—"

"Mr. Callahan—" The security guard who'd refused her entry ran panting into the room with his paunch bouncing ahead of him. As his head came up for air, he saw her, raised his hand and said, "You!"

Her stomach fell to the floor as panic threatened to close her throat. She frantically glanced between the door, the three men and the now shut window. All escapes routes irrevocably cut off. "I can explain every—"

"Don't listen to her."

"Finnegan, what on earth's going on?" Sean Callahan's voice boomed around the chaotic room.

"You've caught me mid-citizen's arrest, Dad."

Dad? Annika's chest muscles froze and she gagged on bile. Oh, God, why hadn't she known Sean Callahan had a son? Why hadn't she done some research rather than depending on what Nicole had told her? She looked at both the Callahan men, and now that she knew their relationship she could immediately see the genes they shared—the impressive height, the strong, square jaw and the deep brackets around a wide mouth just waiting for a reason to smile. Right now though, given the way both of them were staring at her, that reason was going to be a long time coming.

"I can take over for you, sir." The security guard put his meaty hand on her arm. She struggled not to try and shake it off.

Tell them the truth. Tell them you're the acting mayor of Whitetail. She toyed with that idea for about one tenth of a second. She'd broken into a house, wrapped herself around the owner's son, allowed herself to be kissed senseless and to cap it off had kicked him as hard as she possibly could, treating his shin like a soccer ball. Oh yeah, they were so going to believe her.

TWO

FINN RUBBED HIS throbbing shin and reminded himself to never underestimate someone who claimed to be uncoordinated. He grunted at the security guard. "Ring the police, Jerome."

The usually stoic man looked confused. "Mr. Callahan, sirs, exactly which county sheriff covers this area?"

"Aren't you supposed to know stuff like that?" Finn could feel an egg-size lump rising on his leg.

"In Chicago, sir, but this part of the country is all new to me."

"We're on the border of Lake and Bayfield so take your pick."

Donna sighed, her smoky voice sounding tired. "Actually, it's Lake County. The police chief's number is 555-3228, although it's Saturday night so he'll probably be bowling. He never hears his cell over the noise so best to call 555-5196."

His gaze stalled on her mouth and the way it formed the numbers so precisely, instantly recalling the wild and hot way it had played under his. He ran his hand through his hair, the curls frustratingly snagging at his fingers. Kissing her was supposed to have been a test to see how far *she'd* go in her quest to get what she wanted. Instead he'd been more turned on in three minutes than he'd been in three months. He closed his hand, pressing his fingers into his palm, desperate to shut out the feel-

ing that had been tingling there since it had unexpectedly discovered a soft curve of breast nestling behind
the embroidered bodice. A tingling that had made him
reach for her zipper.

He hated that he'd responded like a randy teenager to
her calculated plan to get a story. But that was over. He
had her number and then some. "Don't believe a word
she says, Jerome."

"No, sir."

"She's right about the county," his father said quietly
as he put his hand on the door handle. "The toasts are
starting, Finnegan. Leave Jerome to handle this."

And it was time to go play happy families—the evening just got better and better. "She's wily, Jerome. Don't
let her near any windows and stay with her until she's
in the back of the squad car."

"Yes, sir."

He could barely look at her but he gave a curt nod.
"I'd like to say it was a pleasure meeting you but we
both know that's a lie."

Her chin shot up and those sparkling blue-on-blue
eyes flashed. "Enjoy the rest of the party, Finn."

Her words mocked him as he stepped out of the library.

BRIDGET MARY CALLAHAN—BRIDEY to her family and
close friends—was now officially engaged. She and
Hank had been quietly engaged for three months but
tonight was the public declaration. She stood barefoot
with thick, soft grass tickling between her toes. The
gentle and relaxing sound of the lake lapped behind her
as she stared up at the house from the bottom of the
garden. Fireflies zipped through the air, drawn to the
tiny white bud lights that adorned the huge maple and

beech trees. Torches surrounded the now-empty dance floor, casting delicious flickers of light and shade, and just beyond, on the terrace, she could make out the silhouette of Aphrodite—the slowly dripping ice sculpture that had graced the buffet table. The scene looked like a magical kingdom and the hours and hours of meticulous planning she'd put into it had all paid off. It was exactly how she'd imagined it. Picture-perfect.

A woman marched onto the terrace and into the picture. Bridey instantly recognized the walk—stiff, tightly wound and perfectly controlled. *Mom.* Then silver flashed in the night light and her father appeared, followed quickly by a woman younger than her mother who immediately slipped her arm through his as if staking her claim and declaring to all, "he's mine." *Stepmom.*

It didn't take long before big brother joined the group, standing next to their mother and flanking her like a protective guard as he always did on the very few occasions the Callahan clan actually came together. The last time had been two years ago when she'd finished her master's and had been accepted into the PhD program to study twentieth-century American literature. She held her breath, willing the picture to hold.

This night had been close to perfect but that had been when one hundred and fifty people had separated her family. Surely they could hold it together for just a tiny bit longer. She glimpsed a man stepping through the French doors, his height equal to that of her father and brother. The lights caught his hair, giving it a golden glow like the sun god, Apollo, and her heart fluttered in her chest. *Hank.* His usual stance—that of a man at ease in the world—held a tremor of uncertainty as he deliberated exactly where to stand. Wisely, he chose Switzerland and took his place between her parents.

She smiled, loving Hank with every fiber of her being. He was her soul mate. She'd been so busy planning their engagement party that she hadn't seen much of him in the last few weeks so she couldn't wait to wake up next to him tomorrow morning and start their vacation together. But right now it was time to rescue him. No one deserved to deal with her family en masse and unprotected. As Bridey picked up her shoes and commenced walking toward the group, her mother's tense voice drifted across the garden. "Where's Bridget? I need to say good-night before I leave."

"You don't have to stay in Whitetail, Kathleen." Her stepmother, Dana, seemed to draw even closer to Sean. "You're welcome to use the guest cottage."

Oh, no, here we go. The scene—picture-perfect when empty—was suddenly shredding at the edges. Bridey knew that a smile-cum-grimace would be pulling the skin taut across her mother's cheeks.

"That's very gracious of you, Dana." The tone said it was anything but.

"Kathleen." Sean's voice rolled out on a growl.

Daddy, no. Bridey knew the exact effect her father's warning tone would have on her mother. *Please don't bring up the divorce settlement and remind Mom how she lost the cottage.* She started to run.

"Sean, I didn't design the cottage for the convenience of your other wives."

"The invitation was well meant." Dana's tone conveyed resignation.

Sean patted his current wife's hand.

Finn's hand rested on the small of his mother's back as if to spin her away. "I'll drive you to Whitetail *now*, Mom. I have to go to the police department anyway."

With his usual lightning-fast decisions, big brother

had come to the rescue of his mother yet again, protecting her against their father even though she didn't need it. Kathleen Callahan had been self-sufficient for years and intolerant of those who were not.

Bridey's feet hit the terrace and she came into the circle of light, grabbing Hank's hand. "What a wonderful party. I just know everyone had the best time."

Her family turned toward her, mouths tightly closed and their silence speaking volumes.

Hank squeezed her hand but his smile was weary. "Mom and Dad are so sorry they missed the party."

A lump formed in her throat, making it hard to swallow, and tears pricked the backs of her eyes, but she refused to cry. She would not cry. She'd wanted everything to be perfect, needed everything to be perfect, and her first attempt had fallen short. Hank's parents hadn't made it and her family looked like they were sucking on lemons.

She gave herself a tiny shake. She knew perfection took hard work and she'd never been one to walk away from that and she wasn't about to start now. Life was a series of steps that needed to be taken in the correct order so that everything fell into place. For her, these steps started with a big engagement party and finished with a huge wedding. Her parents hadn't taken all the steps and their marriage had ended in divorce.

No way was Bridey getting divorced. She was going to do everything right. However, the *tiny* fact that she'd been the one to propose to Hank had her stressing that they'd already started out wrong, breaking the proper order of things—which is why she now had an elaborate plan. A plan to right things in her world, to realign the universe and to appease all or any deities to ensure her future happiness with Hank. Nothing or no one was going to get in her way.

"I'M FINN CALLAHAN and I've come down as requested to check the charge sheet against Donna whoever-she-is." Resignation clung to his words because more than anything he wished he was home in his quiet cabin, free of women, free of family and in a place where he could forget the whole miserable night.

The police chief, looking as weary as most people do at one in the morning, rose to his feet and joined him on the other side of the counter. "Thanks for coming down, Mr. Callahan."

"No problem. This is going to be quick, isn't it?"

"I'm hoping so."

"Hey, Rory, I got us some hot choc— Oh."

What the hell? Finn spun around at the sound of a very familiar smoky voice.

Donna stood stock-still clutching two steaming mugs. Except for her voice, her French nails and a fading black eye, she was unrecognizable. Gone were the high heels and evening dress, and in their place she wore red canvas shoes, ripped-at-the-knee jeans and a blue hoodie. Her face was now scrubbed clean of ruined makeup, making her eyes seem larger than ever, but the biggest surprise was her hair. What had seemed to be a mousy blah color when wet was now a startling white-blond with sun-kissed streaks of gold. Instead of being swept up in a French chignon, it was pulled back in a simple ponytail which made her look ridiculously innocent and wholesome instead of designer and predatory. Then he remembered her mouth—full of delicious sin—and how he'd lost total control.

Anger at himself, as well as her, surged back and he turned around, slapping the counter. "Why isn't she in a cell?"

The police chief calmly stood his ground. "She was wet and cold so I sent her home for a hot shower before she caught a cold. She knew she had to come back."

"She lives here?" He'd assumed she was a stringer from Chicago, plying her trade with the trashy publications of the big city.

"I'll just go sit in the cell." Donna put down one of the mugs and hot chocolate slopped over the side, creating a brown river that snaked its way toward the paperwork. "Oh, sorry." She grabbed a wad of tissues out of her pocket as if they'd been there for the express purpose of cleaning up a self-induced mess.

"No, you need to stay here." The policeman sipped his hot chocolate. "This is good, Anni."

"It's the marshmallows. I whipped them in."

Finn shook his head trying to clear the stands of fatigue that were stealing his concentration. *Anni*? Her name was Donna. Nothing was matching up here except her clumsiness. "Excuse me for interrupting 'top tips for making hot chocolate,' but can we focus on why we're here…" he read the chief's name badge, "…Chief Gunderson. This woman broke into my father's house."

She wriggled her nose like a bunny rabbit and her shoulders squirmed. "Well, technically I did, but not really. I'm sorry for how it looks and I can explain everything."

Cutesy didn't cut it with him but worse than that she was doing that thing she did with her teeth. His gaze slid to her plump bottom lip and his mouth filled with the memory of its cushion softness and intoxicating taste. Part of him yearned to kiss her again. *Yeah, right, like that's really going to help. She's a liar and an information thief.*

He stared at her left shoulder and fought to find his emotionless but analytical thinking that he prided himself on. Did she think he was wet behind the ears? He and his father ran a business that employed thousands of people in and out of the country and he'd pretty much heard every excuse in the book. "It's too late for sorry, Donna, and the only explaining you have to do is to a judge."

She looked him straight in the eye. "Actually, I'm Annika. Annika Jacobson."

He sighed. "I don't care what the hell your name is. It makes no difference to the fact you broke the law." He turned to the chief. "Does it?"

Rory reached for the now damp and chocolate-stained charge sheet. "Technically, no."

Finn smiled. There was nothing like the facts to simplify things and clear them of the chaos of emotions. "There you go. You not only broke into the house with the intention of getting information to sell, you also used an alias and lied about why you wanted to meet my father."

"I'm not a journalist and I didn't lie about why I wanted to meet your father." Her voice was unexpectedly firm.

He didn't believe her. "If that's the truth then you have a funny way of doing things."

"Mr. Callahan, you're quite correct." Rory Gunderson's expression was a combination of paternal concern and professional patience. "Technically she broke the law. However, I'm uncomfortable arresting Whitetail's acting mayor over what I believe to be a misunderstanding."

Finn stared at her in disbelief. Not now, or even when she'd been wearing wet evening wear, had she looked anything like a local official. "You're the mayor?"

Her shoulders rose and fell in a self-deprecating shrug and a faint blush pinked her cheeks. "It's a bit of a long story, but I'm standing in until the next elections."

Heat licked at him, warming his blood. Again. The *only* explanation for this unwanted reaction was it had been way too long since he'd had sex. Hell, he could fix that. He vowed right there and then that first thing in the morning he was heading to Chicago and calling one of his many standby girlfriends who happily dropped everything to have dinner with him. Dinner and sex. Women who didn't wear faded jeans that curved around their ass like a glove.

"Being mayor doesn't absolve you from breaking and entering."

Her chin tilted up and her eyes flashed, all contrition gone. "If AKP Industries had any manners, I would never have climbed through that window!"

Something about the way she said "manners" had him taking it personally. He prided himself on the way he conducted business. "My company." He made a slight correction. "My family's company is run on sound business principles and unlike some people, we don't run around doing what we please under the guise of fairness."

"Sound business principles?" Her voice rose with incredulity. "Does that mean leaving etiquette at the door? If *one* person from *your* company had responded to my myriad of letters, faxes, emails and phone calls about the business park, neither of us would be standing here tonight."

Um, warehouses. A sound bite echoed in his head.

She'd said she wanted to talk to Sean about warehouses. At the time he'd put it down to being part of her play-acting scenario because it made no sense. It still didn't. "What business park?"

"What business park?" She threw her arms out in disgust. "Oh, please, like there's more than one in a town this size? This is exactly the sort of AKP crap I'm talking about."

"Anni," the police chief rebuked mildly. "Take a deep breath."

"Sorry, Rory." She threw him an apologetic smile before turning back to Finn, her lips pursed and her eyes hard. "You and your father owe this town one meeting about your plans for the empty warehouses that you own on the south side of the town."

And right then his world steadied and he was back on known territory—the business. Numbers had always been far more reliable than people and he loved the company. He lived and breathed it, played and slept with it, and, just lately in this economic climate, worried about it way too much. He folded his arms across his chest, a man in complete control. "You've broken the law in vain then, Ms. Jacobson, because AKP Industries doesn't own a business park in Whitetail."

Long, fine fingers slapped her hips. "You're wrong."

He shook his head very slowly, secure in his position. "Unlike you, I'm never wrong."

She hooked him with a gaze as clear as a northwoods stream—one that penetrated deeply and zeroed deep into a place he kept hidden. "Rory, show him the copy of the deed."

Deed? The chief passed him papers that read "Title of the Whitetail Business Park," and a yellow "sign here" note was attached with its red arrow pointing directly to a signature. He blinked twice as if the action would change what he saw but nothing could hide the very distinctive and recognizable scrawl of his father.

Shit. His stomach turned over. Annika was right. He didn't know what he hated more—that she'd just exposed a hole in his knowledge of the company's assets, the fact that AKP Industries now owned a business park in the sticks smack in the middle of the worst economic slowdown in the history of the industrialized world or that his father hadn't told him. A cramp clawed through his chest making it hard to get his breath.

He felt like a fool. How did a whole freaking town know AKP owned a business park ahead of him? What the hell was the old man up to?

The cool indifference he usually held on to when he thought about or had to deal with his father melted under the onslaught of betrayal. He'd been working around the clock, filling in when his father failed to turn up to meetings and Sean was treating him like a mushroom—keeping him in the dark and feeding him manure. It had left him wide open, and he sure as hell didn't appreciate being played or exposed as someone out of his depth and out of control. People were going to pay and payment started right now with someone who had blue eyes, red shoes and the most amazing mouth he was absolutely determined to forget.

WHEN ANNIKA HAD stood under the stream of hot water in her shower an hour earlier, she'd decided that the best thing for her to do would be to apologize to Finn Callahan and admit she was totally in the wrong over the way she'd gained entry to the lake house.

And she'd tried, but when his stormy, coal-black eyes had raked over her, followed up by his self-righteous, rich-man-I-own-the-world high horse, she'd snapped. Victory had been hers when he'd read the documents.

Right now though, with his black stubble darker than ever against cheeks that had paled under a tan, she experienced a slight twinge of remorse. Knowing she still had to secure this meeting for the town, she pitched for calm reasonableness. "Finn, it's late. Let's start over in the morning after we've all had a decent night's sleep."

Silently, he slowly and carefully folded the copy of the deed in half and in half again before sliding it into the inside pocket of his tuxedo jacket. Every action was precise and deliberate, and she suddenly missed the man with the easy and wicked grin who'd pulled her through the window and laughed with her. A trickle of unease turned into a river, flowing insidiously down to every single cell. Perhaps she'd just made a tactical error in showing him the document. Powerful men—any man for that matter—didn't take well to being proven wrong.

He pushed a recalcitrant jet curl off his forehead. "AKP Industries will be in contact."

His voice was quiet and reasonable, and she wanted to feel relieved but she'd heard that phrase over and over from the lips of many without anything ever changing, and she no longer trusted it. Whipping out her phone she said, "As backup, I'll take the contact number of the person in charge of the warehouses."

"That won't be necessary. We'll be in contact. I give you *my* word." His voice deepened as if his word was inexorably linked with his honor.

Be honorable yourself if you wish to associate with honorable people. The old proverb echoed in her head, ramping up her guilt about climbing through the window. *Know when to hold and know when to fold.* She reluctantly forced herself to slip her phone back into her pocket.

Rory smiled the quiet smile he always wore whenever he'd mediated and solved the problem, and unclipped the charge sheet. "So, Mr. Callahan, now you and Anni are finally on the same page and you're taking the meeting, you'll be dropping the charges?"

An ominous black cloud rolled off Finn as his eyes darkened to ebony and stayed fixed on her. "No, the charges stand."

What? Forget guilt and remorse—fury unleashed itself off the back of betrayal. "You bastard, you gave me your word."

"Oh, my word stands, Annika." The chill in his voice formed icicles in the warm, summer air. "You on the other hand have to learn that business has a process, and *that* process has to be followed. Illegal entry, lying and enticement don't even come close."

"Enticement?" She struggled to think what on earth he was talking about and then with a breath-stealing jolt she remembered his question just before he kissed her. *How far are you prepared to go to meet Sean?* Her stomach rolled at the realization and a wave of self-loathing rocked through her, quickly reigniting her anger at him. "You kissed me because you thought I'd sleep with you to meet your father? God, what sort of people do you normally do business with? No, forget that. What sort of person are you?"

"Honorable. I do business with people who follow the rules." His jaw jutted and his eyes flashed with unforgiving intent. "By being charged you get exactly what you want."

Panic tangoed in her belly. "How do you figure that?"

"You get to talk to my father in court."

THREE

At 6:00 A.M. Finn had given up any attempt at sleep and had gone for an early morning run around the lake. The pink streaks of dawn had brought the birds into the sky and he'd caught the red flash of the cardinal, heard the hammering of a woodpecker and watched a flock of Canada geese land on the lake, like planes coming in on an aircraft carrier. Usually, the sights and sounds of the woods soothed him. Not today. If anything the exercise seemed to have increased his sense of disgruntlement.

Hot, sweaty and hungry, he hit the shower in the main house before heading into the kitchen. There was no food in his cabin because he was only staying the one night and as soon as he'd spoken to his father he was on the helicopter back to Chicago. But before any of that could happen he needed eggs and coffee—facing Sean on an empty stomach was inadvisable.

The house was deliciously quiet because the guests had used accommodations in Whitetail and the surrounding county. Sunday was Esther's day off and with the family still asleep after their late night, he was relieved he could have breakfast alone. He whipped open the fridge and examined the contents. He'd just put his hand on the milk when he felt a tug on his T-shirt, and he turned around to see an eight-year-old boy in pajamas holding a toy truck in one hand and a toy sports car in the other.

"I'm hungry." The child announced it more as a command than a statement.

"When I was eight I made my own breakfast," he said automatically.

Logan pushed black curls out of his eyes. "Mommy says I can only make pancakes when there's someone else in the kitchen."

With his hands full, Finn kicked the fridge door closed. "So, go get your mom."

"She's asleep." The boy clambered up onto one of the high stools next to the autumn-brown granite counter, expectation and hope clear on his face.

"Then go ask your fa—" Finn swallowed the word. He didn't want the kid getting their father up. Not yet anyway.

"Daddy's asleep too but you're not."

Finn wanted more than anything to have the kitchen devoid of kid chatter—any chatter—so he could mentally prepare for his "chat" with Sean. That and the fact he had little experience with children and frequently felt out of his depth in their presence. Finn was twenty-five years older than Logan. When that age gap was combined with the fact Finn kept his relationship with Sean strictly business and the Callahan clan rarely gathered together as a family, there'd been few opportunities for the brothers to bond. The result was that his little half brother with the endearing gap-toothed smile was a stranger.

Finn had never cooked pancakes in his life and had no clue how to start. "I'm making eggs. Would you like that?"

"I don't like eggs."

Finn pulled three boxes of cereal out of a cupboard

and pushed them across the counter. "How about you choose one of these instead?"

Logan got a mulish look. "You're grumpy in the mornings just like Daddy."

The comparison stung. "I am *not*." He picked up the box containing the most sugar—a cereal he knew Bridey ate on vacation but he figured any parent would refuse to serve it to their kid. He poured a generous serving into a bowl and pushed it across to Logan.

The little boy picked up a bright green circle of cereal. "Mommy says Daddy has to have his paper, his coffee and his toast before we can talk to him."

A similar accusation had once been leveled at Finn by an ex-girlfriend and he'd denied it then as well. The *only* thing he shared in common with his father was business acumen. He picked up the gallon of milk in preparation to pour it on Logan's cereal.

The boy's hand shot out. "I'm not little. I can do it."

Finn put the plastic container down and turned the handle toward Logan. This was a perfect example of why he didn't get kids. One minute Logan wanted him to cook pancakes and the next he was Mr. Independent, risking sending a gallon of milk spewing everywhere. Kids! He swallowed against the zip of frustration he knew he should curb and tried for conversation. "Why didn't you sleep in?"

The boy stared at him as if he'd come from Mars. "Why would I do that?"

Finn sighed. This was all too hard and with the issue of the warehouses to sort out, he didn't have the head space to try and get to know his brother today. "Why don't you go watch cartoons while you eat that?"

The kid's wide-eyed look told him Dana probably had

a "no TV while eating" ban. "Here, take these cookies too." He shoved a bag of chocolate chip cookies at him.

Logan didn't pause to question this largesse and scooted off with his unexpected windfall.

Finn breathed a sigh of relief and willed the coffee to drip faster. He hadn't cooked in this kitchen in years, but despite different women being in domestic command, some things never changed and that was mostly because of Esther, their longtime housekeeper. He quickly found a frying pan and started cooking eggs.

"Oh, is that coffee?" Bridey walked in from outside dressed in shorts and a T-shirt. "Finn? In a kitchen? Where's my camera?"

So much for a quiet breakfast. "Very funny, just don't tell Esther." He poured the now-brewed coffee into two mugs, took a long slug from one and handed the other one to his sister. "Where's your guy?"

Bridey shot him an infuriated look. "Hank, Finn. His name is Hank."

"Someone's testy this morning." He pressed down the toaster. Hank was the very quiet head engineer at the Illinois plant, and the fact that he'd actually had the balls to propose to his vivacious sister still surprised Finn. The fact she'd said yes had stunned him even more. "Okay, where's Hank?"

"On the phone." Bridey sighed. "He's talking the covering engineer through a problem with machine number four and it doesn't sound hopeful."

Machine four had been temperamental since its installation two years ago but his father had overseen the implementation and dealt with the ongoing issues. It was Sean's problem, not his. "Does Dad know?"

"If they can't get it restarted, he soon will." Bridey buttered the toast roughly. "Sometimes I wish the business would just go away." She stared out the floor-to-ceiling windows toward the lake with a wistful expression on her face. "Do you remember the zip line between the tree house and that old beech tree that crossed the finger of the lake?"

Finn flipped the eggs onto the toast before tossing the pan in the sink. "I remember the yelling and the arguments Mom and Dad had about it. It was the summer they separated."

Bridey didn't seem to hear as she rested her chin in her hands. "I loved it. I loved the way the wind would tear at my hair before I dropped into the water."

"You used to scream like a banshee."

"That was half the fun." She bit into the eggs and chewed thoughtfully. "How long since we had a summer at the lake together?"

The question made him pause and he had to calculate back a long way. "Probably my last year of college. You'd just graduated high school." It was the year his grandfather had died and his father had married Dana.

With the death of his grandfather, he'd lost the reason to visit Kylemore and he hadn't been near the place for years until last year when the island had come on the market. In a moment of uncharacteristic nostalgia, probably induced by the heat of Mexico, he'd bought it at auction, by phone. He only visited when he knew the rest of the family would be in Chicago—his time was winter and fall.

He mopped the broken yolk with his toast, planning one more cup of coffee before texting his father to schedule a meeting. He realized with a start that Bridey was talking again. "What did you say?"

"We should do it again."

"Do what?"

His sister had that starry-eyed look she got when she thought she had a great idea and it was always underpinned by deadly determination. "Have a true Callahan summer here like we used to have when we were kids. One last summer all together before I get married."

The idea gave him goose bumps. "Exactly which summers are you remembering so fondly, B?"

But Bridey was on a roll and either she didn't hear him or she chose to ignore him. "Logan's such a great age now and we could do all the stuff with him that Grandpa did with us. Wouldn't that be great?"

The thought of spending more than one day in the arms of his family made him flinch. "Count me out, Bridey. You don't need me now you've got Hank to play with."

"At least think about it. Two weeks. One even."

Her voice implored the way it did every time she wanted something her own way, but he wasn't his father and he wasn't malleable Hank so it cut no ice with him. Hearing the creak of the front door, he figured his father was up and out looking for the paper. "I came to your party and I'll be at your wedding, but I can't give you a summer." He dropped a brotherly kiss on her hair. "I have to talk to Dad and then I'm outta here."

Ignoring the sage advice of his little brother that their father needed coffee and breakfast before talking to anyone, he walked outside. He met Sean jogging back from the gate looking remarkably fit with the Sunday paper in his hand. Finn begrudgingly acknowledged that for a guy of fifty-seven, Sean hadn't let himself go. Although it was probably more accurate to say Dana hadn't allowed that to happen. The old man still turned heads wherever he went and his Irish charm—when he chose to turn it on—could sell ice creams to Eskimos. Or in his case, paper and packaging to America and beyond. The man was a business legend and from that perspective, Finn had learned a lot from him. But their relationship was much more "business associates" than "father and son." Finn had no problem with that at all.

Last night's humiliation at the Whitetail Police Department circled him and he cut to the chase. "We need to talk."

His father didn't break his stride. "Whatever it is can wait until I've had breakfast."

Finn caught him up. "No, it can't wait." He played the line he'd been raised on. "It's business."

Sean muttered something that sounded like, "It always is," but Finn knew he'd never say that so he must have misheard.

Sean slapped the paper against his hand. "If it's about machine number four, I've spoken to Germany."

The ruthless entrepreneur who'd turned a small business into a mega one cut across his manicured lawn and sat down at a large teak, outdoor table and flicked open the paper. "So you can relax now and enjoy your weekend. I'll see if the Cubs whooped the Brewers."

Finn ground his teeth. "It's got nothing to do with number four and everything to do with your signature on the deed to the Whitetail business park."

"What about it?"

"Letting me know we'd bought it would have been good."

Sean lowered the paper and shrugged. "It's no big deal. I picked up two small warehouses we got in a fire sale when Reggies went to the wall. Think of them as a real estate investment."

Finn pressed his hands onto the table. "The big deal

is they're an investment we don't need when we're currently cutting back in other areas."

His father's shrewd gray eyes suddenly looked interested. "Really? *That's* the big deal, Finnegan?"

The big deal is that a woman with cherry-red lips and cornflower-blue eyes made me look like a fool. No way in hell was he admitting to that. "If I'm to do my job properly I need to be fully briefed. Pulling crap like this makes a mockery of my position of being second in charge."

Sean gave him a long look and eventually cleared his throat. "You're right. You need all the information and I should have told you."

His gut dropped to his feet. It wasn't a reply he'd expected. He couldn't ever recall a time when his father had admitted to being wrong. Feeling totally adrift in a boat full of leaking indignation, he grunted out, "Good, I'm glad we're on the same page then." Only it didn't feel like that at all. "I'm heading back to Chicago."

"Excellent. Take Hank with you and meet the German engineer who's on tonight's plane." Sean picked up the paper.

Finn did a double take. His father was a hands-on businessman and the Illinois plant was his baby. Look out anyone who tried to run it. The two times Finn had brought up succession planning his father had refused to discuss it in any shape or form. "So, you're not coming?"

A voice sounded from behind the paper. "Only if you can't handle it."

Confusion mixed in with disbelief. The fact Sean didn't want to handle it and control everything had his head spinning with a thousand questions. "Of course I can handle it."

"Good." Sean leaned back, paper rustling. "What a

glorious day. On your way out, ask Bridey or Dana to send out coffee."

Finn strode toward the French doors convinced his father was losing it.

"BEING IN COURT will be the ideal place to talk to Sean Callahan because he has to be there, and he has to listen."

Annika addressed the town meeting after *The Bugle*'s online and print edition had published the details of her arrest. To Rory's credit—and he had her eternal gratitude—he'd only released the bare facts but that was enough to require some heavy-duty spin-doctoring. Thank goodness no one had heard she'd been draped over the dark and soulless Finn Callahan, or worse still that she'd been so stupid to be rendered boneless by a mind-altering kiss. A kiss she hadn't realized had been calculated to see how far she'd put out. Her cheeks burned hot at the memory and her conscience berated her.

You have no clue about men. Seriously, no clue…

"The dress is ruined," Melissa grumbled.

"I'll pay for it." Annika restated her earlier promise despite the fact it would totally empty her bank account and she'd have to tell Ellery she couldn't make rent. Again.

You know what to do. Finish the final painting in the Dawn, Day and Dusk *series that the Milwaukee Gallery's waiting on. The one you told them would be done by summer and you haven't even started yet.*

She shoved that particular thought way down deep. It was easier to worry about Whitetail than to think about painting. "Everyone, I've been doing a bit of resear—"

"Will Bridget Callahan be at the court?" Mrs. Norell

interrupted, her face animated. "Perhaps we could put on a mini wedding expo outside to catch her attention."

"That's an excellent idea and I can park my horse and carriage in front of the court," Al suggested. "Prissy will happily stand there for an hour if she has hay."

"I suppose I could dress one of my mannequins in a bridal dress and put it in the carriage," Melissa offered, shooting a telling look at Annika. "I mean it's unlikely to get dirty because it won't be climbing through a window."

"The summer hanging baskets on Main Street are still pretty from Jennifer's wedding," Mrs. Norell effused. "Nicole, you should groom a wig for the mannequin so Miss Callahan knows we can do hair and makeup too. I could mind little Max for you if that helps."

"Thanks, Ella. He always enjoys visiting your garden."

John Ackerman piped up with, "You can use my display boards from the market. Anni, you can pin up some of your invitations and everyone can use the holders for their business cards. I'll ring the chef at the Supper Club and contact Sherri at Lundstrom's bakery so they can put their cards there as well."

A twitter of noise rose as more and more people called out suggestions.

Annika hit her gavel hard on the lectern. She loved these people dearly but they didn't seem to realize that the town needed real jobs. "I love your enthusiasm for this idea but is it realistic? We need jobs *now* and I'm worried this wedding idea won't provide regular jobs that put food on the table."

A grumble rumbled around the hall and Annika let out a long sigh. They were keen to try despite the fact that Bridget Callahan was unlikely to come into town and see the display, let alone commit to marrying in Whitetail. Biting her lip, she weighed up the pros and cons. She valued the fact they wanted to try but she didn't want them to go to all that effort only to be hurt and disappointed. But they wanted to be involved and she appreciated that. So while she was busy securing Whitetail a real industry, where was the harm in a mini wedding expo?

"Sure, why not. I'll put up some examples of my invitations."

WGN TV Chicago

"And to end tonight's news bulletin, some quirky footage from Whitetail, Wisconsin. The small northwoods town set up a wedding display outside their courthouse today as their acting mayor, Annika Jacobson, faced a charge of breaking and entering into the vacation home of Chicago's paper and recycling tycoon, Sean Callahan. With the slogan 'Whitetail—Weddings That WOW,' they hoped to entice Bridget Callahan to marry in their town. The Callahan-Neiquest wedding is tipped to be one of the biggest events on next year's summer social calendar and although the venue is yet to be announced, we think that Chicago's InterContinental can relax."

FOUR

FINN STEPPED OUT of the helicopter, not quite believing he was back at Kylemore again five days after he'd left. This doubled the amount of times he'd visited during the summer in years. Hank was supposed to have been the one on the helicopter, heading back to restart his vacation with Bridey and at the same time, bringing documents for Sean to sign.

But machine number four was still plaguing their life and Hank had to bail on his vacation. Jazz Juice was understandably stressing about their supply of juice boxes and Finn had rescheduled production across all accounts to spread the impact. If that hadn't been enough to contend with, his P.A. had broken her pelvis and was on indefinite sick leave, his lawyer was tied up with his son's Bar Mitzvah, and that left no one else vetted by the company to be trusted with documents, so Finn was back at the lake. He could think of better ways to spend a Friday.

He accepted his bag and laptop from the pilot and walked the short distance into the house. The loud whirr of a vacuum cleaner met him and he smiled. Esther was here, meaning lunch would be delicious and plentiful. He set down his bags and followed the noise.

"Esther."

A large woman with meaty arms looked up in surprise and the next moment he was enveloped in a huge hug, and circled by the scent of cinnamon and spices with a hint of bleach. "Finn, you're back?"

He breathed in the scent that reminded him of the happier moments of his childhood. "Just for a day."

Esther tsked. "You look exhausted. Stay longer, sleep late and let me cook you all your favorite foods."

The idea of comfort food curled warmth through his belly and had him considering the idea for an instant. Then common sense kicked in and he gave her a wide and beguiling Callahan smile. "I'm too busy to stay, Essie, but how about you bake me some brownies and I'll take them back to Mexico."

Esther gave him a piercing look. "Too busy to stay now but not in November?"

He wasn't biting. He'd inherited his family but that didn't mean he had to vacation with them. "So where is he?"

"Your father's outside with everyone."

He nodded his thanks as she returned to the vacuuming and he headed toward the terrace doors. As he approached he could hear a mix of voices and laughter drifting on the summer breeze. Taking a deep breath, he slid on his sunglasses, slid open the screen door and stepped outside.

Through the trees, he could make out a group of people on the huge expanse of lawn. Logan was closest and came running up the moment he saw him.

"Finn, do you want to play T-ball?"

"Sorry, but I'm not on vacation, Logan."

"Come on," Logan wheedled. "We're all playing."

He didn't know who "all" was but he imagined it was the immediate neighbors and maybe Bridey. "That's good, so you've got a team and you don't really need me, do you?"

The kid sighed and the look in his dark eyes was too familiar by far, but he didn't say anything else before running back through the trees.

Finn stomped on a sliver of guilt and immediately justified his actions. He wasn't on vacation and that fact was being reinforced by the hot sun beating down on his chinos making him hot. He wished he'd taken the time to change into shorts and a polo shirt and he would, just as soon as he'd talked to Sean. For now, he rolled up the sleeves of his business shirt and kept on walking.

He saw Dana holding a baseball bat and swinging for a ball tossed by someone he didn't recognize. As she hit it high, people started running and then he heard a deep and victorious laugh. He stopped dead and felt his jaw drop as he watched his father slide into home base. His father who'd never played a game in his life other than deal-closing golf, was playing vacation T-ball.

A voice called out, "I've got it."

No way. Not again. Abject incredulity poured over him and he swung around sharply at the familiar melodic voice. He lifted his sunglasses and squinted hoping that would change the image. It didn't. Annika Jacobson, her blond hair streaming out behind her, stood with her head tilted back, her creamy neck extended and her arms outstretched, all ready for the perfect catch.

He watched mesmerized as the white ball reached its zenith before arcing down toward earth and her open hands. She leaped for it, missed and fell over.

A chorus of, "Are you okay?" went up as everyone started running toward her. With her lush, cherry-red mouth laughing, she rolled over and stood up, her legs stained with green. "I'm fine. Sorry, Captain Logan, I told you I wasn't very good."

Finn stared, rooted to the spot, and desperately tried

to locate his vanished equilibrium. Nothing in this picture matched up with anything close to normal. *She* did not belong here. His father did *not* play ball and it was this disparity that had him stunned and staring. It had absolutely *nothing* to do with the way Annika's slim and shapely legs seemed to go on forever before seductively disappearing under the cuff of very short, denim cutoffs. She bent down to retrieve the ball and his pants tightened.

"Finn!" Bridey shrieked, her voice making everyone turn toward him. "You came back."

Annika's chin rose and those dazzlingly clear eyes met his gaze for a fraction of a second, offering up some sort of challenge, and then Bridey got closer, blocking his view.

His sister greeted him with arms stretched out wide, but her vision reached far over his shoulder and way beyond him. "You changed your mind and you're staying. Thank you." She hugged him hard and then pulled back. "Where's Hank?"

He shook his head. "I'm not staying and Hank's tied up at the plant."

Her hand immediately slid into her pocket and she pulled out her phone, checking for messages. With an abrupt action, she shoved the sleek, black device back into her pocket.

His effervescent sister looked as crestfallen as a little girl whose ice cream had just fallen out of the cone and landed in the dirt. The latent big brother in him surfaced. "He's probably left a message for you with Esther. You know that unless it's life or death, she doesn't run after us if we're not in the house."

Her mouth quirked up on one side as if she only half believed him. She called out a general announcement of,

"I'm going back to the house" before giving a backward wave and striking off through the trees.

Most of the other guests drifted toward the drinks table and Dana called out, "Finn, sit down. Lunch is at one."

He gave a tight smile and nodded. Had everyone forgotten that he wasn't on vacation? He didn't have the time or inclination for a long lunch and he wished he could think of an excuse to get out of it but given he'd just arrived, he had nothing. When he finally turned back to see what Annika was up to, he saw her walking toward the lake with Logan, her head bent low toward his and her white-gold hair shimmering against his black curls. She looked completely at ease with the little boy in a way he'd never known. It shouldn't have bothered him but it added to the utter confusion that swam inside him at seeing his father playing ball. He felt like he was the outsider here and that was plain wrong. She was the person who didn't belong.

He immediately closed the gap between him and his father. "Dad, what the hell is she doing here?"

Sean had mostly been an absent father from the time Finn was twelve, although there'd been occasions when he'd come down on him as the heavy-handed father complete with the lash of his Irish temper. As a teenager Finn had taught himself to ride out the lectures, telling himself there was no point in reacting because Sean would vanish again soon enough. By the time Finn joined the company at twenty-five, he only viewed his father as a business associate and Sean had done the same. It worked for both of them.

But right now, Sean's mouth was thinned in disapproval and he was looking more like a father than he had in years. "This is my home, Finnegan, and Annika's my guest. Inviting her over for lunch after what happened was the least I could do." He folded his arms tightly across his faded, blue Chicago Cubs T-shirt. "I had an interesting morning in court on Monday, and as a result I've spoken to my secretary about not filtering my mail. Now it's your turn to explain. It seems you chose to leave out a few pertinent facts about the night she came into the house."

No way was he feeling any guilt over *that*. "She outright lied."

Silver hair glinted in the sunshine and Sean sighed. "She bent the truth. Some of us do it from time to time."

A sliver of something close to anger tried to pierce his now well-constructed disconnection from Sean as a father—a detachment which had started the day Sean had left his mother for Dana's predecessor. "You'd know that better than me."

Sean stiffened and his eyes flashed but when he spoke it was back to business, just as Finn preferred. "You need to sit down with her and discuss the Whitetail warehouses."

He'd rather swim with sharks than sit down again with Annika of the big blue eyes and the long, long legs. "I could do that but seeing as you bought the warehouses as a business investment, that makes them your baby. I know how much you like to run things your way so it's best you talk to her."

His father's mouth twitched. "I would, except I'm on vacation."

He dismissed that in a heartbeat. "You do deals from the lake every year."

"Not this year. I'm spending the entire summer here, and I'll return to my desk in September." Sean tilted his head and gave one of his penetrating long looks. "You can finally have what you've been wanting for a year now, a shot at running the business. I'm giving you two months."

For the second time in two days his father left him speechless. The earliest memory Finn had of him was in a suit and walking out the door to the office. Sean Callahan was synonymous with work, and even when the setting was recreational, Sean kept working. The fact he was handing over the reins for sixty days in the middle of a production mess was unheard of and totally unexpected. It was also immensely exciting.

An uncomfortable thought took hold despite the fact he and Sean weren't close, and his question shot out abrupt and terse. "Are you sick?"

Sean shook his head and thumped his chest. "No, the doctor gave me a clean bill of health at my physical last week."

Now it was official—Sean's offer made no sense. "Then what the hell are you going to do all summer?"

His father gave him a bemused look and extended his arm out toward the lake. "What do you think I'm going to do? Sail, canoe, read. The choices are endless."

"You'll be bored in two days." Finn plowed his hand through his hair trying to interpret what was going on. "You realize that if word gets out you're doing this the share prices are going to plummet?"

The savvy businessman's eyes took on a calculating glint. "It won't get out. As you pointed out I usually run the company from here every summer so no business analyst or journalist is even going to question my absence from Chicago."

Finn started to pace. "They will when they see my signature on the paperwork and me commuting between Mexico and Illinois."

His father leaned casually against the trunk of a towering beech tree. "Ah, but you won't be. You told me a month ago that the management team down south was working like a dream,
so that frees you up."

"Except I'll be tied up like an errand boy running documents up here."

Sean shook his head. "That won't be necessary. The solution is easy."

"How? I'm not letting your midlife crisis, or whatever it is, affect the company."

Sean's brows rose. "I'm having a vacation, Finnegan, and the solution to all your concerns is right here at the lake."

"You've lost me."

His father gave him the look he gave junior associates in their first week when they knew nothing. "You do what I do every summer and run the company from here."

The thought of spending the next two months up here with family and only occasional trips to Chicago had him ready to run. "No way in hell."

Black brows rose inquiringly. "So you have another idea?"

Of course he did. He had to. He'd…perhaps if…or… While his mind scrabbled for a rock-solid solution, he aimed for another weak spot. "My P.A.'s sick and I'll need help. Dana won't want a stranger in the house and no way am I working remotely with someone new."

His father didn't skip a beat. "Dana will be fine with it as long as your P.A. confines herself to the office. Fly a temp up, rent her a car so she can drive in from Whitetail, or better yet, stick her in your cabin and you move into the house. Problem solved. Anything else?"

Move into the house?

The suggestion stunned him, blanking his brain completely at a time when he needed it to be firing with ideas on how to avoid this very situation.

He closed his eyes running through his options but nothing materialized. He couldn't come up with even one alternative solution. The wily old bastard had him. If Finn wanted a shot at running the company without risking the fallout that happened to businesses whenever there was succession planning, he had to play it Sean's way. He had to do it from the Kylemore.

His father took his silence as acceptance. "Good. That's settled. You can start your stint as acting CEO by sitting down right now with the acting mayor of Whitetail and discussing the warehouses. Then organize yourself an assistant."

There weren't many times Finn hated business, but this was one of them.

"IF YOU WANT to talk about warehouses, let's talk."

A shadow cast itself over Annika and the sandcastle she'd been making with Logan up until he'd gotten hungry and run back to the house. Now she looked up to see the jet-haired and extraordinarily handsome Finn Callahan standing above her, his stubbled cheeks taut, his Irish eyes dark, and even his curls, which should have softened his terse look, seemed lined with steel.

She guessed he'd just discovered that Sean had asked for the charges against her to be dropped and that the municipal court judge had obliged. Annika totally got how that, combined with her being here as a guest, would stick in his craw. *Tough!* He was the one who'd been unreasonably stubborn and had misconstrued everything.

He'd been the one to kiss her and cop a feel before she'd come to her senses.

You didn't. He pulled away first.

The realization rocked her as she remembered him so clearly stumbling away and pouring a drink with an unsteady hand. Now his dark eyes were fixed on hers and in an automatic protective reaction she superimposed fair hair on Finn's perfect bone structure and golden hair on his head. Blond, he was beautiful and unthreatening just like an angel. Albeit a cross and grumpy angel. The gold vanished, and as she gazed at his charismatic darkness she imagined he must look a lot like Lucifer had immediately after his fall from grace.

Right now this devil had her in his sights and she stifled a shiver that wasn't remotely generated by fear. That alone worried her. Almost a week had passed since she'd met him and given that he'd refused to listen to her and had her dumped in a jail cell, her brain should be overruling her body. Only it wasn't. Instead she was fighting the desire to rise to her feet and lean into him. She pressed her hands against the sand to stop the tingling in her fingers that burned to feel again the solid muscles she knew lay beneath his blue Oxford shirt.

At least she recognized that touching him would be the fast track to insanity. Knowing *that* had to help, right? It must, because no one in their right mind would actively put themselves in the path of someone they disliked and who intensely disliked them back. That simple truth had to provide some protection, but she knew she needed a lot more.

She stayed seated and stared out at the lake. "Come to kiss me again and hope you get lucky or are you planning on locking me up?"

A slight crack appeared in his rigid stance and his

voice held regret. "I apologize for the kiss. It was utterly out of line. It won't happen again."

The surprise apology should have made her feel better—less used—but instead she felt a traitorous sadness sneak through her. Furious with herself she blurted out, "But putting me in a jail cell for a night wasn't?" She wrenched back some control and dropped her volume. "Your father's a charming man and a surprisingly good listener. Obviously not a trait you inherited."

The crack sealed. "And you know me so well to judge."

"Putting me in a jail cell set precedent."

A muscle twitched close to his mouth and she imagined how, if he let himself relax, it would wind up as a wide and captivating smile. "Put yourself in my position, Annika. You broke the law and you lied about who you were."

The calm rebuke told her what she needed to say. "I admit my thinking and actions were flawed and I'm sorry about that, but when Rory explained all and you had the opportunity to recant, you didn't."

His jaw jutted. "There are worse character flaws than expecting people to follow the rules."

Granted, she normally played by the rules too but his words were heavily weighted with an unexpected intransigence. What was that about? "Admit it. You were ticked off and you wanted to take it out on someone."

She heard a sharp intake of breath and glanced up at him, glimpsing a look that had a hint of Logan, a touch of Sean and a trace of guilt. Tiny beads of sweat formed on his top lip as his chinos and shirt were much more suited to "casual Friday" in the air-conditioned comfort of an office rather than being on a beach. She patted the space next to her, feeling a twinge of sympathy for him. "It's cooler down here on the sand."

For a moment she didn't think he'd sit but then his hands pulled at the knees of his pants and he lowered his tight behind onto the sand, leaving a space between them. "I'm sorry, Annika. I didn't know Sean had bought the warehouses and you're right, I took it out on you." He ran his hand through his hair—the action jarring and jerky. "I know you'd prefer to speak with Sean but he's having some sort of midlife crisis so, sorry, but you're stuck with me. Let's do what you wanted to do on Saturday night. Let's talk about these warehouses."

The measured businessman was back and giving her the opportunity she'd been waiting weeks for. She took in a deep breath and aimed for concise. "You have two empty warehouses and Whitetail has forklift drivers, assembly line workers and people with logistics experience. It's a good match."

"It would be except for one thing."

"What's that?"

"All of our warehouses are strategically positioned on our major transport routes heading south of Chicago. Whitetail is too far north."

Confused, she turned to face him and regretted it as her thoughts started to addle. No man should be allowed to be so broodingly beautiful. His long straight nose and taut jaw cut an imposing profile and she was reminded of the magnificent works by Michelangelo and Donatello that she'd studied at college. "Then why did AKP buy the business park?"

A band of tightness circled his mouth and ran down his neck and along his shoulders. "Sean bought them on a whim because they were cheap."

No. His father had been genuinely apologetic and

charming at the court, and again today as a host, so she couldn't believe the warehouses were just a rich man's whim. "And to use, surely?"

This time he faced her. "What business are you in, Annika?"

The question startled her and she scrambled to answer. Once she would have said "Art" but that dream had been trampled into the dust and she didn't bother mentioning the Milwaukee Gallery's request because she hadn't told anyone about it. That and the fact she hadn't even started the final painting of the triplet—the lake bathed in summer's dusk. "I have a home business. I use calligraphy to create invitations, logos, that sort of thing. Mostly just for people in town."

"You can live on that?"

Almost. The big fat zero on her bank account's balance told another story but she wasn't going to admit that to Finn. Not when his incredulous expression matched his tone, and sounded all too similar to her brother's regular emails. *You need a real job, Anni. Come work for me in Milwaukee.*

She rolled her shoulders back and sat up straighter. "My main job is keeping Whitetail afloat so it survives the economic slowdown." *So I can stay here.* "This involves finding a replacement for Reggies and AKP has to be that replacement. We have a lovely town on a beautiful lake and people choose to live here for the quality of life, the clean air, pristine water and being part of a community where people know your name and notice if you don't bring in your paper every morning." Her voice rose. "No one dies alone in this town like they do in Chicago. Whitetail is full of good people and they deserve to have work."

"Everyone deserves to have work."

His wide mouth softened and she was reminded of the man who'd pulled her through the window. The man whose mouth had creased into laugher lines before teasing her about her lack of coordination. *And kissed you until you were a puddle of need.*

She tried to forget that last bit and instead returned his smile, relaxing for the first time since she'd seen him arrive. "Wow, we actually agree on something. This has to be a sign of something good."

His gaze grazed her mouth and she got that same quiver—the one that sent a coil of heat through her belly. Heat that had nothing to do with the summer sun.

He abruptly returned his gaze to the lake and tugged at a curl that had fallen across his ear. "I'm sorry, Annika, but it would cost AKP money to operate this far north so the warehouses are staying empty until we sell them for a profit."

Relaxation vanished, taking hope with it. "You can't do that to the town."

He shrugged, the action resigned. "I'm not throwing money into a bottomless pit when we've had to make substantial cuts elsewhere."

After the debacle of falling through the window at the feet of Finn Callahan and not knowing who he was, she'd done an internet search on him and researched the business. "But AKP posted a profit last quarter."

"Just." His hand pressed down on the sandcastle, flattening it. "The pressure's on and my responsibility's to the shareholders."

A vortex of powerlessness spun in her chest, sucking her down. Ryan had put business ahead of her and Finn was putting it ahead of an entire community. "So you don't care?" She heard her voice gaining volume. "You're quite content to sit back and watch a town die? I should have known you were a heartless number cruncher when you dumped me in jail."

Those bottomless eyes stared down at her, registering her outburst of feeling with emotions tightly leashed, but she glimpsed pity. She hated that.

"This isn't personal, Annika. You're confusing sentiment with business and AKP's not a charity."

Art's a business, Annika. You're naïve if you think it's not. The smoking ashes of her past flared up and she wanted to scream but this wasn't about her, this was about the town.

Think!

Somehow, she had to get Finn into town so he could see Whitetail and meet the people. That would take Whitetail from a name on the map to a real place with heart. A place people called home, a place where they watched their children grow and thrive, and when the time came, they buried their loved ones. "Have you seen the business park?"

"No."

She remembered his expression at the police station when he'd first seen the deeds and she aimed for what she was pretty certain was his Achilles' heel. "Isn't a successful businessman one who keeps his finger on the pulse of all aspects of his business?"

His shoulders jerked. "They're warehouses!" His mild tone vanished on a rising inflection. "X amount of square footage with walls and a roof."

Touchy. Good. "Sounds an odd way to do business though. Buying something you haven't even seen."

His lips barely moved. "I told you that I didn't buy them."

She tried to sound beyond casual. "I could give you a tour."

He abruptly shot to his feet sending sand flying and then he extended his hand to her. "Let's go."

Startled, she shielded her eyes and looked up. "What, now?"

"Yes, now." Impatience zipped around him as his hand hovered between them.

She glanced toward the house and then back to him, not wanting to be rude to Dana and Sean as well as being seriously hungry. Paying for the ruined dress had meant skimping on food. "Dana said lunch was at one and that's in five minutes. We can go directly after that."

He shook his head and his curls bounced. "You can stay here for lunch if you wish but this is a one-off, never-to-be-repeated offer. You show me the warehouses now or not at all."

The detached businessman didn't look quite so detached anymore.

"So what's it to be?"

She read the challenge in his eyes. Ditching lunch put her in a tricky position but what choice did she have? None. For Whitetail, she threw her lot in with the devil and accepted his hand.

"So you didn't think to leave a message for me?" Bridey sat cross-legged on the window seat of her room, her left thumb spinning her large, square-cut diamond engagement ring with the diamond-encrusted platinum band, while her right hand pressed her phone against her ear. All week she'd been counting the days until the weekend and now she felt like a little girl who'd been left out of a play date. The adult in her hated how whiney it made her sound.

"I knew Finn would tell you." Hank sounded mystified by her chagrin. "And you know I'd have filled you in on everything when I called you tonight."

She did, which made the fact he hadn't called even worse. Hank rang her every night they were apart. At 7:00 p.m. when his automatic reminder went off. She sometimes wondered if he thought of her at any other time during the day. She leaned her forehead against the window, watching the way the light played through the thick foliage of the trees and tried to stomp on her disappointment. "I miss you."

"I wanted to be on the helicopter, but it's mayhem here."

Hank's calm voice—so unlike her father's and Finn's—usually soothed but not today. She didn't want to be soothed. She wanted Hank here. "Why can't Damien handle it?"

"Darling, you of all people know why. I'm the chief engineer and in a crisis I have to be here. It's a damn mess and we're working around the clock trying to keep things going. You know what it's like when things go wrong, and you know what it means if Jazz Juice pulls out."

She did. Once one big client pulled out, others often followed and although it was never a good time to lose a client, now was not even close to good. She rested her chin in the palm of her hand. She was so very weary of the business. She'd grown up hearing nothing else talked about in her father's house and of course, post-divorce, it had never been mentioned in her mother's. Although Finn sided with his mother over the divorce, business ran deep in his veins and he'd taken to the company like a duck to water. But not her.

Truth be told, part of the reason she'd done her master's and was now doing her PhD was to avoid telling her father she didn't want to work at AKP when she got her doctorate. And to avoid telling her mother the same thing. She didn't want to disappoint her father or please her mother in that particular way, so she was treading water, not having said "yes" and not having said "no"— instead leaving it all up in the air. She'd honored her promise to her father and earned her generous allowance by doing a variety of summer jobs for the company over the years but she didn't view it as training for the future like Sean did. Not that she had any regrets about the work though because it was through AKP that she'd met Hank.

Solid, quiet and often in-his-own-world Hank. The first time she'd seen him was on the factory floor. He'd looked up from a machine that lay in pieces and had given her a gentle smile, his honey-brown eyes warm behind his dark-rimmed glasses. It had been a split-second smile before he'd quickly turned back to the job in hand. Used to the charismatic charm of her father and brother where Irish drama often punctuated the day, Hank had seemed like a refuge. She'd set about to meet him again. And again and again. When he hadn't asked her out, she'd asked him. After dating exclusively for one year she knew exactly what she wanted—a long life with Hank. A year later, with no sign from him that he wanted to move forward but with no signs that he wanted to back out, and with her biological clock ticking loudly, she'd proposed. He'd accepted.

She chewed her lip. "I should come visit and stay with you."

A soft sigh vibrated down the line. "Bridey, you said what you wanted most was a summer at the lake with your family. So take it."

Yes, but you were supposed to be here too. "Won't

you miss me?" As the words shot out she wanted to pull them back. When had she got so needy?

The moment you proposed to him.

She could hear noise in the background and someone shouting his name.

"Bridey, I'm sorry but this really isn't a good time. I'll call you tonight and meanwhile you have fun."

The line went dead. *Fun.* She dropped her phone onto the cushion. This time at the lake wasn't about fun. It was about insurance. All part of the series of steps that started with one happy summer which would lead into one happy Christmas and culminate in one enormous, happy wedding that proved to the world they belonged together. The plan was going to give her and Hank everything her parents had never had, and ensure that she and Hank had a long and wonderful life together.

The roar of a car interrupted her thoughts and she peered through the trees, glimpsing a streak of red disappearing down the drive. Finn's Ferrari California. The sound of the lunch bell tinkled. *Damn it, Finn!* How hard was it to get *one* summer where her family acted like other families and actually spent time together.

FIVE

"And this is the Main Street square."

Watching Annika walking backward in those damn short shorts as well as admiring the way her T-shirt moved over her small but perfectly round breasts, had Finn regretting his spur-of-the-moment idea to come into town with her to avoid Dana's lunch. What had seemed the perfect solution to missing lunch had started to unravel the moment she'd grasped his hand on the beach. Her boundless energy had run along his veins, firing up a reaction of base need he was finding difficult to quash. The not-so-perfect solution had continued to taunt him on the journey into Whitetail with her perfume filling his car and making him breathe more deeply. Adding insult to injury, the AC had blown strands of her long hair onto his arm where they'd stayed, held by a static force sent to mock him.

The insane thing was he didn't like her so his reaction to her made no sense. As soon as his body got *that* message everything would be fine. He hauled his gaze up to the Richardsonian Romanesque–style turret and clock tower that graced the City Hall of a town that fell so far short of a city it was a joke. Its grandeur was in stark contrast to the other buildings which had plain, flat-fronted facades although the cinema flirted with a faux Tudor style. "That's one hell of a building."

"My Swedish ancestors had a vision." Annika looked

up at the clock with a wistful expression on her face and then turned back to him. "I'm starving and you promised me lunch."

"What about here?" Finn glanced up at the faded sign that said Sven's Swedish Smörgåsbord. Välkommen. "Is this place any good?"

"The pickled herring's to die for."

He opened the door for her with a teasing grin. "In that case, be my guest and order yourself a huge plate."

"Actually, I prefer the lingonberry pancakes." With eyes sparkling, she ducked under his arm and promptly tripped over the snow grate that was permanently in place.

His arm shot out to steady her, his fingers wrapping around the waistband of her shorts and brushing up against warm, soft skin. "Did you enjoy your trip?"

Her dry tone matched her eye roll. "Your wit astounds me. Excuse me while I hold my stomach muscles together from laughter."

He grinned. "My friends laugh at my jokes."

"You have friends?" Her mock surprise was followed by her patting his arm. "That's good to hear."

He laughed and as she stepped out of his hold, the scent of her hair filled his nostrils with the uncomplicated aroma of apples and cinnamon. One of the comfort foods Esther had been making him since he was a kid.

Just remember, she's bossy and opinionated—everything you don't like in a woman.

The restaurant was busy and the hostess seated them in a booth with a jug of fresh iced tea and she recommended the Pytt Panna: Swedish roast beef hash served over a hardboiled egg with a side of pickled beets. Finn thought the pancakes sounded like a safe bet.

While Annika sipped her drink she got a familiar

glint in her eye—the one that said, "It's time to talk." She stirred the ice with her straw. "Now that you've seen the warehouses and the town, you've seen the potential and you know you want to use them."

The business park had been a pleasant surprise and it was in very good condition. As an investment it had been a good deal, but then Sean rarely made bad deals—only bad marriages. He shook his head. "Sorry."

Two small lines formed at the bridge of her nose. "So nothing you've seen in the last hour has changed your mind?"

"It's not sound business."

She pursed her lips and leaned forward. "Then sell them now. There might just be a company they're perfect for who would use them and employ Whitetail's workforce."

She'd just echoed one of his emerging thoughts although given how tight things were he'd be stunned if they sold quickly. He rubbed his chin. "I suppose I could put them on the market but I'm not selling at a loss."

"Obviously."

She'd just surprised him. He'd picked her as having no business savvy at all. "I'll call my Realtor."

Annika flinched. "Could you use Ellery Johnston, the Whitetail Realtor? That way, if you sell, some money stays in the town."

He contemplated her suggestion for a long moment wondering if there was any way it might actually work. "I doubt he'd have the contacts and reach of my guy."

She huffed out a breath as if he'd just insulted her. "Whitetail might be a long way north but we're connected to the world. Even our paper is online."

"Still…" He couldn't picture a small-town Realtor with Gavin's killer drive.

She tapped her finger on the table. "Oh, now here's an idea. You could wait until you've met Ellery before you leap to conclusions. You make a lot of snap decisions, don't you?"

"No, I make considered decisions quickly." He wasn't used to anyone being this up front with him but instead of taking offense he found himself enjoying the challenge. He leaned forward, hooking her gaze, and used one of his negotiating tactics—staring down the opposition. "As mayor, shouldn't you be humoring me?"

Vivid blue eyes held his stare. "What are you going to do? Lock me up again?"

Something about the way she said the words in that husky voice of hers had him picturing her wearing only handcuffs and white cotton panties. It shouldn't have turned him on in the least but the restaurant suddenly seemed hot. "Don't give me ideas."

"Hi, Anni. Both Ellery and Nicole are looking for you." The waitress, whose name badge said "Olivia," arrived with a pen in hand and wearing a white blouse, black pants and a long, red-and-white-striped bibbed apron.

She gave Finn an appreciative look from under thick, dark lashes. Exactly the sort of glance he'd been receiving since high school and one he was completely at ease with, unlike the combative one he'd just got from Annika. He returned Olivia's flirtatious peek with an easy smile.

She fluttered her eyelashes at him as she asked, "Who's your handsome friend, Anni?"

Annika glanced around as if looking for someone and then said with a cheeky grin, "Oh, you mean Finn? Livvy, meet Finn Callahan."

Olivia beamed. "Mr. Callahan, it's so great you're

going to provide jobs for Whitetail. My boyfriend was about to leave town for work so thank you."

Finn opened his mouth to deny everything when Olivia called out to the half-full restaurant, "Everyone, this is Finn Callahan."

A murmur buzzed around the room and people rose and headed over to the booth, each of them wanting to shake his hand and tell him their story of how a new employer would mean their brother, father, sister, cousin, aunt, uncle, niece, nephew and every other relative in between would be able to stay in Whitetail.

Throughout the introductions, Annika had stayed completely silent but he could feel her gaze on him.

"So when will you be opening?" John asked.

Annika spoke, her voice firm and crisp, reminding him of his media consultant. "AKP Industries has no plans to operate out of Whitetail and are putting the warehouses on the market."

The warm reception from the locals turned frosty.

"Typical Callahan."

He heard the vitriol in the man's voice and it raised his ire. "Would you care to explain that?"

John leaned his hands against the table. "My father and your grandfather used to fish together but that was back in the days before that big house, private helicopters and the Callahans thinking they were above the town."

"John, please." Annika put her hand over the market owner's.

Finn instantly defended Grandpa. "My grandfather loved the lake and he drove a rusted-out truck. He had *nothing* to do with the Kylemore of today. That was built by my father."

John snorted. "And don't we know it. Your father turned his back on this town from the moment he used contractors from Chicago to build that house. He's hardly put a cent into the economy and now you're following his lead."

A murmur of agreement rumbled around the restaurant.

He only accepted being compared to his father in terms of being a successful businessman. He'd never liked what Sean had done to Kylemore or the way he'd gone about it. "No, I'm not."

"Then give me an example of how you're contributing to Whitetail?"

"He's using Ellery as the Realtor to sell the warehouses." Annika's voice sounded unexpectedly conciliatory, as if she was on his side.

Surprised, he glanced at her but her expression said, "You agreed to that, remember."

The market owner wasn't impressed. "That's it? That's your contribution?" He turned to the gathered diners, his voice full of disgust. "He's not even going to employ one Whitetalian. I'm telling you, he's his father's son."

Finn pressed his thumbs hard into his temples. He admired Sean's business sense but not the rest of the way his father lived his life or his many marriages. Going on the derisive curl of the market owner's lip, John wasn't making any distinction between business and the man. Finn refused to be cast in the same collective light as his father and he'd prove the difference right this second even if it went against his better business judgment.

He stood up, looking straight over the older man's head toward the group. "I need a P.A. for the summer here in Whitetail. I'll employ the person who knows their way around data processing and spreadsheets, is absolutely reliable and not afraid of hard work. Who fits that description?"

"Anni." Several voices spoke at once.

Annika made a choking sound.

"She's the fill-in when people take vacations." John nodded. "You can't go wrong with Anni. She's always helping out."

Shit. Numerous pairs of expectant eyes were glued on him and after his grandstanding statement no way could he renege on his promise without risking being lynched by the townsfolk of Whitetail. The idea of Annika Jacobson as his P.A. and working closely with her had him all itchy and scratchy and hot and cold. He knew the best way to get over this foolish attraction was by simply not seeing her because once she was out of sight she would be out of mind. Working with her would make that impossible. How the hell was he going to get out of this mess?

Sneaking a quick glance at her, he immediately let go of a breath he hadn't realized he'd been holding. As it whooshed out he felt a surge of laughter bubbling up in his chest and somehow he managed not to grin widely. Annika sat opposite him, every part of her rigid and screaming that the idea of being his P.A. more than appalled her.

He instantly relaxed as he realized there was no way in the world she'd take the job. Even better than that was the fact that *this* had become a win-win situation for him. She'd find him a P.A. that wasn't her and at the same time inadvertently save him from being held up as his father's son.

"No, this isn't going to work." Annika finally found her voice amid her gasping surprise and absolute horror at the idea of working closely or to be more precise, in close proximately with Finn Callahan. It had been hard enough sitting next to him in the confines of his low-slung sports car surrounded by the seductive scent of leather and the suddenly sexy scent of Tide. How did the man convert the clean smell of fresh laundry powder into a turn-on?

She was seriously losing it and she had to put a stop to this nonsense right now. She appealed to the town. "Are you forgetting this is the man who insisted I spend a night in the cells?"

Melissa pursed her lips. "Well, to be honest, Anni, it was pretty silly trying to climb through a window in one of my most expensive dresses."

Her voice rose. "I've paid for it." *And I'm flat broke with no phone service and nothing else to fall back on.*

"You also told us everything was all sorted out." Olivia turned and batted her eyelashes. "There're no hard feelings, are there, Mr. Callahan?"

This time Finn was the one to choke but he rallied quickly and gave the crowd his winning smile. The one that looked guileless, but she knew better.

"Absolutely. All that misunderstanding is water under the bridge." He rubbed his chin thoughtfully, his expression full of consideration with a hint of challenge. "Although, if Annika's uncomfortable working for me then I *totally* understand and I'm happy to employ someone else."

And there it was. He'd just turned it all back on her.

"She needs a paying job." Mrs. Norell clucked like a mother hen and gave Finn a beatific smile.

Annika surely didn't need "help" like this. "Mrs. Norell, I'm doing just fine."

"Honey, we know you'd like more work just like everyone else around here, especially as your calligraphy work has been quiet too."

Oh great, tell Finn Callahan everything. "I don't have time to work for him when I'm acting mayor." Her voice sounded loud and defensive and she blew out a long breath. "That's a full-time job in itself."

"Is Anni here?" Nicole's voice called out from behind the group which parted to let her through. She rushed forward seeming oblivious to Finn and the fact that everyone was standing around their booth. "I've been chasing you all morning. Why didn't you return my messages?"

Annika didn't want to publically admit to not being able to pay her cell phone bill but she didn't have to as Nicole rushed on.

"Never mind, I've found you now. Guess what? I've got two brides who want to talk to you about invitations."

Annika frowned trying to think who it could possibly be. "But no one's got engaged since Thea and Jason."

Nicole squealed with excitement. "That's the thing. Two women called today after seeing us on TV and they're seriously considering getting married in Whitetail. They're driving up to visit on Wednesday and they want to meet with everyone to get quotes."

Mrs. Norell beamed. "See, Anni, we *do* have a new business so you don't have to worry. Now you can work for Mr. Callahan and help him, as well as doing your invitations."

Annika rested her head in her hands for a moment and silently counted to ten. When she looked up she spoke slowly and calmly. "That's great news. It really is but two wedding inquiries don't make a business. They're inquiries and they might lead nowhere. Let's be realistic here. You don't have a website or a brochure outlining what is on offer. You don't have a central person to pull everything together and you don't even have a place where brides can come to discuss their ideas."

"The town can have the use of the warehouses rent-free, until they sell."

All heads snapped to Finn.

"Really?" Melissa checked. "What about utility costs?"

"I'll pay for lighting and normal use but if you start using more than just basic office equipment we'll discuss that."

Annika groaned. As much as she liked the idea of a wedding business, it wasn't a remotely practical solution to Whitetail's employment needs. Even if it did start to take off, it would be slow to build and probably only generate income for a select few. The town needed so much more and quickly. It was hard being the only person who could see the big picture because it made her sound like a pessimistic naysayer, but they'd asked her to be mayor to guide them through this crisis so it was up to her to lead them. How was she going to tell them that a warehouse was hardly a romantic place for brides to come and discuss their fairy-tale wedding?

She took a long look at Finn who suddenly seemed almost too relaxed as he leaned back in the booth drinking a soda. She wished she knew what was going on behind those dark, enigmatic eyes. Why his sudden largesse with the warehouses? Why the unexpected surge of generosity? She hadn't been able to get anything out of him and now he was offering something, but it did little service to the town. Tilting her head, she signaled frantically with her eyes and then slightly tapped his shin under the table for good measure, hoping he'd get the message and retract his offer.

He didn't. Instead, he smiled at her before addressing the crowd. "As Annika pointed out to me earlier, the warehouses are of no value to anyone empty. Letting you use them until they sell is the least I can do for Whitetail. I'll throw in some IT equipment too, if you want it. We've recently upgraded the Chicago offices so there's some going spare." He pulled out two business cards and gave one to Nicole and the other to Melissa.

Nicole smiled and her face lit up again for the second time in a week. "You've been incredibly helpful, Finn. We'll be in touch."

"Best go through whoever's my P.A. She'll be handling it all." His gaze swung to Annika as his foot connected lightly with her shin.

Now he was the one doing the warning off. Under normal circumstances it wouldn't have even been necessary. Sure, she needed the money. She badly needed the money but not even possible eviction would have been enough to propel her into the job of being Finn Callahan's P.A. But nothing about this situation was normal. As mayor, the town depended on her and she in turn had to protect the people of Whitetail. She needed to keep a very close eye on things from a business perspective and there was only one way to do that. Even if it meant risking her sanity.

She raised her hand and her voice. "You can go through me. I'm his new P.A."

Finn's jaw tensed and his eyebrows hit his hairline, but it was the flash of fire in his dark, dark eyes—fire which flared for a moment before quickly being doused by stony resignation—that sent butterflies somersaulting in her stomach. It was going to be a very long summer.

IT WAS MONDAY morning and Annika tried to listen as
Finn paced across the office. His wide mouth and tempting lips that had featured in more than just one dream,
moved continuously as he outlined her job in crisp and
precise detail. She'd expected a grilling from him on why
she'd taken the job but from the moment he'd stepped
through the doorway, he'd treated her like she was any
ordinary employee and had immediately launched into
orientation. They could have been in Chicago and the
only nod to the fact they weren't was his clothing.

Gone was the more formal business shirt of yesterday. Today he wore an apple-green short-sleeved shirt
which sat square on his broad shoulders and had the unsettling effect of making his eyes far more chocolate-
noir than inky black.

She shifted in her seat and crossed her legs. Watching those eyes and that mouth was far too distracting on
so many levels that she didn't dare count. Instead she
moved her gaze around, trying to pin it to a wall or the
blinking light on the fax/scanner/printer/copier, but it
kept flitting between Finn and the lake. The house was
built on a point and this afforded almost every room a
view, including the office. Today the summer sunshine
shimmered against the blue water which sparkled and
danced like a shower of silver glitter. The recreational
sounds of vacationers drifted on the air—the distant
buzz of motorboats, the delighted squeals of children
splashing in the water and the thwack of balls as they hit
the strings of tennis racquets. Every part of her wanted
to be outside and she wondered how any work ever got
done in this light and airy room.

Finn didn't appear to notice the blue-blue sky, the
vivid green of the trees, the silvery glistening lake or
even her. Nothing it seemed could distract him from

work, which was probably why he had millions of dollars in the bank and she had less than nothing.

Just start the final painting for the gallery exhibition you agreed to and earn some money that way.

The thought had her ducking for cover. *No time. The town needs me and that means working here.*

Finn rubbed the back of his neck. "I usually use an agency to hire temporary staff so I'll have to ask someone in payroll to organize a contract for you and get your social security details and all that stuff. Payday is the end of the month."

Money. That snapped her attention back on task. She checked the desk calendar—there was far too much of the month left and too little money to cross the gap between now and payday. She tucked her hair behind her ears and tried to sound casual. "That sounds like a lot of trouble for such a short period of time. I mean, it's not like I'm getting any benefits so why not make it easier and just pay me cash?"

He stopped pacing, turned his head and just like a marksman, he held her in his sights with those delicious cocoa eyes.

Her heart leaped and her breasts strained against her bra. She quickly crossed her arms, desperate to hide any telltale signs that her body craved him with an intensity so strong it strayed way beyond the boundaries of common sense. So far from the boundaries that it scared her more than she cared to admit. Arguing with him was a lot safer. That and the fact it would distract him from getting to the truth that she was stone broke. *No one* needed to know that. She didn't need pity or a lecture; she got enough of both from her brother.

He cocked one eyebrow. "Avoiding the IRS, are we?"

She tossed her head. "You're really determined to think the worst of me in every situation, aren't you?"

His palms flattened against the side of the desk but his mouth twitched at the corners. "If the boot fits."

She swung her sandal-clad feet up onto the desk as if giving him the bird. "Oh yeah, I'm up there with the top criminal masterminds of the twenty-first century."

His eyes stalled on her brightly painted toes and his voice rumbled lower than ever. "I've met the rest of the masterminds and they're far more coordinated than you."

Suddenly it felt a lot more like flirting than disagreeing. Planning to put her legs back on the floor and act more like the P.A. she now was, she abruptly moved her legs and immediately felt the wheels of the office chair skate out from under her. "Ohh!"

Her bottom slid forward until her spine sat flat against the chair and she hung precariously between the chair and the desk, her arms not long enough to reach the wooden top to save herself from falling.

Rich, vibrant laughter erupted around her before strong arms rescued her, helping her rise to her feet. Finn grinned down at her. "I rest my case."

"My klutz-like tendencies are just part of my cover with the masterminds." She brushed her Capri pants free of imaginary lint to hide the fact she was a trembling mess just from seeing him smile and having his warm hands on her arms. She voiced the unspoken elephant in the room. "I'm surprised you're even letting me work for you."

He leaned forward, his breath tickling her cheek and his voice deep and low. "I like to keep my enemies close."

A wave of heat dumped over her so fast it stole her breath and the tingling aftershocks made her head spin.

His lips hovered so close it would only take a small move to the right and a slight tilt of her chin and her lips would be brushing his. Tasting him again, feeling her body come to life under his touch as he infused her with—

Stop it. This is so not a good idea. At the very least he's your boss and if Ryan taught you anything it was never mix business and pleasure. Ever. Again.

She stepped back, desperately needing the distance, and she walked over to the windows. "Only we both know I'm not your enemy because you ran a police check on me. Trust is a big issue for you isn't it?"

He shrugged, the businessman back in action. "It's standard business procedure. AKP can't afford anyone selling secrets."

Surprise lit through her. "Does that really happen?"

"It can. We're in an enviable market position at the moment but business is fluid and it can change in a heartbeat. Which reminds me—you need to sign a confidentiality clause stating that everything you see, hear or read while in my employ stays here. Will that be a problem?"

She shook her head. Keeping secrets wasn't a problem for her; she kept plenty of her own. "Not at all. So we're agreed. I keep your information safe and you pay me cash every Friday. Deal?"

Finn watched Annika wind the ends of her hair around her fingers and the memory of those silken strands caressing his palms four days ago had him curling his fingers into a tight ball, trying to crush the simmering desire that refused to leave him. Damn it but he'd almost kissed her again a moment ago and that was after the grand total of twenty-five minutes of working together.

He still couldn't believe she'd accepted the job and

he'd decided not to ask her straight up why she had. No, he'd wait and see what panned out because if he'd learned one thing over the last few days it was that she *always* had a reason for her actions no matter how crazy. And he'd been right—a hint at the reason hadn't taken long to emerge. He didn't care how she got paid but he found it interesting that she was so insistent on cash. "Is money why you took this job?"

"As everyone explained, I'm the best person for this job." She gave him a beaming smile. "You really do ask a lot of questions but it's my turn now." She flicked open his diary. "I'm going to make an appointment for you to meet with Ellery tomorrow to discuss the sale of the warehouses, and speaking of warehouses, *why* did you offer the town their use?"

He did a double take at her irritated tone. "Hang on a minute. You've harangued me long and hard about not using them and not providing employment for the town so why am I suddenly the bad guy for offering them rent-free?"

Her eyes flashed silvery blue daggers, in sharp contrast to the smoky hue that had almost made him kiss her a few moments ago. "I get that everyone is excited about the wedding idea, but, try as I might, I really can't see it being the financial savior of the town."

"Some of the most successful companies have started out as ideas most people swore would never work out."

Her forehead creased in deep furrows. "Yes, and a million more have failed. This wedding plan would be okay if it was *one* person starting out and risking all, but the entire town is pinning its hopes on it. I'm really worried it will fail and cause them even more heartache. Whitetail can't afford that, not financially or emotionally, and as acting mayor I have an obligation to protect the citizens."

He rubbed his chin wondering why she was so agitated about this, especially as she had a business herself that would benefit from the wedding-town idea. "As mayor you need to listen to what the town wants."

Her face tightened. "And if what they want isn't in their best interests? What then?"

"This is a democracy. You're the mayor not a dictator."

She shot him a withering look. "I'm well aware of that, but to survive, we need full employment *now*, which is why you're meeting with Ellery. We're going to try and attract a big company to buy and use the warehouses like other small Midwest towns have done."

He didn't like her chances but he didn't care that much to disabuse her of her ideals. "Part of your job with me is to be my liaison with the town and I'm not reneging on my offer so you need to be involved. Besides, I thought you'd be pleased because even if they only get one wedding out of this then it's income for your calligraphy business."

She threw her hands out. "This isn't about me—it's about the town. Someone has to have a broader vision."

Something in her voice touched a place in him he didn't visit very often. "Why do you care so much?"

She stared at him with confusion in her eyes, and it was as if she didn't really understand the question. "These people mean a lot to me. They're family. Wouldn't you do anything to help your family?"

He wasn't so sure that he would.

SIX

THE FOLLOWING DAY, Annika finished the work Finn had left for her by eleven. She hadn't seen him during the morning, which was probably a good thing for her peace of mind but he'd been whizzing emails to her all the same. As she was expected to be in the office during business hours, she was now using the time for Whitetail. While her fingers flew across the keyboard composing a letter outlining all of Whitetail's attributes to go along with the information pack about the warehouses, she recalled the huge argument she'd had with her mother when she was sixteen. Her mom had insisted she take a semester of typing in her sophomore year when she'd lost interest in everything academic, preferring instead to spend every waking hour drawing. Annika hadn't agreed but had lost out.

Today, the irony wasn't lost on her—now she typed more than she drew. *You do everything more than draw, paint, collage—* She sucked in a deep breath, trying to ease the ache that sat in her chest like a lead weight and she ended up rubbing her sternum. Nothing shifted it.

"Shouldn't you be taking a break?"

She looked up in surprise to see Finn standing in the doorway, his feet clad in leather boat shoes. "How do you manage to walk silently on wooden floors?"

He winked. "It's my ninja training so I can sneak up

on P.A.s and make sure they're doing what they're supposed to."

She huffed out a halfhearted indignant breath which lost out against a smile. "All your work is done."

"I'm sure it is."

She tried to read the message behind the mild words but his handsome face gave nothing away. "Besides, with all the restrictions you gave me on where I'm not allowed to go on the property it's just easier to stay here."

His teasing humor faded. "I'm sorry, but it's Dana's house."

She shrugged, wondering why he even felt the need to explain. "I'm staff and it's her vacation. I get it. It's not a problem."

"But it doesn't mean you work through." He strode over to a work area and slid open what looked like a cabinet door but was actually a dumbwaiter. "I got Esther to send up lunch."

The thoughtful gesture stunned her. "Thank you."

This time he shrugged. "As soon as we've eaten we'll drive into town to meet with your real estate agent."

We've eaten? She studied the contents on the tray that was clearly set for two. "You're not having lunch with your family?"

The tense set of his shoulders matched his brusque words. "I don't have time for long lunches."

The sound of pummeling feet made them both glance toward the door and the next minute Logan barreled into the office. "Annika! Dad said you were here again."

She returned the boy's big smile. "Hey, dude, how are you?"

Excitement poured off him. "Dad just taught me how to do a somersault off the diving platform and I wanna show you now."

Finn gave a tight smile but when he spoke his tone was quiet but firm. "We're working, Logan."

The boy's mouth formed a stubborn line and he scuffed his sneaker-clad toes against the polished boards making a loud and defiant squeaking sound. "I came to see Annika."

"Logan." Finn sighed as if he was bone weary. "Now's not the best time. Maybe later."

Why? It wasn't like Logan was interrupting something important. Wasn't that the point of a home office during vacation time when things were more casual? "I can come and watch you dive after work, Logan, but only if it's okay with your mom and dad."

Logan beamed. "'Course it's okay. It was Dad's idea and Mom said you should stay for supper because we're having a cookout. You'll stay won't you? This time we'll finish the sand fort."

As she dealt with her astonishment at the unexpected invitation, she thought she heard Finn groan. "I'd love to come. I'll bring my bathing suit so I can swim out to the platform too."

"Awesome." Logan bounced up and down in anticipation.

"Fabulous." Finn's voice sounded strained.

Annika wasn't totally certain if Finn was against the idea of her as an employee spending time with his family or if his issue was with Logan but her natural inclination to "help" kicked in. She raised her hand for a high five with the child. "I need to get back to work now, dude, but I promise I'll see you tonight."

"Okay. See ya." The happy boy ran out of the office, his voice echoing back to them as he called out, "Mom, she said yes!"

"You know, you didn't have to do that." Finn handed

her a plate covered by a massive Reuben sandwich and she realized just how hungry she was.

"Do what?" She watched mesmerized as he bit into the rye bread and how his tongue chased a strand of melted cheese that clung to the bow of his top lip.

"Offer to swim with him."

That jolted her out of her lust-fest. "I wouldn't have suggested it if I hadn't wanted to do it. Diving off platforms with kids is all part of summer fun, right?"

"Oh yeah, right up there with mosquitoes." He wrenched the top off a bottle of apple juice and took a slug, his Adam's apple moving up and down—rhythmically and hypnotically.

She tried to stay focused on his words rather than his deliciously gorgeous body and she couldn't believe what she was hearing. She loved summer. It was her favorite season, although she enjoyed sunny winter days skating on the lake and cross-country skiing in the woods, and she absolutely adored fall. *You love it all.* But Finn didn't seem to share her feelings.

"Geez, what happened to you in summer as a kid to make you the Scrooge of vacation?"

That familiar tension that often circled him appeared again, vibrating like electricity buzzing down a line. "I'm not *on* vacation."

Now she was seriously curious. She finished chewing and wiped her mouth with the cloth napkin that had been rolled into a pewter ring with a *K* engraved on it. Everything in the house spoke wealth. "So if you're not on vacation, why are you working in your father's vacation house?"

"Company politics and business strategy."

His words shot out as if spoken by an automaton and they didn't tell her anything. "Oh of course, I should have made the connection given I was just reading all about it in *Forbes* the other day."

His lips curved into a smile and the strain lessened. "*Forbes*, eh?"

She tried not to sound breathy despite the fact her heart skipped a beat. "A mayor has to keep up." She nibbled the edge of some lettuce. "But the article also talked about cutting little brothers some slack when they called by the office."

The tension shot right back like a bow being stretched tight by an arrow. "If you read the *Wall Street Journal* you would have seen the article on the fact they don't belong in the office and if you want to keep the job as my P.A. you need to respect that."

During his orientation yesterday, he'd never sounded so serious or so resolute about any topic—not even the confidentiality clause. She desperately wanted to ask him why the rule but given the set of his mouth, and the jet of his eyes, she'd save that question for another time. Right now, she needed the job too much for herself and for Whitetail. The fact it came with money was a bonus she was coming to appreciate. She only hoped Ellery would be okay waiting until Friday for a half payment of the month before last's rent.

She gave him a mock salute. "Yes, boss. I've got your back and I'll protect you from scary eight-year-olds."

He smiled. "Just make sure you do."

The smile didn't quite reach his eyes or match the tone of his voice and she realized he was actually serious. Why was he so ill at ease with a child?

"That's enough about little boys, Annika. Grab your file on the warehouses because we're leaving in five minutes."

While she double-checked she had everything they

needed for the meeting with Ellery, Finn reloaded the plates back into the dumbwaiter. Just as she'd slid the documents into a bright pink folder, Bridey strolled into the office wearing a bikini top and a multicolored sarong tied low on her hips.

"Hey, big brother, I just got a text from Mom and she'll be here this afternoon."

Annika watched Finn's finger go rigid on the dumbwaiter button and he stabbed it as if his life depended on it.

"You've got to be kidding me?"

"You know I never kid about Mom."

He turned to face his sister. "I don't understand. She *never* comes up here anymore and we only just got through your party." He ran both his hands through his hair. "Oh God, Dana and Kathleen in the same space. Dad will go off his head and—"

"She's not going to be staying here, silly." Bridey's smile seemed overly bright. "When I invited her, I booked her into a B and B."

"What?" Finn's roar ricocheted off all the glass. "You invited her?"

Annika jumped at his volume but Bridey didn't even blink. It was as if she'd expected this reaction.

Finn threw his arms out. "You invited her up here? Have you completely lost it, Bridey?"

"No." Her eyes glinted with purpose. "I'm planning a wedding and I need my mother around for that."

He stalked toward her. "Damn it, Bridey. It would have made more sense for you to go down and visit her in Chicago."

Bridey folded her arms across her chest and got the same mulish look her brother could specialize in. "This is *my* vacation and I can do what I want."

"What? Cause chaos?"

Bridey pursed her lips. "Her plane arrives at three so we can meet her and then take her out for coffee at that quaint diner in Whitetail. She'll love that both of us are spending time with her together. We'll leave at two-thirty and that gives us plenty of time. We'll use my car because Mom's bound to have brought more than one suitcase and your status symbol is hopeless for trunk space."

Annika felt like she was at a tennis match, watching the ball pass between two expert players and culminating with a lot of frenetic volleying at the net. Bridey was like a dog with a bone and a vein in Finn's neck pulsed. Perhaps it wasn't only eight-year-olds he wanted to be protected from.

His relationship with his family was intriguing but none of her business. She was employed to do what he asked and because she needed the job, she picked up her satchel, swung it over her shoulder and said, "I'm really sorry but Finn's got an important meeting in Whitetail at three."

Bridey's smile fell and she suddenly had the air of a forlorn child. "Oh. Can't you change it?"

Annika instantly felt sad on Bridey's behalf and she wanted to make amends. She opened her mouth to say Finn could meet them at the diner at four when she felt Finn's hand firm against the small of her back, and all coherent thought vanished.

With gentle but determined pressure, he guided her past his sister. "Sorry, sis, gotta go. Tell Mom I'll call her later."

Annika swore she heard delight in his voice.

"I use the Multiple Listing Service and I can handle the sale or the leasing. All you have to do is sit back and watch the cash appear in your account. Yes, sir, you don't have to be in the heart of a big city to do big business these days."

Annika listened to Ellery giving his spiel to Finn and watched both men closely. Finn had taken this meeting under sufferance and she knew Ellery would have to win him over. Some people thought Ellery too hometown-country with his warmth, sincerity and lack of guile but they'd be the fools. When it came to sales, Ellery was the man. Right now as he moved the red dot of his laser pen across the spreadsheet pointing out pertinent numbers and statistics it was enough to make the heart of any businessman sing.

Finn sat in his chair with his elbows resting on the desk and his fingertips pressed together in the shape of a diamond. Occasionally he asked questions but mostly he listened with an intensity that had every part of his body centered on Ellery.

Annika took advantage of that to sneak occasional glances at Finn, justifying to herself that there was no danger in window shopping. She watched the way recalcitrant curls formed at the back of his neck despite a neat cut and how they tickled his collar, taunting the crisp and tidy look he cultivated. She noticed that despite a close shave in the morning, by three in the afternoon ebony stubble touched his tanned cheeks and she knew by nightfall he'd have the sexy rumpled look of a pirate that he'd worn the night she'd met him. What was new to her today was the way the band of his polo shirt sleeves seemed stretched by his upper arms but that shouldn't have surprised her given those same arms had once lifted her up as if she was a featherweight.

Finn rose from his chair, his long-limbed body unfolding like a scissor lift, and he extended his hand. "You put a good case forward and I'll give you two months to show me what you can do."

Ellery shook his hand. "I'll have the papers drawn up and bring them out to Kylemore for signing tomorrow."

Annika suppressed the urge to give a loud and emphatic whoop of delight. It was a minor victory in a huge battle but it was a start and either way, lease or sale, some money would stay in the town. "Ellery, we need to meet to talk about strategies to catch the attention of medium- to large-size companies. I'm tied up during the day but what about tomorrow night? Bring Elspeth and come for supper."

The large Realtor suddenly looked uncomfortable. "Anni, have you been checking your voice mail?"

No, because I don't have any cell credit. She went for noncommittal as she collected the documents she'd brought to the meeting. "Hmm, why?"

Ellery hesitated, looked at Finn and then back at Annika before speaking softly. "So you know tomorrow night won't work out at the cottage."

She had no clue why that would be so she played along. "Sure, so how about the night after?"

"Where?"

She smiled. "Same place, my place."

Ellery turned to Finn. "Mr. Callahan, would you excuse us for just a moment?"

Two deep lines appeared on Finn's forehead as if he wasn't used to being asked a question like this. "If it involves the warehouses I'd prefer to be present."

Annika recognized his business tone and she didn't want to risk Finn pulling out of the deal. "Ellery, it's fine. Just say what you need to say."

"I've been waiting for you to call me back since yesterday, Anni." His tone was both accusatory and apologetic. "The Hoffmans have decided to come up from Milwaukee and use the cottage this summer."

Her mouth dried. "My cottage?"

Ellery nodded slowly but firmly. "I'm sorry, Anni, but because you're two months behind in your rent I couldn't argue against it. They're moving in for the entire summer."

Her legs turned to jelly and she sat down hard on the chair. The Hoffmans hadn't used their cottage in two years and she'd come to think of it as hers. "When?"

Ellery put his hand on her shoulder and spoke softly. "Tomorrow. I've been trying to contact you since yesterday to tell you."

You're homeless.

The familiar ring tone of Finn's cell both pierced her shock and backhanded her with an extra dose of indignity. In her stunned state she'd forgotten he was in the room. Her head fell into her hands. Oh, God, now Finn Callahan knew she was virtually destitute. Life just got better and better.

She raised her head. "Ellery, I'll have money on Friday which will go toward my back rent and I have a job for the summer so I'm good for the rest. I don't mind where I go. I'll even take the unleasable cottage near mosquito flat."

"I'm sorry, Anni, but we've had a rush on vacation rentals this year because Illinois folk who used to travel overseas are tightening their belts and staying closer to home. I don't have a single cottage available."

She pressed the heel of her hand against her forehead as if the pressure would make her think more clearly, and she tried to run through her choices. She no longer had family in town. Her parents had sold up and moved to Arizona when she'd left for college and had started a business in retirement travel. They spent more time out of the country than in it, and currently they were in Australia, loving every minute of their "third age." Like the emails from her brother, Axel, the content of most of her parents' messages usually urged her to leave town and reiterated the same theme of "restart your life." But her life *was* here now and she wasn't going anywhere. Any number of townsfolk could help her out for a night or two but moving every few days held no appeal, and she couldn't impose on anyone for an entire summer. Everyone was hurting financially as much as she was.

A wave of weariness rolled through her as a lump formed in her throat. Fighting the good fight when she had no reserves herself was wearing her down. She wanted to be totally self-indulgent and sit and sob but she had no time for that—she had a cottage to vacate. She rose slowly to her feet, tucked her hair behind her ears and faced Finn.

"It appears I need the rest of the afternoon off to move house."

"WHAT ABOUT THIS?" Finn picked up a dusty and battered wooden box with a brass handle unsure if it was part of the cottage's furnishings or Annika's private property.

He'd fully intended to drop Annika off at her cottage and drive straight back to Kylemore, leaving her to sort out the mess that appeared to be her life. But there'd been something about the slump of her shoulders that was so unlike her usual take-charge attitude that he'd felt compelled to stay.

Still, he couldn't believe that he was here helping her pack. He never got involved in his staff's personal lives.

You never get involved in anyone's life period. He shut down the unwanted voice. Thinking of Annika in terms of "staff" was supposed to be helping him *not* to think about her in any other way, but watching her walk past him holding an armful of clean laundry with a white sports bra dangling from the load, wasn't helping. His thoughts strayed to the memory of plain white panties and long smooth legs.

Her gaze flicked over the case he held up and her usually clear eyes clouded for a moment. "Yes, that's mine."

He saw her look beyond the case and noticed a folded-up easel. "Do you paint?"

"Passing phase." She dumped her clothes into the open suitcase on the couch before picking up some rolled-up canvases and putting them quickly on top and snapping the lid closed. "That's it."

Bridey had more gear in her vacation bedroom at Kylemore. "Your possessions are two suitcases and five boxes?"

She tilted her chin. "Some of us have a smaller carbon footprint than others. Even so, it's not all going to fit in that car of yours with its pocket-handkerchief trunk."

"So sue me. Had I known you were moving I would have got you a pickup." The moment he spoke, he caught the spark of an idea light up those glorious eyes like the white light of a sparkler. He silently groaned.

She tilted her head and strands of hair brushed her cheek. "Great idea, thank you."

"You don't have a car?"

She shook her head and put out her hand. He caught the flicker of embarrassment that she immediately squashed with the reality of survival. "I can organize a truck though. I just need your phone to do it because mine isn't working."

He knew that was code for, "I haven't paid the bill." Annika having her own set of wheels and being independent of him made perfect sense but for some reason he found himself saying, "You don't have any money for gas."

"It will come with a full tank." She hooked his gaze with a straight-up and honest stare. "Look at it this way. It frees you up to get back to Kylemore and back to work."

Work which wasn't messy and disorganized like this. She was giving him an out and one he should probably take.

She suddenly spun around to face a large clock and her hand flew to her mouth. "Oh, no, I promised Logan I'd watch him dive tonight. Can you please tell him how sorry I am and tell him I'll go swimming with him later in the week."

She seemed more distressed by letting Logan down than by being destitute, which he didn't understand at all. He thought of all the times when he was a kid and his father had promised he'd come to school concerts and basketball games. On hearing the promise his young self would get a rush of excitement edged with anxious anticipation, which was invariably followed by resigned disappointment when Sean failed to arrive.

"Logan will cope." He had to or he wouldn't survive being a Callahan.

She wrinkled her nose. "I'm sure he will but I gave my word and I want him to know that I haven't just blown him off. Or your parents. Will you pass on the message?"

That would involve having a personal conversation with Logan, Dana or his father—something he never put his hand up for. He tossed her his phone. "Call them from the car on our way to the car rental company."

An hour later, Finn was behind the wheel of a brand-new truck and Annika was at a loss to work out exactly how this had happened when *her* plan had been that he was the one renting the vehicle and *she* was the one driving it.

"So where am I taking you, ma'am?"

She imagined him in overalls with a tool belt slung low on his hips—an image she instantly regretted as her breath hitched in her throat. "You're enjoying this aren't you?"

He grinned. "Who knew driving a pickup would be this much fun."

She rolled her eyes and muttered, "Rich boys and their toys," before taking a deep breath and trying a different tack. She didn't want to tell him where she planned to live and she sure as hell didn't want to have him deliver her there.

She shifted in her seat. "This is really taking you out of your way and I'll just have to drive you back to the lot to collect your car. So now you've had a turn at being a regular Joe, take a right here and we can double back."

"It's no problem. What sort of boss would I be if I didn't make sure you were settled?"

"A normal one."

"Hey, AKP values their staff."

He looked slightly offended and she built on it, hoping he'd get pissed and leave her alone with the pickup. "You just want to avoid your family."

A muscle jerked against the dark stubble on his cheek. "I want to make sure you're settled so you can concentrate on being my P.A. instead of taking afternoons off to sort out your life."

A niggle of guilt burrowed in. She should feel grateful that he was helping her. Plenty of people in town would have happily helped but they'd have had pity and defeat in their eyes, because her failure to financially survive in Whitetail would be yet another reminder that most people couldn't do it without an industry. It made her even more determined to get Whitetail up and moving again so folk could rediscover their spirit and pride. The fact that Finn knew she had nothing was somehow easier to bear, probably because of their natural antipathy.

Antipathy with a lust chaser.

Only she knew if she dared to be honest it wasn't even close to antipathy. Behind that sexy but brusque business facade lay a very likeable man who needed to get out more.

She crossed her arms, refusing to admit to anything. She had to stick to her game plan. "Geez, it was two hours and I'll make it up tomorrow, which by the way includes a brides' meeting at the warehouse." She poked the air with her forefinger. "There's another reason I need this vehicle. I'll be in late and you can't dock me for being out of the office because you insisted I oversee this wedding-caper idea."

But his offended air seemed to have vanished and he just smiled as he slowed at a four-way stop. "I have no plans to dock your pay."

"Great. I've got an even better idea. You could pay me in advance."

He checked the rearview mirror, braked and threw the gear stick into Park before leaning toward her with his palm flat on the bench seat next to her hand. His expression was all business. "That would be unwise. First rule of commerce is never pay before services have been rendered."

Desperately trying to ignore the fact that the air between their hands pulsed with electricity, she spoke without thinking. "Why? I'm good for it."

His jet-black eyes flared with something a long way removed from business, and his voice dropped five tones as he seemed to move closer. "Oh, I'm sure you're better than good."

The words caressed her skin with a delicious shiver and then dove deep. Suddenly the roomy cabin of the truck felt as small and cramped as his Ferrari California and she swallowed hard against a dry throat. Every breath she took filled her with him—the spice of his cologne, the musk of his all-male body and the undisputed scent of delicious danger. It called to her. It marched all over her reason and her common sense with its entreaty and delectable promise that a kiss right now would equal the one the night they met.

God, she wanted to feel like that again. She wanted—craved—to have a moment where nothing existed except sheer wonder and amazement. His eyes darkened to hypnotic ebony and every part of her wanted to fall forward into his arms and onto his lips. With a sigh, her eyelids fluttered closed in delicious anticipation.

The truck suddenly lurched forward and her eyes flew open as her seat belt locked and jammed her against the back of the seat, slamming her with a hefty dose of rational thought. Finn's words boomed in her head. *It was out of line and it won't happen again.*

And it hadn't. As much as she'd wanted him to kiss her and he'd looked for all the world like he wanted to kiss her, Finn was a man of his word. She should have known that especially after their argument at the police station when he'd told her through rigid lips he was an honorable man. He'd rather walk through fire than kiss her again.

She must shake off this insane attraction. She needed to use his self-control to her advantage considering she had none of her own. She needed an immunity booster shot against a dark-haired, dark-eyed Irishman with dimples, and she had to re-find the grim determination to avoid relationships that had successfully protected her for the last two years. The solution was obvious. She just had to make sure she didn't spend any more time alone with Finn than was absolutely necessary.

"I need directions."

She sighed at his hoarse request with defeat licking at her. She'd almost panted while waiting for him to kiss her and now, to add salt to the wound, she hadn't even managed to deflect him from dropping her at her new home. "Take a left just up here."

"A left?" Finn checked because his brain was still re-filling with blood after he'd almost kissed those ready red lips. Hell, twice in two days was two times too much, given he'd promised her he wouldn't kiss her again. She was working for him and kissing staff wasn't P.C., especially when the thought of stopping the kiss once he'd started was harder than not kissing her at all. And damn it, why did he even want to kiss her when she irritated the hell out of him?

He flicked on the indicator. "Doesn't that road lead out of town?"

"Yes."

Her teeth snagged her bottom lip and he took the corner too fast.

She raised a chestnut brow. "The brake's that big pedal on the left."

He grinned. "And to think, someone's actually prepared to have you and your smart mouth in their house." Except the houses were getting farther apart but as she'd been on the phone the entire time he'd been completing the rental agreement, he figured one of her friends or family must live out here.

She didn't fire back her usual quick response. Instead, she said quietly, "Turn right up here."

As he slowed, he recognized the grove of maple and birch trees. "This is the entrance to the business park."

"Well done. You've just graduated Whitetail Geography 101."

Her sarcasm lacked bite, which made him sneak another look at her. Fatigue and worry lines hovered around her eyes and as he killed the engine, he said, "I don't recall any houses out here."

"That's because I only gave you the warehouse tour." She threw him a bright smile. "So now you know my location, pull in here and we'll swap drivers and I'll take you back to your car."

"Not before I've carried in your boxes." His feet hit the blacktop and he met her at the back of the truck bed.

"Thanks, but there's really no need because my friends will help me unload later. Like I said, time is marching and business calls. I'm surprised you're not a barrel of anxious tics from not checking the six messages that came in over the last half hour." She crossed her arms. "I don't want to be the one responsible for your meltdown."

He was fine with ignoring the phone because none of the emergency ringtones had sounded. She, on the other hand, was a barrel of tics and as skittish as a deer. Even when she'd fallen through the window she'd had more poise than she had right now. He stared over her head looking for a manager's house or something similar but all he could see were the walls of the two warehouses. He ignored her and started walking.

"Finn, you're going the wrong way."

He didn't believe her. He kept walking and when she jogged up alongside him, his hand shot out automatically to steady her when she inevitably tripped over her feet.

He rounded the corner of the farthest warehouse and met a towering field of green corn. He knew there was no house between the entrance and here, and suddenly all her agitation made sense. "You're *not* staying here."

Her chin lifted. "You said you were happy for the town to use the warehouses and I'm part of the town."

He tried to keep his voice even but it wanted to rise on a wave on incredulity. "I meant them to be used for business not housing."

Annika squared her shoulders. "The partitions from the Reggies offices are still here as well as a kitchen and a bathroom. It's everything a girl needs to set up house."

"There's no way in hell you're staying out here." He pulled his phone out of his pocket. "Call your parents."

"They don't live here."

That surprised him. Although he spent his life avoiding his family he knew many people had families they wanted to spend time with, and he'd assumed her family was part of the attraction for her living in Whitetail. "Brothers? Sisters?"

She shook her head and he recognized the stubborn glint and failure to back down that had burned them both the night at the police station.

Confusion circled him. "You've been extolling the virtues of Whitetail from the moment we met, so even without family, someone will put you up."

"I can think of twenty people who'd offer in a heartbeat, but I'm not imposing on any of them. They've all

got their own set of worries and I'm not adding to them."
She blew some hair out of her eyes. "I'll pay you rent."

"I don't want freaking rent." He could just see the
headlines in the local paper: Callahan in Kylemore Luxury
While P.A. Lives in Warehouse Squalor. He knew
enough about Annika Jacobson to know she'd fight hard
for what she wanted and despite being taken to the lowest
point, she was determined to try and survive without
taking charity. But even a woman who stretched his
patience to the nth degree didn't deserve to squat in a
warehouse. Hell, it wasn't safe out here in the middle of
nowhere. "I'll pay for your accommodation." He made
a quick call to the Whitetail Motel.

"I'm sorry, Mr. Callahan," the apologetic clerk explained.
"It's the musky fishing tournament in Hayward
and we're full with overflow accommodation. You could
try the B and Bs."

He called them. Same deal. No vacancy.

Shit.

She rubbed her arms as the cool of the evening settled
over the heat of the day. "Once I get a coffee maker I'll
be very cozy here."

"I'll have Rory evict you if you even try. This time
he'll agree with me."

For the first time since he'd met her, she seemed at a
loss for words. The woman who thought on her feet and
was his equal in quick thinking, was strangely silent.

She ran interference with Bridey and Logan today.
The thought shone like a light bulb in his head. If she
was at the house out of business hours she could do that
even more. "You can stay at Kylemore."

Her blue eyes widened in disbelief. "I can't just move
into Dana's house."

He shrugged. "My father has a guest cottage and it'll save you a long commute to work."

He watched her thinking about it. Her expressive face hid nothing as she ran through all the aspects of the offer, even though she virtually had no choice.

She suddenly stiffened. "And I'd be sharing with?"

He laughed, understanding completely. No way would he have been offering if it involved her staying with him. He'd have no chance of honoring his promise not to kiss her. "The guest cottage is down by the lake and you'll have your privacy just like I have mine at my cabin."

She hesitated and he could clearly see the war of housing need versus imposition. He threw her a line. "You can pay my father rent."

Her hand shot out. "Deal."

SEVEN

"SHE'S WHAT?"

Annika had heard the shock in Finn's voice a moment before he slapped the side of his head with his palm as if it would somehow alter the words he'd just heard Bridey speak.

They'd arrived at Kylemore a few moments earlier and she'd expected everyone to be down by the lake enjoying the cookout she'd unfortunately missed. Instead, chaos reigned. The sound of raised voices coming from the kitchen sizzled, and Annika recognized Sean's velvet voice being answered by Dana's softer but equally determined one. Added into the mix were the occasional words spoken by Bridey.

Annika's feet had frozen on the threshold of the terrace's sliding doors, not wanting to intrude on what was clearly a domestic dispute, but Finn had cupped her upper arm and propelled her forward. "Don't mind another happy Callahan vacation. I'll just grab the key to the guest cottage and we'll get going."

At that moment, Bridey had stepped out of the kitchen and straight into her brother's arms. She'd given him a quick hug, which he'd returned warmly before jerking his head toward the kitchen. "What gives?"

"They're adapting to the news that Mom's in the guest cottage."

That bit of information had rendered Finn momentarily speechless before he'd spluttered out, "She's what?" Then he'd slapped himself on the side of the head. "What the hell is she doing there?"

Bridey sighed, and Annika noticed strain around her usually bright green eyes. "Mom missed the last step as she deplaned and she's sprained her ankle pretty bad. The B and B had stairs," she added, as if that explained everything. "They were able to rent the room right away because of some fishing thing so we didn't lose the deposit." She caught sight of Annika. "Oh, sorry, Annika. Hello." Curiosity clung to her cheeks but she stopped short of saying, "Why are you here?"

Finn interrupted. "What about flying Mom home and employing a nurse?"

Bridey rolled her eyes. "That's exactly what Dad suggested and Dana went ballistic saying, 'Kathleen stays in the cottage until she can walk out of it.'"

Finn paled. "How long is that going to be?"

Bridey turned her hands palms up. "I don't know. The doctor in Whitetail said it was a bad sprain."

Annika recalled the numerous times she'd slipped on ice, tripped on curbs and stumbled on sidewalks. "Soft tissue injuries can take a long time to mend." As she spoke, the sound of her words crashed into her, suddenly making the situation crystal clear. With a shudder, she realized that her promised accommodation was no longer available to her. She glanced at Finn and opened her mouth, but Bridey spoke first.

"I think Dana's being totally amazing letting Mom stay. I'm just going back to check on her now. Come with me, Finn, and say hi."

Not wanting to intrude, and suddenly seeing an escape route, Annika reached out her hand with a smile.

"Hey, boss, if you give me the keys to the truck, I'll get out of your way and see you in the morning."

Finn jerked around and looked at her as if he'd just remembered she was there. His eyes narrowed. "You're not going anywhere."

Sean strode out of the kitchen looking thunderous but he seemed to give himself a shake when he saw Annika. "So you made it for the cookout after all, Anni?"

Confused, Annika waited for Finn to explain about the now-defunct guesthouse plan but he stayed unexpectedly silent. She didn't have to fake her surprise when she said, "Hello, Sean. I thought the cookout would be done by now."

Sean shook his head. "We've been delayed with my ex-wife's unexpected arrival."

Finn made a strangled sound.

Bridey gave her father's arm a squeeze.

"Dad, I think Dana's being amazing given the circumstances."

Sean's smile was stiff. "That's one way of looking at it, not that Kathleen will thank her for it."

"Do you really expect her to?" Finn's voice was polite but distinctly cool.

Sean suddenly looked unaccountably weary but his voice was one of command. "Go visit your mother. She won't want to see me."

"You've got that right," Finn muttered quietly, dragging his hands through his hair though his feet stayed still.

Sean shrugged. "Sadly, yes."

Bridey immediately swapped arms from her father to her brother in an action that spoke of peacemaking. "Come on, Finn. Let's go see her."

Finn leaned in close to Annika. "I need you here when I get back because China's just getting up."

She interpreted that as code for "don't even think about leaving me here with my family." Although it could have been "I'll haul you out by your sweet ass if you stay at the warehouse."

"Food first, Annika. China can wait." Sean graciously opened the sliding doors for her and ushered her out onto the terrace. She snuck a glance at Finn, whose taut expression made him look like she'd just abandoned him on a sinking ship.

"WHATEVER WAS SHE thinking painting these walls this color?" Kathleen's gaze touched everything in the room with a critical eye.

The age-old spasm of tension that coiled through Finn every time his parents got within a mile of each other, settled in with its iron grip. Even on neutral territory it made his chest tighten and Kylemore was so far from neutral it qualified as a war zone. How had his ordered life—the one where he controlled the amount of time he spent with his family—managed to turn into a nightmare in the space of ten days? Excluding Sean's second wife, he now had his entire immediate family in the same place, and to add insult to injury, he'd just lost the one place Annika could stay.

He ran both hands through his hair, welcoming the discomfort at his scalp as his fingers snagged and pulled.

"Finn?"

He glanced around abruptly to see Bridey looking at him from her place on the bed.

"What?"

"I was just saying to Mom that she needs to look at the sprain in a positive way."

"How's that exactly?"

She smiled. "We get to spend some time together. Mom's accident has a sort of serendipitous air to it given we're both up here at the lake for the first time in years."

He fixed his sister with a glare that said "I know your plan" before asking his mother, "Are you sure Bridey didn't trip you?"

"Finn," his mother reproved. "What a dreadful thing to say."

Bridey grinned. "See, it's just like old times."

Kathleen's mouth tightened. "Except, I'm a guest in what was once my own home."

Bridey fluffed the pillows behind Kathleen's head. "Think of it as a vacation in your own private villa. You have to admit it's much better than the B and B. Tomorrow morning Esther will be back to fuss over you and once you've had her French toast, life will be brighter. Then you can sit on the deck in the sunshine with your leg up, with a view of the lake, and we can go through the bridal magazines."

"But it's not *my* private villa, is it? Staying here will never feel like a B and B, and Esther will be far too busy at the main house. I'll be left here alone."

His mother's unusually tremulous words sparked a brilliant idea. An idea which would solve a massive problem for him. "My P.A. can stay here with you so you're not alone at night."

Bridey gasped. "Finn, you can't just tell Annika she has to stay."

He rolled his eyes at his sister's horrified look. "This has nothing to do with me being her boss. Two hours ago I promised her the cottage after hers got sublet out from under her." For some reason he didn't quite understand, he closed his mouth before mentioning her rent arrears and the eviction.

Sympathy settled on Bridey's round face. "I'm really sorry to hear that's happened to her but she can't stay here. After the day Mom's had, she needs the cottage to herself."

Kathleen flinched. "I'm quite able to make decisions for myself, Bridey."

Hope flared and Finn smiled at his mother. "I knew you'd prefer to have someone here with you, especially overnight. I'm on the island so I can't get here quickly if you need anything."

"There's an intercom." Kathleen's tone was back to being firm. "If I need anything, which I doubt I will, Bridey can get it for me."

Finn pressed on. "But if you fall no one will be right here."

"I'm fifty-five, Finnegan, not eighty," Kathleen snapped. "I've already negotiated the bathroom and I'm not having a stranger staying here with me."

An amended brilliant plan evolved. "Then I'll stay with you." *And Annika can have the cabin.*

"Don't be ridiculous." Kathleen shifted on the bed. "I know how much you value your own space and after working all day you need the quiet of the cabin."

His phone beeped.

His mother's hand shot out and an imperious forefinger pointed. "And I don't want your phone here going off every three minutes."

"It's settled then," Bridey soothed. "I'll make up a schedule so there's always someone available."

Kathleen flinched. "Not Dana or your father."

"Mom, they might want to help."

Kathleen's hand fisted on the edge of the light blanket

that covered her legs. "Bridey." The warning tone could have triggered an earthquake. "Let things be."

Finn sighed. "I'm working, Bridey."

Bridey threw him a look that brooked no argument. "You're *on* the schedule."

He knew there was no point disagreeing. "Fine. Make it midafternoon because that's usually the quietest time of day."

He stood up, giving it one more shot because he knew if he and Annika had to share his cabin, he'd be permanently hard and having at least five cold showers a day. "Mom, are you sure you're going to be okay overnight, alone?"

"For heaven's sake, Finnegan. I've never known you to fuss and now isn't the time to start. I'll be perfectly fine and I have Bridey not far away. Now both of you, please go. My ankle's throbbing and I just want some peace."

Stifling a sigh, Finn leaned down and kissed his mother on the cheek. "I'll see you tomorrow then."

She nodded silently and closed her eyes as if to say the discussion was over.

He stepped out onto the large deck and stared out at the lake wondering how he'd get through the next few days. The sun was dropping but there was still enough light in the sky for water play. He heard Logan's shout of "watch me" drift across the air and he turned to see his little brother execute a fair dive off the platform. The same platform he'd learned to dive off at much the same age under the tutelage of his grandfather because his father had always been too busy. Lucky for Logan, Sean didn't appear to be too busy now.

He heard Annika's cheer before he saw her. He brought his hand up to shield his eyes from the sun and his eyes scanned the beach and the lake. When his gaze finally found her, she was climbing out of the water and pulling herself up the steps of the platform. Water sluiced around the soft curves of her breasts, across the womanly swell of her belly and down her long, lithe legs.

His whole body tightened and his palms burned to outline her body, following the exact same path as the water.

"Now it's your turn," Logan instructed.

Annika laughed. "I think you're the champion diver here. You don't need to see me dive."

Logan crossed his arms and his bottom lip pouted. "None of the grown-ups ever dive."

Annika ruffled his hair. "I tell you what. I'll give it my best shot."

Finn instantly went on alert. Surely she wasn't going to try and dive off the platform. Hell, she couldn't even walk in a straight line without falling over.

He heard her throaty laugh ring out as she ran the length of the platform and threw herself off the edge. The loud thwack of her belly hitting the water had him running as fast as he could toward the lake.

WRAPPED IN A towel, in the bow of a small aluminum boat, Annika tried not to lose her recently regained breath while she watched Finn row.

"What possessed you to try and do a flip?" Finn asked the question she knew had been hovering on his lips for a good ten minutes or more, while he'd waited for her to recover from being badly winded.

A black curl fell across his eye and he tossed his head to move it. "Actually, I think I know. It's always important to give it your best shot, right?"

Her head jerked up as she reluctantly pulled her gaze

away from watching the ripple of muscles across a taut chest. She met dark-chocolate eyes that glinted with something close to begrudging admiration. He'd just quoted something she'd said to him the first night they'd met. "Actually, Logan dared me."

His eyes widened with surprise. "And if I dared you to do something stupid, would you comply?"

A shiver of anticipation skated through her as her mind went immediately to the memory of his kiss. "That would depend on the dare."

"Is that so?" His lips tilted in a wicked smile that made her acknowledge that if he asked her to kiss him right this minute, she'd be just as reckless as she'd been with Logan.

She hastily returned the subject back to the little boy. "He's a kid in an adult's world and he's desperate for a friend."

"So you, who have the coordination of a giraffe on ice, decided to act like an eight-year-old?"

"No." She tilted her chin trying to feign indignation because at least she was putting some effort into playing with the boy. But she failed, grinning as she lost out to the reality of the situation. "More like a twelve-year-old, really."

He laughed, and for a moment his usual deep worry lines vanished, making him look far less uptight. Making him look way too gorgeous, approachable and friendly, which was far too dangerous for her peace of mind.

She tugged the towel around her, needing to do something with her hands so that they didn't reach out and touch him. "Seriously though, that kid needs someone his own age to play with."

"Not my problem and not yours either." The brusque businessman was back. She should be pleased because he was slightly easier to resist, but the traitorous woman inside her sobbed, longing to see the relaxed man again.

"Thanks for picking me up but I would have been fine to swim back after a bit of a rest."

He shrugged as he continued to pull at the oars. "No problem."

She'd been so mesmerized watching him row that she only just realized he was heading away from the shore where the family was gathered. Instead he was rowing toward an island in the lake. She thumbed behind her. "Um, Kylemore's that way."

"I'm well aware of that." He kept rowing.

Perhaps he wanted the exercise. "How's your mom?"

"Cross, sore, cranky and impossible to help."

"A severely sprained ankle hurts."

"Talking from experience?"

"Totally." She gave a wry smile. "Growing up, Dad bought me my own pair of crutches because he said it was cheaper than renting them all the time."

He shook his head gently as a lazy smile roved across his cheeks and she let that delicious image wash over her along with the gentle sound of the lap of the oars slicing into the water. The high-pitched chirp of an osprey made her look up and she watched the magnificent bird flying above them. "He's heading home for the night."

Finn tilted his head toward a huge tree on the island. "He's home. He swoops in every night at this time."

"I love these birds."

"Do you want a closer look?"

"Sure."

He rowed around the other side of the island and the boat hit the pebbly beach with a thud. Finn stowed the oars before vaulting over the side. Annika didn't even try to hide her admiration for his easy athleticism.

Gripping both sides of the boat and spreading her feet wide, she prepared to stand but before she'd pushed up, Finn's hand hovered in front of her. She thought of how her knees turned to jelly whenever he touched her. "Thanks, but I grew up around boats and I'll be fine."

He quirked one brow and his hand stayed put. "You grew up around sidewalks too but they still trip you up."

His teasing held an absolute truth and did she really want to end up facedown looking like she was kissing his feet? It wouldn't be a good look on so many levels. She took a deep breath and slid her palm against his. His firm grip held her and his strength flowed through her, along with the pop and fizz of tingling and enticing heat. It spread through her limbs and then raced to a sweet spot between her legs. She pressed her thighs together to try and stop the wondrous throb.

"Ready?"

Very ready. The part of her that had been deeply asleep since Ryan's betrayal—the part that had stirred and had been drowsy from the moment Finn's lips had touched hers last Saturday night—woke right up with a pant of longing. Annika tried to send her straight back to sleep by thinking of the long list of reasons why getting it on with Finn Callahan would be a seriously bad idea but the twinkle in his jet eyes sidetracked her. She somehow managed to nod her reply.

Dimples carved into the black stubble that graced his cheeks. "That means you have to stand up."

"Right." *Get it together, girl.* She forced liquid legs into an upright position but as she stood, the boat tipped and despite his steadying hand, she wobbled. "Ohh." She tried to lean back as a counterweight, but fell forward and the next moment her free hand was clutching his shoulder and her bikini-clad chest was pressed firmly against his. Her nipples puckered in anticipation and the rest of her sighed in bliss. God he felt good.

His laugh rolled around her and the deeply textured notes thrummed through her, adding to the wildfire of need that already burned brightly and threatened to race out of control. Then his arms wrapped firmly around her waist and he lifted her out of the boat.

As her feet hit the beach, she looked up at him trying to sound as normal as possible despite the fact that her heart hammered as fast as a hummingbird's, and her body was quickly melting into his. "Th-that seemed to go fairly well."

He stared down at her, his gaze not quite as focused as normal and when he spoke, his voice was unusually husky. "Technically, you didn't fall."

"No. Just into you."

His thumb grazed her bottom lip as his eyes held hers. "Do you want to go and see the nest?"

His touch detonated a million tiny explosions of lust. It took every ounce of willpower not to moan, and the effort drained her reserves completely.

She'd spent four days around Finn in a constant state of heightened awareness and sexual-sensory overload, and she was exhausted. She wanted him to kiss her to defuse the tension. She wanted *one* moment in her truly crappy day just for herself, and this was it. One kiss and then she'd worry about where she was spending the night and the rest of the summer. One kiss and then she'd worry about Nicole and brides, Whitetail and industry, and the future.

Ignoring the forest of red warning flags that shot to attention in her mind, and turning two deaf ears to the piercing tornado-siren that screamed in her head, she raised her palm against his rough cheek. "I do want to go and see the nest."

He cleared his throat and then swallowed hard—his Adam's apple moving jerkily. "We should go now before we lose the light."

She held his desire-filled gaze with her own. "I guess we should."

But neither of them moved.

Apart from his breathing, he was perfectly still. But every breath he took expanded his chest into hers, caressing her breasts and sending his heat and lust spinning into her.

She asked the question she knew the answer to. "You're not going to kiss me, are you?"

"No." The tiny syllable came out on a croak of overstretched restraint.

Her fingertips skated across his jaw propelled by her need to touch him. "Because you gave me your word?"

"That's right." His lips hardly moved and it was as if they'd had difficulty framing the words.

His code of principle and honor bound him as tightly as if he was tied by ropes, and she could clearly see the battle waging in his eyes. The battle not to kiss her.

She realized she could have some fun *and* be kissed at the same time. "So, no matter what I do or say, you're not going to kiss me?"

"No." He shuddered out a breath. "I'm not going to kiss you."

"I understand." She ran her hands down his arms to his waist and after a quick flick of the cotton, she slid them under his shirt where they touched smooth, hot skin. It scorched her hands and she wanted to feel more.

He stiffened against her as every muscle tightened, and his erection pressed against her bare thigh. Any lingering doubts she might have had that he didn't find her attractive, fled.

"What if I kissed you? Would you kiss me back?" She smiled as her hands pressed against his lower back, and her thumbs gently kneaded the skin. "I mean, that's still kissing me, right?"

A growling sound came from his throat and a wild look tore across his face. As his hands slid back to her waist, she worried he'd pull away. She'd had her fun but now it was time to put him out of his misery. Put herself out of her misery. She rose on tiptoes and pressed her lips softly against his closed mouth. She tasted sunshine, a hint of peanuts and a shot of desire. She wanted more and her tongue ran along the seal between his lips.

His hands tensed against her sides and his mouth slackened slightly. With anticipation, she dove in and started to explore. Heat dominated and it seared her before infusing her with a myriad of flavors. All of them tasted like need.

He groaned against her mouth but he stayed perfectly still, amazing her with his self-control. She flicked out her tongue, driven by a memory and wanting to revisit a place that had given her so much pleasure. She traced the tip of her tongue slowly along his inside cheek, trawling it across his teeth, and then with deliberate, lazy intent, she outlined the groove in his tongue.

His hands instantly shot to the sides of her head and his thumbs gently pressed against her cheeks. Then he angled her mouth for perfect access and took control. His tongue stroked hers for a moment and electricity arced between them, lighting her up with bliss. Then he started a concentrated exploration of his own. Her hands curled around his neck as she hung on to the most delicious onslaught of sensations she'd ever known.

His left hand pulled at the ties of her halter top, and her breasts, heavy with aching need, fell from their scant support and she sighed. With his mouth still on hers, he cupped her breasts with his hands and his thumbs drew tiny circles across her nipples until she was wet and throbbing and thought she'd come on the spot. She fell to her knees, impervious to the feel of the pebbles on the beach, and he came down with her. With a jerky tug, she pulled his shirt over his head and as his mouth moved down her neck she pressed her mouth to his shoulder. He was beautiful—tanned skin over toned muscle—and she wanted to kiss all of him and then go back and trace him with her tongue.

His mouth closed over her breast. Exquisite fire lit through her and her head fell back with a moan as colors exploded in her mind. His arm pressed against her back for support, and his erection pressed against her belly. For a second, she wondered how her knees could still hold her upright but then she lost herself in the touch of his hands, the heat of his mouth and the pure wonder of him under her fingers. Nothing mattered but this moment, and all her muscles throbbed for him with all-consuming need.

He pulled her onto his lap and she felt his erection firm under the material of his shorts. She wanted him inside her. She wanted to grip him tightly and ride him until she shattered into a thousand tiny pieces of pure and unadulterated pleasure. Without hesitation, she wrapped her legs around his waist. The hard cotton of his shorts pushed up against the thin material of her bikini, caressing her, and her body started to rock against him.

With a groan, his mouth returned to hers as if it was home, and his tongue continued its rampage, as did her own. Nothing existed except his mouth on hers and she'd never been kissed like this before. Their hands roamed all over each other as they moved together and then his fingers tangled with the ties that held her bikini briefs together.

Somewhere, something deep in the recesses of her mind yelled, "Stop."

It was supposed to be a kiss. Sex wasn't part of the plan. Her hand covered his as she hauled her mouth away.

Wild-eyed and panting, he seemed to be staring at her as if he was a long way away. "What?"

She scrambled off his lap. "I'm sorry." Seeing his gaze on her breasts she hastily retied the halter top and shivered. "I'm cold."

Deep dimples curved into his cheeks and his mouth pulled into a lazy, yet wicked smile. "Sweetheart, there's enough heat between us to warm Alaska for the next seven winters."

And so help her but she knew he was right.

He reached out his hand and skimmed a finger down her arm, and she jumped at his touch. Her words came out on a wail. "We don't have any protection."

"You have got to be kidding." A sigh shuddered out of him. "I've worked hard to keep my hands off you for four days, so exactly what did you expect was going to happen when you kissed me like that?"

She bit her lip, hating that she'd put them both in this position of mind-altering lust but without protection. "I didn't think it through."

"No." His voice was hoarse and his eyes held an agonized look of unwanted control. "Next time you try and seduce me, please have a condom handy."

The image of her straddling him with her head thrown back took the breath from her lungs. *You fool.* Guilt made her snap. "I don't make a habit of trying to seduce men and this was a one-off aberration. There won't be a next time."

He laughed. "Now that I know you can't keep your hands off me, there'll definitely be a next time. Come to think of it, I suddenly feel the need to visit White-tail Drug."

To her shame, the thought had her instantly hot and tingling and she scraped her wet hair behind her ears, hoping it would cool her down. "I think we should go back now."

He winked at her. "Sadly, Whitetail Drug won't be open."

Another thrill shot through her. *Oh, God, why are you so damn gorgeous?*

Can you please just focus? The sensible voice in her head drove her back on track. "Very funny." She crossed her arms in an attempt to stop her breasts tingling and to try and look serious. "I meant we should get back to your family who'll be wondering where we are. Plus if you remember, I need to organize a place to stay tonight."

He spoke quietly, his previous teasing vanishing fast. "We're exactly where we need to be."

His answer made no sense and she studied his suddenly tight face. "I beg your pardon?"

Weariness clung to his voice. "With my mother in the cottage, and Dana's 'no staff in the house' rule, the only place with an available bed is on this island." He pointed to a path that disappeared up from the beach and into a stand of birch trees. "In my cabin."

Silver spots danced in front of her eyes and she heard her sharp intake of breath. A few minutes ago they'd been seconds away from having sex and now she had to share a cabin with him? She wanted to sit down and cry. How the hell had she got herself into this mess?

Lust.

Shut up.

She tried unsuccessfully to hide the desperation from her voice. "Please tell me you have a spare room."

He shook his head slowly. "Not even a sofa. Just a queen-size bed."

As his words sunk in, she heard the cry of the osprey calling for its mate and she looked toward the tree in the distance. It was a crying shame she couldn't fit into that nest.

EIGHT

THE LIGHT ON the bow of the boat glowed yellow across the dark water and besides the slip of the oars, the only other sound was the haunting wail of the loons. Finn could have used the motorboat to get Annika's stuff, but he'd chosen to row and to row hard. His body still hummed with her wholesome scent of apples and cinnamon, and her exotic taste of hot and heady need. Did she have any clue how sexy she was when she'd looked at him with those liquid blue eyes and asked, "You're not going to kiss me, are you?"

It had been nothing short of torture feeling her hands on him and her lips against his, and given he'd known they had to share the cottage there'd been no way he was going to kiss her back. He'd managed to stay strong right up to the moment she'd deepened the kiss. Then her hunger for him had hit like a force-five tornado, totally undoing him and firing up his craving for her to the point he thought he'd either explode or go insane. So he'd kissed her back. It still stunned him how fast and how quickly the kiss had become a catalyst for something so much bigger. Had it been left to him to pull back, he wasn't sure he could have.

But she'd pulled back and now he was pulling oars. He couldn't believe that he didn't have condoms in the cabin but why would he? He'd never brought a woman there. The cabin was his domain and one he didn't care to share with anyone, not even family. The boat hit the beach with a thud and he sighed. That had just changed. Now he had to spend the night in the cabin with Annika, knowing it wasn't safe to touch her because if he did, he wouldn't be able to stop until he'd buried himself deep in her hot body, and lost himself in oblivion. His body tightened at the thought.

Don't go there. He jumped out onto the sand as the boat hit the island's beach and he hauled the boat beyond the water line, before picking up her suitcase, extinguishing the light and heading up the path. Solar lights and a huge moon lit his way and the cabin's porch light was on but the rest of the place appeared to be in darkness. Had Annika gone to bed?

Bed. He didn't want to think about Annika in bed. *His bed.* He'd left her an hour ago with the suggestion she take a shower and he'd set out one of his T-shirts and an old pair of running shorts for her to wear until he returned with her clothes.

The squeak of the screen door sounded overly loud as he stepped inside. He switched on a lamp, expecting Annika to be curled up in one of the old but comfortable club chairs watching the way the moonlight played across the lake. "Hello?"

But there was no reply. Surprised, he made his way to the bedroom. The bedside lamp was on low and Annika lay asleep. Her chestnut lashes brushed her cheek and her hair spread out on the pillow like a white fan edged with gold. She looked peaceful which was hard to believe given how manic they'd both been on the beach. Her huge day must have caught up with her and he imagined losing her home was more stressful than she'd let on. He admired her ability to keep on going against the tide of the economy but he wondered if her staying in Whitetail was the best thing for her.

She'd pulled his Egyptian cotton sheet right up under her chin and the light blanket reached her waist. He could see the hint of deep blue from his Yale T-shirt where the sheet fell from her shoulder, and as his eye followed its curve it stopped short on the rounded edge of a bolster pillow. He moved into the room and saw an uneven line running parallel with her back. Annika had stuffed the bed with pillows, creating a barricade.

He swallowed a chuckle and smiled. Did she really think some feather down and cotton slips were going to stop them from having sex? For the first time since he'd realized he had to share the cabin with her, he felt calm. He kicked off his shoes, shucked his shorts and shirt and slid into bed with a blissful sigh. They would have sex. It wouldn't be tonight, but it was going to happen and for now that knowledge was enough. He dumped the pillows onto the floor and drifted into a deep sleep.

ANNIKA WOKE UP slowly. She was loathe to leave behind her dream where she was curled up on a chair on her cottage's veranda, warm and content, and at peace with the painting on her easel. She knew without a doubt that the painting was good, and that feeling had been gone so long she wanted to stay in the dream and hold on to it with both hands. But the dappled morning light tickled her eyelids and she moved to stretch her arms and legs to greet the day. Her limbs stiffened so fast she risked injury. Her leg lay along the length of another and that leg wasn't waxed, so it wasn't hers. All traces of sleep vanished and she realized with horror that instead of her top arm being curved between her breasts it was curved around a waist, and her fingers were caressing a narrow trail of hair that disappeared under an elastic waistband.

Finn. She was wrapped around Finn like gift wrap.

No, *no*, *no*. She rolled away so fast she tumbled out of the bed, falling heavily onto the hardwood floor. "Ouch."

A sleepy businessman rolled into the space she'd just vacated and stared down at her with delicious bedroom eyes. He gave her a long, slow smile. "I see you're starting the day as you plan to continue."

She stumbled to her feet, tugging on the edge of the T-shirt he'd lent her, which smelled so much like him and barely covered her bare bottom. Backing out of the room, she walked straight into the doorjamb, adding another bruise to her fast-growing collection. "Coordination comes with coffee."

"Really?"

She shook her head and gave him a wry smile. "Sadly no. Not even on the days I drink too much."

He swung two deeply tanned legs out of bed and rose to his feet in an easy, fluid motion. Her eyes immediately dropped to his boxers, which were pushed forward magnificently by his early morning erection.

"Sweetheart, my eyes are up here."

Her skin burned and her head jerked up to his laughing face. She was totally out of her depth so she went into damage control, which came out snarky. "Where's my suitcase?"

He ambled toward her and rested his hand on the door frame above her head. "And to think *I've* been accused of being grumpy in the mornings."

She tried not to breathe in too deeply. "Not just the mornings."

"Touché." He stroked her cheek. "I left your bag in the other room."

His touch sent tingles skittering and turned her mind to mush, but she somehow managed to stammer out, "Thanks."

He stepped to the side and the teasing softness disappeared and the efficient businessman slotted back into place. "I'll use the bathroom now and leave you to get yourself organized. You'll find space in the dresser and wardrobe for your clothes. There's enough food to make breakfast but we'll need to shop so make a list of what you like to eat. I know you're meeting with the brides this morning but I need you to format some documents first. Can you be ready to leave at seven-thirty?"

"Absolutely." Glad to be firmly back in her role as his P.A., which was a lot less confusing than the rest of her life, she fled into the main room.

She'd explored the cabin last night while Finn was retrieving her stuff—not that she'd needed a compass or a map. Unlike Kylemore with its many large and generous rooms, this cottage was a very simple rectangle. One third of the space was taken up by the bedroom and a small bathroom with a tub, which had such an amazing view of the woods that it was like bathing outside. The rest of the cabin was open living space which included the kitchen, an eating nook and a sitting area. A large stone fireplace with a hand-hewn pine mantel dominated one side of the room and on the other was a huge double-glazed window, providing an enormous view of the lake. White ash paneling gave the space light and warmth and the obligatory game and fishing photos graced the walls. She especially liked the one of young Finn holding aloft a big musky and standing next to a man who looked like an older version of Sean.

The living space extended to the outside where a large veranda with a herringbone log rail ran around the four sides, almost doubling the livable area. There was a glider seat, numerous Adirondack chairs and a barbeque. Annika had instantly fallen in love with the cabin and had she been able to live here alone it would have been the most perfect accommodation.

But it came with Finn. Finn who had her so flustered she could hardly think straight and she knew she couldn't walk straight.

Now that I know you can't keep your hands off me, there'll definitely be a next time.

His words from last night boomed loud in her head. Only a fool would complicate her life even more than it already was right now. Sex with Finn might be what her body wanted more than oxygen but it had disaster tattooed on it with indelible ink. During the day she was safe but she knew she'd cave if she had to spend another night in Finn's bed. She needed to take steps to keep herself out of harm's way. During the day that was tricky because she worked for him but the moment the brides' meeting was over she was hotfooting it to the camping store and buying a sleeping bag and an air mattress so she could sleep alone. Her body would just have to deal with it.

ANNIKA PUSHED OPEN the plain side door of the warehouse, which led directly to what was once the office, and immediately noticed that the Reggies sign had been taken down. Nicole and Melissa were going to have to do a lot more than that to wow brides. As she stepped into the foyer, she stopped short. Gone was the reception desk and office equipment that had once sat in front of a feature wall with the Reggies logo. The wall now had white tulle cascading from a fixed point—tumbling down the partition like a waterfall, before flowing around the edges of the room, and winding around the base of three familiar wooden pedestals which held huge vases of white peonies, stocks and calla lilies. Their scent filled the air with the promise of magic. Comfy chairs circled a low table, which completed the space, making it the antithesis of the previous dull but functional area. Now it was an enchanted room that spoke of bridal dreams and assured a wedding full of romance.

Annika stared, not quite able to get her head around the change, and behind her the door slammed shut.

Nicole looked up from displaying magazines on the table. "So what do you think, Anni?"

"I...I think it looks incredible. No one would expect to walk into this when they open the utilitarian outside door."

Nicole beamed. "I know, right? It's taken Melissa and me days but I think it says exactly what you suggested. That we're serious about our brides."

"Where did you get all this stuff?"

"The reverend lent us the pedestals, the chairs are from Mrs. Norell, and Emily did the flowers." She paused and her expression suddenly dropped from excitement to concern tinged with sympathy. "I heard about the Hoffmans, Anni. You know you could have spent a few nights with Max and me." She flinched slightly and added, "We'd have enjoyed having someone else in the house."

The sad look on her face was the *very* reason Annika hadn't asked. Nicole's house echoed with her grief for her husband who'd died serving his country so very far away in Afghanistan. "If it had been for a few nights, of course I would have asked but the Hoffmans are here for the entire summer. Please don't worry about me. I've got a room at the Callahans'." She didn't elaborate on the fact it wasn't in the safety of the main house or that she'd woken up draped over Finn like a second skin.

A flash of heat tore through her at the memory. She quickly blew out a breath and refocused, ignoring the quizzical look from Nicole. "Since I don't have a car, staying out there means I'm not imposing on anyone in town and it means I'm closer to the office for the early starts Finn insists on." She sent an apology into the ether because so far Finn as an employer had been more than reasonable.

"I guess being P.A. to a high-flying businessman is a lot of hours. But are you sure you're okay staying so far out of town?"

She wasn't sure about anything to do with Finn Callahan but she nodded just the same.

Nicole got back to business. "We know you're really busy but could you paint the door to look more bridal? You know, to hint at what's in here?"

Annika hadn't picked up a paintbrush in months but this sort of art she could do. "Sure, I'd love to. I can paint golden hearts entwined on a white background which would really set the scene."

Nicole's brows drew down. "Actually, we're thinking more on the lines of Main Street with the flower baskets in full bloom and a happy couple in the horse-drawn carriage. That way the brides can picture one of the unique things we offer the moment they walk through the door."

An unusual jab of irritation prickled all the way through her. Nicole, along with everyone else in Whitetail, usually agreed with her suggestions so the fact that she was rejecting Annika's idea was completely unexpected. Annika wasn't certain she liked the feeling at all but she reminded herself that Nicole had taken on board her suggestions of making the offices more bride-friendly so she agreed to painting the streetscape. "I can use a photo from Jennifer's wedding."

Nicole turned on her notebook computer. "Thanks. To help you juggle the jobs, I've sent the schedule to your email with all the appointment times."

She blinked. Appointments? "You mean there's more than just today?"

Nicole laughed. "We've got the two brides today and then another one wants to come on Friday if she can get her fiancé to take the day off work."

While Annika was trying to get her head around that bit of news, Melissa rushed in breathless and carrying three enormous white dress bags.

"Look what's just arrived in time. Sample dresses." She sank onto the chairs, almost smothered by the bags and bubbling with excitement. "I spoke to one of the brides the other morning about what she was looking for. When I hung up the phone I thought what if she could try a dress on? Then she'd feel like a bride and that feeling might just extend to her choosing Whitetail."

"That's a great idea, Melissa." Nicole squeezed her on the shoulder and then turned to Annika. "Anni, put your invitation folder down on the table next to my brochure on hair and makeup." Her phone buzzed with a text message. "Oh, the brides have just left Hanson's corner. How long do you think it takes a horse and carriage to get here?"

Annika was having trouble keeping up. "Why are they coming by horse and carriage?"

Nicole beamed. "We're giving them the full experience of what Whitetail can offer so we've combined the horse and carriage ride with a tour of wedding service venues. They're riding down Main Street then past the churches, the gazebo in the park and Mrs. Norell's garden. Just like you said, warehouses don't exactly say 'bridal' from the outside, but coming up through the grove of trees on a sunny day will soften it all. Plus, Al gave them both a glass of champagne when he assisted them into the carriage."

Annika sat down hard on the chair Melissa had just vacated, stunned and impressed at how comprehensively they'd thought things through. Dazed, she arranged her sample invitations, fanning them out on the table.

Nicole chewed her thumb. "Of course they might not decide to get married here but at least we've done a dry run and we'll be all set for Bridey Callahan. Has she shown any interest yet?"

Annika told the truth. "I haven't really seen her to talk to her about it."

Melissa turned from hanging the dresses up on a portable rack next to a screen. "But you will, right?"

Annika didn't want to encourage something she thought was only going to lead to a dead end, especially when her focus was on the bigger picture, but she didn't want to rain on their parade, especially after all the effort they'd put in. "If the opportunity presents itself, I'll say something. But please—"

"They're here!" Melissa cut her off with a shout and raced to the kitchen to get the coffee tray.

"Okay, girls, let's do our best!" Nicole smoothed down her dress and opened the door.

Within a quarter of an hour, Melissa had both brides wearing a bridal gown. As the two brides-to-be sat and each talked about their vision for their ideal wedding, Nicole, Melissa and Annika listened carefully and offered up suggestions. Annika outlined her thoughts for the invitations and save-the-date cards, tailoring her ideas to suit one bride's desire for a vintage wedding theme and the other bride's more modern style.

"What about the thank-you cards? Can you supply them on the same stationery with our initials entwined?" Jessie, the bride who wanted the vintage theme, fingered the most expensive paper in the portfolio.

Annika had never done that before as most Whitetail brides bought some pretty cards at the drugstore. "If you wanted me to, then I could certainly do that. You might want to consider having me calligraphy your initials into a monogram and use that on your invitations too."

"That's such an awesome idea. Oh, could you do napkins?"

Annika glanced at Nicole who was nodding furiously. She guessed she'd worry about the logistics of printing later. "Sure. If that's what you'd like. You might also want to consider having some extra cards printed with the monogram for use in the future." Annika heard the entrepreneurial words pour out of her mouth and for a moment wondered who was talking. "What's your fiancé's name?"

"Daniel Roberts."

"Are you keeping your name?"

Jessica shook her head. "No. All my life I've had to spell out my surname so I'm grabbing Roberts with both hands and holding fast."

Annika smiled. "One idea for the monogram would be to combine the *J* of Jessica with the *D* from Daniel and tie it all together with the *R* for Roberts."

Jessica's eyes misted over. "I love it!"

Now on a roll, Annika continued. "As you're going with a vintage theme, then I'd suggest ivory or wedding white and triple crown quality paper."

For the first time, the bride hesitated. "It's going to be

a big wedding so I'm not sure I can afford every single invitation to be handwritten."

Annika knew about budgets. "There are processes that print from an original handwritten invitation and avoid the cost of an engraving plate."

"But then my invitations are just like everyone else's."

Annika countered gently, "No, they're not. For example, I could use thermography to raise the monogram and make it any color that you like. Gold on ivory would be stunning. You could also consider wax or gold filigree seals on the envelopes."

Ashley, the other bride, sipped her champagne. "Do you calligraphy the envelopes?"

Annika's hand cramped at the thought. "I'm sorry, I don't do that because of time and it would seriously add to your cost."

Ashley pouted. "Oh, but I'd want everything to match."

"I can use a calligraphy computer font and print your envelopes so it looks more like they're handwritten." She dug into the back of the portfolio and found her envelope from Jennifer's wedding, which was the first time she'd ever used a fancy computer font. "Like this."

"That's gorgeous." Ashley picked up the heavy and tissue-lined envelope. "Feel the weight. It says 'special occasion' before you even open it."

An hour and a half later, Whitetail—Weddings That WOW had just taken two bookings with the first wedding in midautumn, and Annika had orders for not just two weddings but urgent save-the-date cards for Ashley that needed to be sent out by the end of the week.

Suddenly she had more calligraphy work than she'd ever had in one time frame. An edge of panic scuttled through her. She'd only ever done handwritten invitations for small weddings, and now she had two big weddings. Jessica's invitations would need a thermography machine and she'd have to go to Duluth for that, which would take a full day. How was she going to balance that against being Finn's P.A. as well as working on her business hunt for Whitetail?

There's also that painting to finish.

And sex with Finn.

But neither of those two things belonged on her ever-increasing to-do list.

FINN HUNG UP his phone, ending a long conference call with Hank and the German engineer. They were close to testing the new machine and hopefully Jazz Juice boxes would be back in production by Monday. All week he'd been listening to clients vent and then reassuring them that the impact on them was minor. Some of the old-timers wanted Sean but he'd got around that and, fingers crossed, no one would walk. He couldn't lose an account—not on his watch. Not when companies were folding around him. The business world was full of stories of big-brand companies considered part of the fabric of American society and now they were closing their doors.

One generation to lose. He would not be that one.

He quickly checked his messages but miraculously there were none. His stomach gurgled and he looked at the clock. With a jolt, he realized it was one o'clock and Annika still wasn't back from her meeting.

The office had seemed almost dead without her constant activity and as shallow as it made him, he cheerfully admitted to having missed watching the way her rainbow skirt moved across her tight behind and outlined her legs when she bent down. Not to mention the occasional glimpse of a brightly colored bra when she leaned forward. He had plans to see a lot more than a glimpse of that bra. He picked up his phone to call her, only to put it straight down again. Damn, she didn't have a functioning phone service.

You don't have any work for her so it's not like you really need to talk to her.

Who was he kidding? Work or no work, he just wanted to be able to pick up the phone and hear her smart mouth and sexy voice.

He thought of how he'd woken up to the luxurious feel of her smooth, long legs wrapped around his and he smiled. Annika had turned into an amazing surprise package in his summer from hell. A saving grace in fact. They could have a lot of fun together and he planned to make sure they did, starting with getting naked as soon as possible.

Decision made, he quickly put in a call and express-ordered a smartphone, and then rose to his feet. He'd go into town and have lunch with her there. He picked up the sports car's keyless remote and suddenly pictured the scene on Main Street—a circle of curious people admiring the car. Some things in life needed to be done inconspicuously. He dropped the remote back into the small bowl and ran downstairs where he grabbed a cap off the hat stand and a large key from the rack. He'd travel into Whitetail the way his grandfather always had—by boat—and he'd halve the traveling time.

Finn had recently had his grandfather's classic wooden powerboat restored but he hadn't yet taken it out for a big run. He loved being in the boat and a zip of anticipation shot through him at the thought of the wind whipping his body as the hull sliced smoothly through the water. As he cut across the lawn, he heard his name being called and turned to see Sean walking toward him holding a fishing pole in one hand and a tackle box in the other.

"How are things, Finnegan?"

His father never used the contracted version of his name and when Finn had been a teenager, he'd hated that. Ironically, now they worked together, the more formal use of his name epitomized their relationship perfectly. "Testing for number four starts tomorrow afternoon at the latest and I've got everything else under control."

"I don't doubt it."

Finn examined Sean's words, unsure if they were a compliment or a criticism.

His father smiled and held up the tackle box. "Logan and I are going fishing with strict instructions from Dana to catch supper. Why don't you come with us?"

The invitation almost shocked him to silence as it was wrong on so many levels—the first one being that Sean was going fishing. He couldn't remember his father having ever done that before. Finn might have wanted to fish with him at ten but by fifteen and after constant disappointments, he'd accepted that fishing was yet another thing he did with Grandpa. Now the thought of sitting on the dock or in a boat with Sean and his little half brother came as close to his idea of purgatory as it got. "No, thanks. I'm working."

Sean's keen gaze took in his boat shoes, knee-length shorts, polo shirt, cap, sunglasses and the boat's distinctive wooden carved key ring that he held in his hand. "You don't look too busy to fish."

He was thirty-three years old and long past being grilled as if he was a thirteen-year-old. Especially by a man who hadn't been around much when he'd actually been that age. "I'm collecting Annika."

Surprise flashed across Sean's face. "I thought she'd taken the truck."

How the hell did he know that? He didn't want anyone in the family noticing what Annika was doing because that would lead straight back to him. It was time to throw out a red herring. "Dad, if your days have become so dull that you're reduced to finding interest in who took what vehicle, then perhaps you need to come back to work."

Sean's brows rose but he spoke mildly. "That would mean you giving up your opportunity to run AKP and I can't imagine that's what you want. For now I'll stick to fishing and car watching."

Logan ran up clutching a small cooler. "I've got the bait and drinks, Dad."

"Good man." Sean slung his arm around his younger son's shoulder and spoke to Finn. "If you change your mind on the fishing, Logan and I will be over by the point."

Yep, not gonna happen. Finn watched them walk along the path toward their destination. At least Logan was benefitting from Sean's midlife crisis or whatever the hell it was and he was getting to spend time with his father. The weight of the heavy key in Finn's hand reminded him of where he was headed and he spun on his heels. He'd taken two steps when the sound of Sean's mellow chuckle at something Logan must have said hit him like a short, sharp slap.

His breath caught. *What the hell?* He hated the feeling that filled him, taking him back to when he was twelve. Damn it, but he was an adult and he'd got over not going fishing with Sean years ago. Yet, despite knowing that, the stinging feeling lingered and he wanted it gone.

The need to move, to do something, propelled him forward and he ran hard and fast down to the dock. He untied the rope, jumped into the boat and, gunning the engine, he roared out of the small cove, daring the wind to tear every single feeling out of him.

NINE

According to John Ackerman, whom Finn had spoken to when he'd done the marketing, Finn had missed Annika by five minutes.

"She bought some crackers and tuna fish and said she was going to the post office."

Karen at the post office told him, "She used the yellow pages and asked me to hold her mail. I don't know where she went after that."

Nicole was back in her salon cutting hair and had given him a warm smile when he'd asked her about Annika. "She's got a list a mile long so she could be anywhere in town. The meeting went fantastic, and Annika says we need a website so she's looking into that. Thank you so much for the computers and the wireless modem."

"You're welcome." And he meant it. The few times he'd met Nicole, he'd sensed a pervading sadness but it seemed to be tempered some when she spoke about weddings. If a few computers helped her, then he was more than happy to assist. He wondered at the fact Annika was taking on a website when she'd insisted Whitetail needed more than weddings, but then again, she rarely said no to anything. For some reason that bothered him far more than it should.

After making an appointment to get his hair trimmed, he crossed the street to the drugstore. "Have you seen Annika Jacobson, my P.A.?"

Randy Nuertsin, the pharmacist, said she hadn't been in. That slugged Finn with a burst of surprise. There wasn't a doubt in his mind that she'd been in as much agony as him last night when they'd stopped on the cusp of sex, so he'd been absolutely certain she'd have done the responsible adult thing and gotten prepared. Apparently not. So he did it for her along with a huge array of toiletries—most of which he didn't need—in an attempt to camouflage the point of the purchase.

The young sales associate flicked her gum as she scanned the condoms. "Those ones are good. I like the cherry flavor."

Finn tried not to choke as he handed over a fifty, grabbed the bag and made a hasty exit. No one ever commented when he bought condoms in Chicago, not that he'd bought many recently but still, the last thing he needed was the town talking about what he and Annika were or weren't doing. That was something he planned to keep strictly between the two of them.

He scanned the street looking for the distinctive red truck but couldn't see it or Annika anywhere. How hard could it be to find someone in a town that pretty much had all its businesses on the Main Street? He raised his sunglasses and noticed Rory ticketing a motor home with out-of-state plates that had been parked across the policeman's driveway, blocking him in.

"Hey, Finn. Good to see you. I was pleased to hear you gave Anni a job. She needs it more than she'll ever admit."

Finn shook the police officer's hand, getting a strong parental vibe. "Are you related to Annika?"

He shook his head. "No, but her father and I are good friends. Ever since she moved back to town, she's been busy looking out for everyone."

"And as her father isn't here, you're looking out for her."

"Got it in one."

Finn leaned against the side of the motor home and tried to sound casual. "Any reason she didn't move with her family?"

Rory ripped the ticket off the pad. "She left first when she went to college and her folks moved after that. No one ever expected Anni would choose to live in White-tail again after living in Chicago for eight years and making a name for herself there, but here she is." Rory stuck the ticket under the wiper with a practiced flick before giving Finn a look that said, "I've talked enough."

It effectively cut off the question, "Why did she move back?" A question that teetered on Finn's lips. *Making a name for herself?* He mentally added "Type Annika Jacobsen into a search engine" to his to-do list.

"If you're looking for Annika, she left ten minutes ago and said she was heading back to Kylemore. You have a good day, Finn, and remember the speed limit on the lake." Rory moved off down the street as he spoke into his radio making a request for the motor home to be towed.

Damn it. He'd talked to half the town and missed the one person he'd come to see. He checked his watch. Even keeping well within the waterway's speed limit, he was certain he'd make it back to Kylemore before Annika. He planned to be waiting in the circular driveway when she pulled in and then they were going straight to the cabin.

His phone beeped and Bridey's name came up on a message. *Mom wants some Swedish pastries. Buy, deliver and stay for coffee.*

His plans took a hit as he realized it was midafternoon already, and he was on mother duty.

WHEN ANNIKA ARRIVED back at the office, relief flowed through her that Finn was nowhere to be seen. "Put off today what you don't want to do tomorrow" hadn't always been her mantra but in many ways it had become one when she'd moved back to Whitetail. She dropped her purse onto the desk and grabbed a can of soda from the bar fridge, realizing she wasn't only thirsty but hungry and she'd left the crackers and tin of tuna fish in the truck. She'd been so busy in town she'd missed lunch and, having stayed away longer than she'd anticipated and not able to text Finn, she'd rushed straight back. She really needed to pay her cell phone bill but the bulk of her first paycheck was earmarked for back rent to Ellery and the rest she'd just spent on bedding. The phone would have to wait.

As she put the soda can down on a coaster, she couldn't miss seeing the bright pink sticky note that was stuck smack-bang in the center of her computer screen. Finn's bold, black and unwavering script scrawled across the fluorescent square of paper with the words *Am at guest cottage. Come immediately. Bring file.*

File? She had no clue what he meant. So far in her job for Finn she'd done some word processing, pumped numbers into a spreadsheet, filed, set up meetings and booked conference calls. The rest of the time had been spent making calls and writing letters to other companies about the warehouses. Did Finn mean that? Or was it something to do with his mother? She checked the documents on the computer and rifled through the filing cabinet, but nothing was marked *Kathleen Callahan* so she picked up the only two file jackets in her inbox and headed back down the stairs.

Turning at the bottom, she walked toward the side door, which was her entrance and exit so she avoided the main part of the house and the family. As she opened the mudroom door, she stopped so abruptly that she banged her shoulder on the door. "Oh, I'm sorry, Dana. I didn't know you were here."

On the few occasions she'd met the current Mrs. Callahan, Dana had always looked as if she'd stepped straight out of the pages of a glossy lifestyle magazine, complete with an air of aloofness that the very rich often wore. Now she stood in rubber boots with a sunhat on her head and a pair of gardening gloves in her hand.

She smiled at Annika. "Logan and Sean are fishing and as the idea of touching bait makes me squeamish, I've been in the garden instead. I'm encouraging my asters by fertilizing and talking to them so they'll put on an amazing late-summer show."

Annika rubbed her bruised shoulder. "Is that enough?"

"I threw in some guilt for good measure by mentioning how stunning the day lilies currently are with their myriad of colors." She hung up her hat and smoothed down her hair. "Are you interested in gardening?"

"Oh, I love gardens but I'm not a gardener. I'm more of a potentilla girl. They're so hardy they flower almost no matter how much you ignore them."

Dana laughed and for the first time Annika saw the warm and friendly woman she'd previously missed. Sean's wife nodded at the files in Annika's hand. "Finn's visiting his mother. Are you heading over to the cottage?"

"Yes, I am."

"Would you mind taking over this fruit basket and these towels? Esther's tied up preparing dinner and I'd deliver them except Kathleen's likely to throw everything back at me and I don't think we should waste perfectly good fruit." This time her smile was wry.

"Sure, I'd be happy to take it."

"You're probably wondering what you've walked into with this family."

"Not at all, I—"

"Just don't judge us too harshly." Dana's usually soft voice sounded strained. "I had stars in my eyes when I married Sean, thinking we'd be one big happy family and a baby would be the glue to bring us closer. But Finn was twenty-one and Bridey was seventeen, and it took me four years to conceive. My biggest regret is for Logan."

She pushed the basket abruptly into Annika's hand and the detached air zoomed back in, as if she regretted her disclosure. "Thank you for doing this and enjoy the rest of your day." She brushed past Annika and walked into the house, closing the door behind her with a firm click that said, "Don't follow me."

Not that Annika planned on following but that didn't stop a ripple of sadness running through her that Dana had shut her out. *My biggest regret is for Logan.* She got exactly what Dana meant—in fact it was exactly what she'd been talking to Finn about yesterday. As she made her way across the lawn—balancing the towels, fruit basket and the files—she decided that getting Finn more involved with his younger brother and family was something she could do to help. After all, helping out was what she did best.

IT WASN'T THAT Finn didn't love his mother; he did, very much. From the moment his father had left her, he'd stepped up as protector and now as an adult, he enjoyed her company. He regularly met her for afternoon tea at

Palmer House, and occasionally accompanied her to exhibition openings, but Kathleen in pain and back at Kylemore was acerbic and out of sorts.

The coffee he'd made was too hot and too bitter, the pastries he'd bought not the ones she'd wanted, and his attempt at arranging her flowers under her precise instructions—"I said move the delphinium to the back, that's a stock"—had him biting his tongue. It had been a very long and patience-testing forty minutes. Where the hell was Annika?

He heard a thump against the glass, followed by an "oof" and his mother said, "Good heavens, it's a walking fruit basket. Finn, go and help."

Pleased to be able to walk away from the floral arrangement he'd seriously mangled, he stood up. Although he could only see a pair of legs because the rest of the owner was hidden by a massive fruit basket and a tower of toppling towels, he instantly knew it was Annika. He gave a silent chuckle. She was deliciously clumsy and he was thrilled to see her. He'd been waiting a long time for her to arrive—not just to give him a valid excuse to end his visit before he said something to his mother he'd regret, but so they could take up where they'd left off last night. Only this time it wouldn't be on a rocky beach, and it wouldn't be stopped so abruptly that his balls would ache for hours. No, this time they'd be in his bed with enough contraception to safely keep them there until they chose to leave.

He caught the towels as they started to tumble off their precarious position on the basket and whispered softly in her ear, "Hey, Legs. What took you so long?"

Her body trembled but she didn't reply. Instead she peered around the other side of the huge basket before turning sharply, which sent a melon rolling across the floor before she reached the safety of the table. "Shall I put it here, Mrs. Callahan?"

"Yes, thank you. Can you pass me the card?" Kathleen looked animated for the first time since he'd arrived.

Finn watched mesmerized as Annika's fingers carefully eased the card off the cellophane by peeling back the tape, and the memory of those fingers touching him last night was so strong he could feel them kneading his back. He wanted them touching him again. Now.

"Mom, this is Annika Jacobson, my P.A." He wafted his arm out in a gesture of introduction but his eyes stayed fixed on Annika. "Did you bring those files I requested?"

Annika pushed the files across the table before handing Kathleen the card. "How's your ankle feeling, Mrs. Callahan?"

Kathleen glanced quickly at the card and smiled before tucking it under her thigh. "It aches a lot. Please, call me Kathleen."

Annika nodded with sympathy clear on her face. "Ice packs for twenty-four hours and then applying heat really helps. So does keeping it up as much as possible."

"You sound just like my doctor."

"I've had a bit of experience with ankles, wrists, knees." Her hands fluttered out in front of her. "Basically, I've pretty much sprained every part of me."

Interest flared on his mother's face. "Do you do stunt work?"

Annika burst into laughter and Finn cut across the conversation, seizing the moment. "Sorry, Mom, but we have to go as I've got a conference call booked for Mexico." He picked up the folders he knew contained Annika's "Find a business for Whitetail" documents.

"Thanks for coming, darling." Kathleen gave him a

wave and immediately swung her gaze back to Annika. "Can you stay, Annika?"

No. No way was this happening.

But Annika had sat down without giving Finn a glance. "Oh, Kathleen, are those pastries from Lundstrom's?" She immediately countered with, "I'm sorry, that was rude. It's just I missed lunch."

"Annika, we have to leave, now." His words sounded unreasonably curt, courtesy of a hell of a lot of frustration. He was the one that was supposed to be getting all cozy and chatty with Annika. Not that he planned to do much talking or at least not the type of conversation his mother was about to have.

Kathleen frowned. "You said you had a conference call so you go do that and leave Annika here."

"She hasn't eaten and there's food in the office."

"Finn, I have a kitchen full of food here."

He knew he was clutching at straws. "I need her to type up the notes on the call."

A pair of cornflower-blue eyes with amusement dancing in their depths, hit him with a look that said, "I know your play and I've got one to match it." "Record the call and I'll transcribe it in full tonight. It will be more accurate that way, especially as I'm a bit light-headed from lack of food. I'd hate to miss something important."

Kathleen passed the platter of pastries. "Good idea. It's all settled then."

"Finn, I booked the call for the office phone, and it's almost four." Annika raised a cup of coffee in a salute to the fictitious conference call.

Finn swallowed a string of oaths, not quite able to believe he'd let himself be out-maneuvered. He took in a deep breath and regrouped. Giving Annika a lazy smile—the one he knew made her back into doorways and bump into kitchen counters—he said, "I don't know what I'd do without your efficiency, Legs."

Her pupils widened at the use of her nickname.

If Annika wanted to play games then it was officially "game on." Only next time he'd reach the end zone.

ANNIKA BLEW INTO the air mattress for the umpteenth time and silver spots sparkled in her vision, making her feel extremely dizzy. Jamming the plug into the half-in-flated bed, she lamented that she hadn't spent the extra money on a pump.

After a very pleasant hour with Finn's mom, who was a fascinating woman with eclectic tastes and interests, and hearing all about her current passion, which was supporting a community outreach program of the Art Institute, Annika had used the kayak to get herself over to the island. The Callahans had every conceivable water toy from human-powered row boats and stand-up paddleboards, to fuel powered Jet Skis and motorboats. Without a moment's hesitation, she'd taken advantage of their wide collection of vessels to stay one step ahead of Finn. She didn't feel one shred of guilt at not having gone back to the office after her visit with Kathleen because she knew there was no post-conference call transcript to be typed. It had all been a ruse to get her naked.

A shiver of desire she couldn't quite quash added to her light-headedness and she sucked in another breath, firming up her crumbling resolve. The reason she'd come directly to the island was so she could have her camp bed all set up before Finn got back to the cabin. It would make the statement of "this is how things need to play out," and back up her words that sex was a bad idea.

Heavy footsteps suddenly pounded up the wooden veranda stairs in a very un-ninja fashion, and the screen door slammed loudly. Still clutching the half-inflated mattress, she scrambled to her feet. Finn stopped just inside the door, his curls in delicious disarray, having been blown by the wind into a sexy, rumpled look. He leaned casually against the doorjamb, crossing his arms over his chest, which sent his biceps bulging against the soft material of his shirtsleeves.

She immediately imagined him shirtless and dropped the edge of the air mattress. "You're back early."

Dimples swirled deep into his cheeks and he gave her a long, seductive smile that reached all the way to his eyes. Eyes which roamed lazily over her, taking their own sweet gazing time, and sparking off a thrill of tingles from the tips of her toes to the top of her head.

"Early for what?" He pushed off the doorjamb with confident ease and walked toward her. She could almost smell his intent and a quiver of lust coiled deep. She didn't fear him one little bit but so help her, she feared herself.

He cocked one brow. "Did you have plans that included me?"

Somehow she managed to stop a breathy "yes" rolling off her lips by shaking her head and jerkily flipping out the sleeping bag. "No. I was just getting organized here."

His jet-black gaze took in the camp bed and he poked the mattress derisively with his foot. "So I see, but you're not going to be very comfortable with it like this." He scooped up the mattress, sucked in a deep breath and started to puff air into it.

She stared and blinked as surprise thundered through her.

She'd been expecting an Irish bellow, similar to the one he'd leveled at her when she'd told him she was planning on sleeping at the warehouse. The sex fiend deep within her pouted that he hadn't scooped her over his shoulder and deposited her on his bed, but the sensible part of her was thankful he was respecting her wishes. Needing to do something so she wasn't tempted to watch him at work, she zippered together her sleeping bag.

Finn plugged the mattress and put it back on the floor. "Man, that's hot work." He whipped off his polo shirt, dropped it onto a chair and then lay down on her mattress. "This feels about right." He patted the space next to him and grinned up at her. "But as you're the one sleeping here, you should check it out for yourself."

Her gaze immediately shot down to his bare chest and lingered on the smattering of hair at the base of his toned abdominal muscles. Black hair that trailed tantalizingly downward before disappearing under the band of his shorts. Lying down next to him was a shortcut to insanity and she wasn't playing that game. She tilted her head and put her finger against her chin, as if deep in thought.

"The thing is, you're heavier than me so you're dispersing more air. To know if it's inflated enough for me, I really need to test it out by myself."

He raised his arms behind his head and matched her thoughtful gaze with one of his own. "Well at least I know it works for me."

"You won't be using it."

"So if I offered you use of the bed in exchange for me sleeping on this air mattress you'd refuse?"

She remembered how comfortable his cushion-top mattress was, and the luxurious feel of his high thread count cotton sheets.

Don't forget how amazing it felt to be cuddling him.
I am so forgetting that!

"It would depend on the deal."

He rolled off the mattress, rose to his feet and stood so close she could smell the peppermint scent of his hair. He stared down at her. "No deal, just a direct exchange."

She couldn't read him, which worried her because it meant she couldn't work out his game. "That would be the *exclusive* use of the bed. If your air mattress springs a leak, you're still on the floor."

"Absolutely. You're the guest and you get the bed."

Generosity infused his words, making her feel small that she'd doubted his motives.

He spun away from her saying, "Change the sheets while I have a shower," and then he disappeared into the bathroom.

The bathroom was located directly off the bedroom, and there was no way she was spending any time in there while he was naked in the bathroom with only a thin wall between them. Even out here in the main living area she could hear the water from the shower and her sex-starved self immediately went into visual overload, streaming images of tall, dark, toned and indecently gorgeous men.

She turned the radio on loudly, not caring what was on as long as it drowned out the sounds of the shower. *Let's talk about sex*, *baby*, screeched through the static. With a lunge of sheer frustration she pulled the plug and started singing, "la, la, la" to herself.

She'd make supper. The idea burst into her frazzled and melting mind and she leaped on it.

Marching to the fridge, she opened it to see if Finn had kept his promise to shop. He had and it was groaning with food. She diced and chopped, happy to have a task, and arranged a garden salad and marinated chicken in soy sauce and honey in preparation for the grill. As she worked she sang through her limited repertoire of show tunes and Sunday-school hymns.

She heard the creak of a door opening and Finn walked out with wet hair—his curls momentarily flat but shedding water fast, which dripped down across his shoulders. He held an armful of dirty laundry. It took Annika a second to realize that the only item of material on his body between his head and his feet was a bath sheet tied low around his hips. The knife she held clattered loudly onto the counter.

He glanced in her direction, his expression obliging. "I'm putting a load on. Do you have anything?"

She picked up the knife again and kept her gaze on the onions, hoping she didn't dice off a finger. "No, thanks."

"Okay." He ambled off to the laundry and returned a few minutes later with empty arms.

Even though she'd known he'd probably still be shirtless and had prepared herself, she somehow managed to knock over the bottle of soy sauce, sending the contents spilling across the counter. Furious with herself, and cross with him, she fixed him with a glare. "Don't you feel debased by resorting to peacocking?"

He grinned. "Not at all. Especially when I know it gives you so much pleasure."

She picked up a cloth and started to mop up the mess. "I've hardly noticed."

His laugh was like the deep, rich notes of the bassoon and stroked her like velvet. "Sweetheart, you've noticed. One dropped air mattress, one dropped knife and now there's a river of soy sauce heading toward the floor. And let's not forget this morning when you fell out of bed and walked into the doorway. There's so much sexual tension sizzling between us, you've become an occupational health and safety hazard to yourself."

And damn it, it was all true. She dropped the cloth in the sink and marched over to the chair where his discarded shirt lay. Her fingers wound it into a ball and she threw it at him. "If you're so worried about me hurting myself then put on some damn clothes."

He flicked the shirt out so it wrapped around her waist and then pulled her gently toward him. "And where would be the fun in that?"

He smelled of soap, shampoo and the promise of wonder.

"This isn't fun for me, Finn. This is torture."

He dropped his head so his lips were next to her ear, and his breath and his words stroked her. "But it's torture of the best kind, right?"

She bit her lip and shook her head. "No." She put her hands on his forearms and leaned back. "Last night, I made a big mistake, Finn. I wanted to kiss you but it got out of control way too fast and I'm telling you, it's not going any further. I refuse to become the cliché of the P.A. who sleeps with her boss. Her very rich boss."

Intelligent eyes studied her. "So this buyer's remorse of yours is to do with ethics?"

"Yes."

"Then quit."

Oh that she could. "You know I need the money."

"Fair point." His fingers played with her hair. "Have you ever slept with your boss before?"

"No." The word shot out on a stream of indignation with a lust chaser.

His gaze burned into her. "Would it help if I told you I've never slept with any of my P.A.s, or any other members of my staff for similar ethical reasons?"

"Little bit." The words came out on a breath as his fingers caressed her cheeks. Her knees sagged.

"So really, both of us are in a difficult situation."

"Difficult." Her lips could hardly frame words.

His fingers dipped into the hollow of her throat, fondling her skin in ever-decreasing circles. "What if AKP was to subcontract directly to Annika's Custom Calligraphy with the express purpose of managing the warehouses and to provide a P.A. to the Kylemore office for the summer?"

Miraculously, there was still one tiny part of her brain that was free of desire-fuelled haze, and she could see exactly where he was going with this. She'd be her *own* boss. "My fee's pretty steep."

"I pay industry rates." He matter-of-factly named a figure.

She was glad she was gripping his arms or she would have fallen at his feet. She tried to look businesslike and composed when she was feeling the exact opposite. "Is that number the truth, Finn, or are you just trying to get me into bed?"

His mouth flattened and a serious look entered his eyes. "By now you should know that the truth is very important to me, and I *never* joke about business."

She recalled their first misguided twenty-four hours and how he'd conducted himself ever since. She should have realized the figure was accurate. "You're right. I do know that about you."

His serious expression lingered. "This agreement's just for the summer, Annika. Come Labor Day, Sean's back in command and I'm back in Chicago or Mexico."

Just for the summer. The words were clear, concise and completely ambiguity-free. A definite end date—that worked for her. This thing between them was all about a summer of sex and given recent events in her life, she deserved some no-strings fun. "Annika's Custom Calligraphy accepts."

"Good." His normally smooth voice was suddenly raspy. "Can we shake on it now and draw up the paperwork tomorrow?"

As much as it would be fun to watch Finn's expression if she said "no," saying that would only mean she'd suffer too and her body was already aching so hard for him that it hurt. A random thought exploded in her mind and she bit her knuckle. She'd been so determined not to have sex with him that she hadn't gone to the drug store. "Do you have condoms?"

"Unlike some people, I'm organized and prepared. The perfect Boy Scout."

"Thank God." As she shook his hand in her right, she whipped off his towel with her left. Her mouth fell open with a gasp. "You—you've had shorts on under there the whole time?"

He grinned at her with dancing eyes. "I was having some fun with you, but I'm not a sleazebag."

Her own embarrassment collided with an edge of disappointment that he wasn't standing in front of her naked, and she mustered up some playful indignation. "I could have severed an artery when I dropped that knife."

"But you didn't." His fingers played with her hair. "Besides, is it my fault that your imagination had me naked under the towel? You should be thanking me for a virtual picture show."

He reached to pull her closer, but she ducked away and rounded the couch. If he thought she was that easy— and heaven help her, she was—she'd make him work a bit harder to get what they ultimately both wanted. "I think this is a case of false advertising."

One black brow shot up. "Is that so?"

He'd tortured her so now it was her turn. She pressed her palms against the back of the couch and leaned forward, knowing the position gave her meager breasts some cleavage and that her scoop-necked T-shirt fell slightly forward. "Sure. It's a blatant misrepresentation of what was really on offer to trick me into making a purchase that I otherwise might have avoided."

His dark eyes swept her breasts and her body fired with heat as he met her gaze. It burned with a need that matched hers and somehow she managed to add, "I'll need to alert the FTC."

"I see." With every part of his height and breadth targeted on her he rounded the couch and moved tantalizingly slowly toward her. "On what grounds?"

He stood so close she could smell his desire for her and her brain almost emptied. "Truth in labeling or manipulation of packaging by using, um," she stammered as she visualized his boxers underneath the shorts, and then vividly pictured what lay under that soft cotton, "too many layers or fillers."

He tilted his head and a curl dipped over his eyebrow giving him the delectably wicked look of a pirate. "Oh, baby, there's nothing false or misleading about this and there are definitely no fillers." His fingers gripped the fastener at the top of the zipper on his shorts and his voice dropped even deeper. "What you see is what you get. All of it. Just for you."

A blast of need hit her so hard she swayed and anticipation had her so wired she could hardly see straight. Liquid heat followed, pouring through her and making her panties wet. "So what are you saying? That if I unwrap the packaging this time I won't be misled?"

She reached out and slid her fingers under his, undoing the fastener. Then her hand slowly slid down the front of his pants and she shivered as she felt his erection under the material.

He groaned and his eyes glazed over. "If you're unwrapping me, you need to do it fast."

She laughed. "But I always unwrap my presents carefully by peeling back the tape and not ripping the paper."

His hands caught hers and he pressed them against the band of his shorts. "If you unwrap this too slowly, you might find your present won't work for a while."

"I can't have that." She shucked his shorts with a quick tug, expecting to see boxer shorts. But he stood before her with the late-afternoon sunshine streaming all over him—tall, tanned and blissfully naked. This time she gasped with wonder and her hand longed to wrap itself around his long, silky length. She couldn't hide the admiration in her voice. "You're beautiful."

He gazed down at her. "So are you."

The soft words made her heart jolt and she instantly went on alert reminding herself that this was just sex. His words were just part of foreplay. She stepped into him, wrapped her arms around his neck and tilted her head back.

His mouth melded to hers and his heat flooded her like the blast from an open furnace—swooping through her like a hot wind on an August day. It instantly fanned all the tiny embers of desire that had been burning deep inside her for days into a raging and out-of-control wildfire. She plundered his mouth with hers, filling herself with his taste of coffee, mint and sex. As she lost herself in his mouth she pressed her hands to his naked skin, touching him and soaking him up like parched land absorbs rain when the drought breaks.

He pulled her down onto the air mattress and straddled her, gently pinning her underneath him. "Now it's my turn to unwrap you."

"Yes, please." She raised her arms and he pulled her T-shirt over her head. A sliver of reality pierced her lust, making her instantly self-conscious about her old, plain bra that was a very faded orange, and had been washed so many times it was ready to fall apart. Embarrassed, she crossed her arms. "I don't have any sexy underwear."

He smiled and slid the straps down her arms. "I'm a lot more interested in the contents than the packaging." Three seconds later, and without a moment of fumbling, the embarrassing article was on the floor lying on top of his shorts.

Thirty seconds after that, her skirt and panties joined them.

She rolled her head back to look at him. "Impressive."

He grinned and his dark eyes flashed with desire. "I aim to please."

And he did. He lowered his head and nibbled her ear and then his mouth roved along her jaw nipping and kissing in a seductive march of branding. She moaned as his mouth closed over her breast and his tongue gently and deliciously lashed her nipple. Pure pleasure streaked through her and her hand gripped his head hard as her body seemed to rise off the bed.

His mouth broke contact.

She cried out as loss rammed her. "Don't stop."

His mouth twitched. "Sweetheart, I'll keep going when your hands stop clamping my head like a vise."

"Sorry." She dropped her hands. "It's just so good."

He dipped his head again and his mouth suckled her other breast. A moment later she bucked toward him and her fingers dug into his shoulders.

His hands caught hers and he laid them tenderly above

her head, keeping one of his hands gently over them. Her breasts rose as her shoulders pressed against the mattress. Part of her felt totally exposed but most of her felt unbelievably desirable. She'd never experienced anything like it.

He kissed her on the nose. "Your hands need to stay here so they don't keep getting in the way and nothing short of fire or flood can move them."

"But I want to touch you."

"And you will, I promise. But right now this is going to work better for you."

She didn't understand. "Why? I mean it—"

"Shh." He put his finger to her lips. "Just trust me on this."

And despite only knowing him a few days she knew she could accommodate his request. "I do trust you."

"Excellent. Now where was I?"

His curls brushed her face as he trailed kisses across her chest and then his tongue wove a slow, meandering path between her breasts and down her belly. Unlike the glorious but almost excruciating pleasure of his mouth sucking her nipples, this had her moaning out a long sigh. Although at first she wanted to touch him and give back to him, she slowly relaxed and totally submitted to his touch—losing herself in every luscious sensation.

His mouth moved past her belly button, moving lower and lower and her body floated on a river of heady arousal. She was vaguely aware of his fingers tightening slightly around her wrist and then his tongue caressed her most sensitive place between her legs.

She whimpered with building need, her hips left the bed and her arms tensed, wanting to wrap themselves around him and hold on tight. Deep inside her muscles throbbed, desperate to have him fill them. She lifted her wrists and his hand fell away but before she could touch him, his mouth and tongue did things to her that she never wanted to stop. Heat spiraled, need burned, sheer and intense pleasure built—spinning faster and faster until she thrashed under his touch, wanting more, needing more, and she greedily took everything he offered. Wave after wave of wonder took her higher and higher until she thought she'd die from exquisite pain. As she tumbled over the edge, she heard a faint scream in the distance and realized it was her, but she was already floating high above herself on a cloud of utter bliss.

As the sensations rolled away, she slowly came back to earth and to Finn. She pressed her hand to his cheek. "That was simply amazing. Thank you."

"You're welcome."

"Only…"

"Only what?" A ghost of anxiety crossed his eyes.

"No, not that." She kissed him hard and fast. "You're unbelievably generous, not to mention talented."

His chest expanded. "Talented. eh?"

She laughed. "Oh, I can see using that word was a mistake." Her fingers skimmed down his chest. "It's just I don't get how that was good for you."

A slight crease marred his high forehead. "Watching you orgasm is an incredible turn-on."

His words stunned her. "Really?"

"Believe me, it is."

He rolled her over and sat her on top of him. She could feel him hard and strong between her legs and she burned to feel him inside her.

He ran his hands through her hair, trailing his fingers through its length that fell to brush her breasts. "You're my Lady Godiva."

She'd never felt so powerful in her femininity as she

did at that moment. She used her hands and explored every inch of his broad, toned chest that had been calling to her from the moment he'd taken off his shirt, and she pressed her lips to salty skin. As she skimmed her hands downward, she felt his tension spearing through her palms.

She gave him an arch look. "Is this bothering you?"

"No." But his hand shot out for his shorts.

She plucked them out of his hand and found the condoms in the pocket. As his hands cupped her breasts and his fingers did delicious things to her nipples, she somehow managed to open the square foil. She rolled the condom onto him, loving the feel of him under her hands and she wanted to stroke him again and again.

"Annika." Her name came out on a guttural moan and she saw his restraint crumbling. "You're killing me."

"We can't have that." She rose on her knees and then slowly lowered herself down on him, feeling herself opening for him and wanting to give to him what he'd just given to her. Wanting to send him spinning out on a stream of mind-altering delight.

He rose up to meet her—filling her—and her body gripped him. She kept her gaze on his face, hypnotized by the line of his jaw, the sheen of sweat on his top lip and the lust burning brightly in his eyes. Her body started moving with his and suddenly she wasn't an onlooker anymore. Her body caught his rhythm, and she was one with him, riding fast toward the stars.

She shattered a moment before he did, but this time her orgasm scooped him up and took him with her. Together, they were flung out into space, circling each other until they fell back to earth on separate paths and rolled away from each other.

As they both lay panting, Finn rose up on an elbow

and brushed her hair from her cheek. He stared down at her with deep dimples carved into his cheeks and a quiet smile on his lips. "No tripping, dropping or stumbling. I think we've just found the one sport you're incredibly good at."

She rolled into his arms laughing. "I was pretty hot, wasn't I?"

"Totally hot."

She traced her finger along his sternum. "And you're very talented."

He grinned. "We're the perfect summer combination."

She rested her head on his chest, feeling the rhythmic rise and fall of each breath. All she knew was that she'd never had sex like it. Not that she'd had many partners and she didn't really count her first time in a college dorm with a boy who'd known even less than she did. Based on that experience she'd always thought sex with Ryan had been adequate and he'd certainly never complained although her needs had often been left behind. She now realized she'd been shortchanged by him more than just emotionally and financially.

Finn shifted slightly and immediately groaned as his elbow hit the floor. "Next time we're doing this in my bed."

She refused to feel embarrassed about the rush of tingles that shot through her at the thought of a next time. She did a quick calculation of the number of days between now and Labor Day and smiled.

TEN

"Nicole said your meeting with the brides went well."

Annika looked up from her sketch of the monogram she'd been toying with for Jessica's wedding and smiled. When hunger had finally driven them from the air mattress, they'd enjoyed a meal together before Finn had been caught up on a work call. Annika had unpacked her pens and ink, lit citronella candles along the veranda and made herself comfortable on the glider swing. Now Finn stood before her holding two glasses of wine.

"Both brides were lovely. I'm still a bit stunned we've got two weddings booked and for me, it's going to involve at least one day, possibly two, spent in Duluth sorting out the invitations."

"Why?" He set the glasses down on a low table and sat down next to her, the swing moving gently under his weight.

"Jessica, one of the brides-to-be, wanted the print on her invitations to be raised so I need to use a—"

"Thermography machine."

She blinked at him—twice—stunned that he knew exactly what she needed. "Yes, but how do you know that?"

He gave her a bemused look. "Annika, exactly what do you think AKP does?"

"Recycles paper." At least that was what most of the correspondence she'd dealt with had been about.

"Recycling's one part of the business and the new plant in Mexico's been my focus while Sean's been taking care of the packaging side. But AKP is *all* about paper." His eyes lit up with a glow of pride. "All kinds of paper. We supply companies with everything from pulp to triple crown stock and I bet we make the paper you use for your invitations."

She immediately thought of the quality paper used for Bridey's engagement party invitation. "And that's how you know about thermography."

"Yep. My grandfather and Sean insisted we spend time working in all areas of the company. I started off in the boutique paper area and I've used a thermography machine."

Finn was full of surprises. "So you know how fiddly it is. I have to quickly calligraphy one invitation at a time in sticky ink, immediately apply the gold powder and then run it through the machine. That's why it's going to take two long days. Longer if the humidity is high."

"I need you here."

The softly spoken words made her stomach flip but when she looked at him she could only see the astute businessman. "I can go up on the weekend."

"What if you rented the machine from AKP? We can write that into the contract and you can set up a studio in the warehouse rent-free."

She couldn't believe what she was hearing. "You'd do that?"

He shrugged. "I told Nicole I'd support Weddings That WOW with some office equipment and this is all part of that."

Of course it was. This wasn't personal at all—just business, and she'd do well to remember to keep the two very separate. She pulled up the inexperienced businesswoman within and started haggling. "I'll need fans for the temperature control."

"Okay. That won't pull much power." He pulled out his phone and started typing a text message. "I can have the machine here in the morning. But we need to have a schedule." He hit Send and turned to her—the quintessential businessman on an organizational roll. "I need you in the office every morning and you can do your studio work in the afternoons. We'll leave the truck at the Whitetail dock and you use the boat to travel back and forth because it's a lot quicker, especially if I need you back here urgently for something."

"Like transposing conference calls?"

But her teasing reference to his made-up call earlier in the day didn't elicit a smile or even a delicious twinkle in those dark and enigmatic eyes. With a jolt she realized he was serious. Of course he was—he was talking about business.

His phone beeped with a return message. "By the way, your new phone's arriving in the morning and your first job is to synchronize our electronic diaries. I need to be able to contact you as necessary and you need to have the phone with you and turned on at all times."

A ripple of irritation shot through her. "Is that in the contract?"

"Damn straight."

She crossed her arms and tried not to raise her voice. "So I can't ever turn my phone off."

"It can be off when mine's off." For the first time in the conversation, he smiled and treacherously divine dimples carved into his cheeks.

She tried to ignore the sweep of heat that whooshed to her toes at his smile. "Oh, right, so that's never."

His eyes burned bright with the same spark of need

she knew lit her own. Holding her gaze, he pressed the off button on his phone and slowly laid it down on the side table.

She watched mesmerized. She'd never known an everyday action to be so erotic. His arms reached for her at the same moment she moved into his lap. Yet again, they didn't make it to the bed.

BRIDEY HAD THREE yellow legal pads on the kitchen table, along with copies of almost every wedding magazine that had been published this month and her laptop was open displaying photographs of wedding cakes. Every day for two weeks she'd been compiling lists upon lists for the wedding and sending Hank emails filled with pictures.

Her father strolled in and gave her shoulder a squeeze as he glanced at the organized piles. "Ah, wedding planning. Having fun, Baby-girl?"

She leaned into her father's hand and rubbed her temples. "There are so many decisions to make and get right. Which cake do you prefer?" She pointed to a more traditional nine-tier cake with a matching cascade of sugar-flower roses and calla lilies that wound around the tiers. The only color was the yellow stamen of the lilies which gleamed gold against the elegant ivory. The other cake could have been mistaken for a basket filled with a mass of spring flowers.

"Honey, it's your wedding so it's up to you. Choose whatever makes you happy and I'll be there to give you away and to pay the bill."

"Yes, but do you have an opinion?"

"As long as they both taste like cake, that's enough for me." He kissed the top of her head and walked into the kitchen.

She tried not to sigh. She should have known better than to ask her father. Although he'd been married three times the weddings had always been arranged by the brides or, in the case of his marriage to her mother, hastily organized by the bride's parents. Finn had been born seven months later.

Her wedding to Hank and their marriage was going to be very different, starting with Hank being involved in every step of the wedding planning. That had been part of her plan for this vacation. But Hank was in Chicago and had been for almost two weeks and she was here. He wasn't responding to her emails about wedding venues or cakes or boutonnieres. When she tried to talk to him about it on the phone he usually sounded so tired that she hadn't pushed him for any opinions, but she was starting to get anxious about it. She wanted his input. She didn't want to make any mistakes in the planning because *everything* had to be perfect. If the wedding was perfect then their marriage would be perfect. But so far the planning of the wedding wasn't going to plan.

Snapping down the lid of her laptop, she also snapped down her disappointment.

So organize the other part of the plan.

Bridey was her father's "Baby-girl," no matter that she was twenty-nine, and her father usually gave her what she wanted—within reason. He'd always been generous with gifts for both her and Finn, although she suspected they came with some of his guilt attached. Growing up, Finn had hated the gifts and had returned many. Bridey had always loved pretty things and felt no compunction in accepting them. As a result, her relationship with her father had fared better than Finn's. In the last couple of years, she'd taken to inviting Sean to her guest speaker gigs at local colleges and most times he'd attended and had then taken her out for dinner afterward. Had she ever been asked the question, she'd probably say that right now their relationship was the closest it had ever been.

"Daddy."

"Yes." Sean poured himself a glass of iced water from the dispenser in the door of the fridge.

"Do you remember the zip line?"

He smiled. "You used to scream like a banshee every time you rode it and then you'd swim back to shore and do it all over again."

"I was thinking maybe Logan might get a kick out of something like that."

Sean sipped his water and Bridey held her breath while silently willing him with a chant of *please, please, please.*

He put the glass down. "That's not a bad idea, B."

Yes! Bridey pulled a brochure out of the back of her diary that she'd carefully placed there a month ago. "Here's the number of a company that installs them. When you call, ask for Jeff."

Sean rubbed his chin, deep in thought. "Actually, Bridey, I don't need the number. The zip line is just the sort of project I've been looking for."

Bridey started. "You're going to build it?"

He laughed at her surprise. "Honey, I did engineering at college."

The loud whirring noise of the helicopter cut off her reply. "Do you and Dana have guests for the weekend?"

"Not that I know about."

Dana came in from the garden, her brows drawn down. "Sean, have you forgotten to tell me something?"

Sean smiled at his wife before kissing her on the

cheek. "I'm in the clear this time. Besides, I promised you this summer is about us, not work."

Dana touched Sean's cheek and exchanged a smile with him that made Bridey feel like an outsider. She loved that her father was happy and unlike Sean's second wife, she really liked Dana a lot, but a tiny part of her still ached for the family she'd lost when her parents had separated. She knew it was silly because Dana was a much better fit for Sean than Kathleen had ever been, but it was moments like this that made Bridey feel she didn't have a family as such, more a collections of parts. Parts that never came together to form a whole unit.

She quickly gathered her stuff and stacked it on a side table.

Dana turned away from Sean and spoke to Bridey. "Oh, have you made your cake decision already? I thought we might have coffee and a browse together."

Bridey appreciated Dana's interest but the thought of more wedding talk combined with the possibility of Kathleen finding out, suddenly intensified her headache and the *one* person she needed to be interested in the wedding wasn't returning her emails and texts. "I need some fresh air. I think I'll go for a swim before spending some time with Mom."

"Another time then. Esther's doing a potluck supper tonight and I thought we could serve ourselves from seven. Kathleen's very welcome."

Her father sighed. "You know she won't come."

Dana's chin tilted up sharply. "I know no such thing. Bridey, it would be great if you could encourage her to come. I've texted Finn but I haven't heard back."

"I think my son might be otherwise occupied."

Bridey heard her father's tone and did a double take. "What has he said?"

"To me? Nothing at all. This is Finn we're talking about. I'm just saying he's a man sharing a two-roomed cabin with a leggy blonde. He'd have to be made of stone not to be somewhat occupied."

"But he didn't want Annika at the cabin. In fact he tried to get Mom to— Oh." Bridey smiled as realization dawned. Finn always kept his private life very, very private and she might have just stumbled onto a bargaining chip to get her brother to start attending some family gatherings. "Dana, I'm pretty sure Finn will be there tonight and I'll do my best to bring Kathleen."

She let herself out, enjoying the feel of the soft, warm grass tickling her bare feet as she walked down toward the beach. Her father's words kept turning over in her mind and she decided she might just kayak over to the island as she did from time to time. Of course while she was there, she'd have to call into the cabin and say hello, because not to do so would be plain rude.

Lost in her scheming, she didn't hear anything other than her own thoughts so when a pair of arms covered in blond hair grabbed her around the waist and swung her up and off the ground, she screamed. It took less than five seconds for her to recognize the strong hands with their neatly trimmed nails and for her brain to decode the familiar earthy scent tinged with a slight tang of oil.

She squealed with sheer joy. "Hank."

Holding her tightly, he let her feet touch the ground and then he spun her around in his arms, never losing contact. Behind his dark-rimmed glasses he looked bone-tired, but his honey-brown eyes smiled down at her. "Bridey."

His lips brushed hers lightly, making her body sing, and she wrapped her arms around his neck, needing to feel his strength against her skin. "I can't believe you're here."

His fingers gently rubbed her neck. "I hitched a ride on the helicopter along with some gear for Finn."

She gave a tiny jump of delight and kissed him hard before catching his hand and pulling him toward the tree house. "Our vacation starts now and we're starting it horizontal."

He laughed and tugged her back toward him, while at the same time glancing around the wide expanse of grass as if he was looking for someone. "Where is everybody?"

"Around. Out. I don't know. Does it matter?" She'd missed him so much and all she wanted to do was strip him bare, touch him all over, hold him and make wild and unrestrained love. Right now. She counter-tugged but Hank had stopped walking, his feet wide apart and firmly planted on the grass.

"We're not having sex in the tree house during daylight hours and risking scarring Logan for life." He slid his palms against her cheeks and traced the jet lines of her brow with his thumbs. "Before we do anything, I should go meet your parents."

She shook her head, not wanting to share him with anyone. "Later."

He matched her head shake with one of his own. "No, now. I'm a guest in their house."

Her frustration built. She hadn't seen him in two weeks and their phone calls had been short, and now his unfamiliar air of distraction had her on edge. "You're not a guest. You're not an employee. You're *my* fiancé."

A muscle in his cheek twitched and an intransigent look entered his eyes. "Actually, I'm all three."

"Hank, please." They had this argument every time

he arrived at the lake or her father's house in Chicago. Usually, she kissed him until he smiled, but today unease scuttled through her, underlining the fact she'd proposed to him. She'd driven the marriage carriage right up to his door. "You're marrying me, not my father."

"That doesn't negate common courtesy, Bridey. I should make my presence known to them seeing as I'm here for the weekend."

Her loop-the-loop of excitement violently crash-landed into a landfill of disappointment. "Just the weekend?" She couldn't stop the moan in her voice. "No, it has to be longer. For once I've got the *whole* family together and you're supposed to be here with me too. We've got wedding decisions to make, like the venue." Her voice rose as the long to-do list scrolled in her head. "And Monday is the cutoff date for the Newberry Library, which I love but it's probably going to be too small. The InterContinental is tempting but Mom's pushing for the Museum of Contemporary Art and—"

He kissed her quickly on the mouth and then said in his calm and quiet way, "It's all going to be fine. We've got an entire weekend."

Breathing deeply, she absorbed the serenity he always gave her and laid her head on his shoulder. "So we've got until Monday morning."

He pressed his lips to her hair. "Sunday afternoon."

She jerked back so fast she wrenched her neck and the pain intensified the moment she saw his resigned yet determined expression.

"Bridey, I was lucky to even get this weekend. The testing on the new number four went well but full production starts Monday. I have to be there at 7:00 a.m." He kissed her on her eyebrow. "Don't let that spoil the time we've got."

He wrapped his arms around her again and his eyes darkened to burnished amber. "Come nightfall, when you and I are alone in the guest cottage, I promise I'll make it up to you not only in the best way I know how, but how you like it best."

Guest cottage. She almost sobbed. "Mom's in the cottage."

Hank paled. "And your room's between your parents' and your little brother's." He swung away from her. "Bridey, not only do I have to work with your brother and your father, I have to face them at breakfast."

That was code for "you're noisy" and "I'm not sleeping with you in a bedroom surrounded by your family." Her plans for the perfect summer took another hit.

She heard the distinctive throb of the motorboat and saw Annika throw the rope toward the bollard and miss as Finn maneuvered the vessel parallel to the dock. She also saw his gaze on Annika's behind as she fished the rope out of the water, and the smile he gave her when she finally got the rope in place.

Her big brother who hated vacationing at the lake had got lucky. Damn it, she was engaged and if anyone should be guaranteed to get lucky it was her. The moment Logan was safely tucked up in bed she and Hank had a date in the tree house.

FINN GRIPPED THE longneck bottle of beer and wondered if a Friday night could possibly go any slower. His plans for the evening had involved him and Annika in the spa bath with champagne and watching the sunset before moving into his bed to do more than just sleep. He couldn't quite believe that for three nights they'd only slept in his bed. They'd had sex on the air mattress, outside on the veranda, on a rug in the woods with the fresh scent of pine around them, and this morning, somewhere between coffee and toast, they'd had sex against the kitchen counter. But in bed they'd only talked and spooned. He wasn't used to having a woman in his bed all night but surprisingly, he'd slept and slept well.

But his bed plans had been stymied the moment Bridey had met them on the dock. While he'd been pulling up the outboard, Annika hadn't waited for him to help her out of the boat and she'd tripped and sprawled front-first onto the dock. Hank had helped her to her feet and Bridey had issued the dinner invitation on the spot. Annika, being Annika, had accepted immediately. That left Finn with the choice of spending time alone at the cabin, time with his mother who'd furiously declined the dinner invitation and had insisted on being "left alone to heal," or time with the rest of his family. He'd chosen dinner as the lesser of the evils.

His father wandered over with a beer in one hand and a fistful of peanuts in the other. "I'm guessing Hank's presence here tonight means things are under control with number four?"

"They're improving. Monday will be the real test."

"Everything else going smoothly?"

"Yes." He studied his father's summer-tanned face but couldn't read it. "Do you want me to email you a full report before Monday?"

"No, thanks." Sean took a pull on his beer. "Smooth is good. It means you can work summer hours."

He heard Annika's laughter from across the terrace and thought about all the many and varied ways they could while away Saturday afternoon and all day Sunday. "This weekend anyway. I'm not holding my breath about next week."

Sean gave an understanding nod. "Seeing as you have

time this weekend, how about you help me build a zip line?"

His response to the unexpected question was instant and automatic. "I don't think so, Dad."

If Sean had anticipated his refusal, he didn't show it. "Hank's offered."

This didn't surprise Finn in the least. "Of course he's offered. It's the sort of thing future sons-in-law do."

Sean shrugged but the rolling motion said he didn't agree. "Bridey thought Logan would enjoy the zip line as much as the two of you did when you were kids."

"I'm sure he will." It didn't mean he had to be part of the build. Memories crowded him and he took a long pull of his beer. "It's a shame Grandpa isn't around to give you construction tips." He started to move away but Sean's reply stalled him.

"You might surprise yourself and enjoy it."

"And pigs might fly."

He made a beeline for Annika, but was thwarted by Hank, who wanted to update him on work, and then Esther rang a small dinner bell, asking everyone to be seated. Before he could reach Annika, Hank was pulling out a seat for her and Logan had snuck onto the chair next to hers. Bridey grabbed his arm so he missed rounding the table before Hank sat down on the other side of Annika.

Finn seated his sister and took the chair opposite Annika, as Dana sat next to him and Sean seated himself at the head of the table. Esther quietly removed the extra place setting that had been laid out for Kathleen and returned to the kitchen. At least one thing had gone his way this evening. He could be polite for an hour and survive the meal. Had Kathleen come, things would have been very different. Her presence and tart response to questions was the one thing that might have had him feeling almost sorry for his father.

Platters of food were passed up and down the long table as the family-style meal commenced, and for a minute or two all that could be heard was the scrape of serving spoons against china, and the murmured requests to pass particular dishes. The fish cakes were the most popular followed by the potato-and-cheese bake. Dana picked up her fork. "Did anyone see how enormous the moon was last night?"

"It's a blue moon." Annika broke open a crusty dinner roll and spread it with butter.

"No it's not. It's white," Logan corrected her with eight-year-old logic.

Most of the adults laughed but not Annika. Instead she met Logan's serious gaze and proceeded to explain—in terms a young boy could understand—about moon cycles and why it was called a blue moon.

Hank, who was usually quiet at family gatherings, said, "My dad used to take us camping on a full moon. It was like trying to sleep with the light on."

Logan's head swung around to Hank. "Awesome. I'd love to sleep in a tent."

Hank glanced up at Dana and Sean, his expression slightly cautious but mostly obliging and respectful. "Maybe we could if it was okay with your parents."

Bridey stiffened in her chair. "We don't have a tent, Hank."

Annika leaned slightly in front of Logan and spoke directly to Hank. "I've got an air mattress and a sleeping bag. It's a glorious night and if you can rustle up another bag, you guys could camp out on the island. I used to camp out with my brother."

Finn shot her a look he hoped said, "What in the hell

are you doing?" but if Annika saw it she chose to ignore it.

Sean took a second serving of the creamy potato bake. "We've got plenty of sleeping mats and bags in the storeroom."

Logan's face was a wreath of smiles. "Can I, Mom? Can I camp out with Hank on the island?"

A hint of a frown hovered on Dana's forehead as her gaze moved between Hank and Bridey. "Are you sure you want to do this on your weekend, Hank?"

"Sure." He nodded and a lock of blond hair fell over the rim of his glasses. "I've had my nose in a temperamental machine for two weeks so it'll be great to spend a night out in the fresh air." He put his hand on Logan's shoulder. "What do you think, buddy? Do you want to sleep under the stars?"

Logan let out a whoop of delight.

Bridey choked on a mouthful of chicken and Finn hit her firmly on the back. "You okay, sis?"

Nodding, she gulped down some water as Hank's hand reached across the table and covered hers. "Coming with us, Bridey? It'll be fun."

Finn saw the tight edges of his sister's smile and he knew that Hank was in serious trouble for planning a campout on his first night back. If this camping expedition was taking place on the island then he'd make sure it was as far away from the cabin as possible so as not to disturb him and Annika. "Hank, there's a pretty beach on the north side which would be perfect for a small fire and toasting s'mores."

Bridey tapped the base of her wineglass with her finger as if she was tapping out a code for those who could decipher it. "It sounds like something out of the Boy Scout handbook. Seeing as us girls are lacking the right equipment, we'll stay here and do girl stuff while *all* the boys go. Dad and Finn, you need to join in too."

Traitor! Finn couldn't believe that in her frustration with Hank, Bridey was taking him down with her. None of them was going to get any sex tonight. He immediately weighed in with, "I don't think that's—" but his words were drowned out by those of his father, Dana and Annika who readily agreed with the plan.

All eyes turned to him, including Annika's penetrating blue-blue gaze that saw more than he thought he'd ever exposed. Normally, nothing would induce him to spend time with his father and little brother, let alone a night camping out. Normally, he'd push back his chair, throw down his napkin and say, "No way," but if he did that now it would leave him dealing with Annika. An Annika asking hard questions and he knew she wouldn't be distracted by anything. Not even sex. He was *not* having that sort of conversation with her.

He swallowed a sigh. If he had to spend a night with Sean and Logan then at least he had Hank as a buffer. "I'll bring the marshmallows."

ELEVEN

"You do realize this is all your fault? We could have been crossing the lake right now, well on our way to having wild monkey sex but no, you had to mention camping."

Annika smiled up at Finn who'd cornered her near the storeroom, and was now using his body against hers in the most divine extortion tactics she'd ever experienced. She fingered his collar. "Actually, it was Hank who mentioned camping."

"I should have him fired." He nuzzled her neck.

His breath caressed her skin, making her dizzy. "He's family."

He raised his head. "And you think family can't be fired?"

His expression said "joking" but she caught a glimmer of buried steel in the depths of his eyes. *Business always comes first.* She grabbed the stark reminder and held on to it like a life preserver in a debris-strewn sea. The fun they had together, the amazing sex they shared—all of it was very, very temporary.

She kissed him hard and then forced herself to break the contact. "Go have fun."

He made a grumbling sound and tried to kiss her.

She ducked and pressed her palms against his chest. "Go. Relive your childhood camping adventures with

Sean and tell Logan all the silly stories about the fish that got away and—"

"I've never been camping with Sean in my life."

The words cracked like a whip and tension shot along his jaw so tightly she wondered how he'd been able to speak. She'd noticed a similar strain tonight when Finn had been talking with his father, although it lessened when they'd spoken about the company. She doubted they were close and yet she'd seen Sean with Logan teaching him to dive and fish—doing the things fathers did with sons that built relationships. Had Finn's parents' divorce got in the way of that?

She breathed in but it seemed hard work, as if she was pushing air against a heavy weight on her chest and she realized the weight was immense sadness for him. She recalled the few times she'd been lucky enough to go camping with her dad—just the two of them—and she treasured those special times when she didn't have to share him with her mom or brother. "So tonight's the time to start. It will help you all get closer, which can only be a good thing."

"Annika." He spoke her name on a warning growl. "I know you have this thing about helping, but don't even think about getting involved in this."

But she already was. With every passing day she was getting more and more involved with the Callahans.

ANNIKA HAD SLEPT with the blinds and windows open, allowing for the cross ventilation of fresh air and better sleep. The downside was the slivers of the dawn light and the cacophony of early morning birdsong woke her. Not that she minded. Between her excitement about setting up the thermography machine, thinking about Finn at the campout, and her arms constantly reaching out across the bed only to find a cold and empty mattress, she was done with sleep. Or to be more accurate, she was done with what had passed as sleep, and she was happy to start her day.

The sound of running feet and a slamming door launched her out of bed.

"Annika, are you here?"

"Be there in a minute." Wondering why on earth Bridey was on the island so early, she quickly pulled on the nearest clothes, which were a pair of her shorts and an old long-sleeved T-shirt of Finn's. She caught her elbow on the doorjamb as she walked into the main room and found Finn's sister in the kitchen rummaging through cupboards.

Unlike Finn's chaotic curls, Bridey's hair was smooth, sleek and neatly pulled back in a ponytail. It swung around her face as she spoke. "Does Finn have eggs?"

Annika tried to focus beyond the fact that Finn's scent filled the T-shirt and the cotton was stroking her body, reminding her that she'd missed him last night far more than was sensible. "Why eggs?"

Bridey levered herself to standing. "They'll want a big breakfast after sleeping on the beach and I thought I'd cook it."

Annika stifled a yawn with her sleeve and found herself breathing in deeply again. She gave herself a shake. Last night at their girls' night in, Bridey had been overly bright as if she was trying to enjoy herself but was falling short. It was odd given that it had been her suggestion to do the pedicures.

She pulled up a stool. "They took food with them and besides, burning breakfast on a campfire is part of the whole camping experience. Surely you don't want to deprive them of that."

Bridey slumped against the counter and sighed. "You're right. I know you're right. It's just I haven't seen Hank in two weeks and his visit is super short. We've got wedding things to work out but instead of spending time with me, he's off camping with my brothers and father!"

"I'm guessing you didn't sleep so good last night."

Bridey leveled a knowing look at her. "Did you?"

"Sure. With Finn gone, I got to sleep in the bed." She didn't want to talk about Finn, especially not to his engaged sister. It was her experience that all brides-to-be viewed the world in terms of future couples, and she and Finn were not a couple. They were just two people sharing amazing sex for a short time. She rounded the counter and banged her hip. "I'll make us some coffee."

Bridey moved out of the way and sat on the couch, hugging a cushion to her chest. "I'm sounding like a rich, spoiled brat, aren't I?"

Annika liked Bridey a lot. She could have been a spoiled rich girl given how much her father was worth, but she wasn't. Instead she was warm, funny and down-to-earth. None of the Callahans seemed to view their wealth as a right, but rather as a privilege. "No, not a brat. You're sounding more disappointed."

The sunlight caught the facets of Bridey's enormous diamond ring which sent a shower of reflections dancing across the walls. "I had such hopes for this family vacation and none of it's turning out how I pictured it."

Annika thought about her own far-flung family. "You've actually got your family all in one spot."

"That's true. Even Mom's here, which hasn't happened since the divorce." She spun her ring on her finger. "But I don't have Hank."

Something about the way she said her fiancé's name made Annika look up from the coffee machine.

Bridey gave her an overly bright smile. "What I mean is, Hank not being here wasn't part of how I saw the summer. I especially wasn't supposed to be planning the—" she made quotations marks with her fingers, "—'Wedding of the Year' on my own either, but that's happening too because Hank's consumed by work."

Annika scooped the fragrant coffee grounds into the filter and set the machine to drip. "I would have thought growing up in your family, work was part of the territory."

Bridey grimaced. "Very true. AKP dominates everything but Hank isn't like Finn or my father."

The comment spiked Annika's interest, especially as Bridey was a striking woman and Hank, with his glasses and serious expressions, came down more on the side of ordinary. "Is that part of the attraction?"

"I don't know. Maybe." A slow wave of red crept up Bridey's neck and washed across her cheeks. "All I know is that from the moment he smiled at me, I was his if he wanted me."

Annika's heart hitched in her chest at the idea of that sort of love and the fact it was being returned. "And obviously he wants you because he proposed and now you're getting married."

But Bridey didn't reply. She didn't even sigh in the blissful way engaged women tended to when they got lost in thought about their future with their soon-to-be husband. Instead, she chewed her nail and then started fiddling behind the cushions until she pulled out a rectangular board. "I was blaming Finn's lumpy couch for being uncomfortable, but it's this."

"Sorry, that's mine." Annika crossed the room to take the board.

"What are you drawing? Is this the view from the

cabin?" Bridey glanced out the window and back again, before taking a closer look at the two pieces of paper clipped to the board. "Oh, and this looks like a vine of hearts entwining the letters *J* and *D*."

Annika avoided commenting on the lake sketch which she wasn't happy with. "It's an idea for a wedding invitation monogram. I've already done the one the bride wants but I was playing around with this idea."

Bridey's eyes lit up. "Can I see the other one?"

"Sure." Annika flipped over her satchel and carefully removed the first fully completed monogram which was more traditional with fleurs-de-lys surrounding the initials.

Bridey jumped off the couch to study it on the table. "Annika, this is beautiful. It's classically elegant, but if I was the bride, I'd want the other one."

"Really?" When she'd been doodling the hearts she thought she might have gone a bit overboard on romance-kitsch.

"Totally." Bridey moved back into the kitchen and poured two coffees. "Do you have any other examples of your work? I'd love to see them because I'm in the market for a wedding invitation designer."

Embarrassment tangoed with pride. Annika wasn't certain how much Finn had told his sister but it didn't take a rocket scientist to work out she was currently homeless and lacking in funds. Bridey was being kind but she was also planning a lavish society wedding and Annika was only a small-town calligrapher.

"Bridey, please don't feel you have to use my services for your invitations. You have plenty of time to check out other designers."

Finn's sister's mouth took on one of a few familiar Callahan looks—mulish and determined. "I want distinctive invitations that represent Hank and me, and at the same time set up the excitement and expectation of our fabulous wedding. You've met both of us and there's not a doubt in my mind you're brilliant with pen and ink. I was thinking oversized hand-torn, champagne parchment with a gold monogram."

Annika instantly pictured the glorious heavy paper. "Rolled, wrapped in gold-and-silver ribbon and hand-delivered in tubes."

Bridey grinned. "I like the way you think."

Annika's brain whirred. Bridey had already mentioned three well-known Chicago wedding venues and Annika doubted she would consider Whitetail despite the town pinning their hopes on the Callahan-Neiquest wedding launching Whitetail—Weddings That WOW.

Still, if she invited Bridey to visit the main wedding office then she'd have done her part as acting mayor. She could show her some invitation samples and Nicole and Melissa could take their shot. Melissa might even be able to weave some dress magic although she had her doubts because she was pretty certain Bridey Callahan would be going haute couture all the way.

Annika sipped her coffee and tried to sound casual. "I'm going to my studio this morning to set up the thermography machine and print some save-the-date cards. Seeing as we've no clue what time the guys are getting back, and texting them isn't in the spirit of camping, why not come with? You can tell me your ideas and we can go from there."

Bridey raised her mug and smiled. "It's a date."

"YOU'RE BURNING THOSE eggs." Sean poked the fire with a stick.

Finn's hand gripped the panhandle. "You think you can do a better job?"

"Happy to try."

"Take a shot then." Finn rose from his crouching position and stretched his back. His sleeping mat hadn't been designed for comfort but to insulate him from the chill of the ground. Who knew sleeping on sand was like sleeping on cold concrete?

It had been a long night, made even longer by knowing that Annika was sleeping alone in his bed only a couple of miles away. It might as well have been a thousand. His father had snored half the night and Logan had kept rolling into Finn. At 2:00 a.m. he'd given up moving Logan back to his mat, and instead had clamped an arm around him and accepted that an elbow in the head was part of the deal. Only Hank had slept as if he didn't have a care in the world.

Finn didn't get it. Hank had known Bridey long enough to know she could sulk when things didn't go her way and that she was probably going to give him hell when he got back. Yet the quiet engineer didn't seem worried or in any hurry to return to Kylemore. He'd risen early, got the fire going and had then taken Logan out in the canoe with the fishing poles and a promise of catching breakfast.

"You want toast?" Sean shoved a piece of bread onto a stick.

I want out of here. "One." He poured them coffee from a blue enamel pot he'd never seen before. "Since when did Kylemore have camp equipment?"

"I bought it for this summer." Sean shoveled the eggs and toast onto plates and handed one off to Finn before sitting down on the sand with the other. "I'm glad you came. It gives us a chance to talk."

A prickle of something he couldn't name made him hot and he gulped coffee. "We talk every day when I give you the daily report."

"I meant talk about stuff other than AKP." His father's intelligent eyes bored into him. "It is possible you know."

"Yeah, it's possible." He bit into the toast. Work was the only thing he and his father had in common. Over the years it had become their sole connection and he was very happy to leave it that way. "Thing is, I don't want to."

Sean stared out at the lake. "I know I was a lousy father to you."

Finn choked on his eggs as the unexpected words snagged him. Words he might have wanted to hear at seventeen but he sure as hell didn't want to hear now. "Lucky for me I had Grandpa."

Sean was quiet for a moment and when he spoke, regret was clear in his voice. "It's part of the reason I took off this summer."

"How do you figure that?"

"I thought if we spent some time together it might help make it up to you."

He thought of his father's bizarre invitation the other day and every part of him froze. "Like going fishing?"

Sean nodded. "And camping."

He spoke slowly as pieces of a puzzle started clicking together fast. "Stuff that fathers do with their kids?"

"Pretty much."

The words melted the veneer of cool indifference he'd spent years cultivating so he could deal with his father. "Fuck, Dad. I'm not twelve."

Sean flinched. "I'm well aware of that, Finnegan."

Are you? Sean had been an absent father with a wake of broken promises trailing behind him and Finn had covered his childhood disappointments years ago by schooling himself to think of his father only in terms of the business and as an entrepreneur he could learn from. Sean had no right to try and change the rules on him now.

"Yeah? Well, your timing sucks." He stood up, his plate falling to the sand. "You're twenty-one years too late."

"That doesn't mean I can't try."

The consummate businessman, the legend who controlled an empire, rose to his feet looking every minute of his fifty-seven years, and a foreign aura of uncertainty hovered over him.

Finn's grip on the world as he knew it slipped slightly. His father was never uncertain about anything and a slither of alarm snuck in, unsettling everything he understood about himself. His anger instantly scorched it. "I don't want you to try. You want to be a redux dad, Sean, count me out. You've got Logan to get it right with now."

Sean's mouth that had charmed so many so often, kicked up at the edges in a grim smile. "Being a parent is fraught with mistakes, Finnegan."

"And you've got a hell of a diploma in that. Fishing and camping just isn't going to do it, Dad."

"I didn't think it would."

Sean met his gaze and Finn saw something in it that he didn't want to see and it sent out malignant tendrils that took hold like cancer. "Me running the company this summer isn't about gaining experience at all, is it? You're holding me fucking hostage so you can sleep at night."

Sean ran his hand across the back of his neck. "The two things are not mutually exclusive."

Finn's chest burned so hot and tight he could barely breathe and all he wanted to do was get the hell away from his father. "What deluded planet are you currently living on? Did you think getting me here and saying sorry was going to be enough? It's too late, Sean. Hell, it was too late years ago. I hope you get your absolution from the great outdoors, because you're sure as hell not getting it from me."

"Dad! Finn!" Logan's excited voice hailed them from farther down the beach.

Every part of him wanted to turn and go but Finn could see the boy running as fast as he could toward them with sand flying, and clutching an enormous fish. A flash of memory—him as a boy with his first big catch—stayed his feet. In the distance, Hank pulled the canoe from the water.

His father hesitated a moment as if he wanted to say something more but he turned toward Logan's excited voice.

Breathless and breathing hard, Logan held his catch aloft. "Look at the size of it, Dad."

Sean's face split into a quiet and proud smile and he slapped Logan gently on the back. "That's quite a fish. We better take a photo to show Mom."

"Finn, can you take the photo of me and Dad on your phone?" Logan asked.

He'd had enough of pretending to play happy families but he thought of the prized photo in the cabin of himself with his grandfather as he held up his first big fish. Every boy needed a record of their first catch and he'd do this for Logan before he left. The only thing that had been good about last night was his little half brother's infectious enthusiasm for everything they'd done, and Finn had enjoyed his role in teaching him how to make a fire.

As he framed his father and younger brother in the viewfinder, his throat closed. Logan stared up at Sean with adoration shining in his eyes. Sean had his absolution.

ANNIKA HAD AN aching wrist, gold embossing powder on her face, sticky ink in her hair and five sample invitations for Jessica to choose from. Working out the speed of the conveyor belt to move the paper through the thermography machine had taken some tweaking, but she'd only had one invitation go up in flames. She was excited to hear Jessica's response to the samples and she couldn't wait to get to the post office on Monday morning to mail the samples. The save-the-date cards had been laser-printed on pretty card stock that Finn had suggested from the AKP catalogue.

Bridey had spent a long time browsing through the sample invitations and as expected, she wanted something totally original. She'd given Annika a check and had commissioned three different designs so she had choice. She'd also chatted with Nicole and Melissa over coffee. The meeting had gone smoothly and Bridey had complimented them on the romantic space they'd created and the ideas they'd put together. Then she'd twisted her enormous diamond ring on her finger and said, "The thing is, it's absolutely necessary that Hank and I have a big wedding. I know we had the engagement party at the lake but the wedding is different."

Nicole had nodded. "Rhinebeck did 'huge' for Chelsea Clinton. We can do huge for you."

"That's very sweet but I've already put a deposit on four venues including the InterContinental. It's very important that I get married in Chicago so everyone knows that Hank and I are taking our first step to a long and happy life together. I have to do it right—*everything* must be done right." Bridey's hand flew to her mouth. "Oh, I'm so sorry, I didn't mean that Whitetail wouldn't do it right, it's just I *have* to get married in Chicago."

"I understand," Nicole had said, but when Bridey had leaned forward to take a cookie from the plate, she'd thrown a worried look at Annika.

Annika agreed with Nicole. She didn't know Bridey well enough to know what was going on but her words, "I have to do it right" struck her as odd. Was there a wrong way to get married?

Still thinking about Bridey, who'd gone to the bakery for her mother, Annika wandered into the kitchen and grabbed a bottle of iced tea. She was just twisting the top when her shiny new smartphone blasted out the piercing sound of an air horn.

She jumped in fright and iced tea slopped all over her hand and down her skirt. Grabbing the phone with her dry hand, she randomly pressed buttons—anything to silence the noise. Finn had given her the phone yesterday, and although she'd only received two calls on it, the ringtone for those had been quiet and classical. Was her phone blowing up? On the third jab the horrible sound stopped and she breathed a sigh of relief. As she washed her sticky hand a Missed Call message beeped.

She couldn't believe that noise had been a ringtone and she didn't know whether to laugh or stamp her foot when she saw it was Finn's number. He must have programmed her phone so when he called it was impossible to miss. She pressed Missed Call and held the phone to her ear.

Finn's voice roared down the phone, his words peppering her like a spray of bullets. "Where the hell are you?"

She pulled in a deep breath to steady herself and sat down. She hadn't heard that tone in his voice since the police station. "Finn, what's wrong?"

"What's wrong is that I've been to the cabin, the cottage and Kylemore, and you're not there."

"I'm at the studio." She couldn't understand why he was so upset. "Why didn't you just call me when you got back to the cabin?"

But his reply broke up and all she could hear was, "Dock now," before the line dropped out.

Five minutes later she pulled up at the dock to see Finn pacing up and down. The moment he saw her he strode toward her, his face set and his feet making the old wooden planks vibrate.

"Hi."

He gave her a quick nod but not even the brim of his cap could hide the melee of emotions in his eyes. He grabbed her backpack and then her hand, and walked them both very quickly down the dock. An onlooker would have seen a well-mannered man carrying a woman's bag for her. Annika saw a man in pain. She was about to ask him what was upsetting him so much when they arrived at the motorboat she'd tied up earlier that morning. She noticed the rowboat tied up next to it.

"You *rowed* here?" Her voice rose in disbelief. The island was a quick row from Kylemore but a good distance from Whitetail.

"Yes." His mouth was a thin line. He handed her down into the motorboat before untying the rope and jumping down himself. Silently, he turned on the ignition and the large engine throbbed to life. With a deft pull on the wheel, Finn accelerated away from the dock.

As the boat gathered speed, the bow lifted, the flag streamed out in its full stars-and-stripes glory, and Annika fell back onto the seat, pushed there by inertia and held firmly in place by the force of the wind against her. The boat breached the lake's speed limit and it hit each small wave with a knee-jarring thud, but Finn didn't seem to notice. He stood, ramrod-stiff with one hand on the wheel and his gaze fixed straight ahead.

There was no point talking because the wind stole every word the moment it was spoken. She might not know the circumstances or the reasons, but she knew with every part of her that he was hurting. His pain radiated into her and she felt it too. Her heart turned over. Without thinking, she reached out and touched him, resting her hand on the small of his back, and started to rub his spine gently with her thumb. At first he didn't move but then his rigid shoulders dropped and his back pressed into her hand. The boat slowed and he pulled her to her feet as they entered a pretty little cove where the pine trees came down to the shore.

"Take the wheel and keep her slow." He tested the knot on the anchor and then threw it into the navy blue water, watching it sink until it was too deep to be seen. Then he cut the engine, pulled her to him and kissed her.

His mouth plundered hers as if he hadn't kissed her in weeks and his hands gripped her arms tightly as if she'd vanish if he didn't hold on to her. The stubble on his cheek grazed her skin, and his lips pressed hard against her own. She automatically leaned back to grab some breath. "Finn?"

"Please don't talk." He growled out the words and moved in again, his hands dropping to her hips and pulling her into him. She swiveled slightly so she fitted against him and he made a sound in his throat—half howl, half moan—an animal in distress.

It tore through her, ripping and tugging like a blunt knife. Right then she knew he needed her. For whatever reason, he needed her and she needed to be there for him. She pressed her hands into his hair, tangling them in his thick curls, and kissed him back. Her tongue dueled with his—thrusting and parrying until both of them were panting for breath but neither was pulling away. He smelled of salt, sweat and campfire smoke, and tasted of old scars and new pain. She wanted to soothe him as well as ride with him on this out-of-control journey, and give him what he wanted.

Keeping her mouth on his, she slipped her hand under his shirt and, gripping the waistband of his shorts, she undid the zipper.

The boat rocked.

He ground out, "Steady" as his hand fought the material of her skirt until he cupped her.

She trembled but somehow managed to release him from his shorts and her hand closed around his silky thickness.

He shuddered and his finger found the edge of her panties and slid into her wetness.

Her hand stroked him.

He stroked her back.

She gasped, "No," knowing she'd come in a heartbeat and she wanted this to be for him.

"Yes."

The boat kept rocking. And tilted.

Her balance shifted and their hands fell away.

The boat tilted back.

"Ohh." She lost her balance completely and as she fell backward she tried clutching his shoulder for support but got his shirt instead. She heard a rip as the edge of the boat hit the back of her knees, and then she was airborne for a moment before being encased by water.

She kicked to the surface, gasping with surprise and the shock of the cold water against her skin.

"Annika! Here." She turned to see Finn's strong arms stretched out toward her from the boat and his face filled with relief. "Are your okay?"

"I'm fine. But I think my sandals are forever part of the lake." Her skirt dragged at her legs like a lead weight so she took it off, balled it up and tried to throw it to Finn. It fell short.

He shook his head slowly as if her miss was completely expected and laughter creased his face, crinkling the skin around his eyes into smiling lines. By the time she reached the side of the boat, he'd retrieved her skirt with a fishing pole. Gripping her wrists he said, "I believe I've done this before. Why am I always rescuing you from water?"

"Just lucky I guess." She tried to smile but her teeth were chattering. "Hurry up already. Deep water is a lot colder than close to the shore."

"You were bossy last time too." But his voice was full of a smile as he pulled her up until she could hold the side of the boat. Then he put his arms under hers and lifted her in.

He rubbed her dry with a towel, wrapped her in another one, sat her down on the bench seat at the back of the boat, and then pulled her close and kissed her on the nose. His dark eyes, which had been filled with torment half an hour ago, now sparkled with fun. "I should have known better than to try and have sex with you on an unstable surface."

She snuggled into him. "If we'd moved back to here I might have been okay."

He laughed. "I don't think so, sweetheart. Lesson learned. It's terra firma for us from now on."

He kissed her again, only this time instead of heat, lust and demanding desire, his touch was infused with something very different from every other kiss they'd shared. Something akin to tenderness.

It circled her heart like a warm glow and she realized with a jolt that if she wasn't very careful, she was at great risk of falling in love with him.

TWELVE

KISSING ANNIKA WAS up there with the buzz of nailing a multimillion-dollar contract, and Finn slowly kissed away every drop of cold water on her cheek before turning his attention to her ear.

"Finn?"

"Hmmm." His tongue dawdled on her lobe because he knew she loved it and she usually responded by seeking his mouth with a moan of wonder.

"What happened this morning?"

His tongue stalled and he slowly lifted his head to find determined sky-blue eyes fixed on his face. He stared down at her. "Nothing."

Her eyes widened with skepticism. "You rowed to Whitetail to find me."

He trailed his finger down her cheek and gave her a long, lazy smile, hoping he could distract her. "Sleeping with Logan's elbow in my head reminded me of how much I missed sleeping with you."

Her eyelids drifted down for a moment and then snapped open. "I don't believe you."

"Suit yourself." He tried to return his attentions to her ear but her hands pressed against his upper arms.

"I am." She shifted slightly and a zip of air darted between them, cooling the heat. "Something upset you."

He hated the way she could read him. "I don't want to talk about it."

She nibbled her plump bottom lip the way she always did whenever she was thinking. "In that case I know it's nothing to do with AKP."

His chest tightened at the truth of her words. "You don't know enough about me or the business to know any such thing."

She didn't deny it but the tilt of her head and the look of sympathy in her eyes made his stomach churn.

She rested her forehead against his. "I think whatever it was that upset you is connected to your family."

This time he was the one to break contact. "Sorry, sweetheart, but you're way off course."

"I'm betting it's to do with your father."

"Good for you." He *so* wasn't going down this road or having this conversation with Annika. He'd found a way to deal with his father which had worked for him for years—right up until today's lapse and that was all today was. A lapse. He stood up, vaulted into the front section of the boat and brought up the anchor. "We need to get back. You need a hot shower."

She stayed seated. "It must be exhausting for you."

He stowed the anchor. "It doesn't weigh much."

Her voice sounded behind him. "Not the anchor. I meant your constant running away."

His hand stilled on the ignition as her words tore into him—their target the barely sealed lid he'd forced shut over the meltdown he'd had at the beach with Sean. Forced tightly shut over feelings he'd only just got back into their holding bay where he thought they'd not only been safely stored for years, but that they'd lost their potency. No way was he allowing any of them back out again to see the light of day. His life was exactly as he liked it. It had taken him years but he'd found a way of dealing with Sean and he wouldn't allow anything to change that, least of all talking.

"We're *all* running from something, Annika. Care to share?"

Her sharp intake of breath sounded loud against the silence of the cove.

He started the engine. "Didn't think so."

ANNIKA SLOPPED A base coat of paint over the warehouse door, preparing it for the mural she'd promised Nicole she'd paint. Using broad brush strokes, she quickly covered the surface. She wanted to find her Zen and get into the spirit of the painting but Finn's inference that her living in Whitetail was running away kept eating into her like acid on paper. She wasn't running away. She was the acting mayor and her job was to find the town an industry that offered full employment.

She flicked her brush over the edges of the door. She would have told him all of that out on the boat except he'd deliberately cut her off with the noise of the engine. By the time they'd got back to the cabin she was shivering so much she'd raced straight to the shower and when she'd finished drying her hair, she'd walked out to find the cabin empty and a note on the table.

At the office. Nothing for you to do so enjoy the afternoon. She wasn't at all surprised that Finn had run to the safety of the office. He'd gone to the one place he felt most comfortable and she could picture him surrounded by the protective force field of work.

As she waited for the base to dry, she stared at the wedding photo of Jennifer and Carl sitting in Al's carriage. Both of them were smiling and waving and Main Street, with its colorful profusion of flowering hanging baskets and fluttering flags, formed the backdrop behind them. They looked happy and so very much in love. A blurry image of a man in a tuxedo with dark, dark eyes wafted through her mind and, with a start, she realized she was biting her lip.

She tasted blood. *This is crazy.*

With a zealous push she pinned the photo to the door frame so she could see it while she painted. She didn't want to get married. The last time she'd toyed with that idea she'd been so badly betrayed it had taken her a long time to recover. Now she was well and truly over Ryan and content with her life—almost content. When Whitetail got a new industry, *then* she could relax and enjoy her life living where she truly belonged.

Two years ago, she'd packed up one very different life and an unworn wedding dress, and she was never going to do something that painful again. Ever. She didn't need a man in her life to be happy. This affair with Finn was exactly what she needed to keep unwanted sentimental thoughts at bay. She blew out a breath and picked up her pallet. It was time to bring Main Street to the warehouse door.

FINN STOOD WATCHING Annika paint. Given that he could barely sketch out a stick figure, he'd been enjoying watching her for the past five minutes, and he marveled at how she made it look effortlessly easy. Under her talented hand what had looked to be brown blobs of paint one minute were suddenly hanging baskets with flowers tumbling out of them.

He'd spent the last couple of hours in the office and as he'd checked figures and cross-referenced projections, he'd finally found the calm that had eluded him all day. Once it had arrived, seeped in and soothed, he'd wanted to see Annika. Not sure of his reception, he hadn't called but had arrived unannounced. He was shifting his weight so he could see around her shoulder, when a stick cracked under his foot. She turned around, surprise clear in the depths of her eyes. Her cheek had a streak of cerise, the hair on her left temple looked faintly blue and her misshapen T-shirt looked like a Jackson Pollock painting. He wanted to pull her into his arms and kiss her until she sagged against him all soft and warm.

She put down her pallet and wiped her hands on an old rag. "I didn't hear you drive up."

He shrugged. "I walked."

Her chestnut brows rose. "You *are* getting a lot of exercise today."

He stepped in close and brushed stray strands of her hair behind her ear. "I guess that means I'll sleep well tonight."

Disappointment raced across her expressive face. "I suppose you will."

He laughed, loving the way she enjoyed sex as much as he did. "I'll need an early night which means you and I have to eat at the cabin, and we're not inviting anyone to sleep over."

"Sounds like a great idea to me." She slid her arms around his waist, rose up on her toes and kissed him.

As her lips touched his, relief slid in. He wrapped his arms around her and kissed her back.

A couple of minutes later Annika used every grain of her self-control and pulled back from the kiss before she ruined the painting by pushing the door open and dragging him inside to one of the couches. "I'll finish this tomorrow. Just give me five minutes to clean my brushes and then we can go."

Finn kissed her gently on the cheek and spun her out of his arms. "It's looking good."

"Hmmm." She wasn't so sure, which was mostly because her heart wasn't in it, although she'd enjoyed the process. "I saw it differently."

He tilted his head. "It looks exactly like Main Street."

She rolled her eyes. "It's supposed to."

"So what's the problem?"

"I had a different painting in mind but Nicole and Melissa want to promote the idea of the town being the bride's for the day."

"That sounds like a good business plan."

She swished her paint brushes briskly in the turpentine. "What if a bride is scared of horses or doesn't want to get married in summer? She's hardly going to relate to this scene then, is she?"

"So what would you have painted?" he asked mildly.

If she was truthful with herself she would probably have said "nothing" because soon the warehouses would be filled with a business that employed a lot of people. *Soon, please, soon.* When that happened, Nicole would have to find another space for Weddings That WOW— that's if it lasted beyond the two bookings they had. But right now Finn was looking at her as if he expected an answer. "I would have painted something that creates atmosphere. Something that announces to the brides-to-be that they're entering an enchanted world."

He shrugged. "But that isn't specific to the town. I think Nicole and Melissa are on to something with their branding."

She couldn't believe what she was hearing. First the town was running wild with the idea weddings would save them and now Finn was saying it wasn't totally off the mark. Her worries about the whole endeavor spilled over. "There's no business or branding plan. This all came from an off-the-cuff comment on a post-wedding high. Sure, they have two weddings booked but that happened only because of a tiny TV news story linked with the Callahan name."

"Successful businesses have started with less." He raised a knowing brow. "And you've got work from it."

She sighed at the dilemma that put her in. "I know, and I appreciate it but I just can't see Weddings That WOW as a viable business that will provide employment for more than a few. I sometimes feel like I'm the only person who really understands how serious things will be if we don't replace Reggies. Everyone's energies should be focused on a sustainable industry rather than running off on a tangent."

"A wedding business can be sustainable because people will always be getting married. Don't ask me why they keep getting married, but they do." He shook his head, sending curls bouncing, and sarcasm leeched out of him. "And more than once as my father has so admirably demonstrated."

She saw the tic of a muscle in his cheek and it reinforced all her beliefs about Finn and Sean's relationship and again she wished she could help. "Twice?"

He shook his head. "Dana is wife number three. Between creating an empire, getting married and getting divorced, it didn't leave Sean with a lot of time for much else, especially parenting. I was fourteen years old at wedding number two, which lasted a solid twenty-four months. Given all that, I have no clue why Bridey wants to even try. I sure as hell won't be."

"She's in love."

His bark of laughter whipped her. "Love destroys more than it ever builds."

And there is was—another reminder that what they

had was very temporary. She stacked it up as part of the wall she was building to protect her heart.

He shoved his hands in his pockets. "So why are you painting the mural if you're not happy about it?"

She folded up her drop sheet. "Because I paint and they don't."

"I thought your painting was a passing phase?" He picked up her paint box and gave her a look that said, "I think you're hiding something." "But that's not strictly true, is it?"

Her heart rate kicked up and she wondered what he knew. The town had always been very protective of her, which was another reason she loved living here. "I dabbled but I'm busy being acting mayor. You know how much time that takes up seeing as you're sponsoring my correspondence with most of America's manufacturing sector."

"You did more than just dabble, Annika."

His quietly spoken words made her fingers fumble as she searched for the truck's keys in her backpack. "I think I know how much I did or didn't paint."

"I did an internet search on you."

A chill shot through her and her voice squeaked. "You've been spying on me?"

He shook his head slowly. "No. I just typed your name into the browser in the exact same way you did with mine."

Guilt pricked her indignation. He was right, she'd done that many times, trying to learn more about him other than Finn Callahan the businessman. She hadn't found out much at all except one article that mentioned him rescuing baby birds when he was a kid. She took a deep breath and decided it was easier to face this head-on. "So what did you find out?"

"That you majored in fine arts and you had a promising career." He smiled and his eyes filled with encouragement. "I saw the photographs of your series of lighthouses on the Great Lakes. They're an interesting fusion of the past and the present."

She bit her lip, instantly recalling Ryan's bitter words about those paintings. "That's *not* how the critics described them."

He shrugged. "Art's subjective. What's one person's pleasure is another's poison."

But she knew what she knew and she crossed her arms over her chest to stop herself from shaking. "So you would have read about how my show brought about the financial collapse of the Raybould Gallery?"

His shot of laughter echoed around the park and then stopped abruptly. The lines on his face deepened to serious and he slowly put down her paint box. "That's what you believe?"

Memories pummeled her. The nightmare of her art being slaughtered by the very critic Ryan had most wanted to impress, and then immediately followed by Ryan's utter betrayal of her. "It's not a case of believing, Finn. I know. My exhibition was an unmitigated disaster and it brought the gallery to its knees."

She hated how the past she'd fought so hard to get over still had the ability to swoop back in like it was yesterday. She'd gotten over Ryan, but she hadn't managed to purge the vitriol of the reviews. Every part of her screamed for her to start moving before she fell down. Blinking furiously, she walked toward the truck on rubbery legs. She would not cry. She'd cried enough two years ago and she was done with all that now. She sucked in a breath to steady herself and one minute she was upright and the next her feet were stumbling and she was pitching forward.

Finn's arms shot around her waist, steadying her. "Annika, stop." His mouth caressed her ear. "Breathe."

She didn't want to be so needy but she was. She let him hold her and she leaned in against him, feeling the steady beat of his heart against her chest. She breathed in his strength and calm.

His hand stroked her hair and then he pulled back slightly, and tilted her chin with his finger. "Did the Raybould Gallery blame you for the demise of the business?"

She swallowed. "That and a few other things."

Flint flared briefly in his eyes and she felt him suck in a deep breath. "Kathleen knows a lot about the Chicago art world, Annika, although her involvement is on the financial and administration side. I know that isn't anything like the world of the artist, but from her I do know that Ryan Raybould ran through his family's trust money like water and he took a Chicago art institution down with him. I'd bet my last dollar your exhibition coincided with the creditors catching up with him, and he used you as handy scapegoat."

She wanted to believe him but she knew better. "If that were true, I'd have known."

"Believe me, struggling businesses don't declare their hand unless they're forced."

She made herself say the words that would declare her a fool in his eyes. "I was living with him."

Surprise crossed his face. "The internet didn't tell me that."

"So I can be thankful for small mercies, then." She tried to lighten the mood. "I, on the other hand, know you dated one of the Hilton sisters."

"If sitting next to her at a charity function is dating,

then yes." He gave her a wry smile. "Ryan Raybould hid his financial woes from everyone until the mess he was in brought everything down on him like a house of cards. I vaguely remember Mom telling me he'd applied for an arts grant and even then there were rumors things weren't good."

She struggled to take in Finn's words but they slowly sank in. That bastard. Ryan had let her take the blame for his mess. "I think I feel even more foolish than I did two years ago."

He shook his head. "Don't. Promise me you'll talk to Kathleen. She knows all about it."

She wondered at his insistence but agreed. "Okay."

He stroked her cheek. "Good. Now tell me one thing?"

"Maybe." She braced herself for the question about how she could have possibly had a relationship with a man like Ryan but when he spoke it was nothing to do with that.

"Did you enjoy painting the door today even though it wasn't what you wanted to be doing?"

She had to admit that she'd got a tiny buzz from it. "Little bit."

"Then create time to paint again."

Finish the Dawn, Day and Dusk *triplet.*

The idea scared her rigid. Ryan's betrayal of her work and herself in an attempt to hide his own situation was one thing. The critics' damning reviews were another beast entirely.

"Annika, paint for yourself."

It was as if he could read her mind but if that was possible he'd know that art wasn't private—it was excruciatingly public and no matter how much her fingers tingled to pick up a brush, she wasn't putting herself out there to be humiliated ever again. "I don't have time."

His free hand curled around the back of her neck. "You might find yourself with a bit of spare time over the next couple of days."

She ran through her to-do list and couldn't think how that would be possible even if she'd been able to block out the critical voices in her head. "Why?"

He sighed as his fingers stroked her skin. "I'm leaving for Chicago in the morning with Hank. Production for one of our biggest clients goes online first thing Monday and I have to be there."

She hated the sink of disappointment that weighed her down but she wasn't going to show him that. "Good. That means I get the bed to myself and can spread out diagonally."

He laughed. "You do that anyway."

She leaned in. "And you hog the top sheet."

"We obviously need more practice in sharing a bed."

His eyes darkened to a delicious cocoa and she let the past and the future slide away. Nothing existed except the fact she was in his arms and she lost herself in the warmth of his eyes and the seductive tone of his voice.

"Oh, yes," she said. "Lots and lots of practice."

"THANKS SO MUCH, Officer Gunderson." Bridey opened the door of the squad car and stepped out onto Kylemore's circular driveway, giving the policeman a wave as he headed back toward the gate. It had been a crazy couple of hours. After buying some pastries for her mother, she'd arrived at the dock to find no Annika and no motorboat, just Finn's rowboat. She'd called everyone but none of her family was answering their phones and she'd been wondering what to do when the Whitetail police officer had offered her a ride home.

In the squad car she'd received the message, *So sorry! Finn commandeered boat. On my way now. Anni.*

Bridey, knowing exactly how Finn could be sometimes, had silently forgiven Annika. She'd texted back, *Am almost home now. No hard feelings. Tell big bro he's bad. B.*

And tell Hank too. It was well into the afternoon and she hadn't heard from him despite sending two texts and leaving three messages. Their weekend was flying past fast and she'd hardly seen him. Added to that they were no closer to deciding on a wedding venue and that decision was the keystone to the entire wedding. They had to get it right—their future depended on it.

She walked into the kitchen hoping that Esther was there just as she'd always been when Bridey was growing up and had a case of "the sads." Esther would always set aside what she was doing, give her a hug and then sit her down. She'd pour freshly squeezed lemonade, serve up some cool and juicy watermelon, chocolate chip cookies and sage advice. The world had always seemed a better place after that and the problem diminished. But today the kitchen was clean and tidy and—apart from the quiet buzz of the refrigerator—silently empty.

Tears pricked at the backs of her eyes. She poured herself a glass of water, sat down and gave herself a good shake. She was being ridiculous. Hank was probably upstairs taking a nap after his campout. She'd go up and snuggle in next to him and when he woke up they could decide on the wedding venue.

"Baby-girl. There you are." Sean strode across the kitchen, kissed Bridey on the cheek and grabbed two beers from the fridge. "Hank and I have been in the library drawing the plans for the zip line."

"Hank's in the library?" Happiness rushed through her and she started walking.

Her father caught up with her. "No, we've finished and Hank just left. I'm not sure where he was headed." He opened the library door for her. "Come and look at the plans and if it's what you want we might just get the order into the hardware store before it closes."

Bridey headed straight to the table and she ran her fingers over the plan—the closest she'd been to Hank all day. This wasn't just a "back of a coaster" sketch. Hank had drawn up the path of the zip line over the deep finger of lake that formed a cove on the west side of the property near the tree house. He'd worked out the stress and weight loads for the wire and the support posts, and his neat script crawled down the side listing everything that was required for the build.

A warm feeling washed through her. One day their children would ride on this zip line. "It looks great, Daddy. Logan will love it."

Sean brought up a browser on the computer and typed in *yellow pages*. "He's pretty excited about the idea that's for sure. He talked nonstop about it as we packed up this morning."

"So how was the great campout?"

Sean's head didn't rise from the screen and two beats of silence passed. When he finally looked up he said, "Logan caught a huge musky."

Bridey understood the significance of the first big catch. "Fantastic. Do you have photo?"

"Finn took one."

Being very familiar with the contents of her phone's inbox today due to constant checking, she said, "He hasn't sent it, or at least not to me."

Sean's mouth formed a wry and weary smile. "He

knows the importance of the first big fish. I'm sure he'll get around to it and if not, Logan will remind him."

He reached for the phone and started dialing and Bridey was about to text Hank again when she noticed a black cell phone on the desk. Hank's phone. She sighed. He was forever getting distracted with projects and leaving his phone behind. Scooping it up, she put it in her pocket, wondering how much of the Callahan estate she was going to have to traverse before she found him.

It only took as far as the cottage.

"Bridey. Darling, over here."

She turned to see her mother waving at her. She lay on an Adirondack lounge chair stacked with cushions and it was positioned under the shade of one of the huge maple trees. With a sunhat on her head, Jackie Onassis-style sunglasses on her face, linen pants and a pastel cotton blouse, she looked the picture of 1960s refined elegance—right down to the Collins glass. Next to her was a table which held a glass pitcher and next to that sat Hank, holding a glass and looking slightly stunned. He rose to his feet and then sat down again.

With a sinking feeling, she crossed the grass. "Hi, Mom. It's great to see you out of the cottage."

"Mint julep, darling?" Her mother wafted her hand toward the pitcher. "Pour yourself one."

Her mother was famous for her mint juleps which invariably packed a punch and left people feeling smashed. "Are you sure you should be drinking when you're taking pain medication?"

"Bridey, I'm not a fool. This *is* today's pain medication." Kathleen patted Hank on the arm. "Are you sure about marrying her, Hank? She can be very contrary."

Hank smiled at Kathleen. "She does like things to be a particular way."

His unexpected words barreled into her, socking her hard. Hank always supported her. The fact he was agreeing with her mother added to her general unease which had been growing from the moment she'd proposed to him. Did he really want to marry her?

You're being ridiculous. He's teasing you with mint julep talk. Of course he wants to marry you. This is the twenty-first century. There's absolutely nothing wrong with a woman proposing to the man she loves. But the reassurance sounded faint and wobbly and did nothing to relieve her anxiety. She looped her hands around Hank's neck and pressed a kiss into his hair. "I've been looking all over for you."

He tilted his head back and his honey-brown eyes struggled to focus. "You found me."

Hank had the occasional beer at social gatherings but he didn't drink much. Even so, his height and breadth meant he could usually handle more than one drink but this cocktail was Kathleen's specialty and she was always liberal with the bourbon. "Did you have lunch?"

He grinned up at her. "No, ma'am. Sorry, ma'am."

"For heaven's sake, Bridey, you're not his mother." Kathleen patted the end of the lounge. "You need to relax. All this wedding planning is making you cross. Sit down, have a julep and start enjoying your vacation."

Hank patted her hand as if she was six and poured her a drink. "They're surprisingly good, Brides."

She stared at her mother and fiancé who were both buzzed and she felt as out of place as the only sober person at a party can. She knew right then she wasn't going to get any sense out of either of them. With a rising sense of panic she realized that the decision on the wedding venue was going to be put off yet again.

THIRTEEN

WHEN BRIDEY SAW Hank come downstairs the next morning wearing sunglasses, she silently handed him a glass of tomato juice and a handful of Vitamin B tablets. He'd crashed before dinner and had slept twelve hours straight. "What were you thinking?"

He took a sip of the juice, shuddered and put the glass on the table as he gingerly sat on a chair. "Don't start, Bridey."

He looked so unwell that she should have been sympathetic, but the unusual warning tone in his voice only ramped up her anger that had been simmering all night. She was furious with him, and her mother, for their impromptu lawn party that had ended up with her assisting both of them into their respective beds.

She folded her arms. "Not drinking on an empty stomach is something they teach you at high school."

Hank's eyes narrowed slightly. "I called in to see your mother who'd been expecting you or Finn. It was obvious she had cabin fever so I offered to set her up outside so she could enjoy the view, the breeze and do some reading. After I'd lugged everything she insisted she needed out under the tree and had arranged everything *exactly* the way she wanted, I was hot and sweaty. She offered me—" his fingers made quotation marks, "—'a refreshing drink.' I'd gulped down a glass before I had a clue what it was."

He rubbed his temples with a sigh. "I thought your family had Irish descendents, not Southern ones. You're the one who should have warned me about your mother's juleps."

"What can I say? The Irish love Irish whiskey, bourbon whiskey, any whiskey." She knew without a doubt she should have visited her mother yesterday morning because Kathleen was finding it difficult being at Kylemore and hated being dependent on people. As a result, her mom was often pedantic and Hank had been the recipient of all those emotions yesterday.

She quickly flattened the flicker of guilt and instead, justified to herself that the previous day's discussions about wedding invitations with Annika was an essential part of the foundations for her and Hank's future. She lugged a pile of magazines and her wedding planner from the side table, and with a thud, dumped them in front of Hank.

He flinched at the noise.

She didn't care. Everything depended on their wedding being perfect and that started with choosing the right venue. That decision must happen today. Flicking open the brochures from the Newberry Library and three other venues, she said, "I sent you the links to all these places last week." She smiled encouragingly. "So, where are we getting married?"

Hank grimaced. "My head's pounding, Bridey, and my mouth feels like the bottom of a birdcage."

"But you've read the information. Surely you must have some thoughts."

Hank took off his glasses and pinched the bridge of his nose. Despite his long sleep, fatigue still cloaked him. "I'm sorry, but I haven't checked out the links. Last week I worked seventeen hours a day and I'm not dealing with this until I've eaten something."

She couldn't stop herself. "If you'd eaten something yesterday we wouldn't be in this position."

He slowly slid his glasses back on his face and when he spoke his voice was cool. "Bridey, what's going on?"

All her frustrations of a delayed vacation and her rising fears generated by the weekend, collided and then morphed into a massive ball of disappointment. Disappointment edged with the golden gilt of fear—fear that Hank was slipping away from her. That he hadn't proposed to her because he didn't want to get married.

She threw her arms up in the air as her insecurities ignited her Irish temper. "*Nothing* is going on and that's the problem. I thought you came up here to see me, but instead you've spent time with everybody else in my family, and I've hardly seen you. Yesterday, when I finally found you, you were hammered. Now you're going back to Chicago and if we're getting married any time next year we've got decisions to make."

"Fine." Without taking a close look at any of the brochures, he picked one up. "This one."

He doesn't care. Her jaw tightened so much she could hardly speak. "Why?"

He sighed. "Bridey, if you're not happy with this choice then you choose."

No, you must be involved. She tried to keep the anxiety out of her voice. "I want to know why you chose this one."

He shrugged. "No particular reason. They all look the same."

Anger spurted. "No. They. Don't."

Hank tapped every brochure's picture of white-clothed tables and chairs. "Yes. They. Do."

With trembling fingers, she gathered up the brochures and shoved them back into the folder. "If you're going to be a jerk about this then don't even bother."

Censure shone in his eyes. "Now you're sounding like a spoiled child."

Shock at his criticism combined with the sting of his words, making her angrier. "I've put down deposits on four venues so we could make a personal choice but all you've done is random selection. Do you have any idea what has to happen between now and next July? How many decisions have to be made about everything from where we get married to the honeymoon, and a million tiny details in between? How can me wanting *our* wedding to be perfect make me spoiled?" Her fist hit her heart. "At least I care, which is more than you do at the moment."

Every hair on his body seemed to rise and he pressed his palms flat against the table as if that action would prevent him from doing something he might regret. He levered himself up slowly, his face as hard as granite. "I can't talk to you when you're like this. When you've got some perspective about the wedding plans, let me know."

For the first time ever, he turned his back on her and walked away.

His unfamiliar anger sent panic swirling through her, bumping and clanging against all her fears. "Hank, wait!"

But he disappeared though the door without a backward glance, and the rigid set of his shoulders told her there was absolutely no point following him.

Her stomach churned and her heart beat so fast it threatened to bruise itself on her ribs. She couldn't believe he'd left. They'd never argued about anything. *Until the engagement.* Her heart cramped. Since their engagement there'd been tiny disagreements, mostly over the party plans, but she'd smoothed them over. Today was very different.

She spun the ring on her finger—the ring Hank had paid for. The ring she'd chosen and ordered because when she'd asked him about rings, he'd kissed her and said, "Choose the one that makes you happy." At the time she'd thought it was the most romantic thing in the world for him to have said. Now her heart quivered with uncertainty. Was this ring just another example of him not caring about the wedding? Not caring about them? Why had he said yes to her proposal if he didn't want to get married?

He works for your father. He's spent the weekend with your family. The traitorous thought seeped into her like poison. The enormous diamond sparkled in the sunshine that poured in through the windows. The ring that represented indestructible love. Her falling tears didn't dent its mocking shine.

ANNIKA LOVED THE serenity of the cabin and the peace of the woods, but she missed Finn. She missed his laugh, she missed the warmth of his arms and, God help her, she missed the sex. Her body quivered at the merest thought of him but without Finn in bed next to her, the attraction of sleeping between the softness of high thread count sheets had faded quickly.

He'd been caught up in Chicago longer then he'd expected but in an act that made her heart sing, he'd made a flying visit late on Tuesday, leaving again early Wednesday. She'd felt slightly guilty when his alarm had gone off at 5:00 a.m. because they hadn't gotten a lot of sleep. The sex had been amazing as usual, but it was the lying in his arms with his fingers trailing through her hair, while they talked through the night, that she treasured most.

She'd kept to their agreed routine of spending the mornings in the office and the afternoons in the studio, but to help the long Finn-less evenings pass she'd pulled a couple of really late nights in the studio. She hadn't done any painting. She hadn't even unrolled the first two canvases of *Dawn* and *Day* because despite what Finn thought, she was far too busy to start painting and just the thought of it had her running scared.

Working late was good on so many levels and when she got back to the cabin she fell into an exhausted sleep which gave her no time to think about anything at all—especially how much she missed Finn. She couldn't allow herself to miss him because all of this was very, very temporary. She hauled her mind back to the computer screen in the office and started checking the email folders she'd created so she could keep the AKP work totally separate from her correspondence connected with Whitetail. Every day she checked in with Ellery and checked her Whitetail mail, hoping there'd be a nibble of interest from the one hundred and eighty information packs she'd sent out.

She hovered her mouse over an email from a Ty Dennison, not recognizing the name. She clicked the left side of the mouse.

"Esther said you were looking for me, Annika?"

She glanced up from the screen to see Sean strolling into the office with a smile on his face.

"Morning, Sean. Yes, I was." She picked up a black folder and handed it to him. "Finn asked me to give this to you."

His intelligent eyes gave her a dry look. "I heard the helicopter at six."

Something about the way he said it made her feel uncomfortable and it had nothing to do with the fact that Finn's family had probably worked out they were sleeping together. "He wants to be in Chicago if anything else flares up with the Jazz Juice account."

He nodded slowly. "Of course he does."

The message buried in Sean's words was clear. Finn spent the least amount of time possible with his father. "I'm sorry, Sean, I can only tell you what he told me."

"When do you expect him back?"

Not soon enough. "Friday."

"Ah." He tapped the folder on his thigh.

She found herself blurting out, "Can I help with anything, Sean?" *I'm already trying to get him to talk to you.*

"Not unless you're a miracle worker." He gave her a sad smile. "I've done a lot of things I'm not proud of and this problem's all mine and mine to fix." He rested one buttock on the edge of her desk. "So, how are things with you, Annika? Sounds like you're busy. I heard you on the radio this morning selling the concept of Whitetail as the new hub of heartland manufacturing."

She groaned. "I was trying hard to but it turns out the interviewer had just got engaged and she was more interested in talking about the wedding expo the town put on the day I went to court."

"Bridey tells me you might be designing her invitations so a bit of free advertising on the radio can't hurt."

She was getting weary of trying to explain her concerns about Weddings That WOW. "I find it hard to imagine that it could provide the level of employment the town needs."

He rubbed his chin. "People spend a lot of money on weddings, Annika. Bridey's almost bankrupted me on deposits alone, and yesterday she was mumbling something about a nine-thousand-dollar wedding cake."

"Nine thous—" Annika choked on her indrawn breath and started coughing violently.

Sean rose and poured her a glass of water before handing it to her with a smile. "That was pretty much my reaction too. I'll let you get back to work."

She nodded her goodbye, still trying to find her breath and after sipping the water she finally read the now opened email.

Dear Ms. Jacobson,

Long River Electronics is looking to expand and is interested in visiting your town. I wish to fly in next week and would appreciate you confirming Tuesday at 2 p.m. I look forward to meeting with you and touring the facilities.

Ty Dennison
CEO and owner of Long River Electronics

Annika blinked and read it three times before she let out a whoop of delight. She grabbed her phone wanting to share the good news. Her fingers bounced over the keypad in excitement and it was only when the call defaulted to voice mail that she realized she'd phoned Finn instead of Ellery. She refused to consider that meant anything more than a momentary lapse due to excitement.

KATHLEEN WAS BOTH bored and worried and the combination made her restless. Almost two weeks had passed since she'd injured herself and the swelling on her ankle had gone down but now the bruising had come up. A swirl of purple-and-yellow tie-dye marked her skin but at least she was graduating from crutches to a walking stick. This should have made her happy, but she was worried about her daughter.

Bridey had visited her earlier in the day with a long list of wedding-related questions but when Kathleen had offered up her requested opinions, Bridey had briskly rejected every single one of them, yet she seemed to be having trouble making any decisions at all. Finally, when she'd questioned Bridey about her almost zealot approach to the wedding, Bridey's face had gone white and tight, she'd gathered up her magazines and computer, and she'd left.

Kathleen knew something was bothering her but her daughter wasn't saying what it was and with Finn currently in Chicago and unavailable to ask, she was at a loss. Not that she was certain Finn knew what Bridey's problem was, or even if he did know, that he'd tell her. Her children had become very self-sufficient during the separation and divorce, and in many ways were now a tight unit that excluded her. As painful as it was to admit, it had probably happened because she and Sean had been obsessed with trying to hurt each other. All that emotional energy had excluded the children. When she'd finally come out of the post-divorce funk and had started rebuilding her life, it had taken every ounce of strength she had. By the time she'd got herself together, the children appeared to have little need of her. She'd spent years trying to make it up to them but she'd never reclaimed all the ground she'd lost. Sean hadn't even tried.

Being back at the lake was one of the hardest things she'd done in years, and she was using every cent of the thousands of dollars she'd spent on yoga in the past decade to stay calm. The loss of the lake had cut deeply and she'd avoided coming to northern Wisconsin for nineteen years but when Bridey wanted her engagement party up here, of course she'd come. When Bridey had insisted she return to help her with the wedding plans, she'd come, never envisaging in a million years she'd have to stay at Kylemore. If that wasn't tough enough, now Bridey was stressing out about the wedding which was still months away.

She sighed and decided that fresh air and a change of scene were needed. She hobbled out to the deck and collapsed onto the lounge chair. Gray clouds hovered, cooling the day and the usually sparkling lake looked like she felt—dull and listless. Remembering her meditation, she focused on a tree on the shore and tried to let her mind empty of everything. Tried to find her hard-earned peace with herself and her life.

Her breath moved in and out, long and slow, and the first sensations of calm trickled through her, seeping in like a restorative balm. Her body sank fully into the lounge chair and she could feel the soft cushion molding to her back. Something hit her. She looked down in surprise to find a small, bouncy ball on her lap and then she heard the sound of running feet.

"Sorry, ma'am. I didn't mean to hit you."

Kathleen had met Logan for the first time at Bridey's engagement party and had been struck by how much he looked like Finn at the same age. "What were you trying to hit?"

His eyes widened. "Nothing. Not you. I mean just the wood." He stared at his sneaker for a moment and then looked up. "The ball bounces really high off this deck," he added by way of explanation.

She smiled at a memory. "Finn used to play with balls like this and he said this deck had the best bounce."

Logan looked unconvinced. "Finn never wants to play with balls."

"He did when he was eight." She rolled the ball around in her hand remembering the time Finn's baseball had gone through the library window. "Would you like a glass of lemonade? Esther put a pitcher in my fridge and if you carry it out here, I can pour us both a glass."

"Awesome."

As Logan rushed into the cottage, Kathleen used her stick and walked into her bedroom. By the time she came out again Logan had the jug, some glasses and a bag of cookies he must have found, all set up on the outdoor table.

Logan eyed the stick. "Can I try?"

She laughed. "Go ahead." She watched him playing with it as she poured the drinks.

He sat back down and politely passed the stick back to her. "It's too big for me."

"One day it will be too small for you. You're probably going to grow as tall as Finn."

"Yeah?" Hope scooted across his face.

Kathleen nodded as she opened up the small photo album she'd retrieved from her purse—the one she always carried with her. "This is a photo of Finn when he was eight."

The boy leaned forward and peered at the picture. "Hey, that's here."

"That's right. I told you he liked to play on this deck."

Logan's face filled with interest. "He showed me how to light a fire. Are there more photos?"

"Sure." She turned the page and started telling Logan the story about each one.

They were halfway into the album when she heard Sean's deep voice calling out, "Logan?"

Kathleen's calm fled and every muscle tensed.

Logan jumped up and waved. "Over here, Daddy."

Sean's long legs took the steps two at a time and if

he was surprised that his son was visiting with her, he didn't show it.

He gave her a stiff nod. "Kathleen."

"Sean." The distance the divorce had wedged between them hadn't altered in the intervening years, only now instead of it being a living, hissing thing that drove her, it was just a deadweight that made her ache. She didn't love Sean anymore but she didn't hate him either as she once had. In fact, these days whenever she thought about their marriage, their divorce, their children and everything they'd lost, she only felt sadness and regret that they hadn't handled it all better.

He turned to Logan. "Hey, buddy, Mom's looking for you so head on home, okay?"

"Okay." Logan stood up. "Thank you for the lemonade, Mrs. um, Finn's mom."

"Call me Kathleen, and you're welcome, Logan. Come visit again."

He ran off with a wave and Sean turned to leave but stopped on the top step and doubled back. "Do you have everything you need, Kathleen?"

A hint of the Irish charm she'd fallen in love with when he'd swept her off her feet at twenty-two, hovered in the question, surprising her. It had vanished with the divorce and for a long time their only communication had been through lawyers. Finally, they'd settled into brief and strained discussions about the children. Of course now Finn and Bridey were adults, they didn't communicate at all. Bridey's engagement party was the first time she'd seen Sean in years. "I have everything I need, thank you."

"You've been comfortable here?"

"The cottage is perfect." She instantly regretted her choice of words as they immediately hinted at the bitter divorce settlement and that hadn't been her intention at all. She braced herself for his reply.

He ran his hand through his hair and silver glinted brightly in the sun. "You did a great job on its design."

His complimentary words shocked her. She loved this cottage and had loved every minute of working on its design and supervising the build. Losing it in the divorce had been like losing a limb. Today was the first time Sean had ever acknowledged her connection to it. She accepted his unexpected olive branch. "Thank you."

He saw the photo album and flicked a page. "Is that Bridey and Finn at breakfast on the farm?"

She leaned in to check. "Yes. Just before she threw up all over my shoes after eating too many pancakes and maple syrup." She laughed. "Good times."

He sat down and kept turning the pages. "We did have some good times."

She thought about their first ten years. "We did, before it all fell apart."

He gave her a thoughtful look. "Do you think we'd have made it even if I hadn't been unfaithful?"

She'd asked herself that question many times and as much as she'd found it hard to admit, there'd been signs before his infidelity that they weren't suited to live together for fifty years. "I think it accelerated something that was inevitable."

He was quiet for a moment. "I've taken a long time to grow up, and I'm sorry for the pain I caused you. Caused us." He gave her a sad smile. "Are you happy, Kathleen?"

His apology and question hit from left field, sending her reeling and she didn't quite know what to say. "I'm comfortable and I live a useful life involved in my community and surrounded by good friends."

His mouth jerked up on one side. "That sounds like

something out of a self-help book. I want to know if you're happy."

She thought about her project with the Art Institute and the fledging friendship with a new man in her life who'd sent flowers and fruit to the cottage and had telephoned her each morning since she'd hurt her ankle. She thought about Bridey and Finn. "For the most part, I think I am. Are you?"

"I'm getting there." His hand stilled on the photo of Finn standing next to his own father, proudly holding up a musky. "I really screwed up with the kids, didn't I?"

She saw the same pain on his face that she knew lived in her heart, and it made her reach out to him in a way she'd never done since he'd betrayed her with his business intern. "We both did."

"You at least made it to the ball games and ballet recitals. I let them down all the time because I was too busy being the hotshot entrepreneur putting the business ahead of them." He rubbed his cheek and sighed. "Over the last few years, Bridey and I seem to have found a middle ground, but Finn, well, he's a damn fine businessman but for all that I know about what's important to him outside of AKP, he might as well be an employee. You're closer to him than I'll ever be."

She heard his regrets and they resonated deeply against her own. "Perhaps, but I feel a distance too. We put it there, Sean. We inserted it when we got caught up in the drama of us, and I think we've lost the opportunity to fix it. I take what I can get and try not to lament the rest."

His shoulders slumped and he finished his son's glass of lemonade. "And now I have Logan. I know I'll make mistakes there too, but this time it won't be because I'm absent."

She stifled the bite of jealousy that Sean had a second chance with a child, and instead thought about how much she was looking forward to becoming a grandmother. She hoped Bridey and Hank didn't wait too long before starting a family. "Logan's a lovely kid and he's at such a great age. They love doing things with their parents at eight."

"Yeah." He pushed up from the chair deep in thought. "Would you come to dinner one night, Kathleen?"

Years of protective armor was hard to drop. "I'm not sure that's such a good idea. Your wife—"

"Dana was the one who insisted you stay here after your accident and she wants you at our table."

She fingered the edge of her sleeve, wanting to attend but still slightly stunned by this mellow version of her ex-husband. "And what about you, Sean? Do you want me at your table? We don't have the best track record of being civil at family gatherings."

He spoke softly. "We've just had a conversation I want to build on, Kathleen."

She recognized his expression—the one that meant he was deadly serious and not about to go back on his word. She knew she wanted the same thing—a chance for their children to be able to enjoy their parents in the same space without the anguish, pain and hurt. "So do I."

He grinned at her. "Let's shock Bridey and Finn speechless."

She smiled. "Looking forward to it."

FOURTEEN

"I'VE GOT SOME great news." Annika addressed the town meeting with a wide smile.

"You've convinced Bridget Callahan to change her mind?" Melissa's hopeful expression was replicated around the room.

She shook her head, swallowed a sigh and tried to think about the best way to get the message through to everybody that Bridey getting married in Whitetail was *never* going to happen. "I think we all have to accept that that train has left the station. Bridget Callahan wants to get married in Chicago and it's time to let that idea go."

Nicole stood up and addressed the room. "We've got four weddings booked now."

"Four?" A clutch of unease gripped her that she was not only out of the information loop but that she hadn't been at the fourth bride meeting.

"You weren't available, Anni, but don't worry, we showed her your portfolio and she's going to contact you." Nicole turned back to the room. "This bride's getting married next May and she wants to have the ceremony in the gazebo, her photos on the town hall steps and then travel in Al's carriage to the Supper Club for the reception. She wants Mrs. Norell to make her cake and she asked if we had a wedding photographer we could recommend. Now that's something we need to think about because right now, Whitetail doesn't have one."

"Anni," Mrs. Norell beamed, "this will please you. See, there's one new job for the town."

One job. One! Annika gripped her gavel in exasperation and brought it down hard on the lectern. The sound reverberated around the room.

Some people blinked at her, others jumped in their seats and as Nicole sat down, she shot her a questioning look loaded with disapproval.

Annika tried not to mind Nicole's expression and justified her action under the heading of "whatever it takes." "And it's new jobs that I want to tell you about. We have an electronics company from Mississippi looking to open a branch on the other side of the Mason-Dixon line, and the owner's expressed interest in Whitetail. He's coming next week for a tour of the town."

A murmur of interest buzzed around the room. "How many jobs, Anni?" Clint Eklund asked. "As many as Reggies?"

She shook her head. "Initially ten jobs but that's ten more than we have right now and ten jobs that are reliable and not seasonal."

"Actually, Anni," Melissa said, "we've had an inquiry about a winter wedding from a bride whose fiancé is a snowmobiler. They want the wedding to be part of a snowmobiling weekend. I suggested a perfect-white, velvet A-line wedding dress with fur trim."

All the women in the room started nodding their approval and Al's eyes lit up. "I could restore the old sleigh. That would be perfect for winter weddings. There's nothing like the sound of sleigh bells tinkling."

"That's if you can hear them over the roar of a blizzard." The strength of Annika's annoyance surprised her. She usually had more patience. "People, a winter wedding this far north is fraught with logistical problems. Who in this town has ever got married in winter?"

Four hands shot up including Nicole's, and Annika's face instantly burned. She wished she could snatch back her words. She remembered that pretty wedding on a miraculously perfect blue-sky winter's day that had dawned after a week of blizzards. Everyone had taken it as a sign—a blessing on a union that would stretch long into the future. Seven years later it had been tragically cut short.

"I'm sorry, I take it back but can we please just focus on Long River Electronics?" She shuffled her papers. "This is really an important meeting for us all. I can't stress this enough so I think we need to work really hard at giving the owner of this company a true White-tail welcome."

Farmer Luke, a good friend of her brother, gave her a smile. "You can rely on us, Anni."

Murmurs of agreement buzzed around the room and no one mentioned weddings. Annika blew out a breath of sheer relief.

Things were finally back on track.

Two HOURS LATER, Annika called into the cottage to deliver a gorgeous arrangement of sunflowers that had arrived for Kathleen. "These have to be the happiest flowers I know."

"They are cheery," Kathleen agreed. "Would you mind filling them up with water for me, please?"

Annika picked up the small plastic watering can and looked at the numerous vases of flowers dotted around the cottage. "Would you like me to go through them all and weed out the dead ones?"

Kathleen's grateful expression said it all. "That would

be wonderful, thank you. I really should tell Geoffrey that I have enough flowers but…"

Annika knew how she felt. "It's lovely to be treasured."

"It is, even if I have no clue how long it will last."

She glanced at the older woman wondering if she was trying to tell her something, which was crazy because Annika knew exactly how long she and Finn had— Labor Day was their end point. "But you're enjoying it while you can."

"Exactly." Kathleen smiled. "Finn tells me you're an artist, which is something you failed to mention when I was rambling on about the Art Institute."

Her heart kicked up but she kept her focus on pulling out the dead flowers which ironically reflected her artistic career perfectly. "I was interested in hearing about the program."

"You're very kind. I do love it and it's one of the things that gets me up out of bed in the mornings."

She wondered what else Finn had told his mother and then she remembered her promise to him a week ago when she'd been painting the mural. "Kathleen, what do you know about the failure of the Raybould Gallery?"

"Ryan Raybould should be shot for what he did to his family's and the city's art heritage." Kathleen's eyes sparked with indignation and her shoulders rolled back. "His great-grandfather would have disowned him and wept, had he been alive when the collection was sold to pay Ryan's gambling debts. That young man's addiction took a lot of people down with him and sadly, many of the artists who held exhibitions there in the last year never got paid."

She'd believed Finn when he'd told her that her exhibition wasn't the reason things had failed but the fact he'd wanted her to hear it from another source made her warm and tingly. Kathleen was looking at her but without any expectation of a comment and she realized Finn had kept her secret and he hadn't told his mother about her connection to Ryan or the gallery. Perhaps it was Kathleen's indignation or perhaps it was just the passing of time, but something made her say, "I exhibited there."

Concern whipped across her cheeks. "Oh, I do hope you didn't lose money or artwork."

"No, nothing like that." *Just my ability to paint.*

"Well that's good to know. Is any of your work part of a permanent collection?"

Annika shook her head as the words *immature*, *derivative* and *lacking substantive style*—words that were carved on her heart—got converted to audio and boomed in her head. "My work is a long way from being in demand."

Kathleen gave a quiet smile. "It only takes *one* painting, Annika."

But she didn't have another painting in her. Annika wrapped the dead flowers in paper and walked toward the door. "I'll take these and put them in Dana's compost bin."

"That's a good idea. Can you tell me, is Finn coming back tonight?"

Kathleen's hopeful gaze sent a thread of sadness through her. Both of Finn's parents wanted to see their son but they seemed to feel they couldn't ask him about his plans. Both were depending on her. The sadness suddenly twisted back on her when she realized she was in a similar position. Finn came and went and she was the one always waiting.

But that's implicit in an affair and you're not family.
The thought failed to reassure her.

As if on cue, her phone chirped, announcing an incoming message, and she pulled it out of her pocket. Reading the liquid display, she hugged a smile to herself. "He says midafternoon tomorrow."

"Perfect. If you'd asked me a few weeks ago if I wanted to be laid up with a severely sprained ankle, I would have said 'no.' But it's giving me extra time with Bridey and Finn, and I had a lovely afternoon with Hank last weekend."

"I'm glad it's all working out for you." Annika could feel water dripping onto her leg through the paper and she slid open the glass door.

"Finn doesn't say much about his life, Annika, but I know for a fact you're the first woman he's ever brought to the cabin."

"Well, he didn't really bring me. I pretty much arrived uninvited when I lost my rental accommodation and he refused to let me stay at the warehouse."

"As it should be. I did *try* to raise him to think of others but he mostly thinks of work. Sean and I didn't give him the best example of marital harmony."

Annika didn't know what to say to this except, "I imagine divorce is tough on everyone."

"I do hope my son is treating you as well you deserve."

Her mouth fell open and this time nothing came out.

"You're dripping water on the floor, dear." Kathleen picked up her book and started reading, signaling the end of the conversation.

Annika tripped over the sliding door flange as she walked out.

BRIDEY DIDN'T HAVE to weigh herself to know she'd lost five pounds. Her face looked longer and her engagement ring spun loosely on her finger.

"I've made your favorite." Esther slid an enormous slice of pie across the counter—deep lemony-yellow custard and a decadent amount of meringue, complete with a hint of a golden brown on the fluffy peaks. "Eat."

Bridey plunged her fork into the pie knowing it would be filled with the wonderful combination of sugary sweet and sharp tangy taste, but when it reached her mouth it lost its flavor. She pushed the plate away. "Just coffee, Esther."

The housekeeper rolled her eyes. "Whatever it is that's bothering you must be catastrophic if you're not eating my pie."

Bridey closed her eyes and thought about the brief and tension-filled phone calls she'd shared with Hank all week. She'd called on Sunday night and apologized for not waiting until he'd had breakfast before starting the wedding discussion. He'd said, "Thank you, Bridey."

Nothing else. Nothing about the wedding, nothing about how he'd been less tolerant due to being hungover, not even an "I'm sorry too"—absolutely nothing.

What did it mean? She felt like she was tiptoeing through a minefield and their conversations—if you could call them that—had been filled with distance and long pauses. Unable to face talking about wedding venues again because she was worried it would bring them back to the argument, she'd sent him an email telling him she'd chosen the InterContinental. His reply had been, "Okay." Four small letters that bruised her heart.

She didn't know what to think and she didn't know what to do. Every time she mentioned the wedding to Hank during their evening phone call, she pictured his face tightening and his eyes closing as if the thought of marrying her was akin to torture. Her mother had actively tried to talk to her about the plans two or three times this week, but her interest and enthusiasm had stung like salt in an open wound. When Kathleen had asked her what was wrong, she couldn't voice the dread-filled words that constantly crawled through her and she'd fled from the cottage.

Now she accepted the coffee mug that Esther had slid across the counter and went for a general answer. "I miss Hank."

"He was here five days ago." Esther briskly filled the sink with hot, soapy water.

That's not what I mean. He's been missing since we got engaged. "I know."

"And?"

And I think he's regretting the idea of marrying me. "And…I don't know. Last weekend he seemed different."

Esther stilled her hands on the edge of the sink. "Honey, he looked exhausted last weekend and, believe me, after two weeks of stress a man is rarely communicative."

Ignoring the memories of the strained phone calls during the week, Bridey clung on to this bit of news like a personal flotation device in a stormy sea. "You think he was just tired?"

"That man was asleep on his feet." Esther scrubbed the large lasagna dish. "The drama at the plant's over now. Your Hank's going to be arriving soon, so stop your moping and go put on a pretty dress. Your father's hosting a party tonight and it's perfect weather for dancing under the stars."

She dreamily thought of how Hank expertly spun her around the floor at their engagement party. "Hank can dance."

Esther smiled. "I noticed. He even made me feel light on my feet."

Bridey stood up feeling a lot happier. Esther always had the best advice and if Bridey had been thinking more clearly earlier in the week, she'd have talked to her a lot sooner. She thought about the new backless dress she'd bought and smiled. It had a bodice that hugged her tight, accenting all the right curves in all the right places before floating out from the waist in layers and layers of gauzy chiffon. It would knock Hank's socks off and hopefully a lot more than that. She instantly pulled out her phone. This weekend she wasn't leaving anything to chance. She didn't care if there were comments and winks. This time she and Hank were going to stay in town at the motel and have mind-blowing sex, no matter what.

Esther inclined her head and the faint buzz of the helicopter got increasingly louder. "Sounds like you don't have to wait any longer."

A whoop of delight spun through her. She gave Esther a kiss and ran out to the helipad, excitement simmering. The shiny, black machine with its enormous rotors lowered down neatly onto the big, white *H*, and then with a slow whine the engine noise died away. The pilot opened the doors and Finn stepped out with a smile and a wave, which Bridey returned as she gazed beyond him.

He gave her a hug. "Hey, sis, where's Annika?"

She distractedly returned his hug. "I'm guessing the office or the studio. She's almost as much of a workaholic as you are."

Finn grinned, pulled out his phone and started to walk toward the house.

Bridey bounced up and down on the balls of her feet and held her breath. Hank would be out next. Hank would stride over to her, swing her up in his arms, kiss her on the lips and say, "I've missed you so much. Let's never argue again."

The sun reflected a golden haze as Hank disembarked but instead of walking toward her, he immediately turned back toward the helicopter and extended his arm inside as if he was assisting someone else.

Had some of her father's guests flown up? She'd thought the party was for the neighbors but she hadn't actually inquired given that her mind had been elsewhere.

She watched in jaw-dropping astonishment as one by one, Hank's parents alighted from the helicopter.

"Bridey." Marion walked toward her with open arms. "Surprise."

Stunned, she hugged the older woman and tried to catch Hank's eye but he was standing next to his father and pointing something out on the helicopter.

Marion hooked her arm through Bridey's. "We were so sorry to miss your party and very touched that your father invited us up this weekend."

"Dad invited you?" As she tried to absorb that bit of news, she glanced over her shoulder at Hank.

He crossed the short distance between them and kissed her on the cheek as if she was his sister. "Hello, Bridey."

Before she could say anything, Bob's voice hailed him. "Hank, come on back. The pilot's offering us a seat in the cockpit."

Marion shook her head and with a conspiratorial air, she leaned into Bridey. "Boys and their machines."

Bridey could see herself about to be separated from Hank and there was no way was she allowing that to happen. "Actually, Marion, I love helicopters."

"I expect you do having grown up around them but

it's all new to Bob and Hank." Her future mother-in-law patted her hand. "Let's leave them alone to talk engines and we'll have a lovely, cozy chat about the wedding."

No!

Bridey opened her mouth to suggest a counter plan but her brain drained at Hank's wide mouth curving into a quiet smile—the one she'd fallen in love with the day she met him. A silent sigh wove through her and she knew that Esther's prediction was correct. Hank was here and everything was going to be all right.

"If you're talking weddings," Hank said, "then I'm definitely staying with Dad." He walked off with a wave.

The fear that had been momentarily waylaid by her conversation with Esther, barreled back into Bridey with the force of a tsunami, making her sway on her feet.

"Oh my. Is *that* the house?" Marion's eyes lit up and she tugged on Bridey's arm and started walking. "I'd love a tour."

Bridey had no choice but to follow.

HAD KATHLEEN'S ANKLE allowed it, she would have been pacing. As it didn't, she sat stabbing a cross-stitch sampler with a needle and thread, but she was unpicking more than she was keeping. Tonight, Sean was throwing a small party for Bridey's future in-laws and she was going. She shouldn't be nervous. Last night she'd faced down the beast of her anxiety and spent an hour with Dana and Sean. Logan had implored her to go to his cookout and without Bridey or Finn in attendance, she'd had to summon all her courage to go. Although she'd only stayed an hour and had spent a lot of it chatting with Logan, she'd unexpectedly enjoyed herself.

Sitting down with Dana had seemed surreal and they

hadn't done much more than discuss the weather. Dana had inquired politely about the Art Institute program and Kathleen in turn had asked about Dana's children's charity. To an outsider it would have sounded like polite, social chitchat but it had been so much more than that—it was a new beginning. Sure, at the start, she'd felt on edge but it had faded quickly once she recognized in Dana a mutual desire to find a level of connection they could both feel comfortable with. What that was exactly, she wasn't certain.

A rap sounded on the glass and she looked up in surprise as it was too early for the quad bike transportation to the party. Dana stood on the other side of the glass with a traveler coffee cup in her hand and a nervous look on her face.

Kathleen thought she probably wore the same look. She waved and called out, "Come in."

Dana gave a tentative smile and slid open the door. "Hello, Kathleen."

Hostess Kathleen kicked in. "Hello, Dana. Have a seat. That coffee smells good."

"It's hazelnut. My guilty pleasure. Sean says it's…" Dana trailed off and her face pinked up.

"'A poor excuse for coffee.'" Kathleen finished the sentence. "A poor excuse being anything that Sean doesn't like."

Dana nodded. "I'm sorry, I shouldn't have mentioned—"

"Don't be sorry. You're married to Sean and of course you're going to mention him in conversation. You've made a better success of things with him than I did."

Dana shrugged. "Perhaps I was lucky enough to meet him when he was finally ready to settle down."

"And you didn't *have* to get married." Kathleen

smiled. "Thankfully, there was another wife in between us which means you and I have no reason to dislike each other." She fiddled with her own coffee cup and decided on honesty. "Although, you should know that I envy you Kylemore. A lot."

Dana met her gaze. "I understand. I love this place too."

Kathleen could see and hear the truth of Dana's statement and she made herself give this warm woman the compliment she deserved. "You've done a wonderful job with the garden."

"Thank you." Dana's smile lost some of its tentativeness. "I guess you put yourself into this cottage like I've put myself into the garden. I know a part of me would shrivel if I had to leave it behind."

Kathleen's hand tightened on the sampler. "I felt like I'd lost a limb." She blew out a long breath. "I'm very sorry I was so rude to you at Bridey's engagement when you offered me the use of the cottage. It's just it brought back a lot of unhappy memories which, ironically, my sprained ankle has made me face."

"We're just glad you're here," Dana said simply.

They lapsed into silence that combined fledgling companionship with a thousand unasked questions.

Dana lowered her cup. "I guess you're wondering why I'm here. It's Bridey."

Kathleen frowned. "What about Bridey?"

Dana sucked in a breath. "I know things can get fraught a few weeks before a wedding but she's at the early planning stages and—"

"She's already flipping out."

"Yes. I'm so glad you've noticed too."

"I've tried to talk about it with her but she's not saying anything, but that's not unusual with Bridey. She tends to hold everything in." She sighed and voiced a hard truth. "Or perhaps she just holds it in with me. Have you asked her about her extreme focus on all the minutiae?"

"I wanted to check with you first."

Gratitude rushed in. "Thank you for that consideration. Please *do* ask her because she might tell you more. I just want her to be happy. I want both my children to be happy."

Dana nodded. "So do I."

IT WAS GETTING late and the jazz band Sean had hired for the evening shifted down a gear. Finn pulled Annika in close as the slow number started and the saxophone crooned its long and sexy lament. Not that they were on the dance floor any more—he'd danced her away from it during a fast set and they'd taken off their shoes and wandered hand in hand along the shoreline until they'd reached the base of the tree house, which was a good distance away from the main house. The moon was waning but it was a clear night and its milky light danced on the water.

He leaned against the tree, breathing in her scent of wildflowers with a hint of Indian ink, and loving the touch of her against him. He'd missed that so much that he'd flown home midweek just so he could have her warm, relaxed and sleeping body snuggled in against his. Sex with Annika had exceeded his wildest dreams and, not that he had anything against the comfort of making love with her in his bed, but he also knew how she loved it when they gave in to the rush of getting naked where they stood.

With that in mind, he'd spent the week organizing something for Annika and he'd needed some time before dinner to check the arrangements, so today he'd been the one hurrying Hank along so they could leave Chicago on time. It was going to be the perfect end to a huge but fulfilling week. Everything was finally back on an even keel at the Illinois plant, and all their customers were happy. Finn was in a celebratory mood and returning to the lake had never felt so good. Even so, he'd kept Annika close at dinner, expecting the usual fireworks seeing as Sean and Kathleen were within a ten-foot radius of each other. But that had been the biggest surprise of the night.

He wound strands of her hair around his finger loving the idea that he didn't have to leave the lake or Annika anytime soon, and the weeks between now and Labor Day stretched out before them to be enjoyed. "You might not realize it but tonight you witnessed a miracle."

She lifted her head and smiled at him. "And what was that?"

"My mother and father managed to sit down at a table and share a meal without any cutting remarks or rapid-fire put-downs. Bridey and I are in shock."

Slight reproach filled her eyes. "You're exaggerating, right? With Hank's parents visiting, of course they're going to be civil."

He shook his head. "Sean and Kathleen set the record for post-divorce public scenes no matter who was present including a very well-known New York billionaire. We barely got through the engagement party so tonight was not only bewildering but totally unexpected."

Her fingers played with the cotton of his sleeve. "I hope for all your sakes it's a new beginning."

A bristle of unease prickled him. "Things are fine the way they are."

Her brows rose but all she said was, "It was nice of

Sean to throw a mini party tonight so the Neiquests got a feel for the party they missed."

Tension started to coil in his belly like a snake. "I think you'll find it was Dana's idea."

She shrugged. "Even so, he didn't have to go along with it."

The snake struck. "You might think you know my father, but you don't."

"I know the side I see, and I think that it's different from what you see."

"Damn straight." He could picture his evening vanishing into an argument which he did not want so he immediately changed tack. "Why are we talking about my father when we could be making out?"

"Because maybe you need to talk about him."

Like hell I do. "So tell me, Annika, how's the painting coming along?"

She tensed in his arms.

Bingo. Her reaction was exactly as he'd expected. Although he knew she'd duck the question and change the subject, it made him sad. Annika had a huge amount of talent and she was hiding from it.

She smiled at him brightly. "Did I tell you I've got two companies coming up next week to tour the warehouses? I snagged one with my mass mail-outs and just after the town meeting today, Ellery called me with another. Just think, Whitetail might be in the middle of a bidding war and how good would that be for the town?"

"That would be great for the town." And he spoke the truth. It would indeed be great for the town but he wasn't so sure it would be great for Annika.

"So we've both had a good week."

He gazed down at her. "I know the perfect way to end it."

"Do you now?" Her eyes glowed and she rose on her toes, pressing her lips to his. He immediately tightened his arms around her and lost himself in her softness, taste and heat.

Annika sighed into Finn's mouth as she relinquished control of the kiss and allowed him to take charge. She opened up to the wonder he sent surging through her body. His tongue took a long, slow and tantalizing journey, exploring every nook and crevice until she was weak with longing.

He finally raised his head and with a thick voice filled with desire said, "Can you climb the tree house steps in that dress?"

"If I can't, I'll take it off."

He groaned softly. "You're every man's fantasy."

She laughed, hugging the compliment to herself. "I aim to please." Already shoeless, she accepted a boost from Finn and started climbing. Ten steps later she was standing in the penthouse of all tree houses, complete with a balcony.

Finn arrived behind her, immediately opened an old tin box, pulled out a flashlight and switched it on. She saw a small cooler, some candles and a box of matches. The hiss of the match filled the air with a puff of sulfur and then by flickering light she saw masses of cushions.

Surprise and gratitude filled her. First a lovely evening where he'd been amazingly attentive, followed by a dusk walk along the lake, which was her favorite time of day apart from sunrise, and now all this. He'd set up a romantic space in the canopy of an ancient tree. "How did you manage all this?"

"I had help. Logan hauled the cushions."

"Logan knows that we're...?"

"God, no, he's eight."

For the first time, she glimpsed brotherly affection on his face.

"My half brother is all Callahan. I told him I wanted to sleep over in the tree house just like when I was a kid. Of course I hadn't thought that through very well because he wanted to come too. So to cut a long story short, Logan and I are going kayaking together tomorrow and sometime soon, I'm spending a night here with him. That kid drives a hard bargain."

Her heart quivered. Finn, who'd started the summer avoiding his little half brother, had now cut a deal with Logan just for her. "You really are a Boy Scout."

He grinned. "Being Prepared is far more useful than your 4-H stuff."

"Is that so?" She hooked her hands around his waistband and unhooked the fastener on his pants. "So you don't want me to pledge my hands to larger service."

He gazed down at her with the flicker of light reflected in his eyes and spoke softly. "I want all of you."

He kissed her gently as if she was porcelain and would shatter under his touch, and then, unlike every other time they'd had sex, he undressed her slowly without any trace of urgency. He slid her dress off her shoulders, unhooked her bra and drew it reverently down her arms, and then he stared at her in the candlelight. "I never get tired of looking at you."

She'd never felt so treasured. She reached her arms up around his neck and he caught her around her waist and laid her down on the makeshift bed. He used his body to worship her and it was only when she was racing toward her third release and begging him by name, that he entered her. Hard and sleek, he eased into her so slowly that it was sheer torture and she sunk her fingers into his shoulders, demanding in a whispered scream that he fill her hard, and fill her now. Only then did he oblige and she cried out in sheer relief that he was finally hers.

"Annika." He gasped her name as he drove into her.

Her body shuddered around him, gripping him tightly as his rhythm swept her up and took her soaring with him. She shattered into a thousand pieces of utter bliss.

Finally, when her breathing had slowed and the fragments of herself had reassembled, she realized that her heart was missing one piece—the part she'd given to him.

Somehow she managed to swallow her cry of shocked surprise and dismay. She'd thought she was so clever and so safe with this affair. She thought she'd protected herself completely but it was all just smoke and mirrors. She had no protection at all—her barricades were trampled and her moat completely drained. She loved him. She loved the way his eyes crinkled when he smiled, and how he teased her about her clumsiness but caught her when she stumbled. She loved how he lay in bed with her nestled in his arms and talked about his work but also took the time to ask about hers. She foolishly and unwisely loved him with every breath she took.

She didn't know whether to laugh or cry, so she did the only thing she could. She kissed him.

FIFTEEN

Bridey had the feeling she was floating outside her normal world—an observer of her own life except she didn't recognize much of it. Kathleen had come for dinner, which wasn't unexpected because the party was being thrown specially for Hank's parents, but what stunned her was the fact her mother hadn't left the moment it was polite to do so. Sure, Kathleen had mostly chatted with Finn and Annika and the Neiquests, but she'd also passed pleasantries with Sean and Dana. Used to seeing Kathleen with shoulder-squaring tension, Bridey was disconcerted to find her mother almost relaxed. She'd even had a sit-down game of catch with Logan before excusing herself when the dancing started.

"Bridey, that was my foot." Hank's hand tightened on her waist as he steadied her.

"Sorry. I was thinking about Mom."

"Yours or mine?" He spun her out.

"Mine." She wished the band would play a slow number so she could snuggle up to Hank. "I think her being at Kylemore might have actually helped her and Dad a little bit."

"Isn't that what you wanted?"

"Yes, but I never thought it would happen." Not that her parents were doing more than circling each other politely but it was better than what used to happen. She thought of Marion and Bob whose affection for each other was in sharp contrast to her parents. "When did you find out your parents were coming up?"

"When they arrived at the plant." He dipped her and pulled her back, giving her a smile. "They're so excited about this weekend that they're like two kids at a theme park. It was really nice of your father to do this."

She danced out and came in again, her back snuggling against his front. "It was, but I was hoping we could steal tonight just for us at the Whitetail Motel or B and B."

He twirled her around and his face wore a slight frown. "This party's for us and my parents so they can celebrate our engagement. We can hardly disappear."

But what about us? We haven't had sex in weeks. She ran her hand up into the back of his hair which she knew in the past had made him kiss her. "What if we left at midnight and were back by six? No one would even miss us."

He shook his head. "Your father's organized a dawn fishing trip."

She couldn't believe it. "Why did Daddy have to choose this summer to take up fishing?"

But if she expected Hank to show any signs of frustration that yet again they were going to have to sleep in separate rooms, he didn't. Instead he just laughed and kept dancing.

But her enjoyment had lost its gloss. She stopped abruptly and pulled away before walking back to the table where the Neiquests sat with her father and Dana. Hank followed her with an audible sigh and when he'd seated her, he took the chair next to hers and slung his arm over the back of her chair. She leaned into him and he absently pressed a kiss onto her hair as if she was a child. Bridey wanted to shake him. She wanted to tell him that she was right here, an adult, and his for the taking, but the seeds of doubt yelled, "He's getting cold feet."

Bob slapped Hank jovially on the shoulder. "Well, son, you've fallen on your feet here."

"Dad, I think you've probably done enough celebrating," Hank said mildly, and poured his father a glass of water.

Bob just grinned and leaned forward. "Bridey, my dear, Marion and I are thrilled Hank finally got around to popping the question."

Hank shifted in his seat and a chill darted through Bridey.

"Oh, yes." Marion beamed. "And we're even more thrilled that you said yes. We've been hoping for a while now, but you know Hank. He has to consider something from every angle and he won't be rushed."

Sean laughed and squeezed Dana's hand with affection. "That will temper the Callahan tendency to make snap decisions."

Bridey sat up straight, rigid with anxiety. "I don't make snap decisions."

This time Hank laughed. "What would you call the doughnut maker you had to have and is now waiting to go to a thrift store?"

Dana smiled. "But the one time she used it, the doughnuts were very good."

Bridey threw a grateful look at her stepmother. "See, you can't argue that."

"And we can hardly accuse you of snap decisions about the wedding," Sean teased. "At last count she had seven different wedding favors she couldn't decide between and fourteen dresses."

"Seeing we're talking about the wedding, and they

don't come cheap," Bob said, "Marion and I would like to make a contribution."

Sean waved his hand. "That's very kind, Bob, but not at all necessary."

Marion reached over and put her hand on Bridey's. "We got sidetracked by the tour of the house and never did have that chat about the wedding. We'd like to offer you our garden."

The Neiquests' garden was beautiful but the unanticipated gesture caught Bridey by surprise, and she was slow to form a response.

Hank sighed. "Mom, we've talked about this. Bridey wants a big wedding."

"Well, darling, we had one hundred thirty people for your sister and it wasn't a crush."

"Try triple that." Hank poured himself a drink.

"Four hundred people?" Marion asked faintly.

Bridey finally found her voice. "It's important that our wedding be a statement. Your offer's very thoughtful, Marion, thank you, but we've already paid a deposit on a venue."

Sean winked. "I think I paid four holding deposits, Baby-girl, because you couldn't decide."

Marion and Bob exchanged a glance and then both of them stared at her with expressions of slight injury as if she'd somehow kept a secret from them.

Marion took in a breath and with a tight smile said, "So where *are* you two getting married?"

Bridey waited for Hank to tell his parents but a beat extended into two and then morphed into an awkward silence. Her heart hammered faster. Why wasn't he saying anything? He knew exactly where they were getting married. He'd texted, *Okay.* Her future in-laws started frowning and she couldn't stand being thought to be the "bad guy" who'd withheld information so she blurted out, "The InterContinental."

Marion blinked.

"It's going to be wonderful. Perfect in fact," Bridey rushed on, determined to convince everyone that her vision for the wedding was exactly what she and Hank needed to start their life together. To cement their relationship. To avoid a divorce. "The theme's traditional Old World elegance. Masses of white roses, tulips and gardenias, chandeliers, tall silver candelabras with cascading floral centerpieces and tall white candles, gold charger plates on ivory damask cloths, tulle and gossamer on the ceiling and walls, a string quartet for the ceremony and a big band for the reception."

Marion looked slightly stunned but patted her hand. "It all sounds very…romantic, dear."

Bridey relaxed. "Thank you. I think so and the men will wear black tie and tails and my eight attendants—"

"Eight?" Hank stiffened against her.

"Yes. Eight." The words shot out between tight lips. "I did tell you this."

His sober gaze held hers. "I didn't think you were serious."

Bob laughed and slapped Hank's shoulder. "Just as well this extravaganza's a year away. You're going to need all that time to rustle up a few more groomsmen, son."

"I think Hank's just learning that weddings are for the bride." Sean raised his glass to Hank in a gesture of camaraderie.

Everyone laughed and Hank's mouth tweaked up tightly on one side but he didn't join in the laughter.

Bridey felt his reproach rip into her like the barbs of an arrow.

Dana's gaze flitted between her and Hank and she said in a calm voice, "There's plenty of time for both of you to discuss all the details in private."

But he doesn't want to. He didn't even tell his parents where we're getting married.

Bridey spun her engagement ring as her unspoken words shrieked in her head, deafening her. Panic swamped her—clogging her throat and making it hard to breathe. She tried to push it down. Tried to push away the fact that Hank's interest in their wedding was zero and that probably meant he was gearing up to end their engagement. She wouldn't let that happen. If she got him to agree to the wedding plans now, then that was a sign he was still going to marry her.

Her hand hit the table making the glasses rattle. "Actually, once I'm back at school, there won't be any time which is why," she heard her voice rising and she was powerless to stop it, "we must make decisions now."

This time no one laughed. An uncomfortable silence settled over everyone and neither her parents nor the Neiquests looked at her.

Hank shot to his feet. "Dana, Sean, thank you for a lovely evening. Mom, Dad, we'll see you in the morning." He turned to her, his face stiff and thunderous, and he extended his hand. "Bridey, let's take a walk."

For the first time ever, Bridey didn't want to be alone with Hank. Not because she feared this new, angry version of him, but because every single cell in her body feared what he might say.

I don't want to marry you.

I don't love you.

Not that she'd heard the words *I love you* from him very often lately, but she wouldn't give him the chance to say that he didn't love her. She refused to take his hand.

Instead, she rose as imperiously as Kathleen could, and quietly said her farewells to everyone.

Everyone murmured "good night" and then she felt Hank's fingers grip her elbow and he steered her silently and determinedly toward the house and directly into the library. This was a side of him she'd never seen before, and his stony face brought all her worst fears to center stage.

"Have you been taking lessons from Sean and Finn?" She shook his arm away as he closed the door firmly behind them.

There was nothing mild about him now and he spread his feet wide, standing like a commanding general in the center of the room. "This nonsense has to stop."

"What nonsense?" She paced to the window and looked out, not wanting to see the glare of reprimand in his eyes.

"This *obsession* of yours with the wedding."

She spun around and threw her hands out wide. "I'm not obsessed."

"Yes. You. Are." He ground out the words and they bounced around the room. "From the moment we got engaged you've become a different person and you're behaving like a woman possessed. First it was the engagement party and I let you have your head with that but I watched stunned as you went completely overboard. My God, Bridey, you planned everything down to the last second, including the time it would take for an ice sculpture to melt."

He didn't understand. "It's important that it lasts." *That we last.*

His hands raked through his hair, raising it into blond spikes. "You said you wanted a summer by the lake to relax but you're so tense you're about to explode, and you're jamming my inbox with emails about the color of cake boxes."

He sighed and sadness ringed him. "We used to talk about everything from French literature to the manufacture of paper, but for weeks it's been like living with an event planner who doesn't have a life. You do realize if you keep going this way you're going to get labeled Bridezilla."

The word whipped her, cutting deeply and she ground out, "One of us has to care enough to plan our wedding. Our future."

His kind eyes flared with anger. "You're saying I don't care?"

Yes. "What am I supposed to say? Every time I want to talk about the wedding you brush me aside or you say, 'you decide' or worse still, you question me in front of our parents. I'm starting to think you don't want to get married at all." Her worst fears clung to the words which had shot out without warning. A tremble started in her toes, quickly spreading to her entire body.

"Not if it's going to be like this for the next twelve months, I don't," he muttered.

His words broke over her, sucking the breath from her lungs. "I knew it."

He pushed his glasses up his nose and when he spoke his voice was tired. "Bridey, come on. Don't be ridiculous."

She rolled her shoulders back and clenched her hands into tight fists by her side, finally asking the question that had been plaguing her for weeks. "Hank, have you ever loved me?"

His eyes darkened as black discs of shock absorbed the honey warmth of his eyes. "What the hell sort of a question is that?"

Her heart hammered hard and her head spun dizzily from all the hurt which poured out of her. "A very real one. I proposed to you, Hank. Me. *I* had to ask you to marry me and now I'm not getting any signs from you that you care about me or the wedding at all." Her voice started to crack. "And you can't deny it. I mean, you program your phone so you don't forget to call me at night. What does that say about us?"

Her legs shook so much she had to lock her knees. "You're not upset that our vacation's been lost and last weekend you did everything possible to avoid spending time with me. I've done the math, Hank, so sue me if those aren't enough reasons for me to ask the question."

"You want me to apologize for spending last weekend with your family?" Disbelief scored his face and he slowly put the glass down. When he spoke, his voice was eerily quiet. "You seem to have it all worked out, Bridey, so tell me your theory on why I accepted your proposal?"

She spun her engagement ring around until the diamond cut into her palm but the pain didn't hurt as much as what she said. "For AKP."

He stared at her for a long moment and she watched his eyes fill with pain—pain she'd just put there. It tore back through her, searing her and shattering her heart. Oh, God, what had she just gone and done? But she knew exactly. She'd got everything horribly, horribly wrong. She'd let all her insecurities and fears come between them and now she'd driven Hank away.

He turned from her and gripped the mantelpiece, his shoulders rising and falling as if he'd just run a marathon and was left gasping for breath. Her own lungs cramped so hard they refused to move air and she stared at his back, feeling powerless and unable to speak. She didn't know how to fix this. "Sorry" didn't sound like nearly enough.

When he finally spoke, he still didn't look at her. "Do you really believe that I chose you because of work?"

She wrung her hands and emotional fatigue threatened to drag her into a heap on the floor. "I don't know what to believe anymore. All I know is that I was the one who pushed for us to get married and with each passing day you seem to move further away from me."

He raised his head and turned back to face her. His eyes, which had always been so warm, were clouded with the swirl of ragged emotions. "Do you still love me, Bridey?"

She didn't have to think. "Yes. Of course I do."

"Thank God." He strode over to her and pulled her in close. "Bridey, I love you. Please know that I love you."

She sagged against him in relief and his arms tightened around her.

He gazed into her eyes. "I've loved you from the moment I saw you walk onto the floor with your father in those shoes that belonged on a catwalk rather than a factory floor."

His emotion spun around her and she stared at him, stunned. "Then why did I have to do all the running? Why didn't you ever ask me out?"

He stroked her cheek. "It's not easy being the chief engineer in a billion-dollar company and in love with the boss's only daughter when even she has occasional thoughts that I only want her for the power and prestige."

Her head fell onto his shoulder and her battered heart tried to beat more steadily. "Oh, Hank. I'm so sorry. I just wanted everything to be perfect. Insurance. But all I've done is make a mess of it all. No one would believe

I'm an academic when I've been behaving like such a silly fool."

His hand trailed up and down her back. "To me you're the quintessential modern woman. You're smart, intelligent and you know what you want, which is why I thought it was wonderful that you proposed to me." He stroked her hair. "Had I realized it had you so worried, I would have told you this story earlier. Do you remember the celebratory dinner we had the night after you proposed?"

"At Le Luna? Of course I do, it was amazing. I could never work out how you got us a table at such short notice." Suddenly things fell into place and she gasped.

He nodded. "The night you proposed, you beat me out by twenty-four hours. I'd booked the restaurant a month prior because I'd planned to ask you to marry me." He gave a wry smile. "Mom and Dad are right. I don't make decisions in a hurry, but when I finally make them, I make them for keeps."

"Oh, Hank. I'm so sorry I ruined your plans."

"No, don't be sorry for that." He shook his head emphatically. "I saw it as a sign of us being in sync and ready to move forward with our lives. You gave me what I wanted most in the world."

He led her to the couch and sat her down. "Bridey, I love you with all my heart, but how did we get to this place tonight? Things have slowly been building to this since we got engaged and I don't ever want to come here again, so let's talk."

"You're right—we need to talk. Where do we start?"

"With your hurt. You said you think I set my phone so I remember to call you. That's not the reason at all. Usually, I've wanted to call you at least four other times in the day but work's been frantic. I set my phone for seven because if I'm still at work and the day's gone to hell in a handbasket, everyone on the floor knows that from 7:00 p.m. to 7:15 p.m., I'm completely unavailable to everyone except you."

Her heart lurched. How could she have been so stupid to think he didn't love her? Just like a light being shone into a dark corner, she could now see her recent behavior clearly. "You're right, Hank. I've been obsessed and I almost let it ruin everything."

She took in a steadying breath as she realized how close she'd come to losing him and tried to explain. "I was scared. Mom and Dad had a shotgun wedding and it ended, well, you know how it ended." She sighed. "I got this idea in my head that if our engagement and wedding were perfect then it would be like insurance and we'd be together forever. Just saying the words out loud makes me realize how dumb it was and how crazy I've been."

He slid his hand along her cheek. "I'm sorry I've been distracted with work and I know I'm not very good at telling you I love you, but I do. From this moment onward, I'm going to be telling you every day and every night, but, Bridey, there's more to love than words."

"I know, but my filter's been out of focus and it fuzzed up everything."

He pressed his lips to her forehead. "Last weekend, all I wanted was to be with you, but you've been telling me for two months now how important this family vacation is to you, so I made sure I spent time with your family. I was trying to bond outside of work." He gave her an ironic smile. "Granted, I probably overdid it some, and I'm never drinking a mint julep again."

She laughed. "Overdoing things is a Callahan trait."

"Very true. The reason I spent so much time with

your dad, Logan, Finn and your mom was because I wanted to get to know them. For you."

Her heart expanded so much she thought it would burst and she hugged him hard. "I don't deserve you."

He teased her with dancing eyes. "Probably not." Then his face sobered. "Bridey, we have to keep talking. The way we always did before we got engaged. If you're happy, sad, worried, scared, I need to know."

She nodded, absolutely secure in his love. "You're right. I've missed us."

"Me too." He ran his thumb over the diamond on her engagement ring. "You and I are not your parents, Bridey. We're us, and we do things *our* way. I want you to be happy because the last two years with you have been the best of my life. The next fifty will be too."

She couldn't stop the flood of tears that poured down her face and she buried her face in his shoulder. "Oh, Hank, I love you so much. We don't have to get married. Let's just live together."

He shook his head and pulled back so he could see her face. "No, we're getting married."

"But you've hated all the wedding stuff."

"No, I've been worried that you thought we needed the biggest wedding of the year. We don't need that but I want to stand up in front of the people we love and publically declare my love for you. I want to see you in a beautiful white dress. I want to watch you glide down the aisle toward me on Sean's arm, knowing that you're pledging your love to mine. But do we really need it to happen in front of four hundred people with eight attendants on either side?"

She shook her head. "No. All I need is you."

He brought his mouth down on hers and as his tongue made pledges to be honored later, ribbons of pleasure ran along her veins and then burrowed down deep, stroking memories and demanding new ones. His hands deftly pulled her thin shoulder straps down and she sighed as her breasts spilled into his hands, soaking up his touch that she missed so much.

She lay back on the leather couch and pulled him down with her. This time he didn't pull back or worry that they were in her father's house. This time he slid his hands under her skirt and his fingers worked their magic as his mouth branded her as his.

She was panting and wet with need, and her hands fumbled with his trousers before she guided him into her. It felt like coming home. He filled her with himself, with his strength and with his love. With each stroke, she rose with him until she tightened around him and gathered him up. Taking him with her they flew off the precipice together and out into the future.

When he finally raised his head, his eyes glowed with the color of polished oak. "The library's sound-proofed, right?"

She laughed. "Actually, it does have thicker walls because Grandpa wanted to block the noise from the house so I guess it works both ways."

He grinned. "In that case, I think we're going to be doing a lot of reading this weekend." He cuddled her close. "Do we have to wait until next July to get married?"

"I guess not." In the languid post-sex haze, an idea exploded in her head. "What about at the end of the month?" She wriggled under him. "Annika's friend asked me if we'd like to get married in Whitetail. Of course I was obsessing at the time so I said no but, why not? My family's here and your parents are home for the rest of the summer. We can fly in our closest friends and the people our parents want to have and cap it at two hundred. Given the short notice, they probably won't all come. We can give Nicole some broad guidelines and color schemes and then let her arrange everything. All we have to do is turn up."

"Okay, but when you're organizing your dress don't go casual on me because I'm wearing a tux to our wedding."

Her hand snuck under his shirt. "You know I always go weak at the knees for a man in black tie."

His hand trailed along her inner thigh. "Darling, I can make your knees weak right now."

And he did.

SIXTEEN

ANNIKA LEANED OVER to turn off her office computer and knocked a stack of folders off the desk. "Damn it." She'd been clumsy all morning and after spilling coffee on two shirts, she'd resorted to wearing one of Esther's aprons. With a sigh, she slid off her chair and started pulling the papers back into the correct folders.

Finn, having ended his phone call, bent down to help her. When all the folders were back in a neat pile, he hauled her to her feet. Gently holding her by her upper arms, he hooked her gaze. "Breathe, Legs."

She bit her lip. "Everything hinges on my meeting with Ty Dennison going well. I lost Ellery's guy to Superior-Duluth because of the port and I need this industry. Without it, Whitetail will die."

Finn frowned the way he always did when she talked about Whitetail. "*You* didn't lose Kugals. They did their sums and the port won because it offered them exactly what they needed. That's business. You've done your preparation for Long River. You've put in the long hours and that's all you can do because you can't control Ty Dennison's decision."

"I wish I could." She stepped into him, wrapping her arms around him, and needing to feel his heartbeat against hers. Loving him way too much.

He stroked her back. "Life doesn't work that way, Annika."

I wish it did. She looked up into those fathomless dark eyes and tried to read them, but once again he'd carefully hidden away all his emotions like he always did. Almost always did. The memory of his meltdown after the campout stayed strong.

He traced his thumb along her cheek. "Do you want me to come with?"

She shook her head, even though part of her wanted him there by her side. "Thanks anyway, but Whitetail has to do this on its own. We organized who's doing what at the town meeting and Ellery's representing your interests."

"That he is."

"I'm meeting Ty at the airport, giving him a tour of the town, calling into a few stores where everyone will make a huge fuss of him, and they'll showcase true Whitetail spirit. Afterward, we'll meet Ellery at the warehouses."

"Sounds like a plan." His phone rang and he gave her arm a squeeze, released it and then took the call. "Finn Callahan."

She heard the pause and saw the moment he became the CEO he was destined to be. "There's a flaw in that plan, Henrico. Let's talk it through so it's visible to you."

Annika watched him stare out the window as he listened intently and knew that even though he was standing looking at one of the country's prettiest lakes, he wasn't seeing it. He was in another world where he belonged and she was firmly in Whitetail. Her town. Her place. A town that after today would hopefully have a new industry and new jobs.

She was acting mayor and she must look the part so instead of arriving windblown from the motorboat, she'd brought the truck back yesterday. She picked up the keys.

Finn turned at the jangle and mouthed, *Good luck*.

His support made her heart roll idiotically in her chest. *It doesn't mean what you want it to mean.* All it meant was that Finn was a caring man. A caring man who didn't love her. She forced a smile onto her face, gave him the thumbs-up sign and carefully made her way down the stairs.

An hour later she turned the truck onto Main Street with Mr. Dennison sitting next to her. She was looking forward to seeing his reaction to the banner she'd organized—the one that said Welcome Long River Electronics. But the banner strung between the post office and Peterson's Market read Whitetail Welcomes the Callahan-Neiquest Wedding.

What? Every instinct had her foot slamming down hard on the brake, but somehow she managed to hold back, which was just as well because giving a potential town investor whiplash wasn't a good idea. *Bridey and Hank are getting married in Whitetail?* She couldn't believe it. Why didn't she know this? After all, she was the one designing invitations for a Chicago wedding which was a year away. She racked her brains for clues or snippets she might have heard to indicate their change of plan, but she came up blank. The last time she'd seen Bridey and Hank was at the party. The bulk of her weekend had been spent on the island with Finn, pretending the real world wasn't just across the lake. The only time they'd had any real contact with his family was when Logan had come to visit after his and Finn's kayaking adventure.

The brothers had lit a fire and then she and Logan had enjoyed a great time teasing Finn about getting sticky marshmallows everywhere except between the graham crackers when he was making s'mores. It had been Annika who'd taken Logan home when Finn had suddenly needed to make a vital phone call—one she was certain wasn't very vital at all, but got him out of having to see Sean. When she'd arrived at Kylemore it was Esther who'd received Logan with a hug and had told her that everyone was in Whitetail. Annika assumed they'd gone berry picking as Marion had been talking about it on Friday night.

On Monday morning, when she and Finn had been cuddled up in the post-dawn chill, they'd heard the helicopter leaving. Finn had mentioned that Bridey was heading back to Chicago for a few days with Hank. Nothing had been mentioned about the wedding being moved forward a year or that the venue had been changed to Whitetail. Surely she'd know if it had?

Why? You're not family. She bit her lip against the truth. She'd fallen in love with Finn and she adored his family, but she wasn't part of it. A shot of acid burned her stomach, making her feel ill.

A rogue thought suddenly pinged her. Late on Saturday, Nicole had texted the first of two messages. Messages she'd ignored because she'd either been having fun with Finn or frantically preparing for today. Had the Callahans and Neiquests been in Whitetail on Saturday planning the wedding?

"…pretty big event." Ty's Southern drawl brought her back with a jolt.

"Excuse me?"

"This wedding." He pointed to the shop front of Whitetail Market and Video, which had hearts all over the windows, and Nicole's salon, which had white tulle with tiny golden hearts filling the display area.

"Ah, yes, the wedding." She smiled tightly as she pulled into a parking space in front of the imposing town hall. "But today's all about Long River Electronics. Please come and enjoy a tour of the town and meet some of the business leaders."

Ty waited for her to alight and then met her on the sidewalk. The plan had been for the aldermen to meet her here, and then together they'd escort Ty and introduce him to the more prominent business owners. The aldermen were there and so was half the town. Relief flooded her. She had no clue what had happened to the banner but it seemed that Whitetail was on track after all.

Mrs. Norell was the first person to notice her. "Anni." She waved and walked over. "This is marvelous news, isn't it?"

Annika was aware of Ty standing next to her and as nothing had been decided she carefully said, "We mustn't get ahead of ourselves. Mr. Dennison hasn't even seen the town yet."

Ella beamed at Ty. "It's wonderful that you're spending some extra time in our town before the wedding. Which side are you on?"

"I'm sorry, ma'am, but I'm not part of the wedding." Ty glanced at Annika with a questioning look.

Annika tried not to grind her teeth and frantically used her eyes to signal everything they'd discussed at the town meeting. "Mrs. Norell, Ty represents Long River Electronics."

The woman nodded and looked slightly disappointed that Ty wasn't connected with the wedding. "Pleased to meet you. If you'll excuse me I have to run. Miss Bridget Callahan wants to have some of her wedding photos taken in my garden and I've got my work cut out for me to have it looking perfect for our bride."

Ella hurried away and Annika hastily called out to John Ackerman who came over beaming. Before she could introduce Ty, John said, "Anni, can you believe it? The Callahan wedding has ordered all their fresh produce through me. The times they are a-changing."

If it had been possible to shoot daggers through her eyes she would have done it. "That's great, John. This is Ty Dennison of Long River Electronics and if they choose to expand in Whitetail then your market will prosper as a result."

John shook Ty's hand. "Good to meet you, Ty. Are you married?"

Ty looked taken aback. "Ah, no, sir, I'm not, but I'm considering it."

"Well, you keep us in mind when you pop the question to your girl. You couldn't choose a better place than Whitetail to tie the knot and we can take care of all your wedding needs. Bridget Callahan has chosen us ahead of all those swanky Chicago hotels because we give our brides the key to the town for their day."

Annika silently groaned and was about to steer Ty away when Nicole rushed up, gripped her arm and with an accusing tone said, "I thought you'd sorted out your phone problems, Anni? We need an urgent meeting. There's so much to do in such a short time and the invitations have to go out yesterday."

Annika stifled her scream of frustration. Had everyone forgotten how important today's meeting was? That Ty Dennison held the future of Whitetail in his hand with the offer of jobs. Real jobs. She couldn't believe the town would risk jobs because of a wedding.

She shook off Nicole's hand. "I'll call you later when I've finished meeting with," she emphasized the words, "Long River Electronics."

Nicole's chin shot up. "Make sure you do." She extended her hand to Ty. "I'm Nicole Lindquist and my salon's across the street. However, I'm also the coordinator of Whitetail—Weddings That WOW. Annika probably hasn't told you but," she threw her hands out to encompass the town, "we've just scored a major wedding and the publicity it's going to generate will cement Whitetail as 'the' place to get married."

Ty shook Nicole's hand. "Congratulations, ma'am."

Annika heard the tightness in his Southern hospitality. If she'd had a flue as a body part, smoke would be pouring out of her. She was fuming with Nicole's grandstanding and so furious with the town for letting her down that she was ready to spit. She frantically glanced around trying to find someone who would focus on Ty instead of Bridey's wedding. Someone who would help her rescue what was starting to look like a runaway disaster.

Luke Anderson—bless him—was crossing the street toward them. After college and spending five years working for an agricultural company, Luke had returned to Whitetail and taken over the running of the family dairy farm. He loved the farm and the town in that order and could trace his ancestors back to the first Swedes who settled in the district in 1846.

"Luke, may I introduce you to Ty Dennison of Long River Electronics."

Luke gripped the Southerner's hand firmly. "Welcome to Whitetail. We might be small but we're big on service."

Ty returned the greeting. "That's good to hear. I grew up in a small town and my company has small-town values which I won't compromise on. My staff's like family."

"Then you'll fit right in here." Luke smiled. He gestured to the town hall. "My forefathers arrived here to make a new life and community has always been a strong part of Whitetail. We're keen to expand that to encompass new ventures."

The three of them strolled along the street with Luke calmly and quietly adding important details to Annika's commentary about Whitetail. This was fortunate because as they passed each shop and she saw yet another wedding window display with a sticker that said Official Supplier to the Callahan-Neiquest Wedding, she was having trouble keeping her mind on selling Whitetail when Whitetail had sold out on her.

It was a relief to finally meet Ellery at the warehouses.

As they stepped through the doorway with the now-finished mural, Ty stopped short and stared at the bridal wonderland.

"I was under the impression the warehouses were empty."

Annika rushed to reassure him. "Technically they are. This is just a goodwill gesture for Whitetail—Weddings That WOW."

"The town's business?"

"I'd hardly call it that. They have a couple of weddings booked is all."

Ty shot her a look. "It feels more than that, Ms. Jacobson." He turned to Ellery. "If I choose Whitetail, I'd want the entire space."

"Absolutely."

Ellery started talking square footage and Annika went ahead thankful she'd closed the door on her studio, and she headed down the corridor to the actual warehouse. She hauled open the heavy door and stopped short. Al Larson's carriage and limousine were parked inside. Huge metal poles lay on the ground along with a sea of white industrial PVC that she'd swear was a massive marquee.

Ty strode past her, pointedly walking around the marquee frames before zigzagging between the vehicles, and then he kept on walking. The rigid set of his shoulders clearly stated that he wasn't happy.

Ellery pressed the big, red loading dock switch and, with a clank, the large door started to roll up. A truck was parked in the loading zone, and a deliveryman with a sign machine walked directly to Ty.

"Chairs for the Callahan-Neiquest wedding. Where do you want them?"

"I don't," Ty ground out.

The delivery guy looked confused and Annika ran over. "I'll sign for them."

Ellery quickly walked Ty down the stairs to show him the other warehouse, pointing out the features of the truck bay and the possibility to extend. She heard their receding voices and stretched her hand out for the signing tablet.

"Miss, I need you to count the chairs as I unload them."

"What? Can't I just sign for them?"

"No. Count first, sign last."

"But I don't even know how many…"

But the guy had disappeared behind the truck where his buddy had already started unloading.

Inwardly seething, she started counting. Where was Al or anyone else from the town? *Seventy-five.* Why weren't they here doing this job? Damn it, but she picked up the slack for everyone in this town. *One hundred and twenty.* If they were so convinced that this wedding business was Whitetail's savior then why weren't they here to accept a delivery?

The men put down the last two stacks of chairs. "Did you get two hundred, Miss?"

"I did." She quickly signed the liquid display on the machine and ran down the steps. She found Ellery and Ty deep in conversation on the blacktop that stretched between the two warehouses.

Panting, she gasped out, "I'm so sorry about that, Mr. Dennison."

He merely raised one brow but the action spoke volumes. "Miz Jacobson. If Long River was to establish itself here, what sort of incentives would Whitetail be offering?"

Annika thought about how empty the Whitetail coffers were and chewed on her lip. "What sort of incentives did you have in mind?"

Ty tapped his foot and squinted at the warehouses. "A significant decrease in the rent."

Annika glanced at Ellery who shook his head. "Mr. Dennison, I'm sorry but the warehouses are privately owned."

The businessman frowned. "I was under the impression from your correspondence, Miz Jacobson, that the town owned the warehouses outright and that you were in a position to negotiate."

Annika looked imploringly at Ellery.

"There's some room to move on the leasing details," Ellery said, and named a figure.

Ty immediately lowered it.

Ellery shook his head and added a thousand dollars to Ty's figure.

The CEO of Long River Electronics didn't even consider the counteroffer. "Then I'll be saying no thanks and goodbye. I'm just not feeling the love, which is ironic given this town's fixation on weddings."

SEVENTEEN

Annika had driven Ty directly to the airport and the moment his plane had taken off, she'd somehow managed to get her shaking fingers to type out a text on her phone—*town meeting now*—and had sent it to the entire town. She'd left fury behind a long time ago. Now she was incandescent with rage. *She* was the acting mayor. They'd asked *her* to take on that position, and she'd accepted it with the same pledge she'd made all those years ago in 4-H—*to better living, for my club, my community, my country, and my world.* As Whitetail was pretty much all four to her, she couldn't believe they'd let her down this way. She'd worked so hard to give them what they needed and she'd only asked them to do one simple thing. Make a fuss of Ty Dennison.

As people filed into the town hall, all she could hear was wedding chatter and it ramped up her anger even more. When the last person took their seat, she slammed the gavel down hard and said, "I call this meeting to order." But that was as far as her meeting protocol lasted. All her anger poured out in full-flight berating-mother mode.

"I can't believe what you all did to me today." She caught sight of Luke and backtracked slightly. "Not Luke or Ellery, but the rest of you—" she pointed accusingly, "—hung me out to dry. I've worked my butt off for weeks trying to get an industry for this town, for all of you, and when I finally get someone to actually visit, you blow them off." Her hands flew up. "Ten jobs. You just blew off ten jobs for what? *One* wedding."

People stared at her in shocked silence. There was no scraping of chairs, no shuffling of feet and even the sounds of breathing were muted. Nicole rose slowly and rolled her shoulders back.

"We appreciate that you've tried to find us a business, Anni, but you've just lost two prospective customers and—"

The unfair criticism fired her brain into action. "The town lost us Long River Electronics today by talking about weddings instead of electronics!"

Nicole waved her hand in a "whatever" action. "The important thing is that while you've been trying to find us an industry, we've created one. We've now signed five brides and our fifth is the one that will change everything."

A murmur of agreement ran around the room but the agreement was siding with Nicole, not Annika. She could feel a level of animosity radiating off the townsfolk and lapping against her in small waves. It unnerved her and she shifted into conciliatory mode just to get over this hump. "You're pinning an awful lot on Bridey's wedding, but let's be realistic here. It's still only *one* wedding."

Nicole shot her a disbelieving look. "Anni, this wedding will feature in bridal magazines around the country. Bridey's dress will be examined and discussed, and so will the cake, the amazing view of the lake from the marquee and the menu. Not to mention the rehearsal dinner and the groom's cake. But most of all they'll talk about how we threw a lavish wedding and protected Bridey and Hank's privacy all at the same time. All of that will mean we'll continue to get bookings."

Annika gripped the gavel, not at all certain that Nicole was correct.

Nicole continued. "You did a lovely job on the mural and we're grateful."

Annika smiled. She knew her town well and all Nicole had needed to do was vent. Given the mural was a totally different picture from what she'd thought would work best, she'd been reasonably pleased with the result. She'd even managed to work a tiny vine of hearts deep in the picture. "I'm glad you like it."

"We do. And the website you started—"

"Yes, it's on my to-do list to expand it, but so far it's looking pretty good." Annika hadn't had time to get much more set up than four basic pages but the contacts were all linked to Nicole's phone and email.

"Actually—" Nicole paused and glanced around at the crowd who nodded at her encouragingly before she turned back. She lifted her chin. "We think the colors are wrong and the photos you've used don't make Whitetail look as romantic as it needs to be."

Annika breathed in sharply. *Wrong?* She'd chosen shades of blues and greens for the website to tie in with the lake and the northwoods. It represented the town perfectly. Her heart rate picked up as indignation swirled. Colors had been her world up until her art had become too painful to face, and though she had trouble painting now, she didn't doubt her color abilities. Her calligraphy clients rarely questioned her color suggestions. People in Whitetail never questioned her. Her voice rose. "What do you mean the colors are wrong?"

Nicole's voice firmed up. "The site should say romance. Right now it looks like a tourism page."

"Nicole's right, dear," Mrs. Norell added her two cents, and more murmurs joined her.

Annika's fingers curled around the edge of the lectern. She'd created a basic website for them because they'd asked her to and now they were criticizing it? *Stay calm.* "I'm sorry—"

"No need to apologize, Anni, you did your best," Al said.

Her jaw was so tight the ache radiated through her teeth and up into her cheeks. "Set up a meeting, Nicole, and we can discuss what it is you want for the website."

Nicole's expression became half determined and half pained. "Anni, we know you're really busy so we've spoken to Joshua about the website."

The name wasn't familiar to her. "Who?"

Eric, the editor of *The Bugle*, waved his notepad. "My grandson."

Melissa added, "Remember, he took the paper online and he's ready to take your start on the website and really romance it up. Make the site really wow and reflect our slogan of Weddings That WOW."

Something akin to dread crawled over her simmering anger and rampant indignation. She heard her voice rise. "But you asked me to do it."

Melissa crossed her arms. "I know, but Joshua's more in tune with the town's vision for the business than you are."

"Vision?" This time her voice came out on a squeak. "A vision is securing a real industry for Whitetail."

Nicole suddenly stood taller. "Anni, the budget for the Callahan-Neiquest wedding is two hundred and fifty thousand dollars."

Annika gaped, too stunned to say anything. "The... that's a lot of money."

"It is, and Sean's thrilled because he says he'll be saving money." Nicole's triumphant look was justified. "This wedding will involve and benefit the *entire* town, including our accommodation businesses." She waggled her fingers at Wade Anderson who owned a B and B. "The out-of-state guests will use the accommodations in town and the overflow in the county. Almost every business is playing a role in staging this wedding. Jason's linking all the accommodation from the website and everyone needs to organize a photo-pictorial for their businesses so he can create a page for each one of you."

Ella Norell started clapping. "It's really happening. The good news for you, Anni, is that you can stop working so hard now."

"How do you figure that, Mrs. Norell? It sounds like there's an enormous amount of work to do to pull all of this together."

The entire crowd looked to Nicole who stepped up to the lectern next to her.

"Anni, you've never really believed in our whole-town wedding idea and you've indulged us with your time. But this is a real and legitimate business, and we need people who believe and who are passionate about its success. You're our public representative of the town but because of how you feel about Weddings That WOW, we're not sure you're still the best person for the job."

Annika's throat tightened as she watched fifty heads slowly nodding in agreement with Nicole, and the tiny wave of animosity she'd sensed earlier became a tsunami of disapproval. It rolled over her, roaring in her ears, streaking through her veins and pressing down on her chest like a concrete girder.

The town had always needed her.

They don't need you now.

Her safe place, the town she'd come back to after her life had disintegrated, had just resoundingly rejected her.

Anger, loss and bewilderment spun inside her so hard and fast she could barely focus. "And you all feel this way?"

Mumblings of, "Yes, Anni, sorry, Anni," left her in no doubt.

Nicole touched her arm, her eyes sad. "Please know we're all really grateful for what you've done. We want you to stay involved through Annika's Custom Calligraphy and do the invitations and the place cards."

She managed to get her mouth to say, "Yes, of course."

Nicole stood staring at her and finally said softly, "Anni, sorry, but I need to use the lectern."

The coup was complete. With a shaking hand she laid down the gavel and stepped back. Every part of her wanted to run but she forced herself to walk slowly down the length of the hall, all the while hearing Nicole's firm voice behind her.

"I need everyone's attention. We only have three weeks to pull this all together and I need your complete cooperation, which includes responding to my emails and text messages promptly. Bridey and Hank are organizing their bridal attire and reception clothing, and have given us their color scheme. They wish to be married in the Unity Church and after their horse-and-carriage ride to the dock, they will go by launch to their reception at Kylemore. This will be in a windowed marquee complete with chandeliers and give a spectacular view of the lake. Their housekeeper is designing the menu and liaising with the Supper Club's chef and staff. The Callahans are providing the security and..."

Annika quietly slipped out the door and closed it behind her as a cold emptiness filled her. Whitetail didn't need her anymore and the only thing that kept her legs moving forward was the thought of getting home to Finn. *Finn*. The man she loved. The man who wanted her. Relief at still being needed flowed into her and she clutched at it. He might not know he needed her on a conscious level but he truly did, and it wasn't as a P.A. Anyone could do that for him but going by how hard he held her hand whenever they attended a Callahan occasion, he needed her to cope with his family. With Sean.

With her head spinning, she swung herself up into the cab of the truck, started the ignition and sent up a vote of thanks. She still had a job to do. She'd fix the estrangement between Finn and his father and prove to him how much he needed her in his life.

FINN CAREFULLY FED another invitation through the thermography machine. Initially, he'd come to the studio because the thought of an evening without Annika seemed oddly lonely. He'd arrived with the idea of chatting with her while she worked, but he'd quickly found himself helping. She was doing a rush job for Bridey's wedding invitations. Hank had sent out a "come to our wedding" email to everyone they were inviting, along with the promise of an "invitation following in the mail." Annika was almost killing herself to get them done in forty-eight hours and had been virtually living in the studio.

Given the time constraints and with Bridey's agreement, she'd tailored the invitations to be printed with a raised monogram, rather than being exclusively handwritten. He had no clue why the sudden rush for the wedding. Bridey hadn't told him much except to say that they wanted to "get married now" and then she'd hotly denied—along with a reinforcing punch—that she was pregnant.

Bridey wasn't the only person playing their cards close to their chest. Annika had been very quiet since Long River Electronics had rejected Whitetail and all he'd been able to get out of her was, "He wanted more incentives than we could offer." Ellery hadn't been much more forthcoming. All of this was in stark contrast to the time when Kugals had decided against Whitetail, and Annika had talked long and hard into the night about her worries for the town. She'd quickly responded to that disappointment by planning new strategies, but this time when he'd tried to draw her out, she'd kissed him like every man's fantasy and the conversation had stalled right there. The sex had been electric.

"Do you want to swap jobs?" Annika asked from the table where she sat surrounded by a sea of gold ribbons and pre-addressed mailing tubes.

"No, you tie a much better bow than I do." He turned to the high-speed digital printer and duplicator, and picked up the next invitation with its wet ink mono-gram. "Besides, I don't want to stop now that I've found my mojo. I've got it all timed perfectly. The moment one invitation rolls out of the thermography machine com-pletely finished, the next one's being printed with wet ink, and that all makes for perfect powder bonding."

She laughed. "You're enjoying all this."

He acknowledged with some surprise that the sen-sation inside him was happiness. "It reminds me of Grandpa and when I started my first college job at AKP."

"Was he like Sean?"

"God, no."

"Really?" She snipped a length of ribbon with her scissors. "He started AKP, didn't he? He must have had the business acumen that you and Sean share?"

He hadn't ever thought of it in those terms. "I suppose he did. Although Sean and I might share business skills, I'm much more like Grandpa."

"How so?"

"People count, not just the bottom line."

Her brows rose sharply in surprise, as if she might call him on the statement, but all she said was, "People count with Sean. Look at how he and Kathleen have built a bridge for Bridey's wedding and he was really—" She suddenly busied herself with sliding an invitation into a tube.

The same irritation he got whenever she talked about his father returned. "What?"

She shot him a smile that said, "don't get upset." "He was very understanding after you and I had…our initial misunderstanding."

"Two examples of Sean doing the right thing doesn't make up for a lifetime of not."

"What did he do that was so terrible?"

"Where to start? How about adultery?"

She chewed her lip. "I agree that one's not good, especially for your mom, but people make mistakes. We all make mistakes. He and Dana seem really happy together so perhaps he learned from his two marriages, and surely it's what we learn that counts."

Being a parent is fraught with mistakes, Finnegan.

He was instantly back on the beach with Sean and sweat poured into his eyes. He mustered up a smile he knew made her smile back. "Can you go grab me a soda from the fridge? I'd do it but it will ruin the flow."

She hesitated. "How about water from the tap?"

He stared at her. She was always so happy to help. In fact he often wished she would cut back on her "helping half the world" approach to life, and take more time for herself. "No, I want cold and sweet."

"Okay." She rose and slowly walked to the closed door.

As she swung it open, she hesitated and he could have sworn she looked both ways, checking the corridor before walking out. It was as if she didn't want to bump into any one of the many Whitetalians who were constantly in and out of the building, pulling out all the stops for Bridey and Hank's wedding. He'd noticed when they'd arrived earlier in the evening, Annika had said a quick hello to Nicole, but had then headed directly to the studio. At the time he'd put it down to her huge workload.

Nicole—who now had a wireless headset permanently attached to her ear—had motioned him over so he'd stayed behind to chat a little. She still wore an air of sadness but she also had a new energy woven into it.

"Finn, we've secured a loan for the official start-up of Whitetail—Weddings That WOW, and I wanted to discuss rent."

"That's great news, Nicole. Good for you. I'll get Ellery to withdraw both warehouses from the market and put the other one up for lease. I promise you a reasonable rate to start off with." He'd smiled. "Of course, once Whitetail's the bride capital of the Midwest and becomes my cash cow, I'll have to increase it."

"I wish." She'd laughed and excitement had flit across her face. "I'm loving this so much but with the short timeline on your sister's wedding it's a huge juggle for me to balance off the salon and my little boy. It's summer vacation and my parents are great but he's exhausting them and—" She stopped abruptly. "I'm sorry. I shouldn't be boring you with all this."

He'd smiled. "It's not boring. Business and home life are always a juggle."

How would you know? You just live work.

"Are you okay, Finn?" Nicole had asked. "You just frowned."

He laughed but it came out strained. "I'm fine. How old's your son?"

"Max is seven."

"My little brother's eight. He's into everything water. Swimming, diving, kayaking, that sort of thing."

Nicole had nodded in agreement. "Max would live in the water if he could."

That kid needs someone his own age to play with. He remembered Annika's comment and before thinking through the logistics, he'd found himself issuing an invitation. "Why not send Max over to Kylemore. Logan would love a buddy to play with and he's got just about every water toy there is."

Nicole's eyes had lit up. "That would be wonderful, thank you. But should I call his mother or…?"

And that's when it had hit him. He'd have to talk to Dana. He'd swallowed his sigh and promised Nicole he'd text her the arrangements, and he'd hurried off to help Annika.

Now Annika was returning in record-quick time from the kitchen with his soda.

"Thanks." He kissed her quickly between the invitations change-over. "You'll be pleased with me."

"I'm always pleased with you." Her eyes sparkled and she kissed him back. "But why especially now?"

"Nicole's pretty busy with the wedding and like you said, Logan needs a playmate his own age so I've invited her little boy over to play."

If he'd expected a hug of appreciation or even a smile of delight that he'd thought of the idea, he didn't get one.

"I'm sure Max will love it," she said in a voice that sounded the exact opposite. She sat down and returned to her ribbon tying with two uncharacteristic frown lines cutting into the bridge of her nose.

Her reaction didn't make any sense. "Everything okay?"

"Totally." She looked up and smiled but it didn't quite reach her eyes. "Almost done. Only twenty more to go."

Only he hadn't been asking about the invitations.

EIGHTEEN

"DANA, DO YOU have a minute?"

Finn had decided to approach Dana in the garden rather than in the house where he might meet Sean. Since the campout he'd avoided being alone with his father. All AKP meetings were conducted with Annika present and he took her to the family functions he had to attend because he knew Sean wouldn't try and discuss their relationship in front of her. However, he wasn't certain Sean would feel quite the same way in front of Dana, which was why he chose to speak to her in a place Sean was unlikely to be.

Dana was planting bulbs and she looked up at Finn from under her sunhat before rocking back on her heels. Dirt clung to her gloves and her knees, but it didn't dent her aura of quiet calm. She jabbed the trowel into the fragrant soil and extended her arm. "For you, Finn, always."

He gently pulled her to her feet and she smiled her thanks. "Do you want some lemonade?" She pointed to the gazebo. "Esther always sets some up for me when I'm gardening. I think it's so I don't track dirt into the house when I'm thirsty."

He laughed. "Yeah, she used to chase Bridey and me with a broom when we ran in dripping wet from the lake."

They strolled over to the gazebo and as well as lemonade in the cooler there was cheese and biscuits along with carrot sticks. Dana poured two glasses and then sat down. "So what's up?"

"Does there need to be 'something up'?"

Dana gave him a direct look. "You rarely seek me out, Finn."

"I guess I can't argue that." He sipped his drink. "I've been thinking about Logan."

Surprise climbed her cheeks. "What about him?"

"He's constantly playing with adults. Annika's played with him. I've taken him kayaking. Mom's been throwing the ball with him—"

"I apologize if any of this has been onerous." Her hand had stiffened around her glass.

He leaned forward. "That's not what I meant at all. If you'd asked me in June if I was going to build a campfire or camp out or go kayaking with my kid brother I would have said no. But I've done all those things and had fun. He's a great kid."

Dana's eyes filled with relief. "You've enjoyed his company?"

It still astonished him that he had, but the more time he spent with the little boy, the more relaxed he was around him. Being with Logan reminded him of the fun parts of his own childhood. "I have. He's good company and because he's used to spending time with adults, his conversation skills are pretty advanced. Still, I was thinking, perhaps he needs a pal closer to his own age. The wedding planner for Bridey's wedding has a kid and I was wondering if the boys could play here at Kylemore?"

Dana looked thoughtful. "Things are going to be hectic here the closer we get to the wedding. If Logan has a buddy it will make my life a lot easier."

"So you're fine with the idea?"

"Absolutely. I love it. As he gets older we can invite his friends to come from Chicago but now he's just a bit young." She put down her now-empty glass. "So how are things going for you this summer?"

He was instantly on guard. "In regard to?"

She laughed. "You can choose the topic, Finn. Personally I want to know about you and Annika, but I know you'll tell me about AKP instead."

He stared at his stepmother who he'd always thought of in terms of "Sean's wife," and "Logan's mother," rather than a person in her own right. A woman it seemed who could be very direct. He hated being pigeonholed so he said, "Annika's mailed Bridey's invitations so I imagine she'll now be returning to her task of saving Whitetail."

"She's got the most community spirit of anyone I've ever met."

"She has, but I'm not totally certain it's for all the right reasons, or at least not the right reasons for her."

Dana nodded her head slowly. "We *all* do things for reasons that might not be apparent to those closest to us."

Her quietly spoken words rolled around him, tugging and pulling and making him uncomfortable. He rose to his feet. "I'll text you Nicole's number."

Dana rose too. "Great. I'll call her and set up the play date."

He nodded and turned to go.

"Finn."

He swung back. "Yes?"

"Thanks for thinking of Logan. It really means a lot."

"You're welcome." And he realized that he genuinely meant it.

ANNIKA HADN'T SLEPT properly in days. Each night she'd make love to Finn and then lie cuddled up in his arms, feeling the soothing rise and fall of his chest as his body slumbered deep in sleep, only to have sleep elude her. She'd spend hours staring out the window and into the night, thinking about everything that had happened with Whitetail before finally falling asleep just as the first fingers of dawn were reaching over the horizon.

"Hey, sleepy."

She breathed in Finn's fresh cologne and opened her eyes, squinting against the light. It took her a moment to realize he was wearing suit pants and a crisp, white shirt.

His fingers deftly knotted his red tie into the broad and somehow sexy Windsor knot. "The chopper's leaving in fifteen minutes and I'll be back in time for supper. What have you got planned today?"

Something I can't tell you about. The first two days after Whitetail had dumped her, she'd kept herself busy with Bridey's invitations, but the moment she'd delivered them to the post office, she'd returned to Kylemore and hadn't left since. Her morning routine remained unchanged but her afternoons were very different. With Ashley's invitations also completed and her next invitation postal date still another two months away, she didn't need to go to the studio, and for that she was thankful. She didn't want to walk down Main Street either. The one time she'd gone for ink supplies, everybody she'd met was overly polite to her. For the first time in her life she'd felt like a stranger in her own town.

The dull pain that was now her constant companion ached. She bit her lip against it and refused to think about Whitetail. Now she was centering all her energies to reunite Finn and Sean. She knew if she brought up the subject, Finn would shut it down like he'd done every other time she'd tried, so subtlety was the key. Each day when she organized the documents that required Sean's signature, she asked in passing what he had planned for the day, especially for the afternoons. Then she set about trying to orchestrate a meeting between father and son.

On her first free afternoon she'd suggested to Finn that they go fishing at Picnic Point. He'd looked startled and had said, "Why would I want to do that? I've never really enjoyed fishing." Nothing she'd said had convinced him and instead he'd taken her out for a ride on the Jet Ski.

The next day she suggested a walk along the bluff and he'd agreed. With excited anticipation she'd packed a backpack of snacks and laced up her hiking boots, only to have Finn cancel due to a client demanding a video conference call.

Today she had a new plan but she wasn't about to share it with him just yet. "Logan asked if he and Max could come to the island and build a fort."

Finn managed to both smile and frown at the same time. "That's great for the boys but I thought you were going to have a phone meeting with that small cleaning-products company you mentioned last week? It might be a perfect fit now there's only one warehouse available for lease."

Ever since the Long River fiasco, Finn had been asking her a lot of "where to now?" questions—questions she'd been managing to avoid or duck. No way was she telling him about Whitetail's decision especially as he'd always thought the wedding idea had merit. She wasn't ready for an "I told you so."

"Chem-Free Cleaning delayed it so I'm free for fort duty."

His eyes strayed to her paint box and then returned to her. "The boys don't have to stay all day."

She rose up and kissed him. "Go catch your helicopter and can you please bring me back a sheet of linen paper? I need it to put into bride number four's sample kit."

"Text me at three to remind me." He squeezed her hand, stood up and left the room.

Her heart quivered before oozing into love-filled mush. Little gestures like squeezing her hand, along with the big ones like the hours he'd spent helping her with Bridey's invitations, made her want to imagine a future with him by her side, and his family a wonderful part of their life. The moment she heard the screen door slam shut behind him, she threw back the covers. She had a million things to organize before he got back tonight.

"And you're sure Finn's okay with this?" Sean's expression was one of surprise mixed with genuine pleasure.

Annika nodded rather than actually replying to Sean's question because she wanted to avoid uttering a barefaced lie. "We've eaten at Kylemore a lot and now it's my turn to cook. It would be fabulous if you and Dana could come for supper. The little boys will already be on the island and while they're eating hamburgers in their fort, we'll be a bit more civilized and dine on the veranda."

"Does he have enough chairs?"

The question implied that Sean hadn't been to the cabin and a tiny nagging feeling dragged at her. She immediately quashed it. This was no time for second thoughts on a thorough and necessary plan. By the end of the evening she'd have both men thanking her. "All you have to do is arrive at six."

Sean signed the documents with a flourish and a

smile, and returned them to her. "I'm looking forward to it."

"So am I."

As he walked out of the room, she slid the paperwork into the black folder labeled "Finn Only" and left it on his desk. That was her last AKP job for the morning and she headed to the kitchen. "Hi, Esther, did that box of food arrive for me yet?"

Esther's finger paused on a line in a recipe book and she looked up. "There's a box of fresh produce in the butler's pantry with your name on it, and the meat's in the fridge."

"Thank you. How's the menu planning coming along?"

The cook-cum-housekeeper smiled. "My gift to Bridey is a wedding menu people will be talking about for years to come."

As Annika had been fortunate enough to eat Esther's food, she was certain this pronouncement would come true. "I won't keep you from great work." She slipped into the butler's pantry and collected her ingredients before heading to the playroom to collect the boys.

She watched them for a few moments from the doorway as they pranced around the room playing pirates. Each of them had a red bandana tied on his head and a plastic sword stuck through his belt loops. They looked really cute and for the briefest moment she hugged to herself the wonder of how it would feel to be taking a curly, black-haired child of her own to the island.

"Hey, me hearties." She laughed to cover up the ache in her heart. "The good ship Anni leaves in five minutes. Grab your pieces of eight."

"Yippee," Logan yelled.

Max ran over to her and gave her a hug. He'd been

doing that ever since his father had died. As she hugged
him back she couldn't work out if he did it because he
was happy to see her or relieved that she was still alive.

"Wait 'til you see my brother's island," Logan said to
Max. "It's awesome."

Max's eyes grew large. "Is there treasure?"

"That depends on your definition of treasure," Annika replied. "Go grab your bag so the adventure can
begin."

A FEW HOURS later Annika felt like she'd been pulled in
different directions all afternoon but she'd managed to
supervise the building of the fort, feed endlessly hungry
boys numerous times and prepare the food for dinner.
She'd created a pretty table with an old jacquard cloth
she'd found buried under the towels and she was certain it had come with the cabin when Finn had bought
it. The centerpiece was a gnarly bit of maplewood that
the boys had discovered when they were choosing the
position of their fort, and she'd teamed it with some
pretty black-eyed Susans with their happy yellow pet-
als. After all of that, she'd even managed to brush her
hair and change into her "thousand shades of blue" sun-
dress. Her wardrobe was severely limited and she only
owned two dresses, but she knew Finn particularly enjoyed seeing her in this one.

She physically ticked off the items on her list and
smiled. She was ready. Her ears strained for the distinctive whoop-whoop sound of the helicopter. As soon as
Finn got home, she'd send him down to the fort to relax
with the boys, and when Dana and Sean arrived, the
three of them would stroll down to join them. It would
all be very relaxed and casual. No crowds of family,
just a small intimate group and a chance to really talk.

She thought she could just make out the faint buzz of the chopper when her phone blared. "Hi, Finn. I can hear you in the distance."

"We're just about to land in Whitetail."

"Oh." Her stomach churned. She really didn't want Finn in Whitetail talking to anyone or hearing about her dismissal. "Why do you need to do that?"

"Bridey's got me playing delivery boy with material swatches. I've got Melissa meeting me at the helipad so I won't be long. See you in ten."

The line went dead. *Melissa meeting me.* Acid seared the back of her throat. Melissa always spoke her mind. Would she say anything to Finn? She immediately scotched the thought, reassuring herself that the pilot wouldn't be turning off the engine for a short stop and nothing much could ever be said or heard over the roar of the rotors. If she needed to worry about something she should worry about her schedule.

Her gaze flew to her watch. Finn's delay was going to make things tight. Still, tight was doable. She'd have a cool drink waiting for him and his casual clothes all laid out. She walked onto the veranda and even though the boys were close by she pressed the call button on the walkie-talkie because it made them feel more grown-up.

A familiar voice sounded a moment later. "Blackbeard, arrrh."

"Anni to Wolves of the Sea, over. Captain Finn will be here soon."

"Yay." Logan forgot to be Blackbeard in his excitement.

She waved to them through the trees and absently adjusted the centerpiece on the table.

She chewed her lip. God, she hoped he was going to get here in ten minutes. She really didn't want him arriving just as Dana and Sean were leaving for the island because they'd suggest he come with them in the boat and that would give the game away completely.

She busied herself by opening the cream for whipping but struggled with the lid and when it finally came off with a jerk, a lot of cream followed. After she'd mopped up the mess with a cloth, she poured the rest of the cream into a bowl and turned on the beaters without checking the setting. The high speed sent cream flicking out everywhere including the counter, the walls, the floor and her dress.

With a wail, she turned it off and started to clean up.

Ten minutes later after restoring order and checking on the boys again, Finn still hadn't arrived. Another ten ticked past and still no Finn. The boys had trekked back to the cabin twice to see where he was and she'd sent them back to the fort with pretzels and drinks. A washing machine on spin cycle would be calmer than her stomach. She was now between a rock and a hard place. She couldn't delay or cancel Sean and Dana because they'd see Finn when the helicopter arrived at Kylemore, but now they were going to arrive on the island before him. She had no choice but to let the evening roll on.

"Hello!"

Sean's melodic voice called out as she heard a heavy step on the veranda followed by a lighter one.

She met them at the door with a welcoming smile plastered on her face that she hoped hid every other feeling that swirled inside her. She accepted the bunch of Dana's zinnias and a bottle of wine. "Thank you, that's very kind." She put them on the small side table by the door. "Finn's not back yet but he should be here soon. The boys are really keen to show you their fort so if you walk down there now, Finn and I will join you as soon as he arrives."

"Have they been good?" Dana asked as she looked toward the trees.

"They've been great but they're aching to show someone other than me all their hard work." She hoped she wasn't sounding as pushy as she felt.

Sean extended his arm to Dana with a twinkle in his eye. "Let's go check out the pirate camp."

Annika watched them walk away, wondering for the thousandth time where Finn was, and then she heard the helicopter coming in over the lake. *Thank you.*

She ran down and met him on the dock. He'd lost the tie but with his jacket slung over his shoulder, he still looked as sexy as a model in a glossy magazine.

"Sorry I'm late." He kissed her in a long, slow kiss that sizzled through her, making her rise up on her toes. "What's with the boat?" He tilted his head toward Sean's boat.

Crap. She hadn't factored that in because if he'd been on time he wouldn't have seen it. She had no choice but to white lie. "Dana and Sean have come to collect the boys and on the spur of the moment, I invited them for dinner."

His previously relaxed expression became guarded. "Why would you do that?"

She linked her arm through his but his eyes didn't twinkle down at her like Sean's had with Dana. "Because we've eaten at Kylemore and it seemed the hospitable thing to do."

"I forgot you were Miss Manners."

She smiled encouragingly and tugged his arm, and they started walking toward the cabin. He would come around and see that tonight was a good idea. "I've got cold beer waiting, supper's organized and all you have to do is kick back and relax. You can give me *some* credit, you know."

His brows rose as if he gave her no credit at all. "Why's that?"

She smiled. "I didn't invite your mother."

He didn't laugh like she'd hoped.

ANNIKA SERVED THE little boys ice creams in cones and then they settled down on the couch to watch *Peter Pan*. Every now and then Logan would jump up and yell out, "Arrgh, me hearties" and Max would say, "Tick-tock." At least they were happy.

As she sliced the chocolate mud cake and arranged it on individual plates with strawberries and cream, she listened intently to the conversation drifting through the open door from the veranda. Her ears were tuned to Finn's rich bass but the only voices she could hear were Dana's and Sean's. Finn had been quiet all evening.

He'd gone down to play with the boys in the fort the moment he'd got changed, but unlike her plan where she and his parents would have joined him, he'd gone to the fort the moment his father and stepmother had returned from it. At dinner he'd responded to his father's questions about AKP and had requested his opinion on the terms a new client was demanding but the moment that subject was exhausted he'd chatted with Dana before lapsing into virtual silence. He'd hardly spoken to her all night.

She bit her lip. This wasn't going anyway near the way she'd pictured it in her head. She concentrated on drizzling strawberry sauce around the edges of each white plate and then surveyed her handiwork. Given the tension in the air she wasn't even going to try and balance four plates on her arms. She carried them out two at a time.

Finn and Sean rose instantly as she crossed the veranda. Finn took the plates from her without a smile and she trudged back for the final two. When she'd returned and had taken her seat, Sean said with a smile, "This meal is worthy of five stars. I'm impressed you managed to cook all this *and* look after two busy boys."

Finn leaned back in his chair but there was nothing casual or relaxed about the action. "Annika likes to keep busy but even she's outdone herself with a spur-of-the-moment invitation."

That particular combination of words should have been a compliment but they slammed into her with the full force of his condemnation about the invitation.

Dana and Sean exchanged glances.

"This cake's divine, Annika," Dana said. "I'd love the recipe."

"I'm sure Annika would be more than happy to give it to you," Finn responded. "In fact she'll shop for the ingredients, come over and give a step-by-step demonstration and then clean up the kitchen for you."

Dana blinked and looked between them. "Am I missing something here?"

Annika rushed to smooth things over. "Finn's just teasing me because he thinks I overcommit."

"That's right." Finn's mouth had an intractable line to it and there was no smile in his eyes. "Like throwing dinner parties and building forts with little boys when you really should be doing *other* things like, oh, I don't know, painting for instance."

"Do you paint, Annika?" Dana's face lit up with interest.

Annika hedged. "At the moment I'm concentrating on my calligraphy."

Finn grunted.

Sean rested one arm on the herringbone veranda rail and looked toward the setting sun which was sending out vivid cerise-and-orange light across the lake. "I can see why you love this place, Finnegan. It reminds me of the original Kylemore."

Finn pushed his plate away. "You mean before you cleared the trees and extended the house so it could feature in *Vogue Living*."

"I was thinking before it had running water and electricity," Sean replied mildly.

"Grandpa didn't mind doing without a few luxuries."

Sean didn't react to the bite in Finn's words and continued on calmly, "Actually, your grandfather bulldozed the first cabin within a week of purchasing the property."

The statement hung between the two of them and if it was news to Finn, he didn't show it. In fact he wasn't showing much at all beyond a stony look.

Sean continued undeterred. "This cabin shares some of the same features and if you're interested, I can dig out some old photos."

Annika smiled. Sean was trying to make connections. This was exactly the sort of thing she'd hoped would happen tonight. "You could also check with the historical society. The two cabins may have been built by the same person and share a story."

"That's true," Sean agreed.

But Sean's attention wasn't on Annika—it was fixed firmly on Finn. She saw something akin to gratitude in Sean's eyes and right then she knew this dinner had been the exact thing they needed. She'd given them the opportunity and the place, and now they were taking the first steps in repairing their relationship so they could look to the future. She hugged the feeling of hope to herself.

Sean leaned forward, his voice filled with sincerity. "I'm just pleased to be here, son. I appreciate the invitation." He squeezed Dana's hand. "We both do."

Tension shot through Finn so fast it ricocheted into her with the slash and burn of a whip on skin. "Annika invited you, Dad." The coolness in his voice chilled the warm air. "I had no clue you were coming until I got here."

The dismay on Sean's face tore through Annika. She immediately put her hand on Finn's arm, hoping to ease him back into the reconciliation. "It doesn't matter who issued the invitation, the important thing is you're both here and—"

"No." Finn moved his arm out from under hers and with his lips barely moving, said, "Dana, I apologize that Annika's ill-advised invitation has put you in this uncomfortable position."

The words didn't touch her because she was still reeling from the way he'd pulled away from her as if touching her was suddenly abhorrent. A little tear bled in her heart.

"Finnegan, I'm sure that Annika was—"

But Dana's hand gripped Sean's and she shook her head as if to say, "not now." "Sean, let's take the boys home."

Hot and cold chills raced through Annika as she walked inside to help the Callahans get the boys ready for the boat. With hands trembling from a combination of anger and disappointment that Finn was throwing away an opportunity, she quickly gathered up toys and towels and bundled them into bags. Dana and Sean quietly overruled the boys' tired and grumpy requests to finish watching the movie and got them on their feet.

Finn stayed standing outside as rigid and as silent as a sentinel waiting for everyone to leave.

"Do you want to come back to Kylemore with us?" Dana asked Annika quietly, concern clear on her face.

Annika shook her head. She wasn't scared of Finn. There was no doubt in her mind that he was angry with her for inviting them to dinner, but it was an anger born out of hurt. His hurt. Sure, he'd yell and she'd listen, and then they'd talk. The rest they'd work out in bed. "Thanks, Dana, but I need to stay." *Finn needs me.*

Dana nodded her understanding and she joined Sean and the boys on the veranda. After some tight and strained "Good-nights" they walked down through the trees to the dock.

Annika expected Finn to yell the moment the motorboat's engine started but as Dana, Sean and the boys disappeared into the night, Finn spun on his heel, brushed past her and stepped into the cabin. The screen door slammed shut behind him. If he thought she was going to let things slide this time then he was sadly mistaken. Taking in a deep breath, she opened the door and followed him inside.

NINETEEN

RAGE BURNED THROUGH Finn hot and strong, scorching everything in its wake, until all that was left was smoldering bitterness that tainted every breath. It had been burning slowly all night despite his attempts to hose it down. He'd thought he'd been doing okay too until he'd seen the look on Sean's face—the one where he thought Finn had invited him to the island and that one action signaled a change between them. It had acted like a hot, south wind and ignited his fury into a roaring wildfire.

He'd stormed inside because he was so furious with Annika that he could barely configure a sentence. He couldn't believe she'd betrayed him. Couldn't believe she'd invited Sean here. *Here*. His hand tore through his hair as if the action would marshal his thoughts but it utterly failed. He heard the squeak of the door.

Shit. You didn't think this through, did you? Why had he come inside to a small, two-roomed cabin? He should have gone for a walk around the island or taken the boat and left the island altogether. He knew the first words Annika said would be, "We need to talk."

Hell yes, they needed to talk. Only this time he'd be the one doing all the talking.

"Finn?" She walked over to him and reached her hand out to his. "I understand you're angry."

Understand? The placating words sounded straight out of Psychology 101 and he crossed his arms to avoid her touch. "Annika, it might come as a shock to you, but you don't understand *anything* about me."

Her expression filled with empathy and she gave a half smile as if she thought the statement really silly. "Try me."

The smile only increased the sensation that he was barely hanging on to everything he understood about his life. "You lied to me. This was no spur-of-the-moment idea, was it? You had no right to invite my father here."

"I'm sorry you feel that way, but—"

"There are no 'buts.'" He threw out his hands. "This is *my* sanctuary. *I* choose who comes here. I've put up with you inviting people to camp out on the island and with you letting the boys build forts, but I will not stand by and allow you to invite my father to my retreat. This time you've gone too far."

"I didn't realize I had no rights as to who I could or couldn't invite, given that you've always told me to make myself at home."

He ignored the flash of hurt in her eyes and overruled the voice in his head that called him a jerk. "I have never wanted my father here."

This time she threw her arms out wide. "I was only trying to help you and Sean bury the past. God knows, you need someone to guide you through it."

His jaw was so tight it ached. "I don't think so."

"I think so." Her chin shot up. "You're blind if you can't see that your father badly wants to find a way to connect with you."

Finn had known what Sean wanted from the morning of the campout. "Yeah, well the only way I want to connect with him is the way I've been doing it for years. Through work." He crossed the room, hauled open the fridge and grabbed a beer bottle.

She followed him. "Don't you think that's a bit immature?"

"No!" He spun the top off a longneck and tossed it into the bin.

"I know Sean was an absent father full of unmet promises but he wants to make amends, Finn. It's clear to everyone he's genuinely sorry but he needs your help too. Can't you at least meet him halfway? If you keep this up you're going to miss the opportunity to have an adult relationship with your father."

He wanted to put his hands over his ears. "I'm fine with the one I've got."

"That isn't a relationship! It's a business arrangement."

"Exactly." He chugged down the amber liquid, cool against his hot, tight throat.

Exasperation and sadness for him swirled in her eyes and she shook her head very slowly as if she'd just worked something out. "My God, for all that you hate the idea of being like Sean, you are your father's son."

He slammed the bottle down. "What the hell is that supposed to mean?"

She pressed her palms down on the counter as if she needed the support. "You're making the same mistakes your father did at the same age and if you're not careful you—"

"Like hell I am." He crossed the room again, agitation pouring through him. "My personal life doesn't even come close to the debacle that was my father's. I'm *not* being unfaithful to a wife and family, and I don't have any children to ignore because I choose not to have any."

She bit her lip. "That part is true, but can't you see? You're putting work between you and your father and hiding behind the company. This way your father can never let you down or disappoint you again. It's so much easier than trying to deal with anything emotional because that scares you to death."

"That's bullshit." But her words skated close to the lid he'd jammed on all his feelings about his father. Skated so close that they almost cut it open and released the hurt he thought he'd shed years ago. He was never going to walk through the emotional minefield that was his relationship with his father. "Who appointed you custodian of how I relate to my father? Why are you all up in my face about this?"

Her face softened. "I just want to fix this for you."

I want to fix this.

I need this industry.

The thoughts rammed into him. This is what she did. And *this* was how she did it. Weeks of vague thoughts suddenly focused and the scales fell from his eyes.

Annika suddenly shivered as Finn's dark and enigmatic eyes stared down at her. "If you're so desperate to fix something, Annika, how about fixing your own life."

"Don't turn this back on me, Finn. My life is just fine."

"Oh, yeah, it's just perfect. You're so busy hiding out in Whitetail and living everyone else's life for them that you're not living your own."

His words hammered her and she hugged herself hard. "I *live* in Whitetail and I've been working my butt off trying to save *my* town. If that's not 'living my life' then I don't know what is."

But his penetrative gaze didn't move an inch. "The saving-the-town bit, it didn't go so well for you, did it? They didn't want to be saved in quite the way you believed it should happen."

For the first time since she'd come inside, he spoke

quietly, and there was something about the way his face had softened that made her stomach lurch. Oh God, he knew. He knew about the town meeting. She tossed her hair and tried not to let the hurt from the town flatten her. "We had a difference of opinion, is all."

He stepped a bit closer. "Melissa told me what happened the day Ty Dennison came. How they asked you to step down. This is why you've been spending more time here and why you're hell-bent on getting over-involved with my family."

Her breath hitched in her throat as her chest tightened and she shook her head hard and fast. "I'm just trying to help. I'm not over-involved."

"Yes, you are." He strode straight to her painting box and picked it up. "If you want to help then help yourself and get involved in your own life. Start living it the way you should be." He shoved the box into her arms. "By painting."

She put the box down. "I *am* living my life the way I should be. Right here, in Whitetail, where I'm needed." *Was needed.* Her throat got a lump in it and she tried hard to swallow around it.

Finn shook his head. "No, you're hiding from it here in Whitetail but they've just released you from your self-imposed responsibility. It's time to stop throwing roadblocks in your own way. I tracked down that review of your work, Annika, and I read it. Are you really going to let one person's opinion rule your life?"

"It wasn't *one* person's opinion. It was three!" She spun away from him, her heart pounding so hard she could hear it loud in her ears.

"So your style wasn't theirs, so what? It doesn't mean you just stop."

His caring voice didn't lessen the impact of his words

and she tried to take in a long, deep breath but she was being spun back in time to the cruel reviews and she couldn't move air in or out. Bitterness spilled over. "I didn't stop. God, I've tried painting. I was asked to paint a series of this lake for an exhibition in Milwaukee but I can't paint what I see. When I try it just comes out bland and lifeless and wrong. Everything about the paintings is wrong and I'm not exposing any more of my failures to the world."

"Isn't that being just a bit overdramatic?"

He stood in front of her, this successful man she loved, and the distance between them had never felt greater. "You have no idea what you're asking me to do, Finn. You've never been publicly humiliated nor had what you believed was your best work thoroughly trashed. And why would you? You're a winner. Under your guidance AKP is weathering a huge financial storm while other companies around you are going to the wall. But not all of us are as driven, or talented, or strong as you are."

His eyes burned her. "You think I don't have problems or challenges? If you believe that then you're living in fantasyland. The only difference between the two of us is that I'm not a quitter and I never took you for a coward."

"I'm not a coward." She knew she was yelling but if she tried to speak more quietly her voice would crack. "I'm making a choice with my life. Right now I'm creating beautiful invitations and making brides happy."

He shook his head slowly and his expression filled with sorrow. Sorrow for her. "Now you're just lying to yourself. Again. First it was saving Whitetail and now you've lost that you're clinging to the calligraphy. You know you're not happy."

She stared at him, thinking about the past few weeks. "Of course I'm happy. I've got you."

The moment the words slipped out she wanted to pull them back and push them down deep where they belonged until he was ready to hear them.

But they hung between them, vibrating loudly, and their message clear.

Finn's face paled under his summer tan and his black eyes seemed huge in his handsome face. "Annika, you and I, we're—"

She cut him off with a forced laugh, not wanting to hear the words she knew would follow. "What I meant to say was I've got you until Labor Day."

But he didn't laugh with her and every muscle, bone and tiny cell on his beautiful body said he didn't believe her. "I never meant for you to…"

It was like a balloon inside her which had been holding her up and it suddenly deflated. She shrunk in on herself. "Fall in love with you?" She bit her lip, hating his shocked surprise. "No, sorry. My bad."

An agonized look crossed his face. "It's been fun, Annika. It's been amazing, but you know we wouldn't work. Not long-term. Like you said, I don't do emotional connections. I don't fall in love, but most importantly, I won't let you live your life through me."

Her heart split in two and the ripping pain seared her like no other pain she'd ever experienced. It stole her breath before shooting down deep to a level never reached before. The man she loved didn't love her. He didn't need her. He was letting her go.

First Whitetail. Now Finn.

Her legs trembled and she gripped the back of the couch so she didn't sink to the floor. *Where to now?*

Somehow, from somewhere, she managed to muster up a spark of dignity. If Finn was blind to what they could have together, if he was so scared of the idea of loving her that he saw no reason to fight for her—for them—then she knew what she had to do. "I should probably spend the night at Kylemore."

He nodded slowly. "That's probably best."

Best? Pain made her numb. Nothing about this was best.

She absently picked up a light jacket. "I'll clear my stuff out tomorrow and make arrangements for someone to work in the office."

He ran his hands raggedly through his hair. "Annika, you can still work for AKP."

She shook her head. "I'm sorry, but I can't compartmentalize my life like you can."

He stared at her silently and then, ever the gentleman, he picked up the boat's keys. "It's dark so I'll take you over."

And the most important relationship of her life ended in a polite and agonizingly silent boat trip.

BRIDEY SNUGGLED IN close to Hank, loving the feel of the soft wool of his tux and the cool satin of the lapels caressing her bare shoulders. Her ivory silk organza gown with its hand-pieced lace tulle overskirt spilled over his legs and filled the carriage, rising to meet the low sides. The horse snorted as Al flicked the reins and the carriage started moving slowly around the town square.

"So did my dress match your tux as requested?"

"Darling, you've outshone my designer tux ten times. The dress is stunning. You're stunning." Hank pressed his lips to hers in a bone-melting kiss.

A cheer went up from the small flag-waving crowd

lining the street and Hank grinned. "Wave, Bridey. It's our day."

With a broad smile, she sat forward and waved, loving every minute of their special day. The sunshine glinted off her shiny, new wedding band and she started laughing.

Hank gave her an indulgent look. "Again? What's funny now?"

"I was just thinking about the church. How many weddings do you think have started with the bridal party on their hands and knees trying to fish the rings out of a crack in the floorboards?"

"Poor Logan." Hank's expression was half sympathy and half humor. "He was concentrating so hard on holding that cushion and he tripped just at the wrong moment."

She could feel tears of laughter behind her eyes. "I could see the rings rolling down the aisle ahead of me, getting faster and faster. From then on it was like watching a comedy of errors as Dana, Mom and your parents threw themselves into the aisle, trying to grab the rings and missing. It was like they had a magnetic force pulling them into the broken floorboard."

He put his hand on the small of her back. "How many brides arrive at the altar doubled over in laughter?"

She giggled again. "I couldn't help it. Everyone's expressions were priceless and besides, it's made our wedding unique. It's a story we can tell our children and grandchildren." A sigh of contentment rolled through her. "A month ago I would have been distraught at the idea of something like that happening but today it didn't matter one bit. I was in a church with you and we were getting married. Not even missing rings could stop that from happening."

He stroked her hair. "For a few minutes there I felt sure we'd be borrowing Mom and Dad's rings but Finn and Logan make a handy team."

"I know, right? Who knew my brothers now carry matching pocket knives that can hook rings."

Al pulled on the reins, and to another loud cheer the horse and carriage left the square and headed down toward the dock where Finn's wooden boat was waiting to transport them to Kylemore.

"It's been a perfect day so far." He pulled her in close. "I can't believe I'm so blessed to have you as my wife."

She looked up into warm and loving honey-brown eyes and she knew she was home. "You've got me forever, Hank."

"It won't be long enough." And he kissed her.

When Bridget Callahan married Hank Neiquest, she carried a bouquet of fragrant gardenias and white hydrangeas which were stunningly replicated in sugar on the four-tier wedding cake. The entire Callahan family was in attendance at the rustic church and the bride's mother and stepmother wore complementing dresses from Chicago's up-and-coming designer Lex. Close friends joined the happy couple at the reception, which was held at Sean Callahan's northern Wisconsin vacation home. Bachelor brother Finn attended alone. According to one source, he was seen on the dance floor enjoying the reception with many different partners.

Annika dropped the copy of *People* magazine onto her brother's coffee table, getting a tiny bit of relief from the fact that Finn hadn't taken a date to the wedding, but what did it really matter? Three and a half weeks had passed since she'd last seen him and she knew it was only a matter of time before he was dating again.

After all, there was no reason for him to be celibate—he hadn't been foolish enough to fall in love and nor did he have a broken heart.

She'd been in Milwaukee for a few weeks now. Her brother had taken one look at her two suitcases and boxes and had welcomed her with open arms saying, "Thank God, you've finally come to your senses." Her mother had emailed from New Zealand. *So thrilled you're working for Axel.*

At least someone was thrilled.

Her phone rang and as she answered it she could hear the noise of a sports bar blaring in the background. "Hey, sis. Just letting you know I'm not home for supper. The guys and I are celebrating."

She asked the question Axel always loved to answer. "What are you celebrating?"

"I sold five of those new apartments off the plan."

"That's great. Party safe."

"Always. You enjoy having the place to yourself. Maybe watch one of your chick flicks."

She smiled as he hung up. Her brother was a Brewers fan, a Packers fan, a Bucks fan, an anything Badger fan—a sports fan period, and the TV was rusted onto the sports channel. Without him here, the apartment was eerily quiet.

She sighed and picked up the discarded magazine. Bridey made a stunning bride and both of the official photos that had been released showed Hank gazing at her with so much love that it made her chest ache. She was pleased that the wedding had gone so well for them and she was pleased for the town too. They'd pulled off an event that usually took months of planning and had done it in less than four weeks.

She'd had almost as long to reflect on how many mistakes she'd made. She'd been so hell-bent on getting an industry for the town that she'd missed the true strengths of Whitetail. She pressed the message icon on her phone and texted Nicole and the town her congratulations.

Almost instantly, Nicole replied. *Thank you. Wished you could have been there. Are you still good for the other wedding invitations?*

Her fingers flew. *Yes. Definitely yes.* Even though she no longer had her own studio and all that lovely AKP equipment, she was determined to find a space because the invitations were the only thing that came close to giving her a creative outlet. Her job as rental manager for her brother's Realtor business paid well but she was often bored rigid. Ironically, between that job and her contract with AKP, she was earning the most money she'd ever earned in her life. Before she left Whitetail, she'd hired Olivia from Sven's Swedish Smörgåsbord to work for Finn. She'd also tried to stop the AKP contract and get the company to employ Olivia direct, but the very pedantic man in the Chicago office of AKP had been adamant there was no valid reason for the contract not to run its course as both parties were honoring it.

With Finn's words about "not living your life through me" ringing in her ears, Annika had promptly given Olivia a big pay rise and had paid off all her debts but it still left her in-front financially. The money made her uneasy.

She hadn't seen or spoken to Finn since he'd delivered her safely to Kylemore, brushed her cheek with a chaste kiss and wished her "All the best." The man she loved had held every one of his emotions in check and bid her farewell like she'd been a valued employee rather than a lover. She'd wanted to push him into the lake. The irony of the whole nightmare was she'd wanted him to open up so he could enjoy a relationship with his father. All she'd achieved was him digging his feelings down deeper into his emotional abyss.

She may not have spoken to any of the Callahan men but she'd received texts from Dana, Kathleen and Bridey each week, asking her if she was "Doing okay?" She appreciated their thoughtfulness but each message brought a fresh wave of pain with it. Finn's family cared for her but the one Callahan she loved with every part of her didn't care for her enough.

The sun had started to drop and the light was fading, making the apartment dim and, given her dreary thoughts, she needed light. Lots of bright and cheery light. She flipped on the main lamp and instantly heard a hiss as the bulb blew, just as it had the night before. "And we didn't buy any new ones," she said to Axel's Labrador, Jet, and rubbed her ears. "Tomorrow we call the electrician, but for now I guess we'll just have to sit in the gloom." But just the thought of it had her changing her mind. "Let's go outside."

Jet didn't seem at all perturbed by any of it and padded out onto the balcony behind her. She'd been sitting there earlier checking figures on the laptop for Axel. She tucked her feet underneath her as she sat down and watched the colors in the sky deepen and stretch further into the horizon. Up until now, she'd avoided doing this because it reminded her of everything she'd lost— the lake, Whitetail, Finn and, less recently, her dream.

The Great Lakes had always fascinated her—massive inland seas which could go from glitteringly calm to roiling waves and pounding breakers. When she'd missed Whitetail at college, she'd had Lake Michigan. The lakes had always inspired her art and she'd walked and camped along the miles and miles of all of their shorelines, but she knew Lake Michigan the best. Industry had scarred them, shipping and fishing constantly took from them and yet they could still throw up pockets of wild and awe-inspiring beauty. They'd been her muse until looking at them had become too painful.

The fiery orange light danced on the water, seeping into its darkness and creating a juxtaposition of color. Light and dark. The dueling of nature. If she was painting this she knew exactly which combination of paints would yield that color.

She heard Finn in her head. *Start living your life the way you should by painting.*

Her inner voice was louder. *You can't even finish the final painting of* Dawn, Day and Dusk.

She huffed out a breath. *Those paintings sucked. People said so. In print. Three times.*

Finn's voice wouldn't be silenced. *So your style wasn't theirs. Are you really going to let one person's opinion rule your life?*

"Yes."

Jet raised her head but when she realized Annika hadn't said "walk" she laid it back down on her paws.

She bit her lip as her life stretched out in front of her—alone and working for her brother. A life devoid of color.

I won't let you live your life through me. A sob rose in her throat. *The town didn't want to be saved your way.*

A sharp pain in her chest made her gasp. Oh, God, Finn was right. She was a coward. She was living her life by believing the words of strangers and she'd actively let them steal away her joy. Worse still, she'd been so desperate to fill her life with something, and stay in Whitetail, that she'd become an overbearing control freak. Her behavior had put her on the outs with her town—a town she loved. With a moan, she dropped her head into her hands as her conduct came under the unforgiving bright light of a spotlight. She'd bossed around White-tail and waded into Finn's life telling him how to live it when she couldn't even get her own organized. Was too scared to even try.

Only hiding out had destroyed everything she held dear. Every time she'd painted in the last two years, she'd done it with a huge question mark hanging over every brush stroke. *Is this right?* It had sucked her dry. But no more. She wanted to paint this sunset. She wanted to paint her lakes. She wanted to show the stark contrast of the wild, rugged beauty against the errors of man. She didn't care if it was "stylized," "derivative" or "imma-ture," she just knew she needed to do it.

She needed to do it for herself.

TWENTY

FINN SAT IN the Kylemore office wondering how Olivia had managed to completely screw up his spreadsheet for the third time in as many days. He'd specifically gone through the steps with her and she'd crossed her heart, telling him that she now understood. Obviously, she hadn't understood at all.

He rubbed the back of his neck and groaned. It was lucky for Olivia that it was two o'clock and she was now safely back at Sven's, waitressing.

You never had this problem with Annika.

God, he missed her. He missed her organization in the office and her body in bed.

You miss more than that.

He refused to acknowledge the thought. *Damn it*, if she hadn't gone and broken their contract of "summer fun" by falling in love with him, she'd still be here on this sunny afternoon, he wouldn't be fixing a spreadsheet and they'd be out on the boat, or sitting in the glider seat or making love in the little cove on the far end of the island. But she'd ruined everything.

The expression on her face when she'd said, "My bad," still haunted him—beautiful and sad. He'd hated that he couldn't tell her that he loved her back, but he didn't love her. He'd loved being with her but that was a long way from love. He didn't do love.

Despite Annika saying she loved him, he wasn't certain she was ready to love anyone until she started valuing herself and her talents. He hated not seeing her reach her potential and if anything good had come out of this mess, it had been that she'd left Whitetail. Perhaps now she could truly start over.

Keep telling yourself that. He pulled his concentration back to the figures, glad to have work. Reliable and dependable work, where problems were solved by logic and reason and not tainted by the mess of feelings.

"Finn?"

He looked up to see Logan scuffing the toe of his sneaker in the doorway of the office. His little brother hadn't done that in a long time. These days he normally just ran straight in and spun on one of the chairs. His visits ranged from delivering a message or making a request like, "can we pleeeease go to the island in the canoe," to showing off a drawing. Today he wore a pensive expression.

"What's up, dude?"

Logan huffed and stayed where he was.

Finn pushed back from the desk and skated his chair around closer to Logan. "That bad, huh?"

Logan's round face wore all the signs of frustrated disappointment. "Yeah."

"So the fish weren't biting today?" Logan had the most amazing luck catching fish and he'd rarely been disappointed that way.

"No, I caught a walleye." His offhand delivery would have made a keen angler despair.

Finn didn't get it. "So what's the problem?"

Logan's face flushed red. "Dad says he's not going to build the zip line!"

Memories rumbled in Finn's gut and he took in a

long breath. "Not going to build it as in not today or tomorrow?"

Logan shook his head. "Not never."

Typical, Sean! His little brother's words released every promise that had ever been made to him by his father and had then been summarily broken. For the first time this summer, his father was finally behaving in character. *I was a lousy father to you.* Cold anger burned. So much for Sean learning from his mistakes.

When Finn was a kid and had been disappointed and hurt by his father's broken promises, he'd always gone to his grandfather. Now Logan was coming to him. Only Finn wasn't going to allow another generation to suffer the same fate. Logan idolized Sean and he didn't deserve to have all that love and admiration destroyed. Not like what had happened to him. He stood up. "How about you go see if Esther's pulled those cookies out of the oven, and I'll go talk to Dad."

"Okay." Logan stared up at him. "I just want to bomb into the water like you did in the picture Kathleen showed me. It looks like wicked, awesome fun."

Finn ruffled his hair. "Me too, buddy."

Finn found his father in the workshop making fishing lures. He hadn't spoken to him face-to-face since the night he'd asked him to leave the island.

Sean turned around as the door hinges squeaked and surprise crossed his face followed immediately by concern. "Finnegan? Is there something wrong at the house?"

He shook his head. "No one's sick or hurt if that's what you mean."

His father's intelligent mind absorbed this bit of information. "That's good to hear."

Sean continued on with wrapping thread around chartreuse bucktail, attaching it to a hook as if he had all the time in the world and yet he wasn't building a promised zip line.

Finn's ire upped a notch. "Logan just stopped by the office."

Sean smiled. "Told you about the walleye, did he? Damn, but that kid can catch fish."

Finn crossed his arms. "He also told me about the zip line. Or the lack of the zip line."

"Ah."

"Ah? That's all you've got to say? Ah? What the hell are you playing at, Sean? You told me you'd been a lousy father. Said you wanted to make amends so I took that as you having learned the basics. Rule number one is don't make promises and then break them. That kid adores you. Don't screw it up again."

Sean tied the thread with a firm tug. "I don't intend to."

"Then build the damn zip line."

Sean took off his glasses and laid them on the workbench. "I would, except that Hank and Bridey are on their honeymoon."

Finn didn't follow. "What the hell has that got to do with anything? Get a contractor in to do the job and Logan can be using the thing by the day after tomorrow."

"Finnegan, the whole point of this zip line was that the family was going to build it together."

He threw out his arms. "So just because Hank and Bridey are away you've told Logan it's never going to be built?"

Sean laughed with affection clear on his face. "Is that what the little schemer told you?"

Finn stilled, sensing a shift in the conversation. "I

asked him if the build had been postponed and he said, 'No, never.'"

"What actually happened was that while we were out fishing, I gave him all the reasons for the delay and I told him it would happen next summer. I guess at eight that counts as never."

"I see." Finn swallowed hard and forced up what needed to be said. "I apologize. I should have gotten my facts right before coming down here."

Sean gave a wry smile. "No problem. It's a rookie mistake, Finnegan. Kids can play you especially if they think it will make things go their way."

He thought of his teenage years. Of his anger and disappointment, and of his need for his father to notice him. "Did I play you, Dad?"

"After the divorce to protect your mother, and I understand that." Sincerity lit up his eyes. "Listen, I'm just glad you and Logan are enjoying spending time together, and I'm even more pleased that you stormed down here to avenge his disappointment and fight the fight for him. It's very brotherly of you, Finnegan. Logan's fortunate to have you."

And this was the side of Sean that confused the hell out of him because he couldn't stick it into any of the boxes he'd made for Sean years ago and continued to use. "Maybe." He pushed off the doorway ready to leave.

"Of course, there's one easy way to temper Logan's disappointment."

"What's that?"

"Build the zip line with me."

The words stopped him in his tracks and he turned slowly and stared at his father. The wily bastard had him. Again. By coming down here, guns blazing, he'd exposed his affection for Logan and now Sean was using it.

Using it to keep a promise.

He ran his hand through his hair, anticipating the same rush of "get out now" sensations that he'd experienced every other time his father had suggested they do something together. But they didn't come. All he got was an overwhelming fatigue. Fatigue and resignation. If he walked away from this, Logan missed out. If he stayed he had to deal with his father out of a work context.

Treat it like work.

He sighed and gave in to it. "Only if Logan's working with us too."

Sean grinned. "I wouldn't have it any other way."

"ARE YOU SURE about this?" Annika's mother's face was blurry on the computer screen but it didn't hide her concern.

"Mom, you've been telling me for ages to leave Whitetail."

"When you were in Whitetail we worried about you in general but never about your safety. Darling, a road trip on your own? It's not a good idea."

Annika smiled reassuringly at the screen and tried a joke. "I thought you'd be happy because as part of the trip, I'm going international. To Canada. Besides, you and Dad travel all the time."

Her mother sighed. "Yes, but we travel together and with our groups."

"I'll be fine, Mom. Most of the places I'm going I won't see many people. It's just going to be me and my sketch pad and Jet for company and protection. I need to do this for me and I'll be back before the weather gets too cold." She glanced at her brother and then back at the screen. "And I promise to check in with Axel every day."

Axel leaned into the computer. "She has to, Mom, or I take my car back."

Annika laughed. "It's your winter car, Ax. It's so full of rust, there's nothing much to take back."

He squeezed her shoulder. "Just come back happy."

"I THOUGHT IT would be ready faster."

Logan had been "helping" Sean and Finn all morning and was desperate for the concrete to dry a thousand times quicker than it was going to take.

Finn pulled Logan's cap down over his eyes. "Go visit Kathleen and bounce the ball on her deck."

"Your mother and Dana have gone into Whitetail to visit two gardens that are open for the day," Sean said. "They'll be back for lunch."

Finn still couldn't quite get his head around the fact that his mother hadn't gone home to Chicago when her ankle had healed, or directly after the wedding, but had stayed on at Kylemore for a real vacation. "Dude, how about you go up to the house and get the cooler from Esther. I could do with a drink."

"Okay." Logan took off running down the track back toward the house.

Sean squinted into the sun and then looked across the lake. "Hank's got a tension line coming from the tree house. The problem's going to be getting the pulley back when Logan lets go over the lake."

"I guess we put a drag rope on it. Bridey and I used to take it in turns to swim it back."

"You also liked to go right through to the second platform and leave her stranded." Sean pulled on leather gloves.

"Did I?" Finn couldn't remember that.

"Yep. One time I came after you and we hiked on up to the bluff."

Finn stared at his father blankly. He couldn't remember that either.

Sean shrugged. "I guess I deserve that you only remember the stuff I didn't do with you, considering there was a lot more of that. Pass me that ratchet, will you?"

Finn passed it over and they worked on in silence, the summer sun making it hot work. He scanned his memories for the hike but he could only remember all the times he'd been ready to go hiking and fishing with Sean and had ended up going with his grandfather instead because his father canceled or was tied up in the office.

He looked out toward the bluff with its gray rocks and windblown pines and a memory stirred. He called out to Sean. "Did we have a picnic at the top?"

His father smiled. "We did. And then you ran down that track like a mountain goat and left me to carry the backpack you'd filled with rocks for your collection."

Logan arrived back clutching the cooler and panting. "Mom's back and she brought Max and we're going swimming, bye." He ran off.

Sean laughed and tossed a soda can to Finn before cracking one open himself. "Well, he lasted longer than I thought."

Working with Sean on the zip line hadn't been as bad as Finn thought it might be. In fact, there'd been moments when they'd actually shared a laugh, but he was still grappling with his father's attempts of casual friendship combined with occasional fathering moments. It made for an odd sensation in his gut.

Finn sat down in the shade of the tree house and tried not to think of the night he and Annika had spent two wonderful hours ensconced up there.

Sean smiled. "That tree house has seen some things. You were conceived there."

Finn groaned. "Geez, Dad, I didn't need to know that."

"Your mother said Annika's in Milwaukee."

Finn spluttered on his drink and bubbles shot up his nose at the link his father was obviously drawing. "I didn't know that either."

"No. I guessed you didn't. Shame. We all liked her."

He tried brushing the comment aside. "It was a summer thing."

"By my reckoning there's still a bit of summer left."

Finn watched the condensation run down the can. "My calendar disagrees."

Sean broke the three beats of silence. "Finnegan, I've been impressed with how you've handled AKP this summer. You had a rugged start with Jazz Juice but you handled it well and the new contract with them lies at your feet."

"Thanks." The compliment surprised him but he was just thankful Sean was changing the topic of conversation.

Sean nodded. "You're a hell of a good businessman and although I've taught you a lot, most of the way you operate is instinctive. You don't depend on anyone and you're your own man. In business, that's one hell of a good trait to have." He sighed. "The thing is, relationships aren't like business. They can be messy but without them life is pretty lonely. I know I didn't lead by example relationship-wise, but I want you to know that despite everything, your mother and I did have some good times in our marriage. But we were young, too young. We handled the breakup badly and we both regret that. A relationship needs maturity to make it work."

Finn really didn't want to hear all of this and he tried keeping it light. "Lucky you've got Dana, then."

Sean smiled. "Dana makes me happy. It's taken me a long time to find that sort of happiness and I saw glimpses of it in you when Annika was here."

Unease shifted in Finn and settled hard and heavy in his chest. "Now you're just sounding old and sentimental. Unlike you I have no desire to get married. Annika and I had some fun and it's run its course. End of story."

His father gave him a direct look. "She loves you and that sort of commitment scares the shit out of you."

"That's crap."

"You wish it was."

THE SUMMER AT Kylemore ended with a party. Bridey and Hank arrived back from their honeymoon in time for Labor Day weekend and Logan finally got to take the inaugural zip line ride. As the little boy had whooped it across the lake and then deliberately dropped into the water on the return ride, Sean had put his hand on Finn's shoulder and said, "We did good."

He didn't shrug the hand away. "Yeah. I think we did."

"Thanks."

"No problem." He'd finally admitted to himself that he'd actually enjoyed building the line. When they'd finished the project, he'd picked up the phone to call Annika, but mid-dial he'd pressed Cancel. What was he going to say after, "Dad and I built the zip line and survived" and "How are you?" She wanted more from him than he could give her.

"I had a good time, Dad, especially when you weren't philosophizing."

"Good." Sean grinned. "We'll have to try fishing next."

Finn smiled. "You and me in a boat? Don't push it, Dad."

Sean winked. "It will have to be golf then." He walked off laughing and started organizing everyone to take a zip line ride.

The afternoon passed with a great deal of fun and laughter. Everybody took a turn on the zip line, including Kathleen who'd screamed almost as loud as Bridey. Nicole and Max had been a welcome addition to the day but the biggest surprise was the arrival of a well-known curator from the Museum of Contemporary Art in Chicago, who'd come to drive Kathleen home.

Bridey had shaken her head in bewilderment as she'd slipped her arm through Finn's. "Can you believe this summer? It's made me so happy. What about you?"

"It's been great getting to know Logan."

She gave him a sideways look. "And Dad?"

He sighed, knowing she wouldn't stop asking until he replied. "And Dad. Yes, little sister, I concede, the zip line was a good idea."

She smiled. "I'm full of good ideas and I've got another one."

He laughed. "Of course you have."

"You should call Annika."

He tensed. "This family might have managed to heal some wounds this summer but we're nowhere near ready to tell each other what to do."

She squeezed his arm. "Annika made you happy. Don't walk away from that."

"Take your newlywed starry eyes over to your husband and lavish your care on him and leave me in peace."

Except peace was something that was eluding him big-time and he couldn't wait for the busyness of the fall work quarter.

ESTHER WAS LEFT to close up the house and everyone headed back to Chicago. Sean moved back into his office and Finn flew down to Mexico for a face-to-face with his team who'd done a sensational job without him. He'd spent two weeks there before flying to Australia and on to China and Thailand, taking meetings and networking for a planned expansion into Asia. The work was all-consuming and the tender process had taken up the month of October, leaving him no time or space to think beyond AKP Asia. There was no doubt in his mind that he thrived on projects like this. He loved the thrill of the chase and nailing down the challenges of the process but despite all of that, it hadn't given him the total satisfaction that he'd expected. So he'd added dating into the mix but after three disastrous evenings where he'd spent more time thinking about Annika than the woman in front of him, he'd given up on that idea completely.

He wondered what she was doing. He'd been wondering that a lot. Usually at 2:00 a.m.

A knock sounded at his door and he looked up to see his secretary walking his way. "Mr. Callahan, your schedule has you blocked out next week for vacation. Are you still taking it?"

His week at the lake. The week he always took when no one was at Kylemore. No Logan to toss the ball with, no Bridey and Hank to hike with, no mint juleps on the deck with his mother, no Dana to chat with in the garden and no Sean to do a project with.

No Annika.

The idea of an empty Kylemore was suddenly unappealing. "I'm not certain I'll go to the lake."

"The Caribbean's lovely at this time of year," Lisa offered up.

Except he'd been flying around the world a lot recently and the idea of getting back on a plane held little appeal. "I'll think on it and let you know but meanwhile don't book in any meetings."

She nodded and left the room, and Finn stood up feeling restless. That had been happening a lot lately. He poured himself a coffee from the pot Lisa replenished regularly so the brew was always fresh. He glanced at the clock. Two o'clock. An image of Annika in her shapeless and paint-stained T-shirt rocked into his head. Why had he thought of that?

At two o'clock she used to be in her studio.

He slammed down his coffee mug, sloshing brown liquid over the side, and picked up his phone. He was sick of unbidden thoughts and images of her coming into his head at all hours of the day and night, screwing with his concentration. To hell with it—he'd just call her. He'd talk to her, find out what she was doing and get her out of his system. Then he could return to his pre-Annika life which had been perfectly fine and ordered. He would get back that level of contentment that was eluding him.

He pressed her number on his contacts and held the phone to his ear. "The number you have dialed has been disconnected and is no longer in service. If you think you have dialed this number in error, please check the number and try again."

He stared at his phone as if it was an alien. He hadn't made a mistake on the numbers. He tried again and got the same message. *Shit.* She'd disconnected from the AKP phone. He ran his hand over the back of his neck.

Of course she had. It was October. The contract with Annika's Custom Calligraphy had been until Labor Day. But once he'd made a decision to do something, he damn well did it. It wouldn't be hard to find her number and given how much grief his sister had aimed at him about her, he'd start there. He got Bridey's voice mail so he tried his mother.

"Do you have Annika's number?"

"Hello, darling, how are you?"

He ground his teeth pretty much like he'd done at fifteen but knew he'd get nowhere without going through the pleasantries. "Hello, Mom. I'm well, how are you? How's Geoffrey?" He was still getting his head around *that* relationship.

"We're both very well, darling. Thank you for asking."

"Do you have Annika's number?"

There was an unexpected silence on the end of the phone followed by a sigh.

"Mom?"

"I'm sorry, Finn, I don't have it."

"But Dad said you'd been in contact with her."

"I had, but before her phone number changed she wrote and asked me very politely to stop. Just like she asked Bridey." She paused. "Why do you want to contact her?"

"I don't know."

"Excuse me?"

God, what was he doing? He was thirty-three years old, second in charge of a global empire and he was talking to his mother about a girl. "Unfinished business."

"If it's AKP business then personnel may have contact details."

"Good idea. Thanks."

"Finn, if it's unfinished business between the two of you then that's a different thing entirely. I'd advise you not to call her."

He stopped pacing. "What are you saying? That I can only contact her about work?"

"That's exactly what I'm saying."

"Look, I just want to know if she's okay."

"You broke her heart and now you want to check she's okay? She's not going to thank you for that."

He plowed his hand through his hair. "Mom, I just think that if I talked to her, knew she was doing okay then I could get back on track—"

"No." He heard the hiss of his mother sucking her breath in through her teeth. "This isn't about you, Finn, unless…"

The pause sounded ominous. "Unless what?"

"Do you love her?"

No. Panic simmered. "Look, Mom, I know you think you're trying to help but this is nothing about being in love and everything to do with moving forward."

"Finn, did Annika tell you she loved you?"

His breath shuddered out of him and he hesitated. "Yes, but—"

"And you told her you didn't love her, so by rights she is the one needing to do all the moving forward, not you. By the sheer fact you weren't invested in the relationship you have nothing to move forward from."

Indignation poured through him. "I was damn well invested. We had an agreement for the summer, a contract and she was the one who broke if off early."

"She isn't a business plan, Finnegan."

People count, not just the bottom line. His words came back to him as did Annika's raised brows. *Finn, that isn't a relationship! It's a business arrangement.*

Sweat broke out on his brow and he heard himself shouting. "Of course Annika isn't a business plan. A BP is clear and concise with goals and an endpoint. Annika's messy and demanding, in my face about Dad and anything else she thinks I should be doing. And she can't even walk a straight line without falling over."

"And yet you want to call her up?"

He heard a smile in his mother's voice and he let out a ragged breath. "Yes." It was all so damn confusing.

"Finn, relationships aren't like work, they're messy and unpredictable."

"Exactly. Which is why I don't do them."

"Except this time you've done one without even realizing."

He loosened his tie which was suddenly choking him. What was it with his family trying to push him toward her? *Dude, you called your mother.* "That's nonsense."

Kathleen continued, "Do thoughts of Annika arrive unannounced when you're in meetings?"

He didn't want to answer that but fortunately he didn't have to because Kathleen kept talking. "How's your appetite?"

Lousy. "I never eat much when I'm busy."

"Okay, well tell me this. At the end of each day do you fall into bed with a sense of achievement and fulfillment or do you have a general feeling that something intangible is missing in your life?"

His mouth dried. Hell, could his mother suddenly see inside his head? He wanted to deny everything. Tell his mother she was way off course and he opened his mouth to do so.

Anything emotional scares you to death.

His stomach rolled and the floor felt unsteady under his feet. He sank into his chair. God, Annika was right.

His heart pounded, sweat poured off him and he was having trouble breathing. For every relationship that he'd ended or had ended for him, he'd never felt like this. Annika knew him better than he knew himself. "Mom."

"Yes."

He swallowed hard. "I love her."

The moment he'd uttered the words his panic subsided. He *loved* her. Loved the way she made him laugh, the infuriating way she made him own up to his foibles, and the way she wrapped herself around him at night and listened to him talk even when she was exhausted and not interested in the different types of cardboard generated from recycled paper.

"Of course you love her, darling. We've all known it for weeks." Kathleen sighed. "Now you need to find her and tell her."

TWENTY-ONE

Bride loves invitations. Now need sample kit 4 casual outdoor wedding in August. Bride in Milwaukee for F2F meet. Can U come to us for Thanksgiving? Max and I would love 2 see you! Nicole x

Send Bride's number for me 2 contact. Thanksgiv would b great. Can I bring Ax? Anni x

ANNIKA PUT DOWN her phone and smiled. The thought of going back to Whitetail no longer daunted her. Whitetail was finding its niche and she was finding hers. She picked up a paint palette. An enormous canvas dominated the small light-filled space she'd rented and the cacophony of colors that swirled, from devastating black to the hope of nature's green, told the story of what she'd seen on her trip and her interpretation of it. She had no clue how it would be received by the gallery that was expecting a traditional *Dawn*, *Day and Dusk* series, but the most important thing was that she'd done it. Almost done it. She still had a ways to go before it was completed but she'd make the gallery's hanging date. Just.

She checked her sketches—the ones she'd made on golden sandy beaches, the ones she'd drawn next to nuclear power plants and Chicago's Deep Tunnel, and a dozen other places around Lake Michigan and Lake Superior. She'd spent three weeks of September alone with only a dog and her sketch pad for company, and she'd found a sort of peace. It wasn't perfect but it was better than what she'd had in years. Ironically, a big part of the new Annika was due to Finn. The man who couldn't love her had been the reason she had her art back and money in the bank. Whitetail was slowly growing her wedding invitation business and her darling brother had "backup" work for her if she ever needed it.

The only thing missing in her life was Finn. She ached for him but without love between them she knew they had nothing, which was why she'd changed her phone and cut her ties with all the Callahans. As hard as that was, it was the only way she knew how to move on. She'd finally confessed all to Nicole on a late-night apology phone call halfway through her trip, and although she doubted Finn would contact her she'd asked Nicole not to give him her number. Cold turkey was the only way she'd survive and grow into this new and more rounded life of hers. She rolled her shoulders back, swiped marine blue onto her pallet and scraped it across the canvas in a big, bold stroke.

"ANY NEWS?" KATHLEEN selected a miniature éclair from the ornate cake stand that was positioned between her and Finn on the table at Palmer House.

"None." No one would tell Finn where Annika was. He'd spoken to her brother who'd offered to sell him an apartment on Lake Michigan but refused to tell him where his sister was. He'd tracked down her parents through their company called Third Age Travel and spoken to them in Fiji. "Anni is safe and well but that's all we can say."

They'd hung up before he could utter another word. Nicole had sounded like she really wanted to tell him but had said she was sorry she couldn't. He'd even trawled through the Weddings That WOW website looking for her phone number, but every inquiry was directed through Nicole. "She doesn't want to be found."

He sipped the Earl Grey tea and wished it had a shot of something stronger in it. He'd spent his vacation searching for Annika but short of doing a line search of Wisconsin he didn't know what else to do. "It's ironic, don't you think, that when I finally fall in love and realize it, I've screwed it up before I've started."

He leaned back from the table, finding the refined atmosphere stifling. The sports bar Sean had dragged him out to the other night had at least been noisy, making it hard to think.

"Don't give up just yet." Kathleen pulled an envelope out of her handbag. "Geoffrey gets invited to just about every gallery opening in Illinois, Wisconsin and Indiana. He brought over a folder of them the other night and asked me if I wanted to attend any of them. I thought I'd go to this one."

She slid the rectangular invitation across the table.

Milwaukee's Waterways Gallery presents a retrospective—Living Lakes.

Annika's name was in the list of contributing artists.

ANNIKA'S STOMACH CHURNED as she walked the short distance from the parking garage to the Waterways Gallery. Agitation pummeled her and it had taken her three attempts to park the car. If she'd thought watching the gallery men carry *Act Now* from her studio into their truck was hard, she realized it had nothing on walking into the gallery and seeing it hung. Seeing other people looking at it and listening to them commenting on it.

She gulped in a breath. She really should have let

Axel come with her. He at least could have parked the car straight, but as much as she loved the support of her brother she knew she had to face down her demons of opening night on her own. It was all part of the new Annika. She stopped outside the gallery's huge and heavy glass doors. *You can do this.* Rolling back her shoulders, and lifting her head, she pushed all her weight on the large silver handle. Her shoulder slammed into the glass with a thud.

Breathe. The sign says Pull.

She rubbed her shoulder. Oh, God, just getting inside the door was a challenge. This time she pulled and stepped inside.

Her throat tightened. There were more people than she'd expected. Muted music played quietly and some of the black-clad waitstaff carried trays filled with glasses of champagne and assorted drinks, while others held platters of tiny canapés which they offered to the crowd of attendees.

"Drink?"

"Yes please." She gave the waiter a weak smile and managed to pick up a glass of champagne without knocking over the other glasses. It was a start.

She picked up a program and started at painting one, planning to work methodically around the gallery, especially given that *Act Now* was number sixteen. She had no rush to see it or hear what was being said about it. All that would come soon enough. There were a great variety of works—some ink and wash, watercolors, fabric art and of course, oils. Most of the scenes depicted either tranquil lake scenes or were season specific. There were quite a few lighthouses and she loved every one of them.

She rounded the partition and came face-to-face with *Act Now.* They'd hung it on the main wall and lit it so that it almost seemed three-dimensional, reaching out to the observer and demanding their attention. It dominated the space and dwarfed the other paintings around it. She knew it would either be loved or hated and there wouldn't be any other emotion in between.

"Annika."

She turned around to see Richard, the gallery owner, walking toward her smiling. "I've got great news. Someone's put in an offer for the painting. In fact they've offered more than the asking price."

Annika stared at him in disbelief. "I'm stunned."

He laughed and then immediately sobered. "You shouldn't be. I've had one critic describe it as 'broad strokes of heartache leaching from the canvas,' and another as 'harsh and questioning yet purveying hope.' I think you'll want to be cutting out tomorrow's reviews and keeping them for your scrapbook."

She nodded but she knew differently. Of course she was thrilled that this painting was being received so well but good or bad, she was never again defining herself by one or two people's opinions.

"We're also very honored tonight to have one of the curators from the Chicago Museum of Contemporary Art and I'd like to introduce you to him. He was quite taken with *Act Now*."

Annika's legs trembled and she sat down on the banquette behind her. "Do you normally get a curator come to your openings?"

Richard smiled. "Not often, but if they're in the area they call in." He turned, quickly scanning the room and then frowned. "I can't see him at the moment but you stay here and I'll go find him."

"Okay." It was all a bit surreal and she stood up again,

accepted another glass of champagne and hugged herself tight. *It only takes one painting, Annika.*

Kathleen had been right.

"It's amazing, Annika."

The deep and melodic voice that was an intrinsic part of her—a voice she'd recognize anywhere—sounded behind her.

Finn. Her heart shuddered and her hand gripped her glass so hard she was amazed it didn't shatter. Without knowing exactly how she got all her body parts to cooperate, she turned around slowly and made herself breathe.

He stood in front of her in a charcoal-gray tailored suit that fitted him perfectly. His curls were tamed and his white shirt and lake-blue tie lightened his eyes to the color of rich, dark chocolate. He was easily the most handsome man in the room and the most handsome man she'd ever met, but it was the lines around his eyes that she noticed most. They hadn't been there the last time she'd seen him. The time he'd stood in the cabin and told her he couldn't love her. *I don't do emotional connections.*

He smiled at her. "Nothing at all like your pretty lighthouses but totally awe-inspiring."

She steeled her heart. "I wasn't in a pretty mood when I painted it."

Finn had rehearsed in his head exactly what he was going to say but from the moment he'd glimpsed Annika, every word had vacated his brain. All his senses were hungry for her, so much so that he barely heard her reply. She was wearing her long hair down and it flowed across her shoulders in a shimmer of white and gold, brushing against her simple, black sheath dress. Her only accessory was a necklace of tiny seed pearls which caressed her throat. Her mouth was as red and lush as ever, only her face was thinner, but it was her eyes that held him riveted. Behind the wariness there was something new—he couldn't put his finger on it exactly but whatever it was it suited her. She looked elegant and slightly remote and a part of him wished she was wearing her misshapen, paint-stained T-shirt or was sleep-rumpled in one of his shirts.

He'd seen her painting earlier—chaos merging with calm—and it had gripped him by the throat. Now as she stood in front of it with her commanding height and the square set of her shoulders, she was having the same effect. She held herself like an Amazon warrior—his warrior. The one who'd fought for him even though he'd been too blind to see it.

A rush of love so strong surged through him, nearly knocking him off his feet. He moved toward her, desperate to touch her, but she took a long drink from her glass and then fixed him with an uncompromising stare.

"Why are you here, Finn?"

Any thoughts of her falling straight into his arms got hammered on the spot and it disconcerted him. "I wanted to see you. See your art."

"To gloat? I'll save you the trouble." Her face hardened. "In front of all these people I acknowledge that you were right. I needed to get out and live my life my way. I needed to paint. *Act Now* is the first step."

He started to sweat. "You really think I'd come here to gloat?"

"I recall some of your last words to me were 'I won't let you live your life through me.' Given that, I really don't know what to think, Finn. Is there a reason that I should?"

A few people looked toward them and heads started

turning. Finn lowered his voice but he couldn't quite keep an edge of anxiety from seeping into it. "Annika, can we please go and talk somewhere more private?"

She sucked in her lips and shook her head. "There's nothing I have to say to you that can't be said here."

He tugged on his collar. "I promise you, I didn't come here to gloat. In fact I'm thrilled you're painting again." He smiled at her expecting to see some softening in her stance when he told her the news. "So happy in fact that I've bought *Act Now*."

Her face drained of color. "No!"

No? That wasn't part of the script in his head.

This time the crowd fell silent and all heads snapped their way with curiosity and interest written clear on their faces.

Damn it, he had to get her into a private space.

With a laugh he said to the crowd, "And people think artists can't haggle over price." Sliding his hand under Annika's elbow he continued talking, "Come on, Ms. Jacobson, let's go and talk privately and find a figure we can agree on."

She gave him a look filled with such utter loathing that he seriously thought she'd prefer to walk on hot coals than to walk with him, but she slowly put her glass down on a tray and took a step. As they walked away, he heard someone in the crowd saying, "Who is that?"

Ushering her into the first door they came to, they were instantly enveloped by the smell of warm wool. He'd found the cloakroom. He quickly closed the door behind him and stood in front of it in case she tried to leave before he'd said what he needed to say. He no longer cared about the script. She'd told him she loved him. Now he loved her so he went straight to the point. "Annika, please listen to me. I love you."

She shrugged as if he'd just said, "I think the Chicago Bears will whoop the Packers." "You don't love me, Finn."

He blinked. "Of course I do."

He reached for her again but this time she sidestepped him. "Okay then, see it my way. The last time I saw you, you looked absolutely appalled at the idea of me loving you and you told me you could never love me. I hear nothing from you in almost three months and now you appear with a declaration of love. Why would I believe you?"

God, why would she believe him? Her withering gaze didn't look like it belonged to a woman who still loved him and it sent terror scudding into every cell. "Because I'm sorry for how we parted and because I've bought the painting."

"You're sorry?" Her chin jutted out in that stubborn way. "Did you buy *Act Now* because you think no one else will?"

"No!" He ran his hand through his hair trying desperately to navigate his way through a conversation that was littered with Stealth Bombers.

She drew herself up to her full height. "I won't let you buy this painting, Finn. I've worked too hard for this and I'm not going to let you steal it from me to make yourself feel better. You once told me I couldn't live through you and yet if you buy this painting you're doing exactly what you accused me of."

Desperation clawed at him as he envisaged his future stretching before him without Annika in it. The pain of that realization almost rendered him mute. "Annika, I bought it because you painted it. Because when I look at it, it's full of you. Your drive and compassion, your laughter and your caring for the people that you love. I see your indignation over things that aren't fair and your

hope that things can change. I see your stumbles and I
see your smile. I see everything I've missed so much
since you left."

"Since *you* asked me to leave."

She wrapped her arms around herself but her face
stayed impassive as if his heartfelt declaration had just
fallen on deaf ears. He'd rejected her love, hurt her too
much, and taken too long to realize she was the love of
his life. He was too late and there was nothing he could
say or do to recover from that. Nothing he could say or
do that would convince her. He felt the ring box in his
pocket dragging him down into a pit of black despair.

Annika could hardly breathe. Disbelief, pain, fear and
utter desolation sucked at her, pummeling every intention she'd had to live her life her way. He had no right to
suddenly appear after three months of silence and drop
a bombshell like this. Not when she'd fought to stay upright and keep going after he'd broken her heart so badly.
And she feared he could do it again. Did he even know
what love was? She gripped her hand around the coat
rail to steady herself.

"Look, Finn, I really don't know where this is coming from or why. But you buying a painting is easy. You
wouldn't even notice the dip in your bank balance. Saying 'I love you' is easy too. Paintings and words just
aren't enough."

He suddenly looked haggard and gray. "You think
me telling you that I love you is easy?" His anguished
voice sliced through her. "God, Annika, you of all people should know that me standing here telling you I love
you is the hardest thing I've ever done."

*I don't do emotional connections. I don't fall in love.
Love destroys more than it ever builds.*

She bit her lip and didn't want to hope.

He sat down between the coats and dropped his head in his hands for a moment before looking up. "The last three months have been hell. When you left you took the rudder of my life with you and I've been drifting. Before you fell into my arms at Bridey's party, I thought I was content but you stormed into my life and my heart and started questioning everything I believed. I'm not proud to admit that scared me witless. You asked me why it's taken three months for me to find you. When you left I was angry. Angry at everyone and everything but despite all of that it seems I'd taken on board some of what you'd said without even realizing."

"Like what?"

"I built the zip line with Sean and it wasn't all bad. We've made a start at having a type of friendship."

The man who held himself apart from everyone had made a connection. Her heart lurched. "I'm glad."

He gave her a wry look. "Yeah. It's been interesting. Last week after I'd spent ten days trying to find you only to have your family and friends block me at every turn, Sean took me to a sports bar. He also got me home after I got filthy drunk."

"I always said he was a good dad." Her heart expanded and sang, not just for Finn and Sean but for herself. Finn, who was always in control, always had it together, had got publicly drunk because of her.

He stood up and gazed down at her, his eyes filled with sorrow. "I know all of this has come too late, Annika, but I want you to know that if my rejection of your love made you feel one tenth of the pain I'm feeling right now then I'm beyond sorry."

He loves you. He honestly does love you.

But could they make this work?

She blinked back tears and held back every instinct

to throw herself into his arms because it was too soon. "Part of me knows you were right. I needed to leave Whitetail. I needed to take this time for me and had you realized you loved me this summer, I might never have done it." She picked up his hand and pressed her palm against it, matching her fingers to his. "But the day you left me on the dock—" she drew in a steadying breath, "—I never want to feel that way again."

His voice was thick with emotion. "Neither do I."

She pressed on, as a tear slid down her cheek. "You once told me that love destroys more than it ever builds."

"I was an idiot."

She gave a half sob, half laugh. "But what about when things get tough? When we disagree? I'll want to talk about how you're feeling and your natural tendency's to push it all down. How are we going to deal with that?"

He rested his forehead against hers. "I'm not saying I'm going to get it right every time, but given my family's been banging me over the head for weeks with the evidence that I love you, I've had a bit of practice talking about my feelings."

She thought her heart would burst. "They have?"

"Oh yeah." He gave a soft smile. "I tell you, once you start letting people into your life they're in your face about things, and I wouldn't have it any other way. You once accused me of being like my father and I hated it but the old man's worked out what's important and you opened my eyes so I could see it too." He slid his fingers through hers, linking their hands together. "You're the best thing that has ever happened to me, Annika Jacobson. Please marry me."

Tears poured down her face. "On one condition."

He tensed against her. "God, Annika, you're killing me. What?"

She stroked his hair. "Tell Richard you're not buying *Act Now*."

He sighed and it shuddered through her. "Okay. I understand you need it out there to stand on its own feet no matter what. Believe me, it's going to stand. Kathleen's Geoffrey is already muttering something about the possibility of it being part of a new artists' expo. I'll rip up the check on one condition."

But he was smiling down at her so she knew she had nothing to fear. "Tell me."

"I want to buy your Lighthouse series, which, according to the internet, never sold."

She gazed up at him. "You want to buy my immature, derivative and stylized offerings that are stashed somewhere in Axel's garage?"

He tucked strands of stray hair behind her ears. "I'm not an art critic. I'm just some dumb schmuck who thinks they're full of love and the promise of the joys, frustrations and delights of an annual family vacation by a lake."

She threw her arms around his neck, loving him more than she ever had before. "Ask me again."

He grinned down at her, his dark eyes shining and his face full of love. "Will you make me the happiest man alive, not to mention making my entire family ridiculously happy, by becoming my wife?"

"Oh, Finn, I most certainly will."

He gave a loud whoop of joy and then he kissed her. He kissed her with love, with his promise to build a future with her and to be by her side always. He kissed her through the sound of running feet, the door being swung open, and a dozen faces peering in at them.

"Sir? Miss? Is everything all right?"

Finn broke the kiss for a moment and grinned. "Everything's perfect. I'm getting married!"

And then he kissed her again.

US Bride

Annika Jacobson, artist and previously of Whitetail, Wisconsin, married Chicago's perennial bachelor, Finn Callahan of AKP Industries, in a low-key wedding, ending years of speculation that the paper magnate would marry and combine love with a business merger. In a surprise move, the couple married in a snowbound Whitetail with only family and close friends in attendance. The bride's parents came the farthest distance, flying in from Peru. The hand-painted wedding invitations were made by the bride. The new Mrs. Callahan wore a white Christmas wedding gown with a fitted full-length fur-trimmed coat. Instead of a veil she wore a small but elegant diamond tiara. Whitetail's stylist and wedding planner, Nicole Lindquist, curled the bride's long hair and styled it so it cascaded gracefully across her shoulders.

According to our sources, the bride slipped on some ice as she was alighting from the wedding sleigh but due to the quick actions of the groom she escaped a nasty fall. The groom's father, Mr. Sean Callahan, was quoted as saying, "We couldn't be more thrilled that Finn has finally found the hap-

piness he deserves." The couple are rumored to be honeymooning in the Caribbean although a helicopter was sighted landing on the small island on Lake Whitetail.

* * * * *

ReaderService.com

Manage your account online!

- Review your order history
- Manage your payments
- Update your address

*We've designed
the Harlequin® Reader Service
website just for you.*

Enjoy all the features!

- Reader excerpts from any series
- Respond to mailings and
  special monthly offers
- Discover new series available to you
- Browse the Bonus Bucks catalog
- Share your feedback

Visit us at:
ReaderService.com

RS13